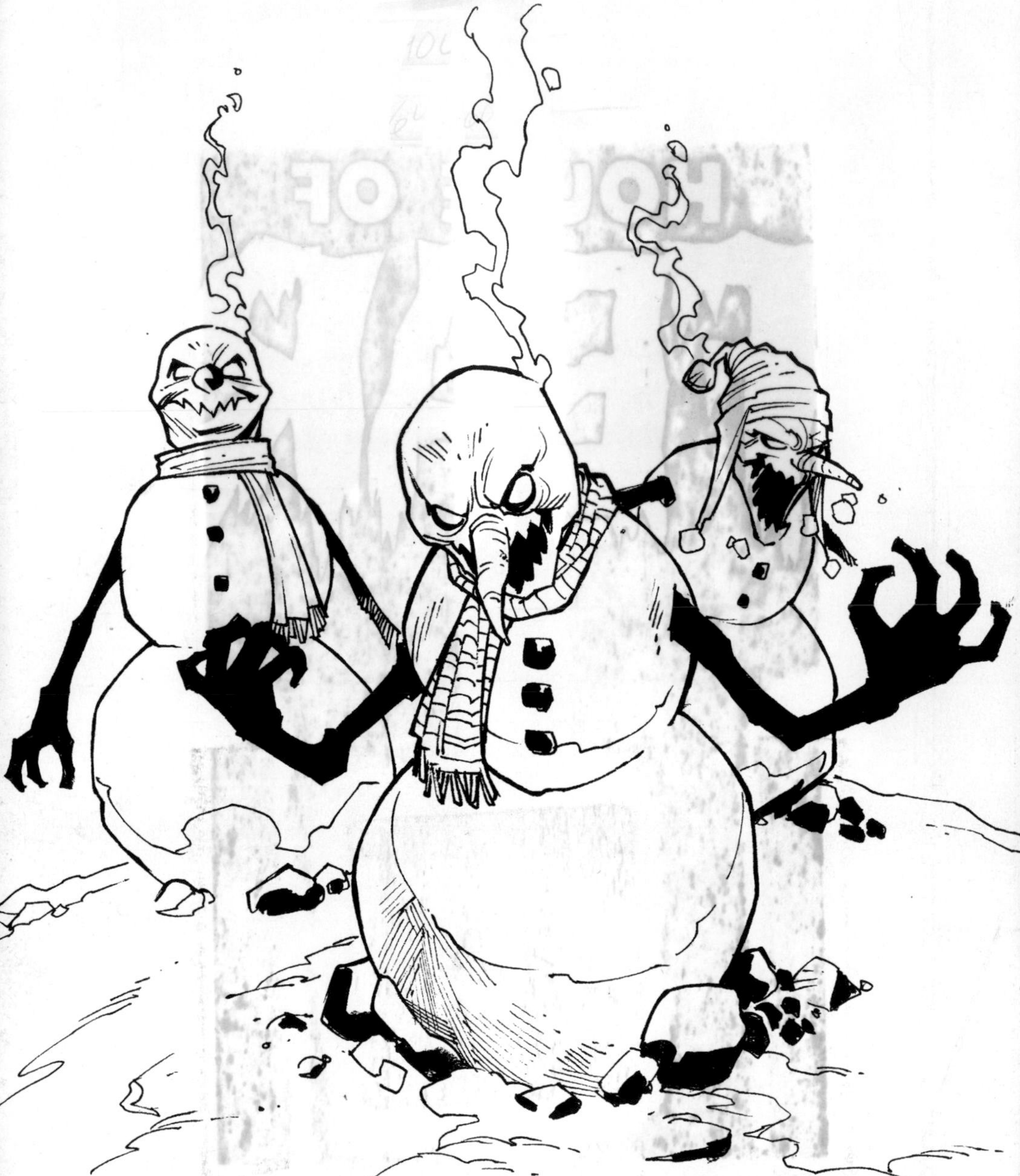

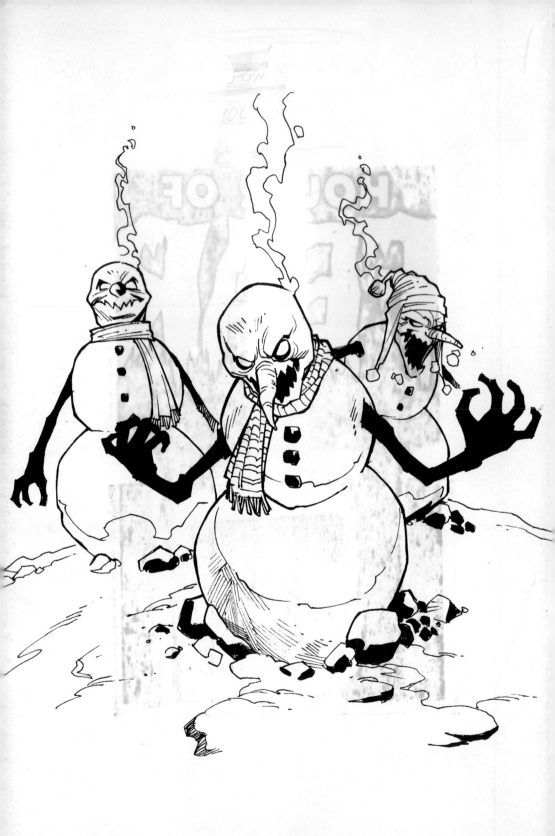

HOUSE OF FEAR

ATTACK OF THE KILLER SNOWMEN

Written by **JAMES POWELL**
Illustrated by **JETHRO MORALES**
Inked by **MIKE ERANDIO**
Bookends Illustrated by **JAMES HISLOPE**
Colored by **JOSH JENSEN**
Lettered & Designed by **MATT KROTZER**

THE CURSE OF COTTONWOOD CT.

Story by **DAXTON** and **JAMES POWELL**
Written by **JAMES POWELL**
Illustrated by **ADRIÁN BAGO GONZÁLEZ**
Bookends Illustrated by **JAMES HISLOPE**
Colored by **JOSH JENSEN**
Lettered & Designed by **MATT KROTZER**

TEETH

Written by **JAMES POWELL**
Illustrated by **JETHRO MORALES**
Inked by **MIKE ERANDIO**
Bookends Illustrated by **JAMES HISLOPE**
Colored by **JOSH JENSEN**
Lettered & Designed by **MATT KROTZER**

DEAD LAKE

Written by **JAMES POWELL**
Illustrated by **JETHRO MORALES**
Inked by **MIKE ERANDIO**
Bookends Illustrated by **JAMES HISLOPE**
Colored by **JOSH JENSEN**
Lettered & Designed by **MATT KROTZER**

THE LEAVING

Written by **JAMES POWELL**
Illustrated by **JETHRO MORALES**
Inked by **MIKE ERANDIO**
Bookends Illustrated by **JAMES HISLOPE**
Colored by **JOSH JENSEN**
Lettered & Designed by **MATT KROTZER**

Original series editing by **CHARLES BARNITZ**, **ANDREW CARL**, and **JASON BOVBERG**

DARK HORSE BOOKS

President and Publisher
MIKE RICHARDSON

Collection Editor
DAVE MARSHALL

Assistant Collection Editor
KONNER KNUDSEN

Collection Designer
SKYLER WEISSENFLUH

Digital Art Technician
SAMANTHA HUMMER

Neil Hankerson Executive Vice President • Tom Weddle Chief Financial Officer • Randy Stradley Vice President of Publishing • Nick McWhorter
Chief Business Development Officer • Dale LaFountain Chief Information Officer • Matt Parkinson Vice President of Marketing • Cara Niece
Vice President of Production and Scheduling • Mark Bernardi Vice President of Book Trade and Digital Sales • Ken Lizzi General Counsel
Dave Marshall Editor in Chief • Davey Estrada Editorial Director • Chris Warner Senior Books Editor • Cary Grazzini Director of Specialty
Projects • Lia Ribacchi Art Director • Vanessa Todd-Holmes Director of Print Purchasing • Matt Dryer Director of Digital Art and Prepress
Michael Gombos Senior Director of Licensed Publications • Kari Yadro Director of Custom Programs • Kari Torson Director of International
Licensing

This volume collects comic books originally published by TEN31 Publishing.

Published by Dark Horse Books
A division of Dark Horse Comics LLC
10956 SE Main Street
Milwaukie, OR 97222

DarkHorse.com

To find a comics shop in your area, visit comicshoplocator.com

Library of Congress Cataloging-in-Publication Data

Names: Powell, James, 1972- writer. | Morales, Jethro, illustrator. | Jensen,
Josh, colourist.
Title: House of fear : attack of the killer snowmen and other stories /
written by James Powell ; illustrated by Jethro Morales [and others] ;
colored by Josh Jensen.
Other titles: Attack of the killer snowmen and other stories
Description: First edition. | Milwaukie, OR : Dark Horse Books, May 2019. |
Summary: "It's Scooby-Doo meets Tales from the Crypt! Welcome to the House
of Fear, your new home for scary comics! Boyle, the creepy caretaker,
presents five frightening tales of startling suspense and thrilling
adventure."-- Provided by publisher.
Identifiers: LCCN 2018060523 (print) | LCCN 2018061005 (ebook) | ISBN
9781506711331 | ISBN 9781506711324 (paperback)
Subjects: LCSH: Graphic novels. | CYAC: Graphic novels. | Horror stories. |
Short stories.
Classification: LCC PZ7.7.P686 (ebook) | LCC PZ7.7.P686 Ho 2019 (print) | DDC
741.5/973--dc23
LC record available at https://lccn.loc.gov/2018060523

First edition: May 2019
ISBN 978-1-50671-132-4
Digital ISBN 978-1-50671-133-1

10 9 8 7 6 5 4 3 2 1
Printed in China

ATTACK
OF THE KILLER
SNOWMEN!

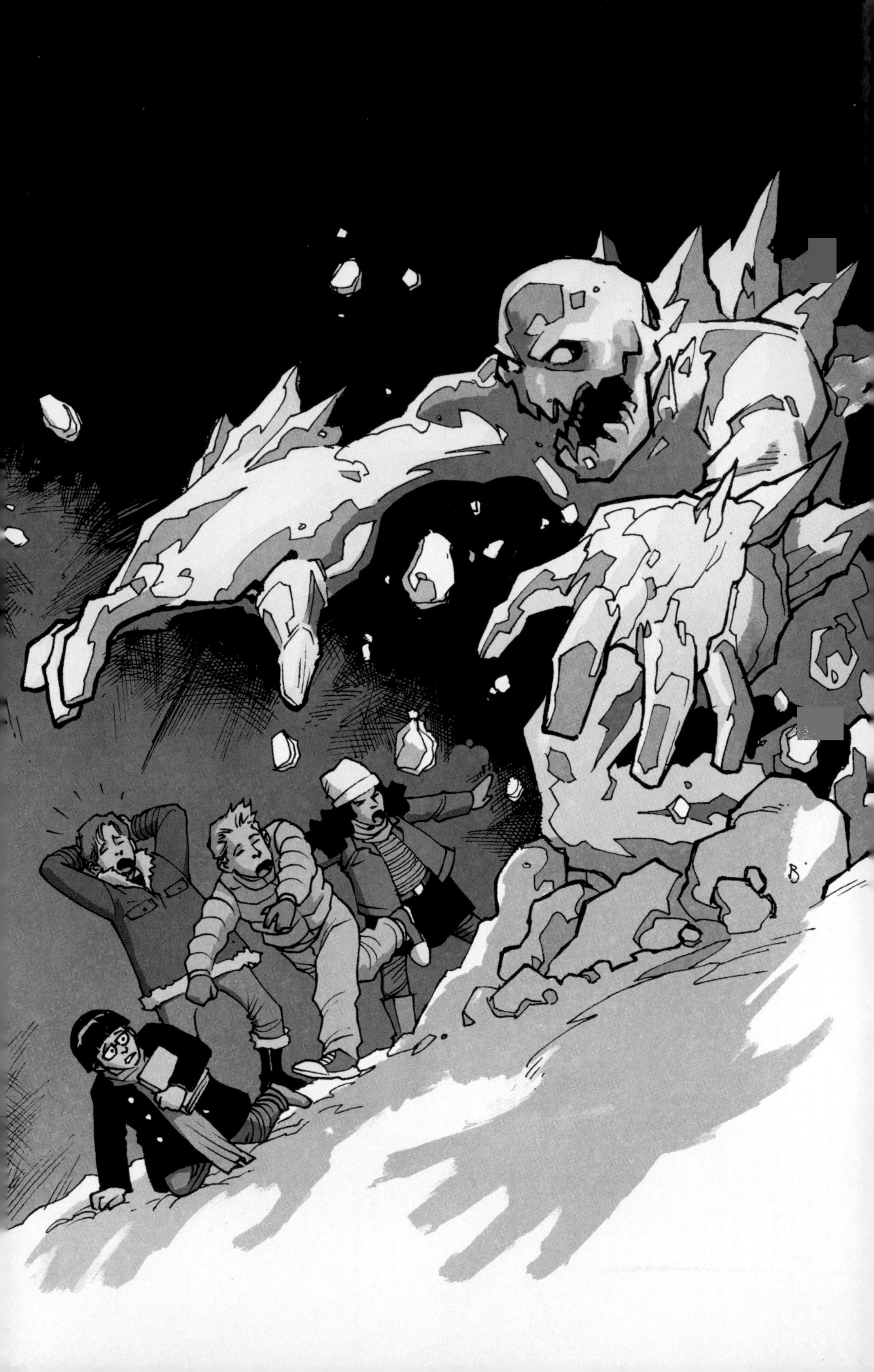

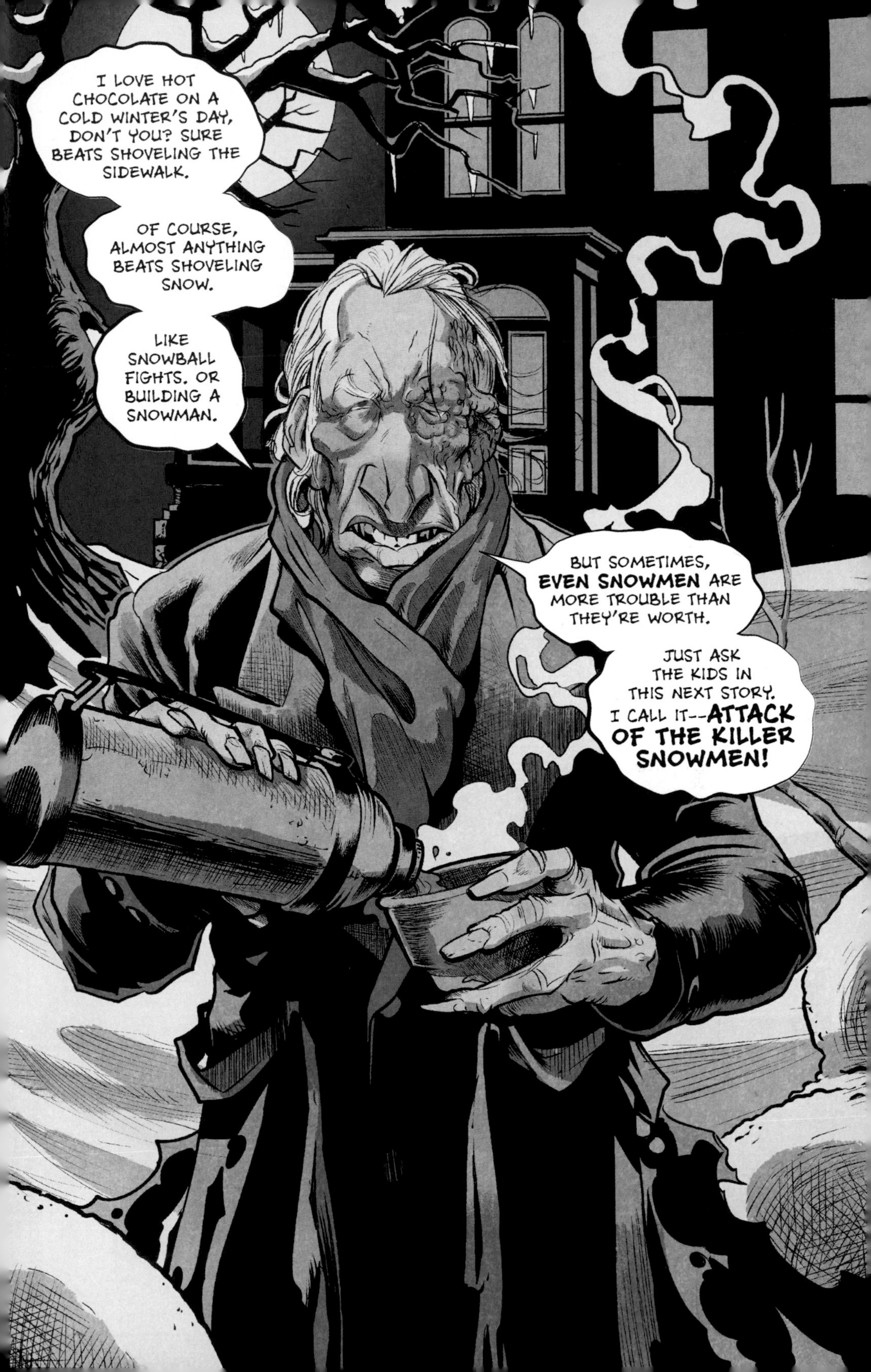
I LOVE HOT CHOCOLATE ON A COLD WINTER'S DAY, DON'T YOU? SURE BEATS SHOVELING THE SIDEWALK.
OF COURSE, ALMOST ANYTHING BEATS SHOVELING SNOW.
LIKE SNOWBALL FIGHTS. OR BUILDING A SNOWMAN.
BUT SOMETIMES, EVEN SNOWMEN ARE MORE TROUBLE THAN THEY'RE WORTH.
JUST ASK THE KIDS IN THIS NEXT STORY. I CALL IT--ATTACK OF THE KILLER SNOWMEN!

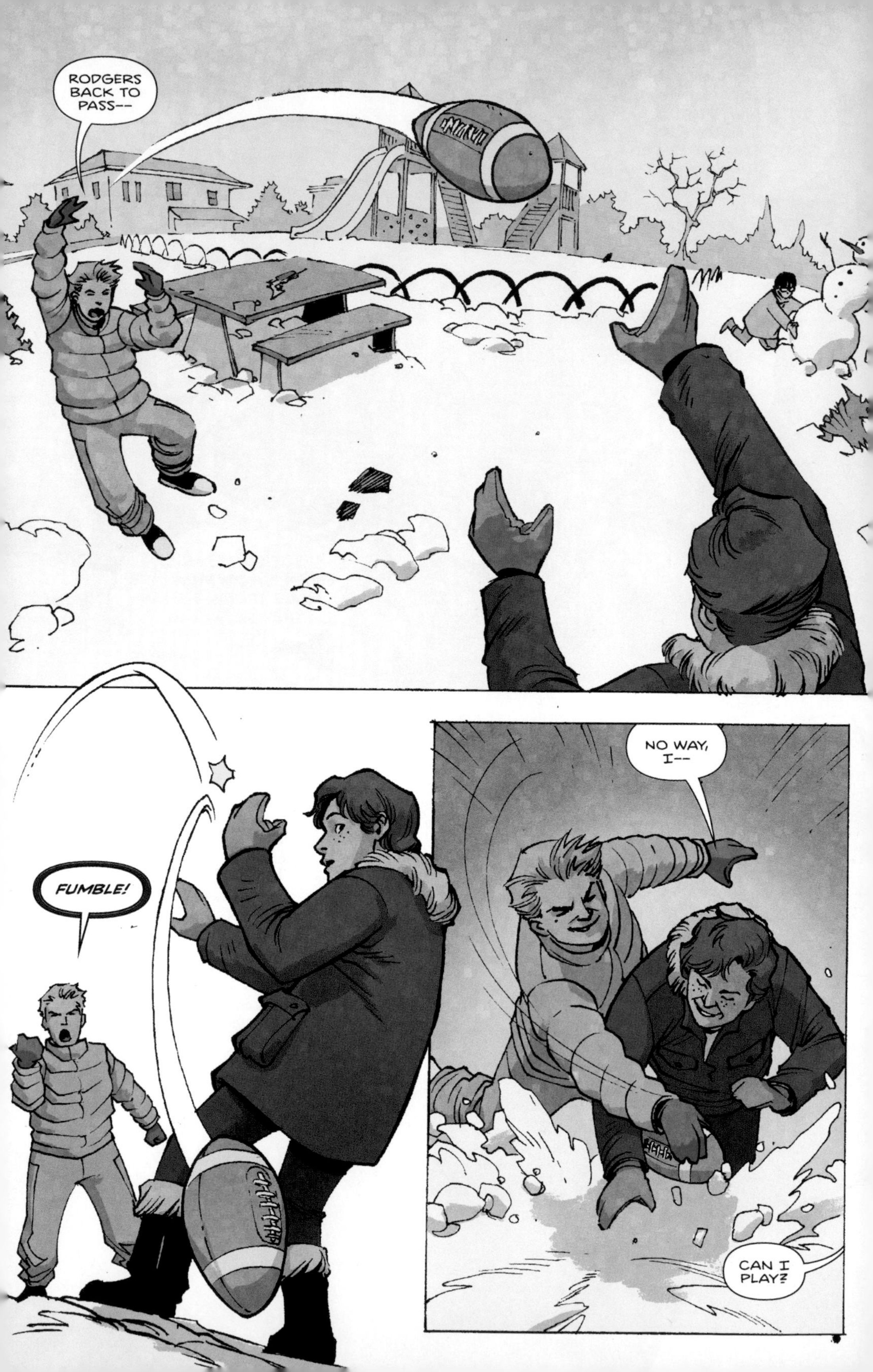
RODGERS BACK TO PASS--
FUMBLE!
NO WAY, I--
CAN I PLAY?

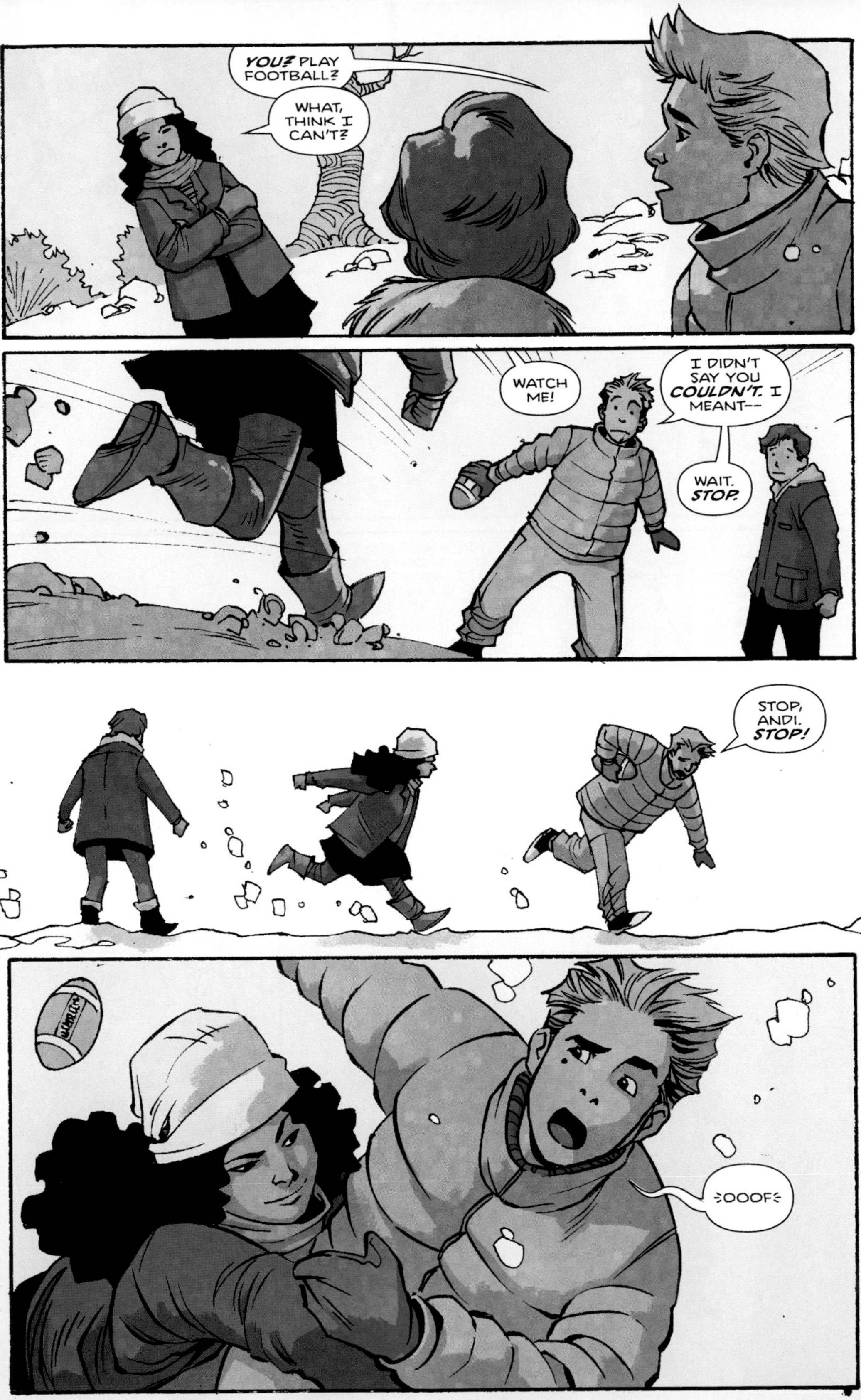
YOU? PLAY FOOTBALL?
WHAT, THINK I CAN'T?
WATCH ME!
I DIDN'T SAY YOU COULDN'T. I MEANT--
WAIT. STOP.
STOP, ANDI. STOP!
OOOF

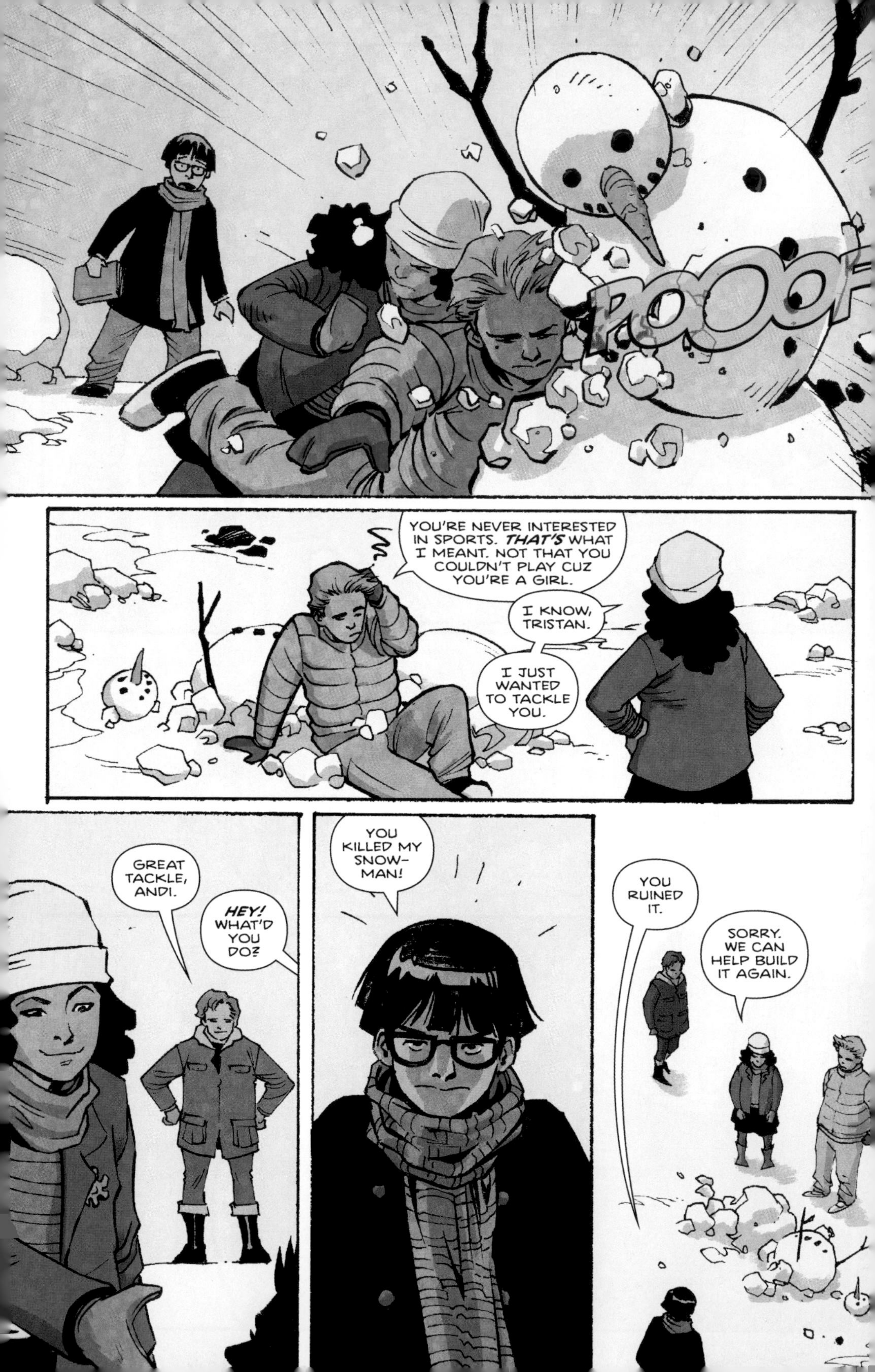
POOOF
YOU'RE NEVER INTERESTED IN SPORTS. THAT'S WHAT I MEANT. NOT THAT YOU COULDN'T PLAY CUZ YOU'RE A GIRL.
I KNOW, TRISTAN.
I JUST WANTED TO TACKLE YOU.
GREAT TACKLE, ANDI.
HEY! WHAT'D YOU DO?
YOU KILLED MY SNOW-MAN!
YOU RUINED IT.
SORRY. WE CAN HELP BUILD IT AGAIN.

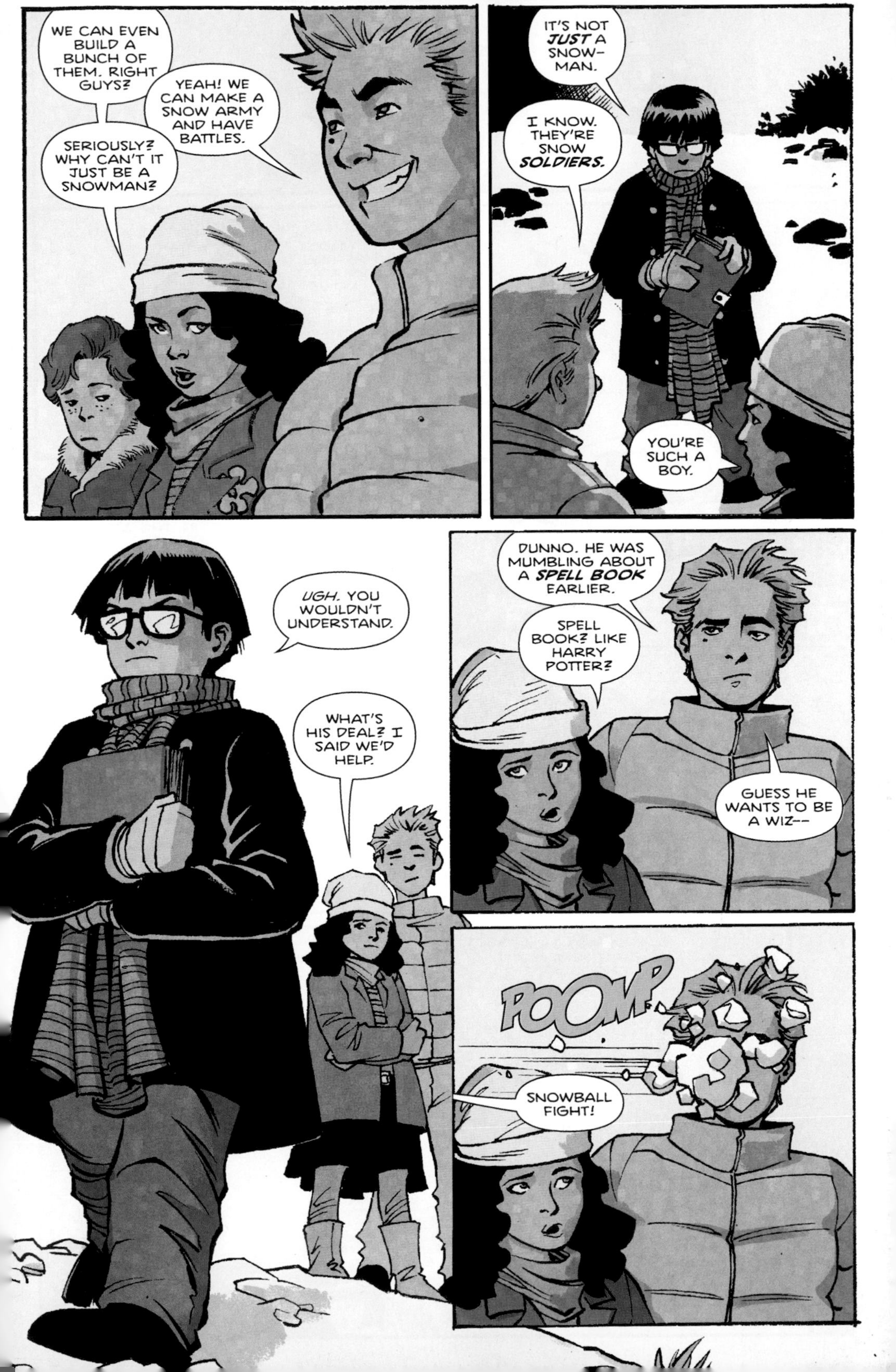
WE CAN EVEN BUILD A BUNCH OF THEM. RIGHT GUYS?
YEAH! WE CAN MAKE A SNOW ARMY AND HAVE BATTLES.
SERIOUSLY? WHY CAN'T IT JUST BE A SNOWMAN?
IT'S NOT JUST A SNOW-MAN.
I KNOW. THEY'RE SNOW SOLDIERS.
YOU'RE SUCH A BOY.
UGH. YOU WOULDN'T UNDERSTAND.
WHAT'S HIS DEAL? I SAID WE'D HELP.
DUNNO. HE WAS MUMBLING ABOUT A SPELL BOOK EARLIER.
SPELL BOOK? LIKE HARRY POTTER?
GUESS HE WANTS TO BE A WIZ--
POOMP
SNOWBALL FIGHT!

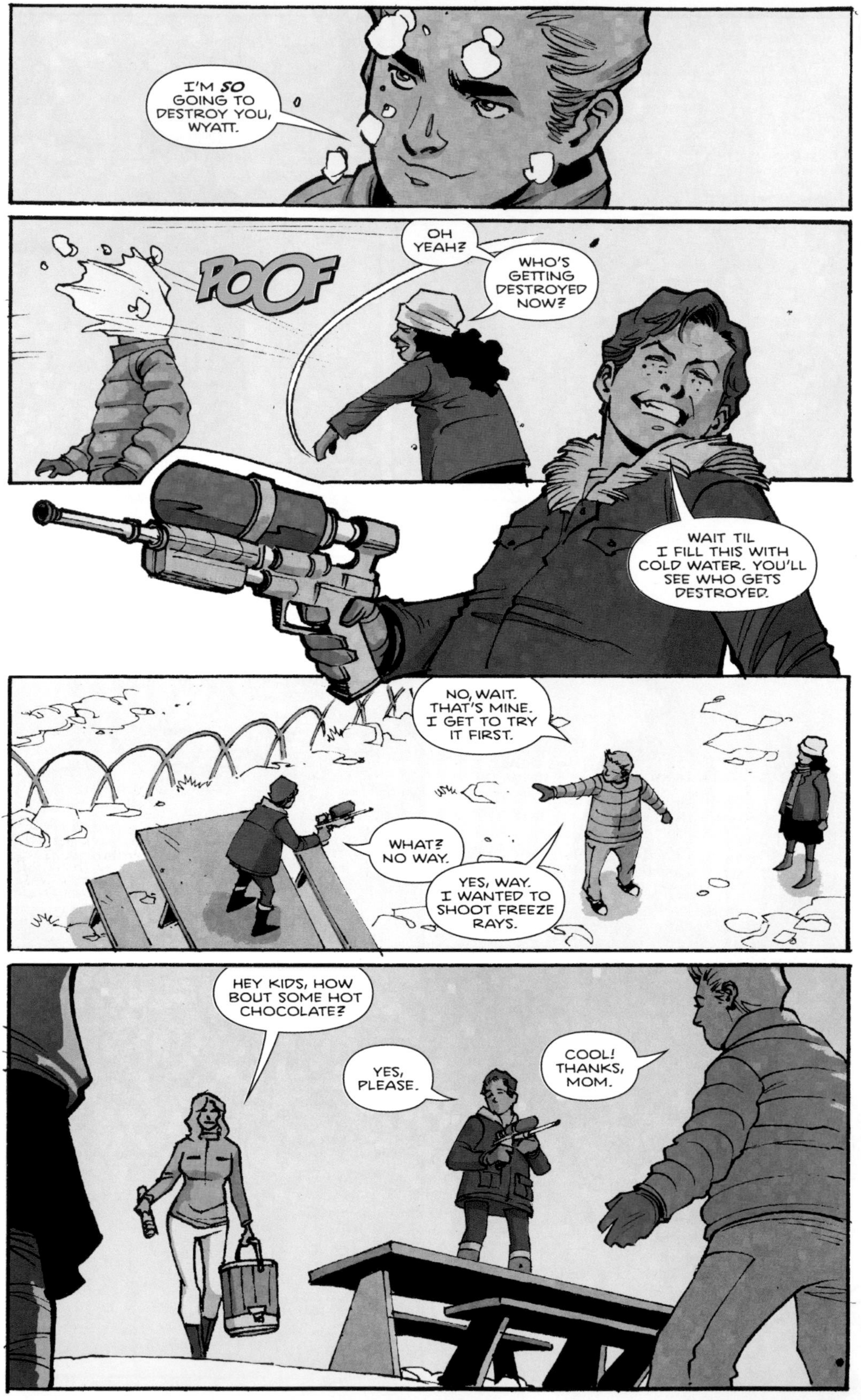
I'M SO GOING TO DESTROY YOU, WYATT.
POOF
OH YEAH?
WHO'S GETTING DESTROYED NOW?
WAIT TIL I FILL THIS WITH COLD WATER. YOU'LL SEE WHO GETS DESTROYED.
NO, WAIT. THAT'S MINE. I GET TO TRY IT FIRST.
WHAT? NO WAY.
YES, WAY. I WANTED TO SHOOT FREEZE RAYS.
HEY KIDS, HOW BOUT SOME HOT CHOCOLATE?
YES, PLEASE.
COOL! THANKS, MOM.

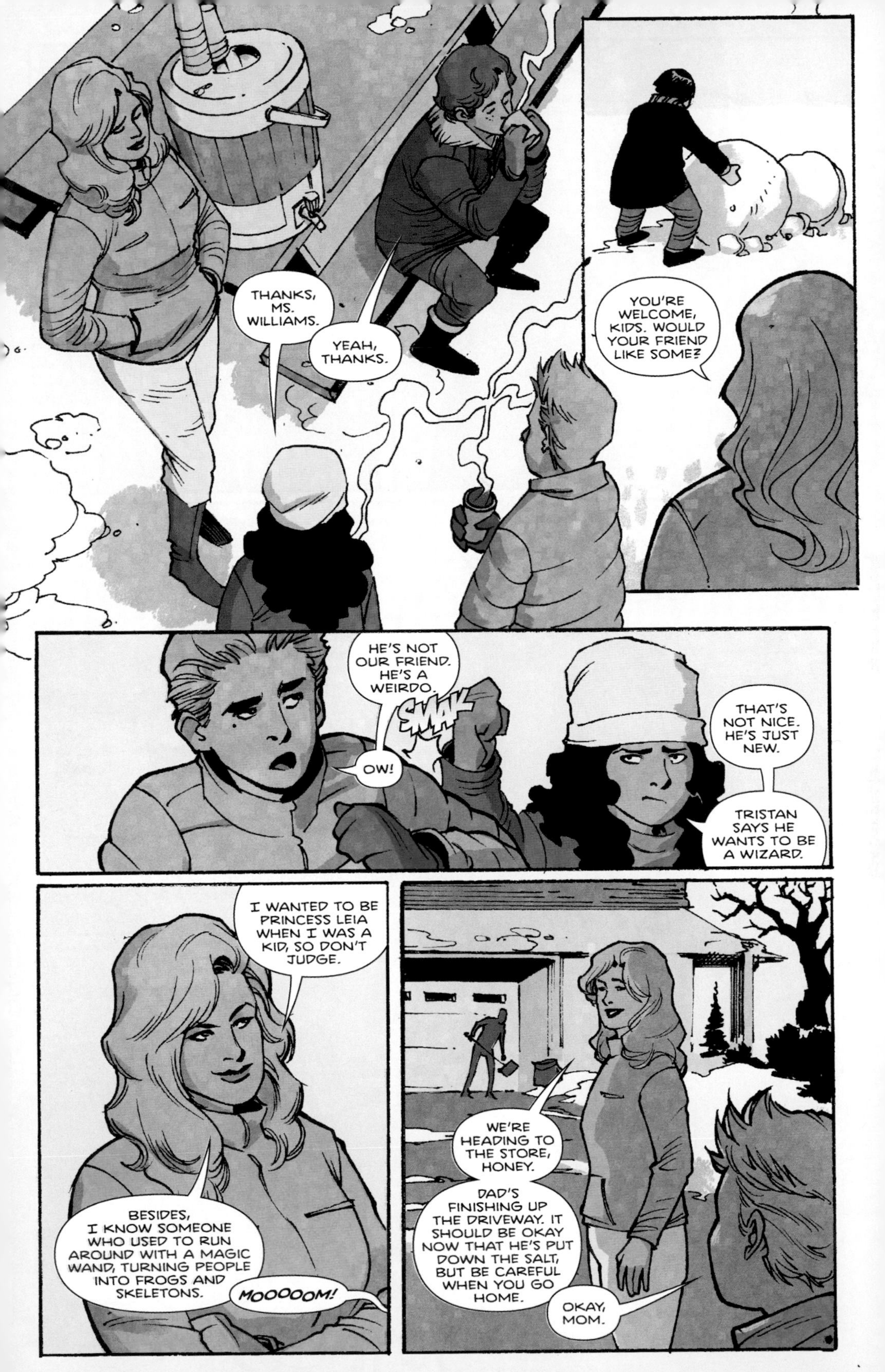
THANKS, MS. WILLIAMS.
YEAH, THANKS.
YOU'RE WELCOME, KIDS. WOULD YOUR FRIEND LIKE SOME?
HE'S NOT OUR FRIEND. HE'S A WEIRDO.
SMAK
OW!
THAT'S NOT NICE. HE'S JUST NEW.
TRISTAN SAYS HE WANTS TO BE A WIZARD.
I WANTED TO BE PRINCESS LEIA WHEN I WAS A KID, SO DON'T JUDGE.
BESIDES, I KNOW SOMEONE WHO USED TO RUN AROUND WITH A MAGIC WAND, TURNING PEOPLE INTO FROGS AND SKELETONS.
MOOOOOM!
WE'RE HEADING TO THE STORE, HONEY.
DAD'S FINISHING UP THE DRIVEWAY. IT SHOULD BE OKAY NOW THAT HE'S PUT DOWN THE SALT, BUT BE CAREFUL WHEN YOU GO HOME.
OKAY, MOM.

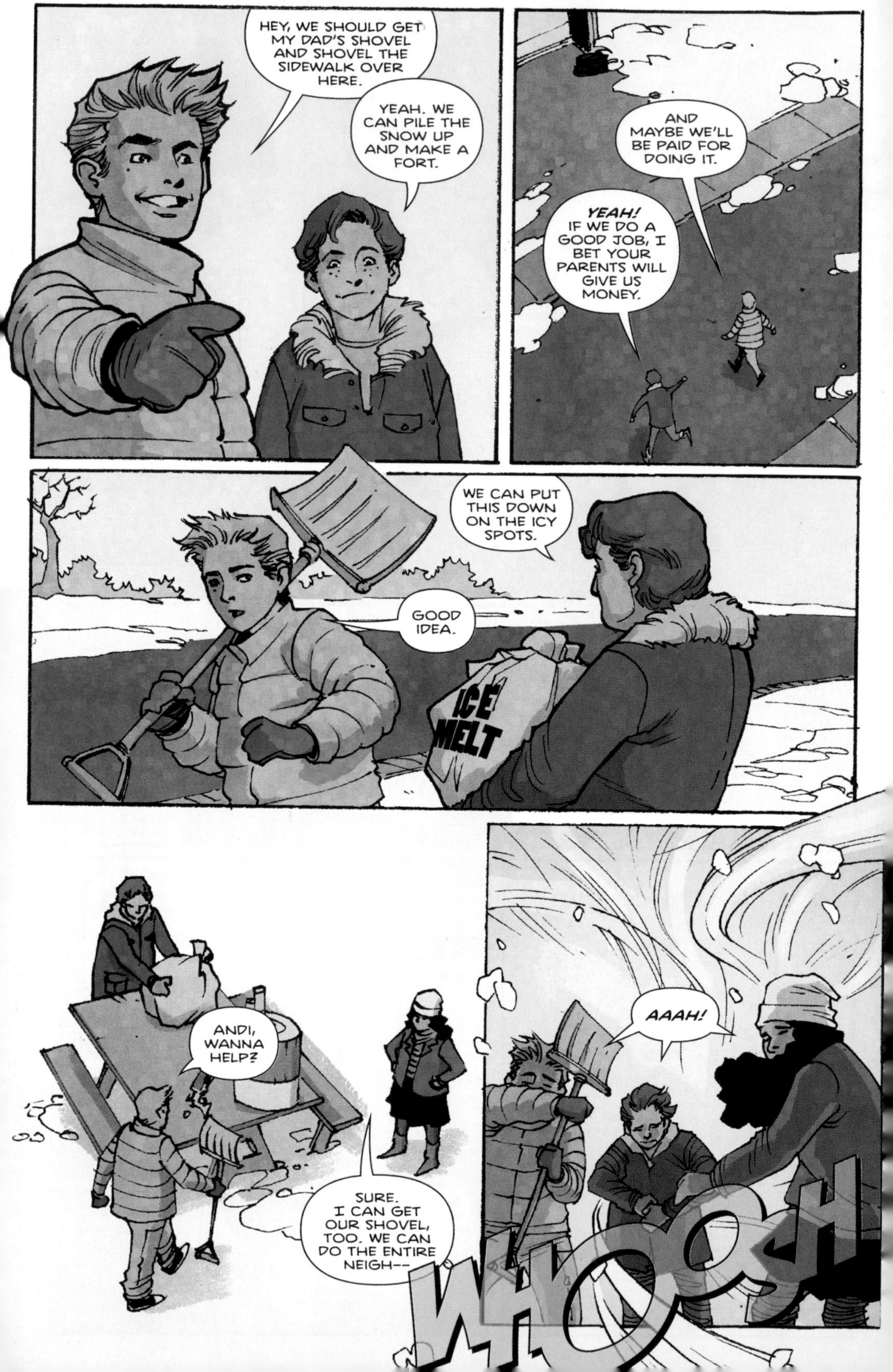
HEY, WE SHOULD GET MY DAD'S SHOVEL AND SHOVEL THE SIDEWALK OVER HERE.
YEAH. WE CAN PILE THE SNOW UP AND MAKE A FORT.
AND MAYBE WE'LL BE PAID FOR DOING IT.
YEAH! IF WE DO A GOOD JOB, I BET YOUR PARENTS WILL GIVE US MONEY.
WE CAN PUT THIS DOWN ON THE ICY SPOTS.
GOOD IDEA.
ICE MELT
ANDI, WANNA HELP?
SURE. I CAN GET OUR SHOVEL, TOO. WE CAN DO THE ENTIRE NEIGH--
AAAH!
WHOOSH

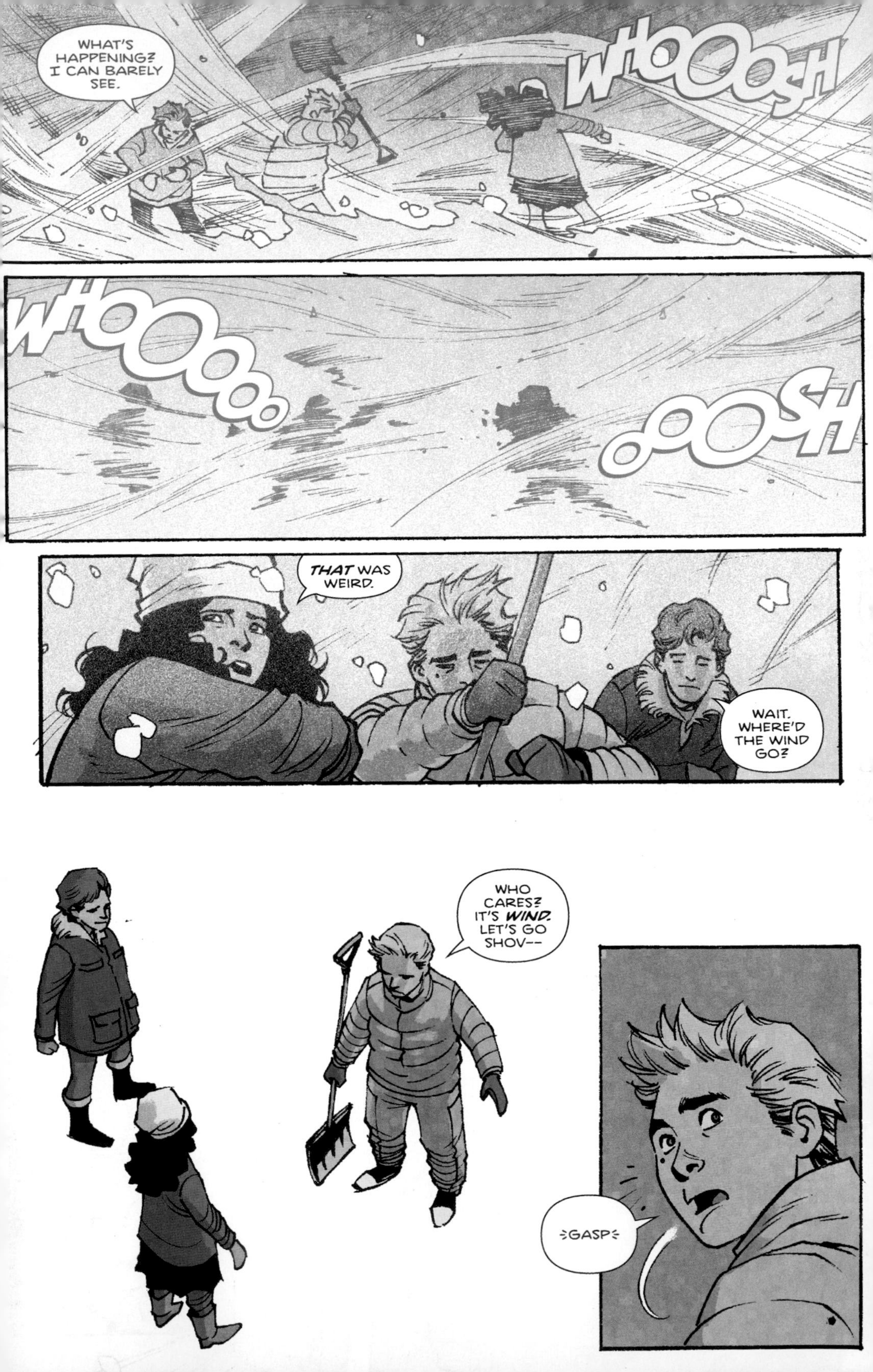
WHAT'S HAPPENING? I CAN BARELY SEE.
WHOOOSH
WHOOOOOO
OOOSH
THAT WAS WEIRD.
WAIT. WHERE'D THE WIND GO?
WHO CARES? IT'S WIND. LET'S GO SHOV--
GASP

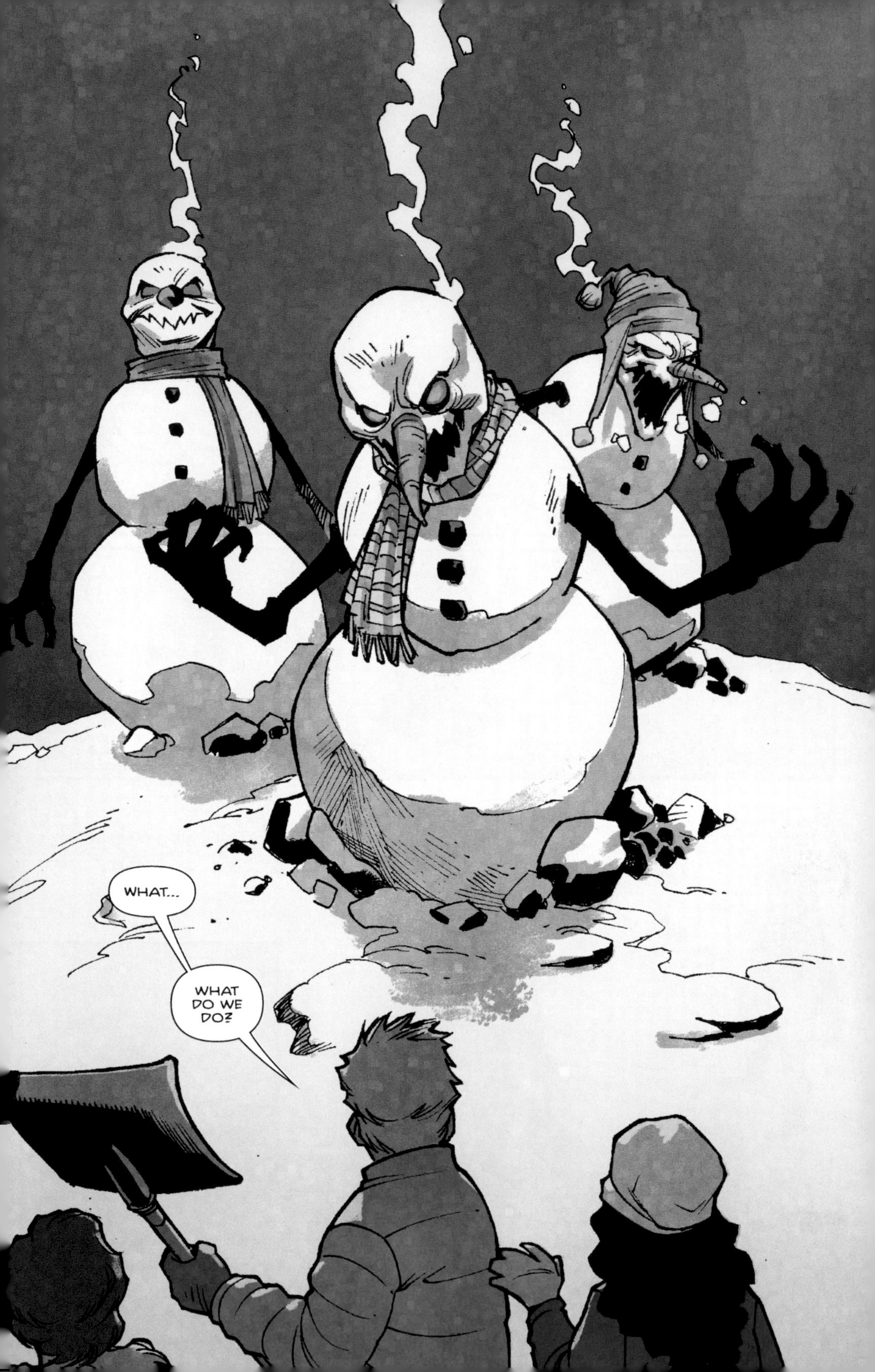
WHAT...
WHAT DO WE DO?

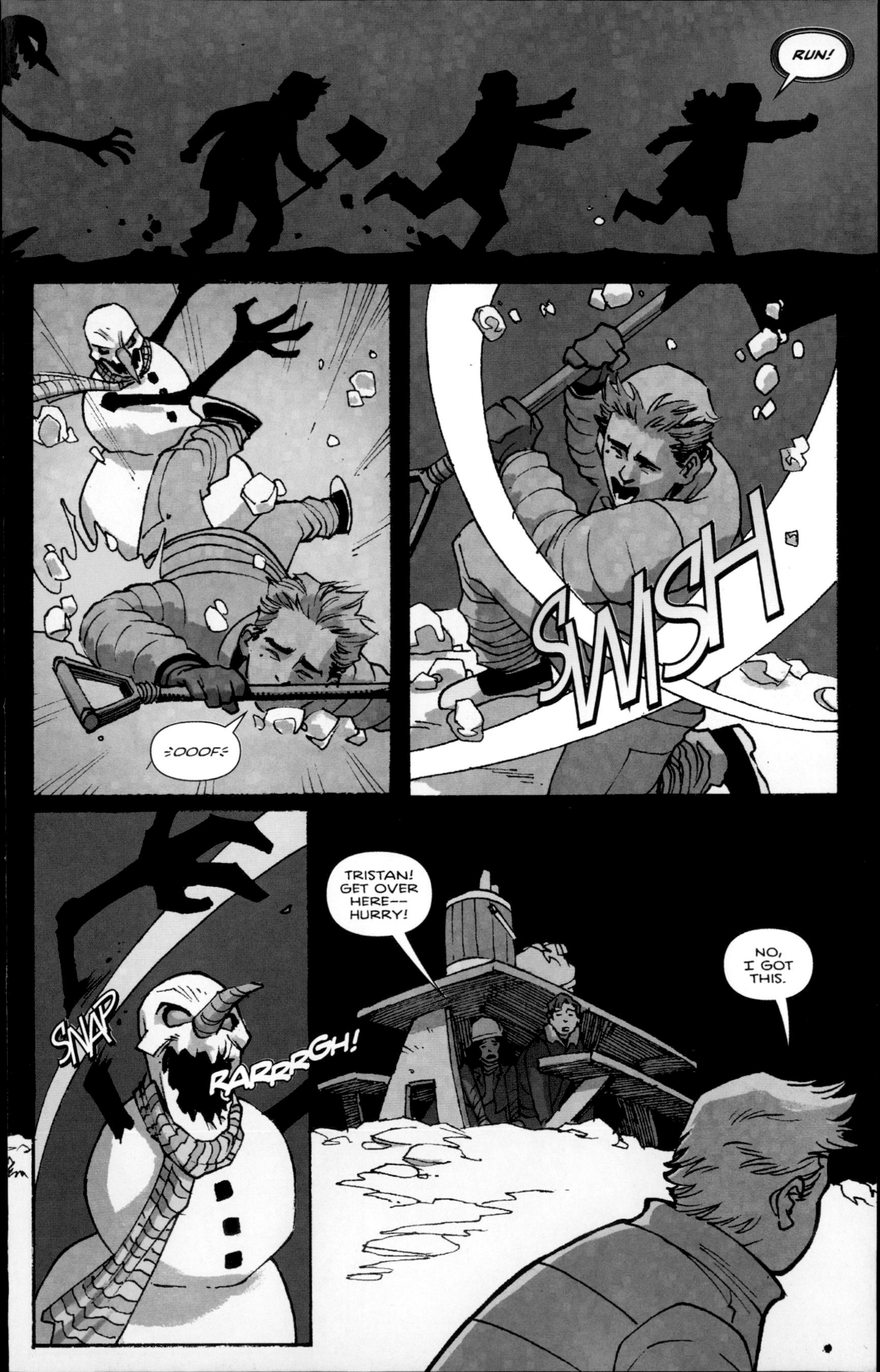
RUN!
OOOF
SWISH
SNAP
RARRRGH!
TRISTAN! GET OVER HERE-- HURRY!
NO, I GOT THIS.

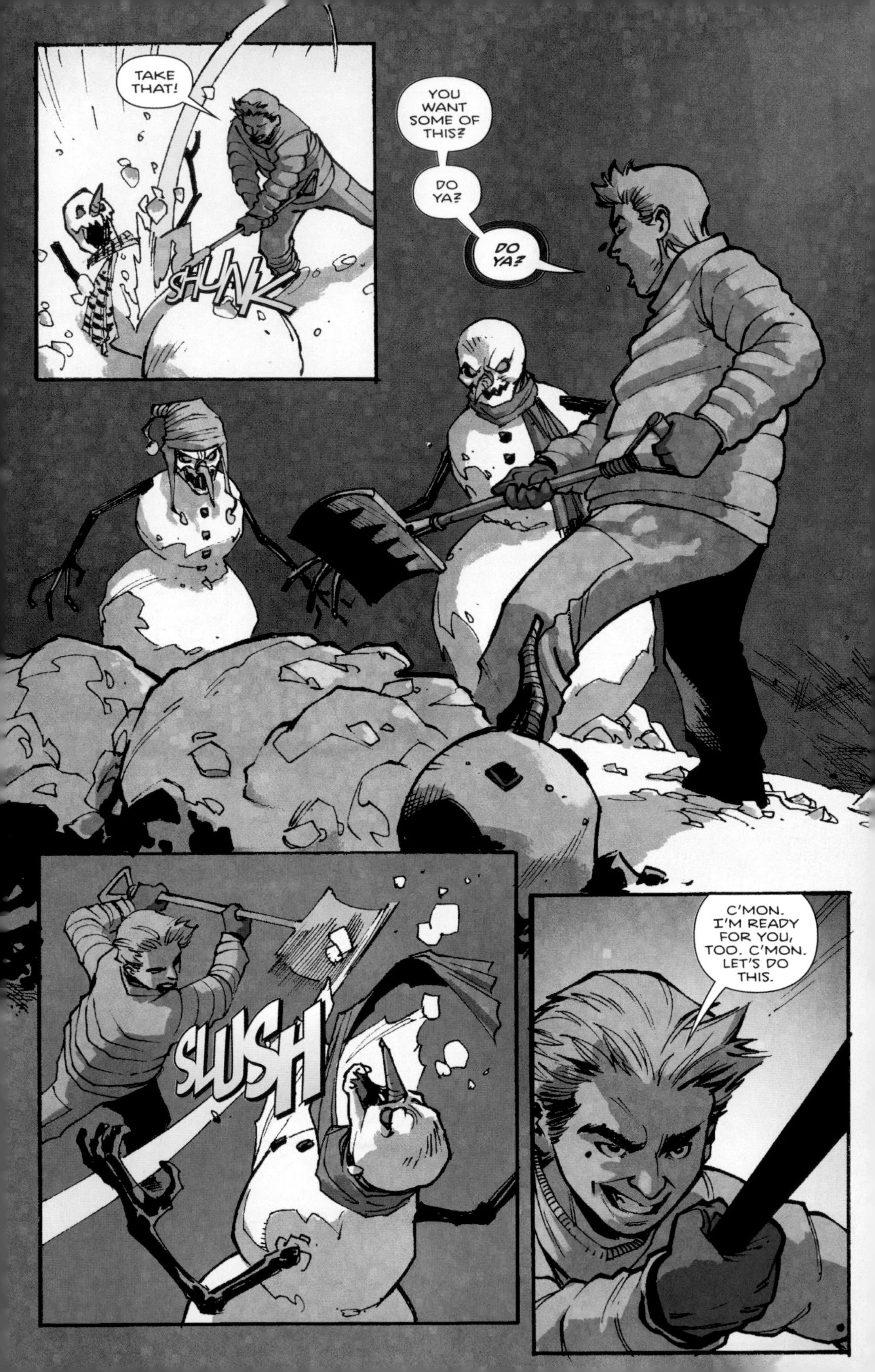
TAKE THAT!
SHUNK
YOU WANT SOME OF THIS?
DO YA?
DO YA?
SLUSH
C'MON. I'M READY FOR YOU, TOO. C'MON. LET'S DO THIS.

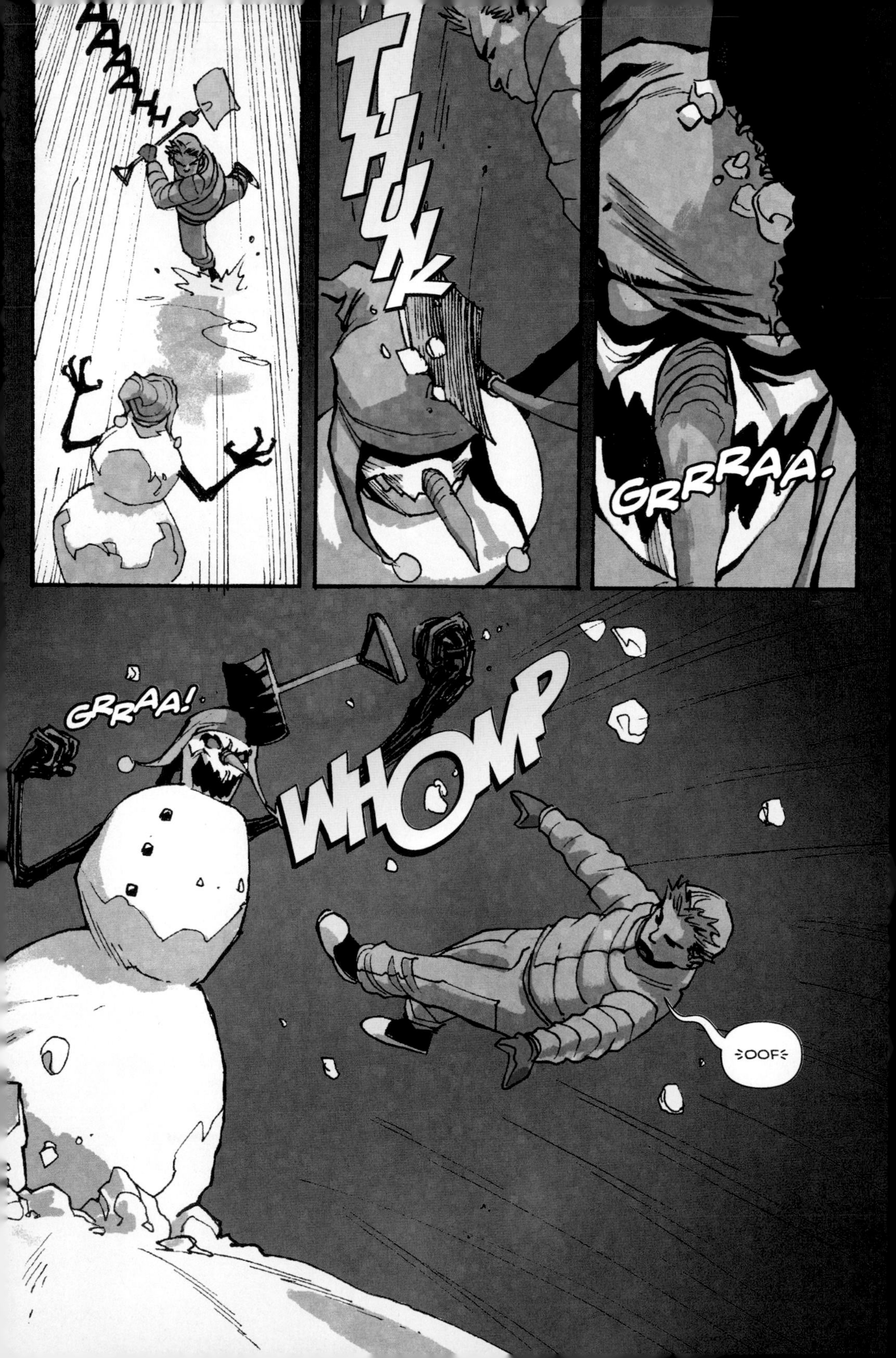
AAAAHH
THUNK
GRRRAA.
GRRAA!
WHOMP
OOF

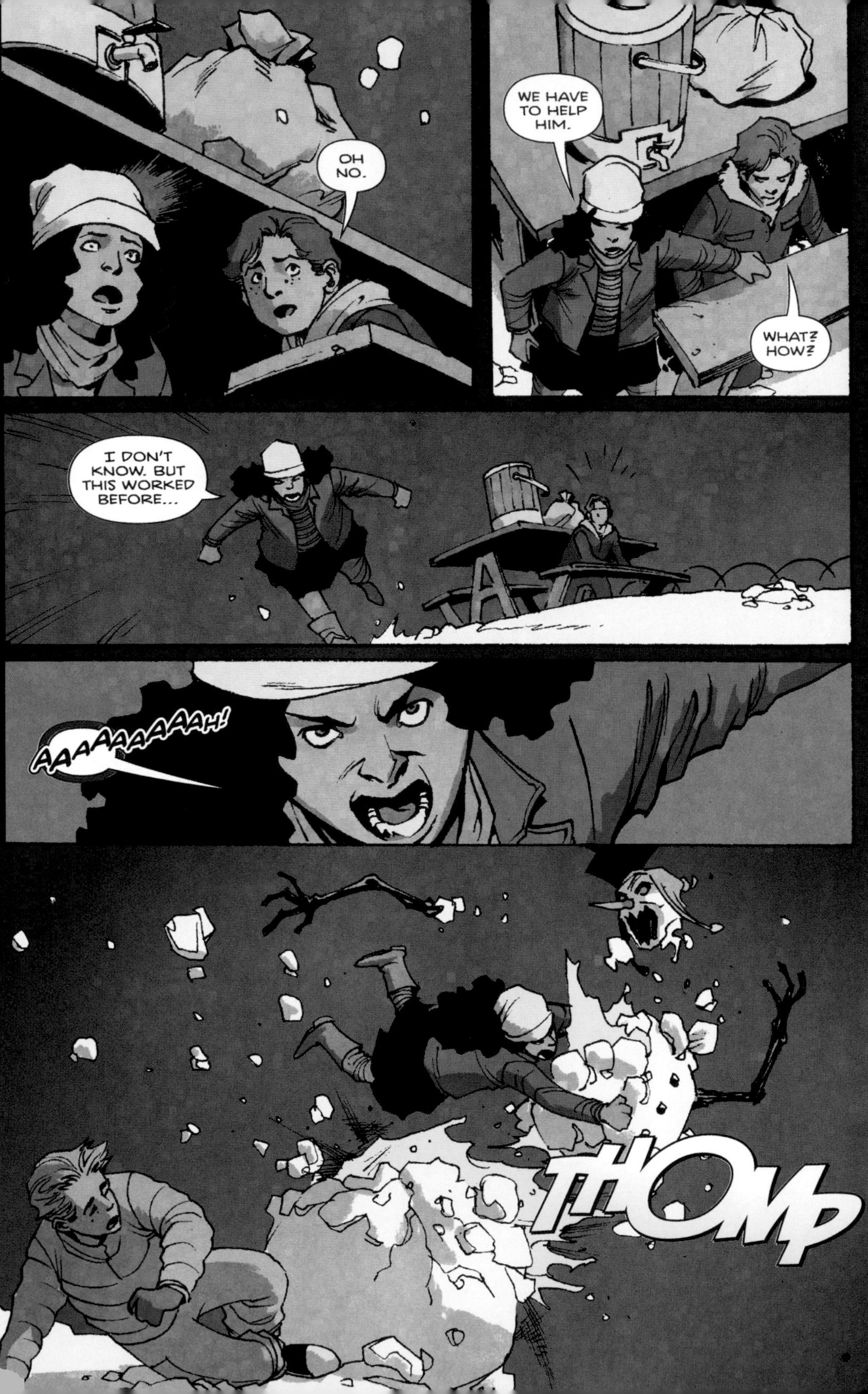
OH NO.
WE HAVE TO HELP HIM.
WHAT? HOW?
I DON'T KNOW. BUT THIS WORKED BEFORE...
AAAAAAAAAH!
THOMP

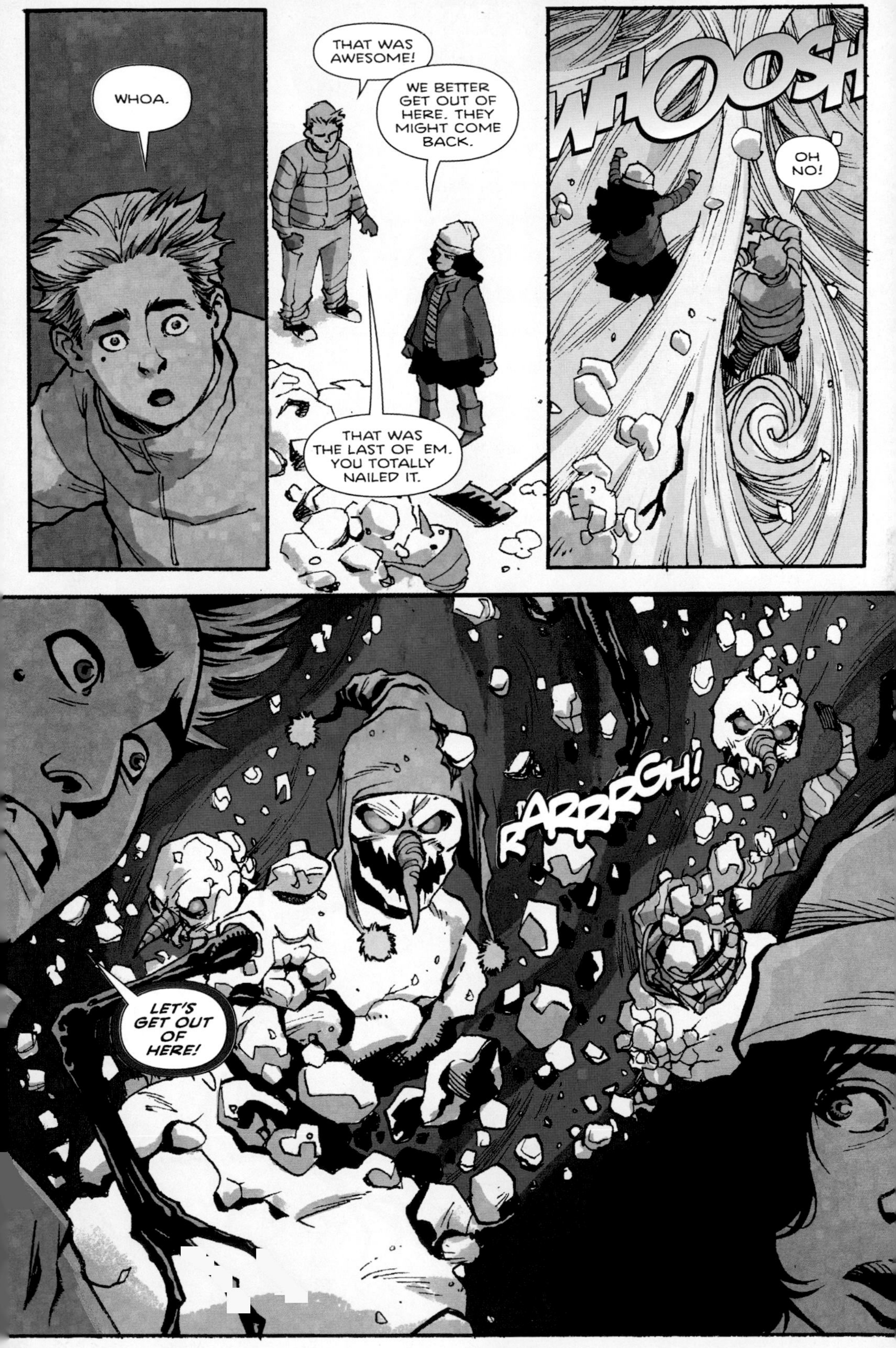
WHOA.
THAT WAS AWESOME!
WE BETTER GET OUT OF HERE. THEY MIGHT COME BACK.
THAT WAS THE LAST OF 'EM. YOU TOTALLY NAILED IT.
WHOOSH
OH NO!
RARRRGH!
LET'S GET OUT OF HERE!

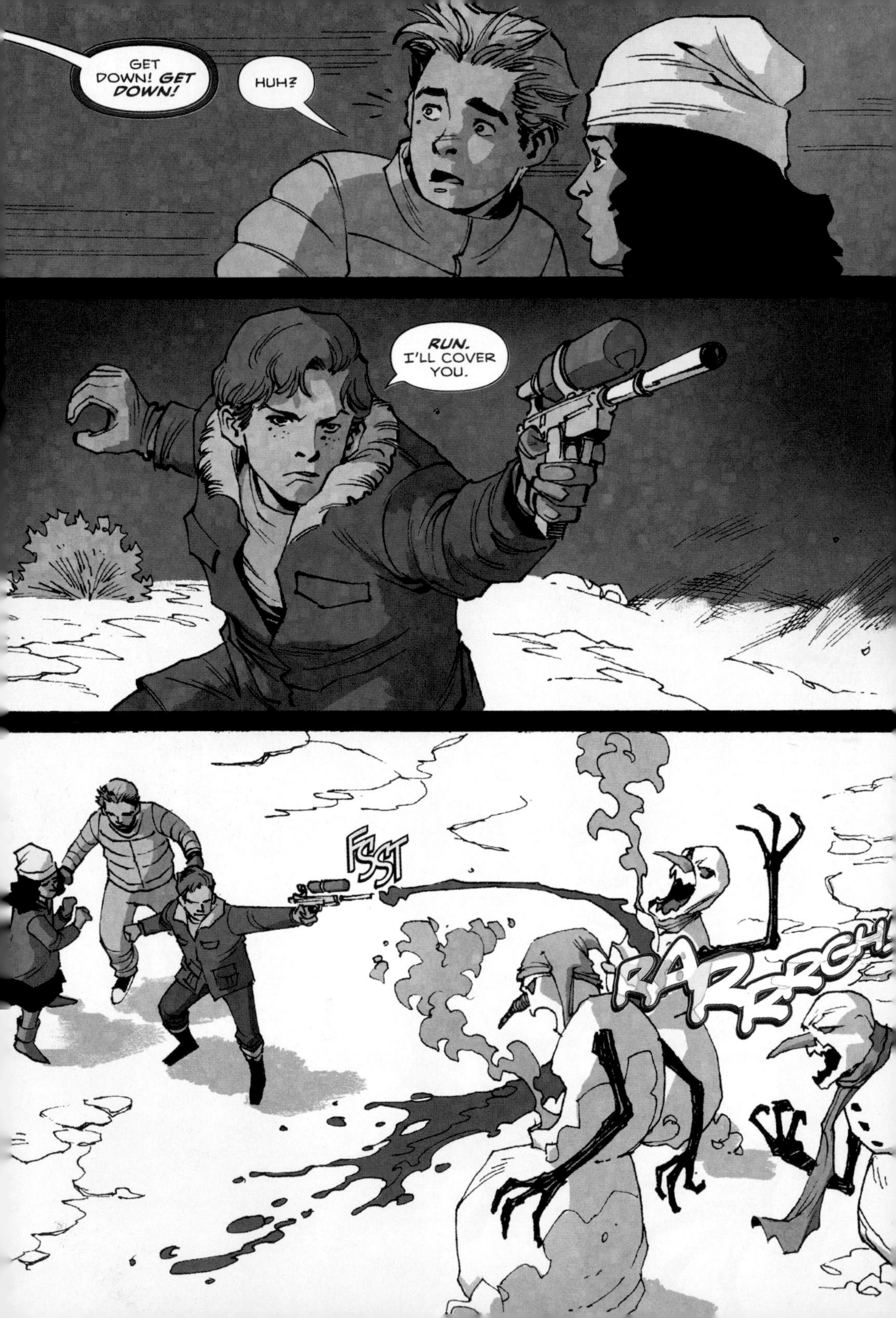
GET DOWN! GET DOWN!
HUH?
RUN. I'LL COVER YOU.
FSST
RARRRRCH

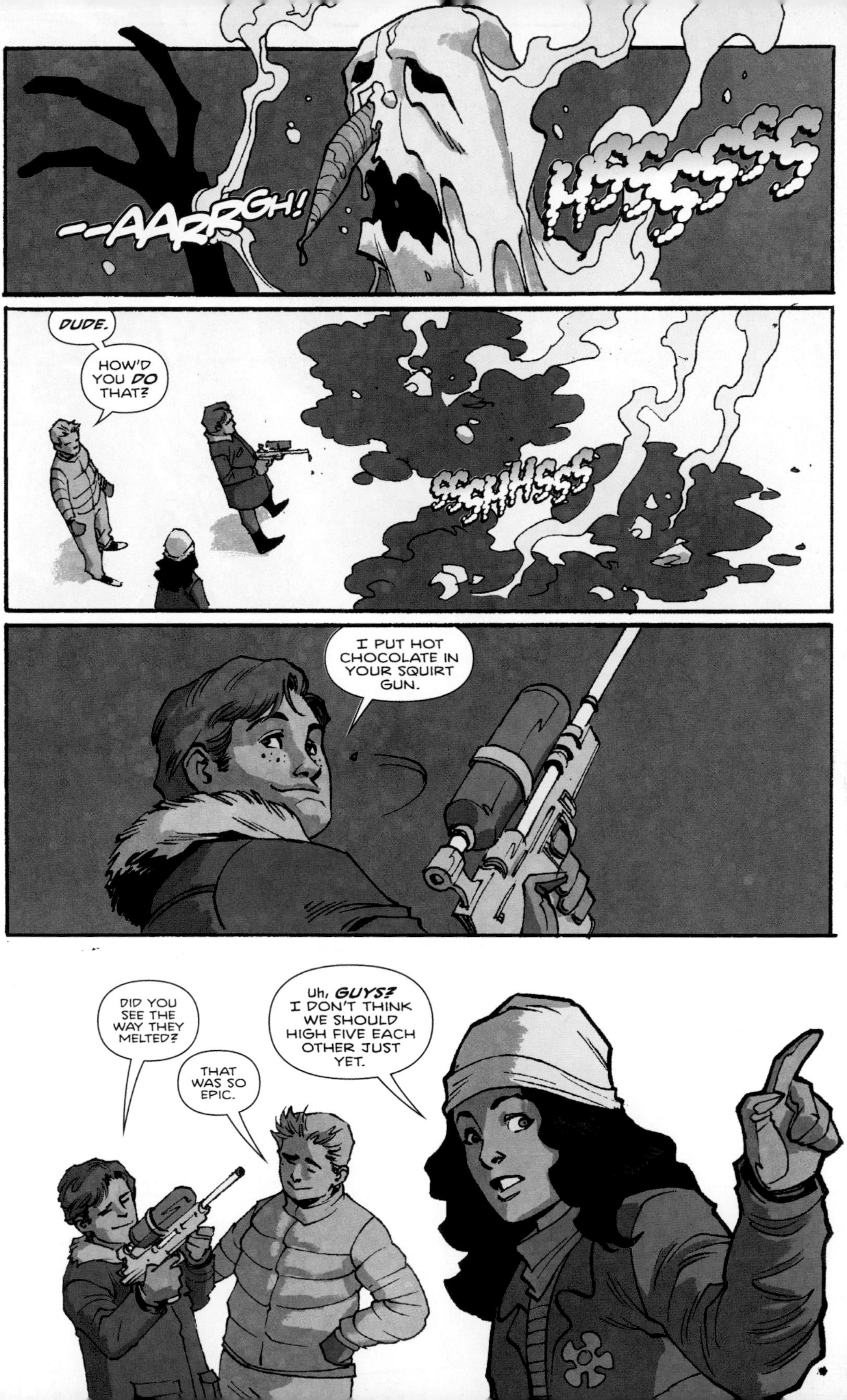
--AARRGH!
HSSSSSS
DUDE.
HOW'D YOU DO THAT?
SSSHHSSS
I PUT HOT CHOCOLATE IN YOUR SQUIRT GUN.
DID YOU SEE THE WAY THEY MELTED?
THAT WAS SO EPIC.
Uh, GUYS? I DON'T THINK WE SHOULD HIGH FIVE EACH OTHER JUST YET.

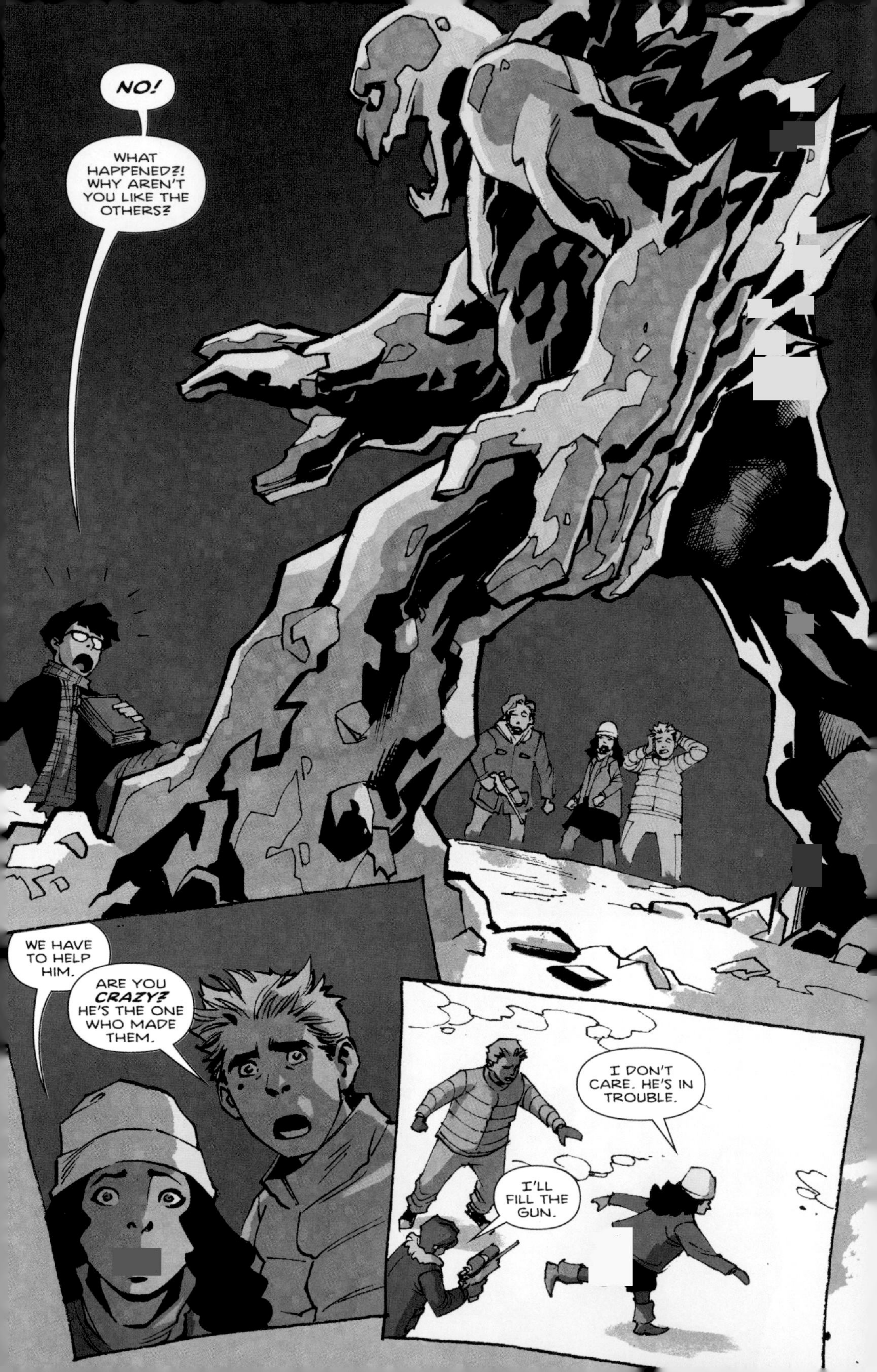
NO!
WHAT HAPPENED?! WHY AREN'T YOU LIKE THE OTHERS?
WE HAVE TO HELP HIM.
ARE YOU **CRAZY?** HE'S THE ONE WHO MADE THEM.
I DON'T CARE. HE'S IN TROUBLE.
I'LL FILL THE GUN.

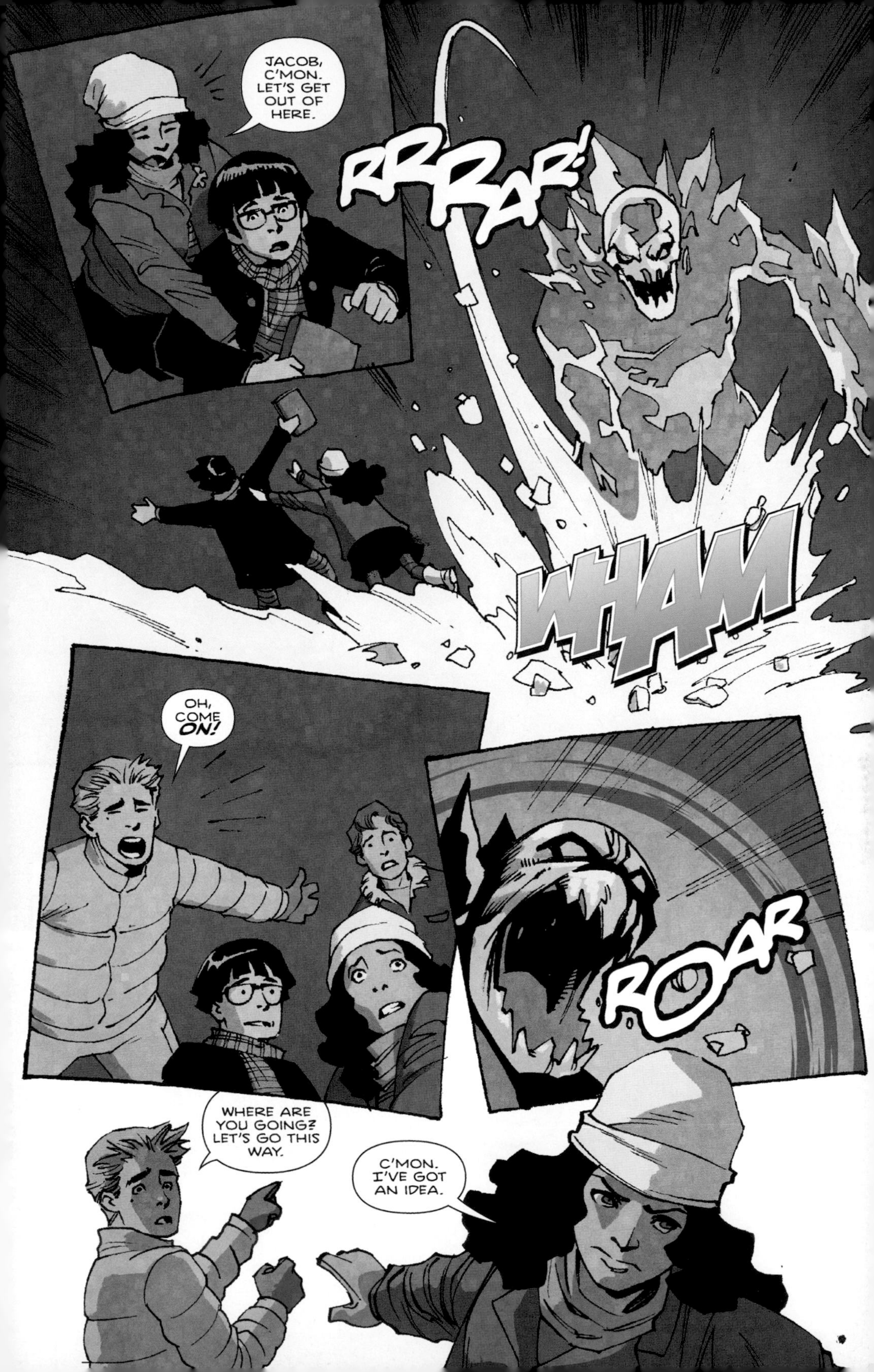
JACOB, C'MON. LET'S GET OUT OF HERE.
RRRAR!
WHAM
OH, COME ON!
ROAR
WHERE ARE YOU GOING? LET'S GO THIS WAY.
C'MON. I'VE GOT AN IDEA.

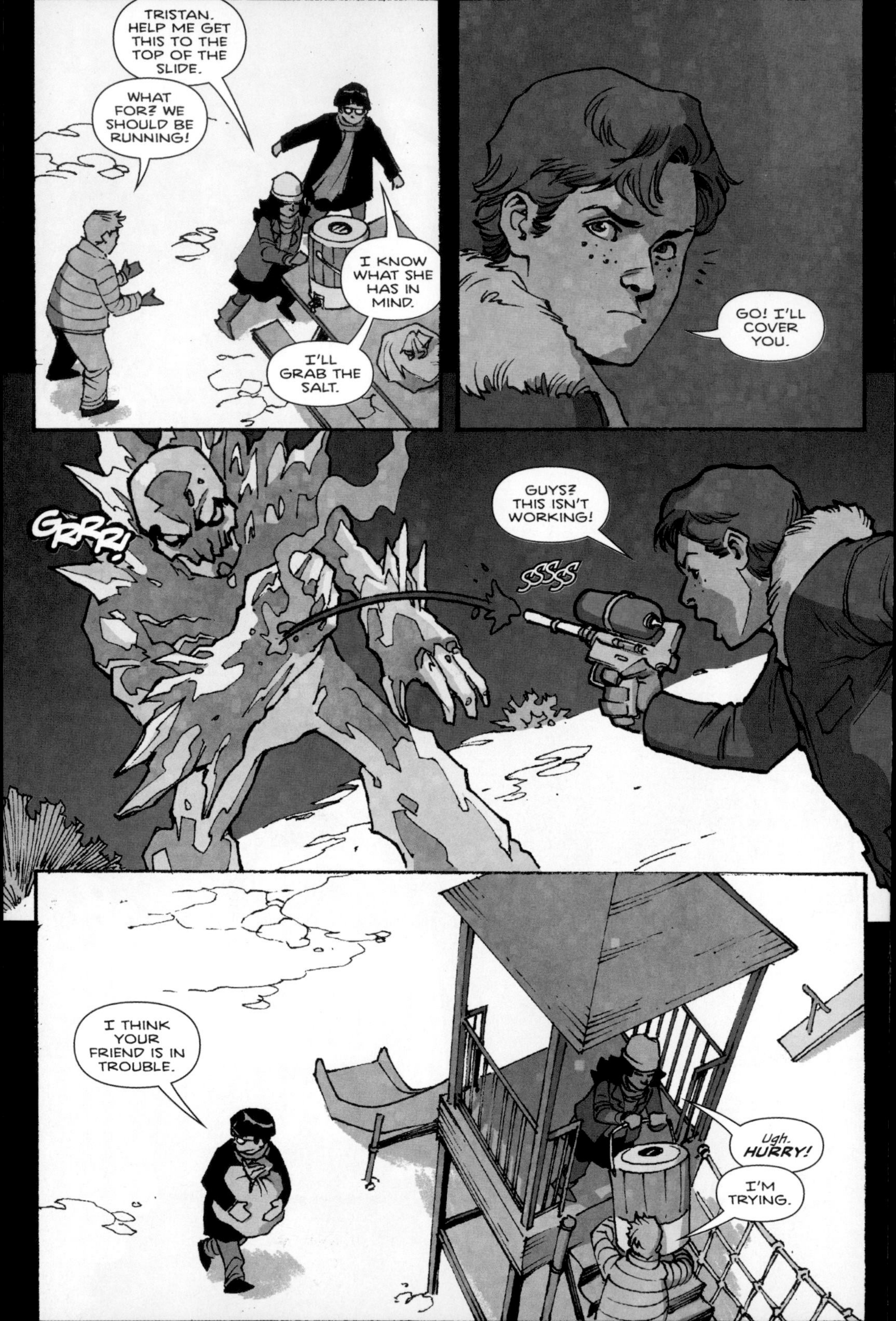
TRISTAN. HELP ME GET THIS TO THE TOP OF THE SLIDE.
WHAT FOR? WE SHOULD BE RUNNING!
I KNOW WHAT SHE HAS IN MIND.
I'LL GRAB THE SALT.
GO! I'LL COVER YOU.
GRRR!
GUYS? THIS ISN'T WORKING!
SSSSS
I THINK YOUR FRIEND IS IN TROUBLE.
Ugh. HURRY!
I'M TRYING.

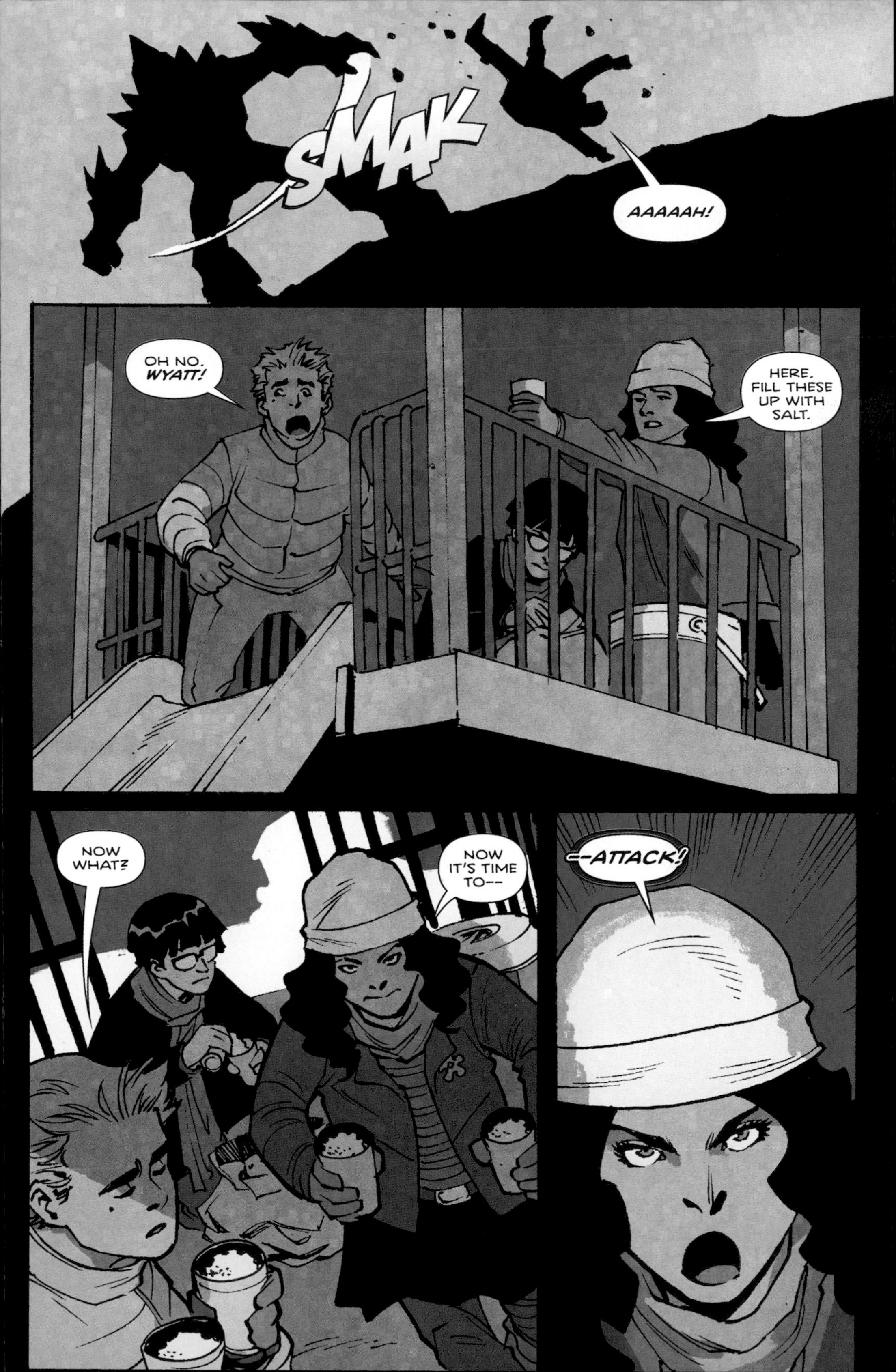
SMAK
AAAAAH!
OH NO. WYATT!
HERE. FILL THESE UP WITH SALT.
NOW WHAT?
NOW IT'S TIME TO--
--ATTACK!

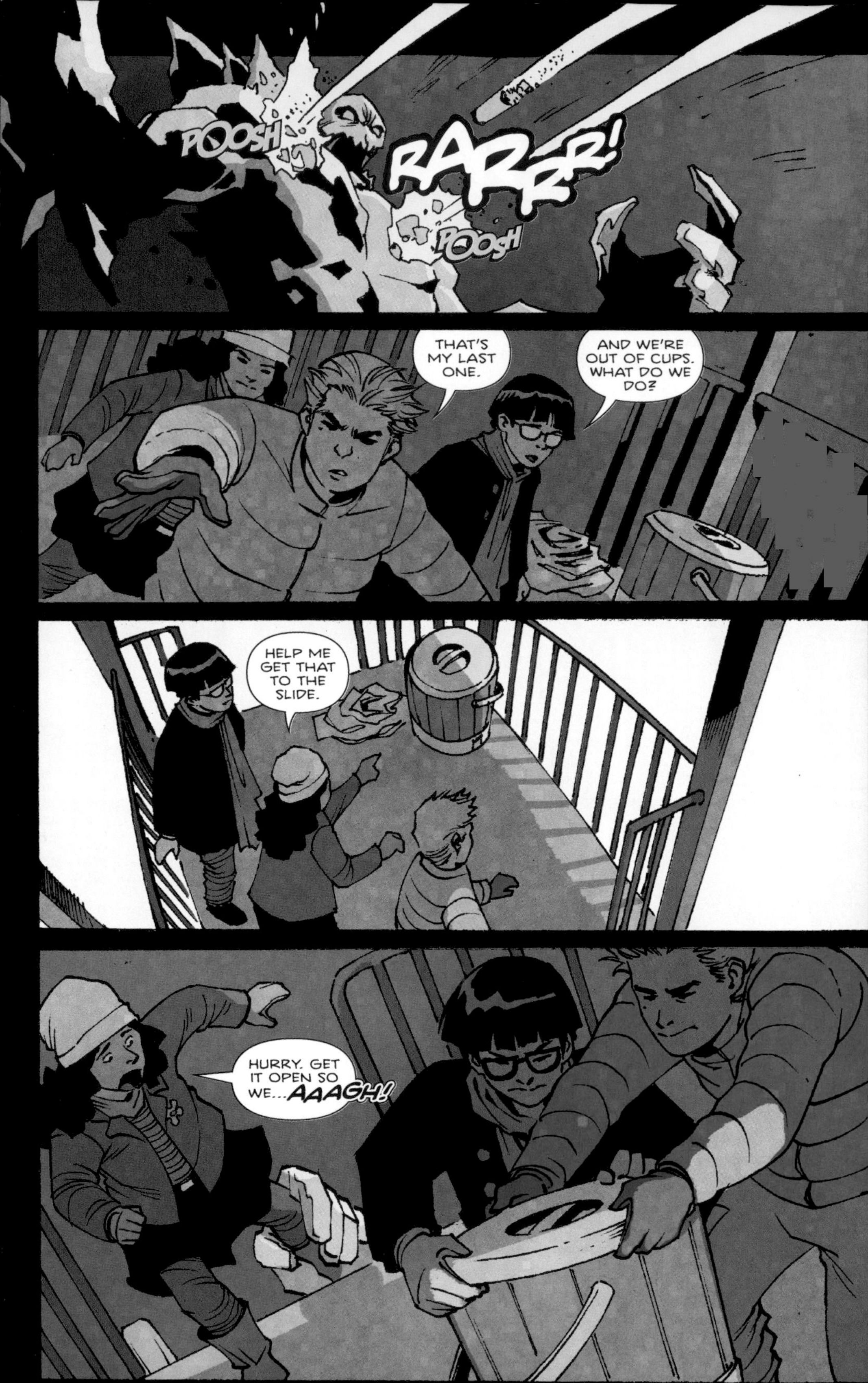
POOSH
RARRR!
POOSH
THAT'S MY LAST ONE.
AND WE'RE OUT OF CUPS. WHAT DO WE DO?
HELP ME GET THAT TO THE SLIDE.
HURRY. GET IT OPEN SO WE...AAAGH!

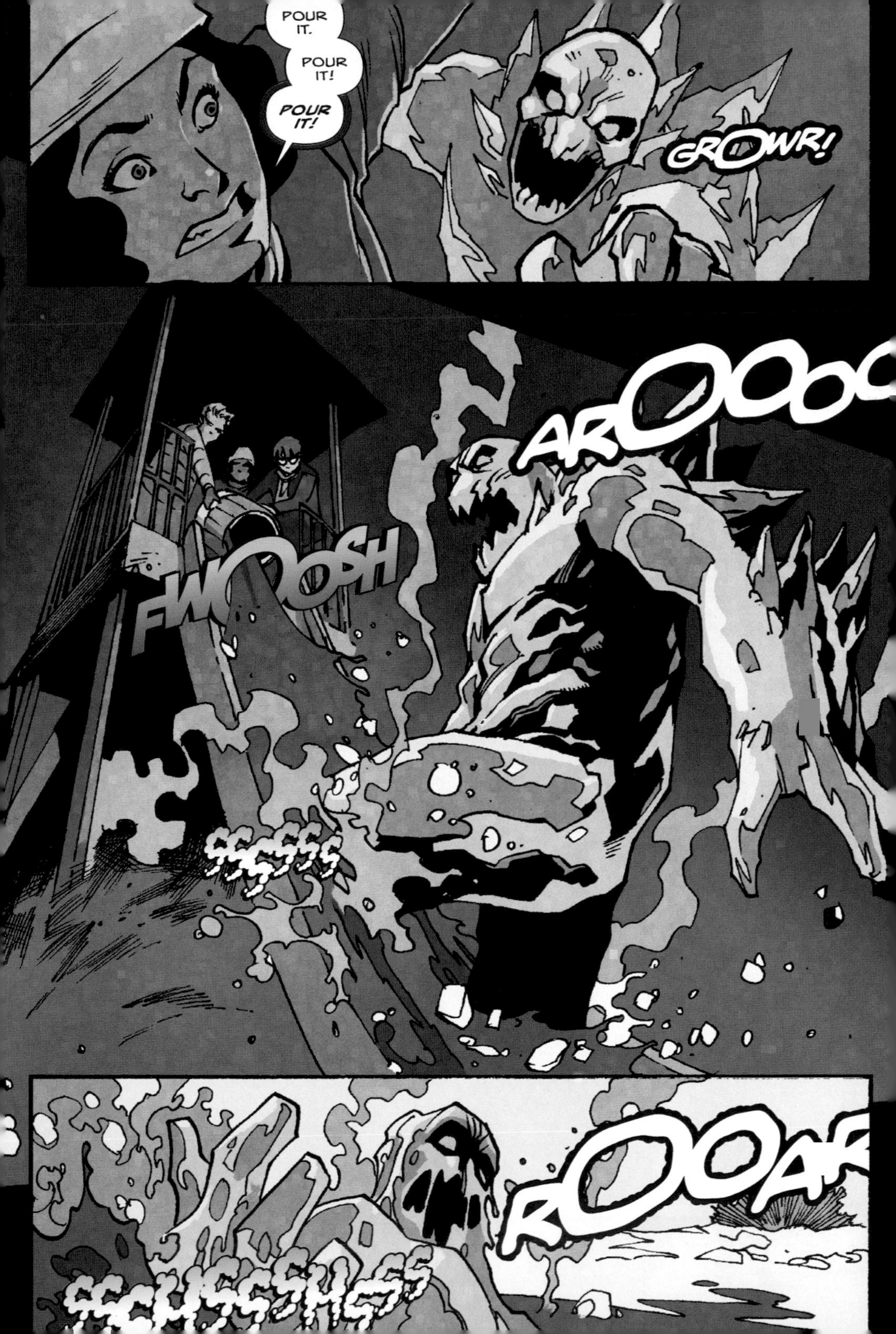
POUR IT.
POUR IT!
POUR IT!
GROWR!
AROOOO
FWOOSH
SSSSSS
ROOAR

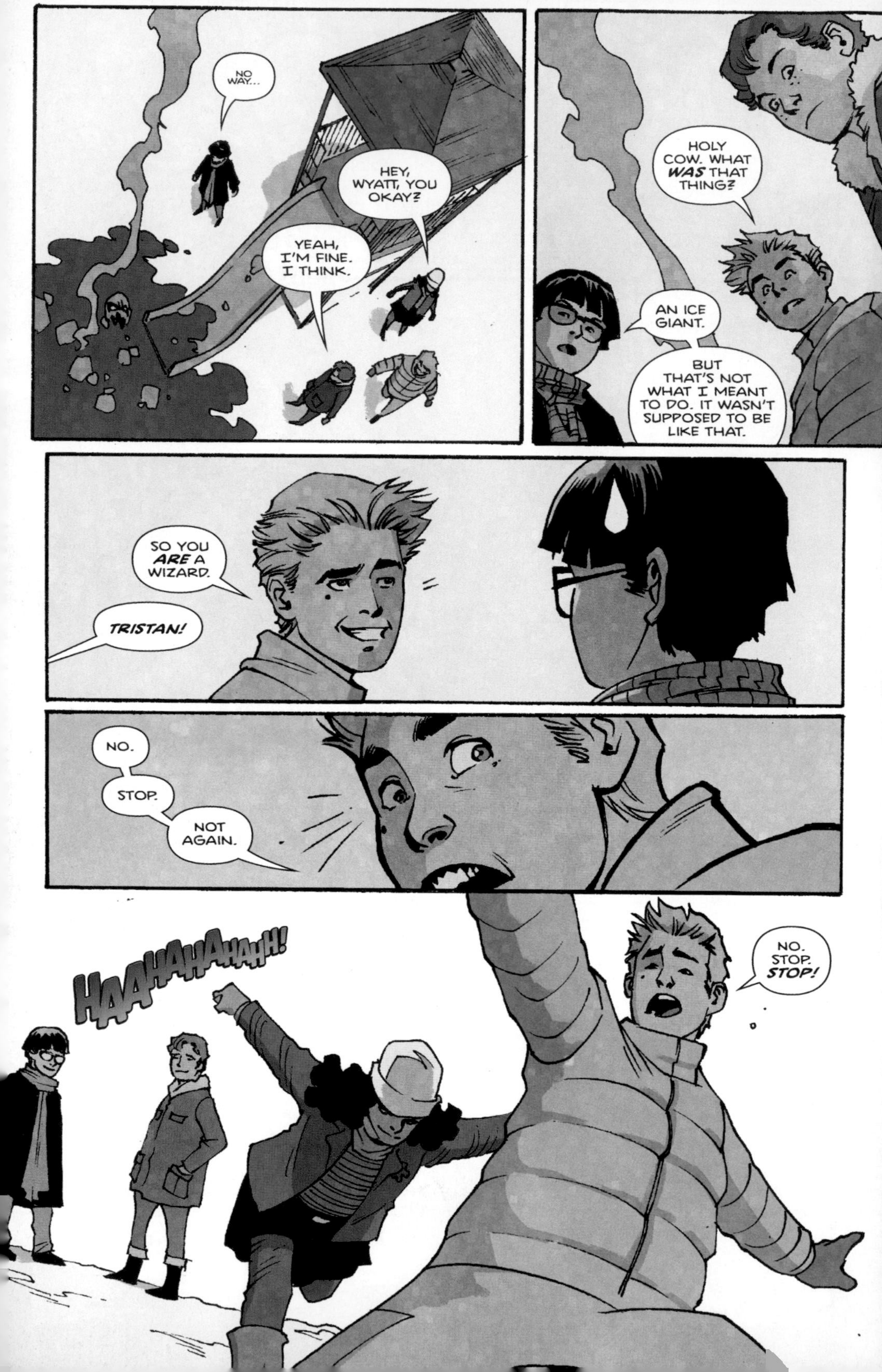
NO WAY...
HEY, WYATT, YOU OKAY?
YEAH, I'M FINE. I THINK.
HOLY COW. WHAT WAS THAT THING?
AN ICE GIANT.
BUT THAT'S NOT WHAT I MEANT TO DO. IT WASN'T SUPPOSED TO BE LIKE THAT.
SO YOU ARE A WIZARD.
TRISTAN!
NO.
STOP.
NOT AGAIN.
HAAHAHAHAHH!
NO. STOP. STOP!

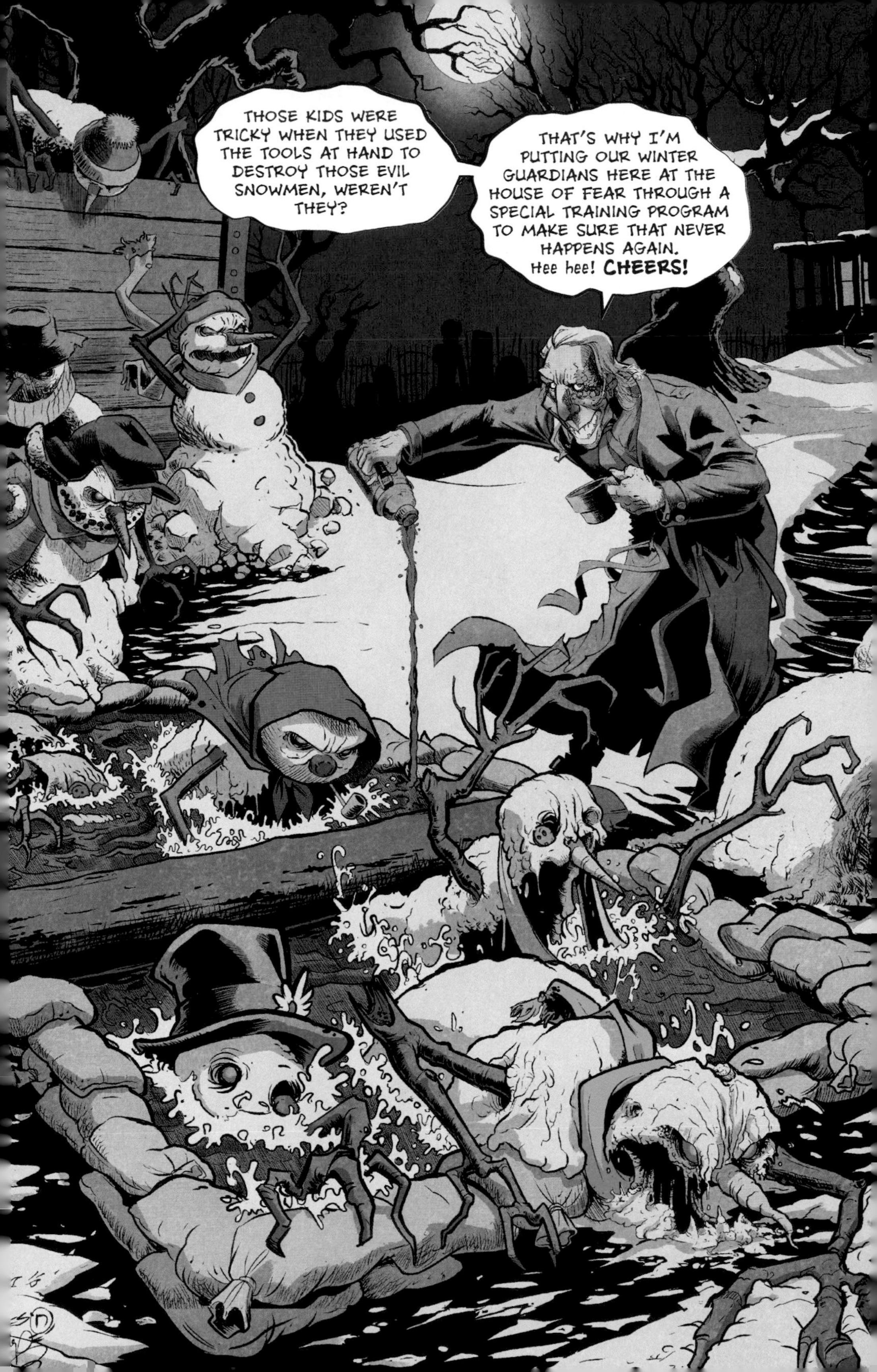
THOSE KIDS WERE TRICKY WHEN THEY USED THE TOOLS AT HAND TO DESTROY THOSE EVIL SNOWMEN, WEREN'T THEY?
THAT'S WHY I'M PUTTING OUR WINTER GUARDIANS HERE AT THE HOUSE OF FEAR THROUGH A SPECIAL TRAINING PROGRAM TO MAKE SURE THAT NEVER HAPPENS AGAIN. Hee hee! **CHEERS!**

DEAD LAKE

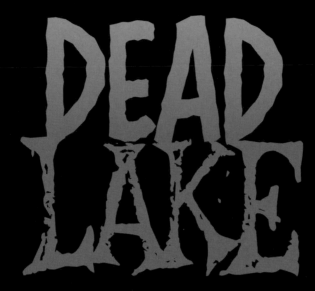

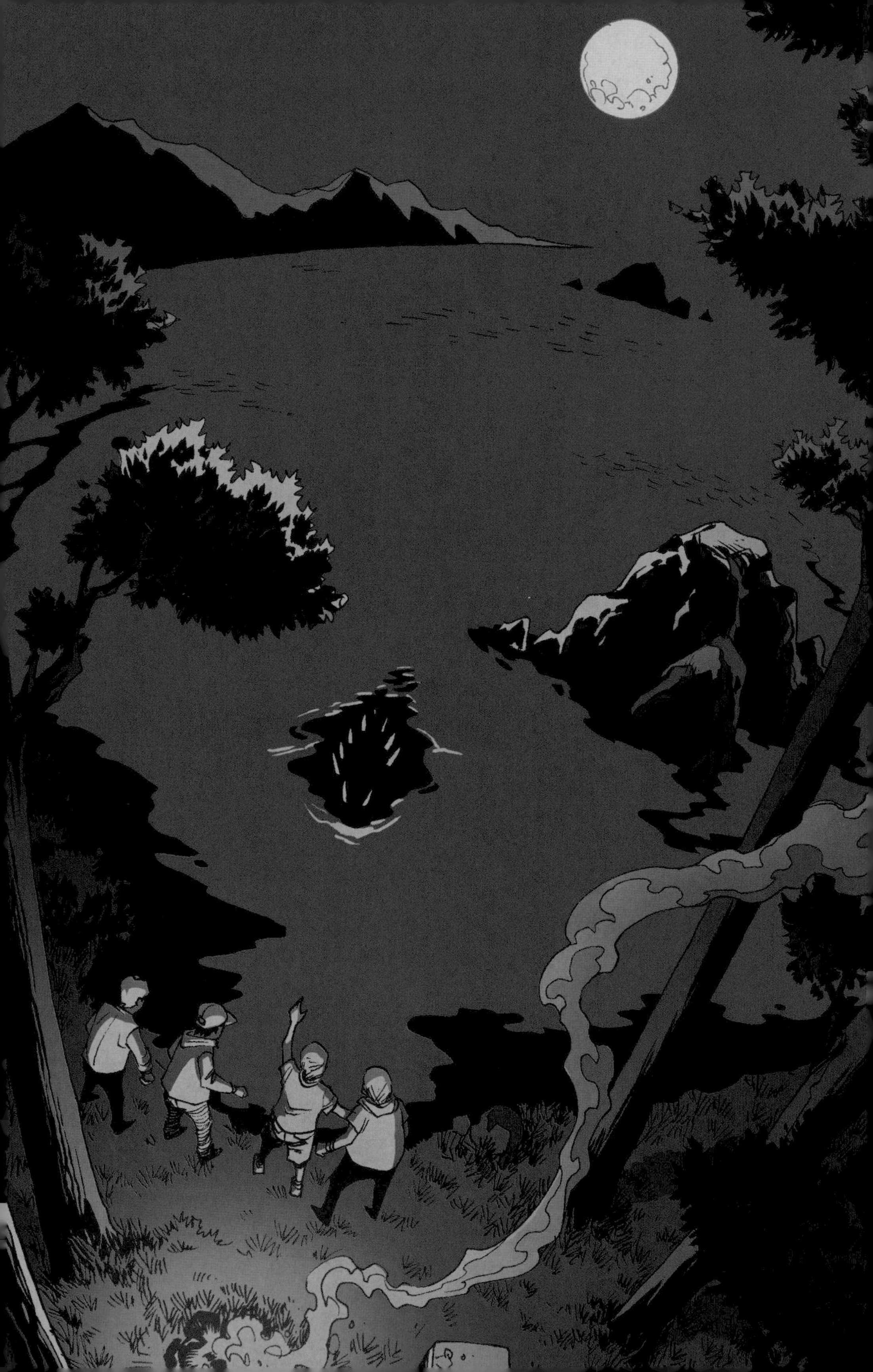

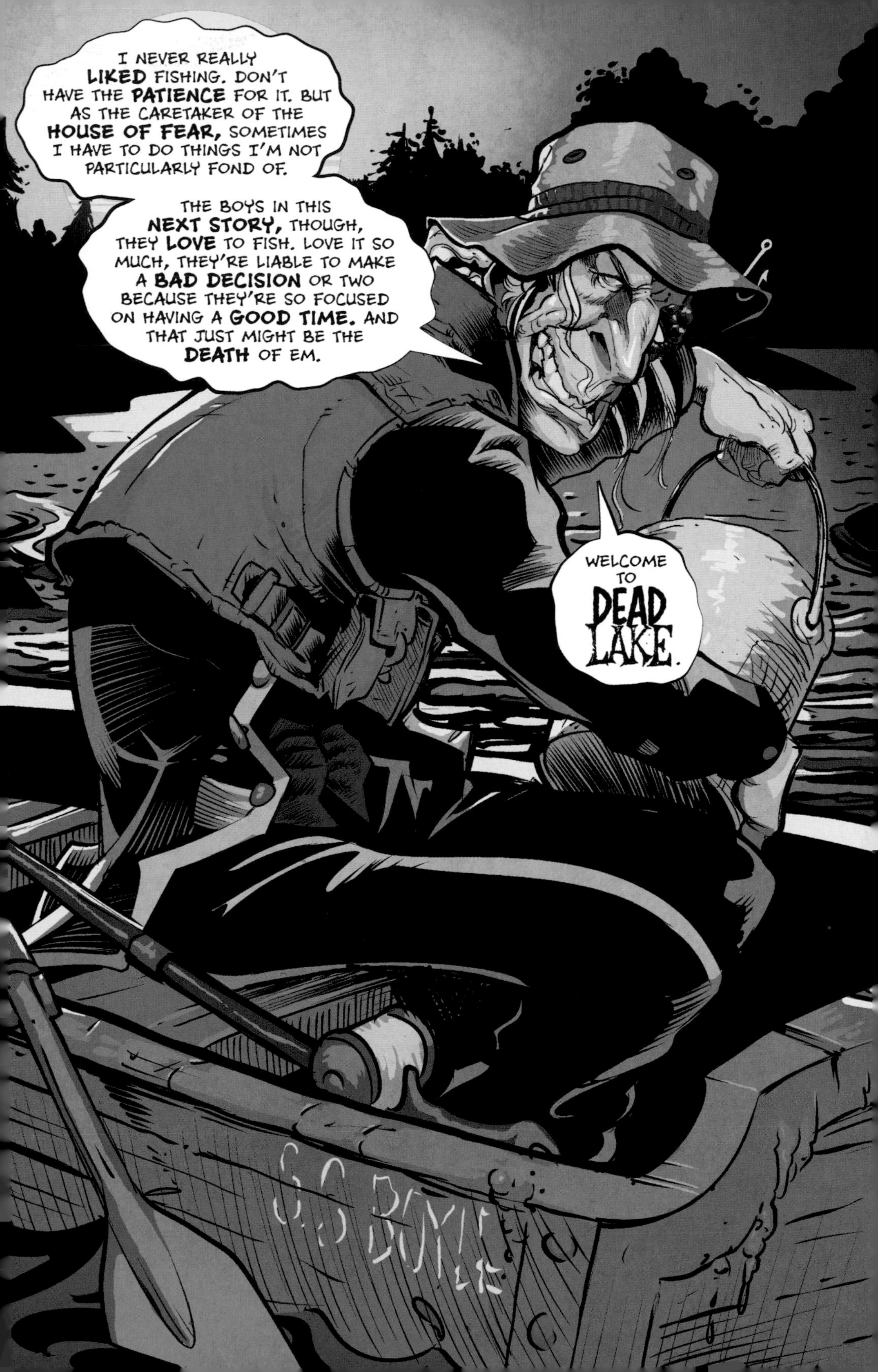
I NEVER REALLY LIKED FISHING. DON'T HAVE THE PATIENCE FOR IT. BUT AS THE CARETAKER OF THE HOUSE OF FEAR, SOMETIMES I HAVE TO DO THINGS I'M NOT PARTICULARLY FOND OF.
THE BOYS IN THIS NEXT STORY, THOUGH, THEY LOVE TO FISH. LOVE IT SO MUCH, THEY'RE LIABLE TO MAKE A BAD DECISION OR TWO BECAUSE THEY'RE SO FOCUSED ON HAVING A GOOD TIME. AND THAT JUST MIGHT BE THE DEATH OF EM.
WELCOME TO DEAD LAKE.

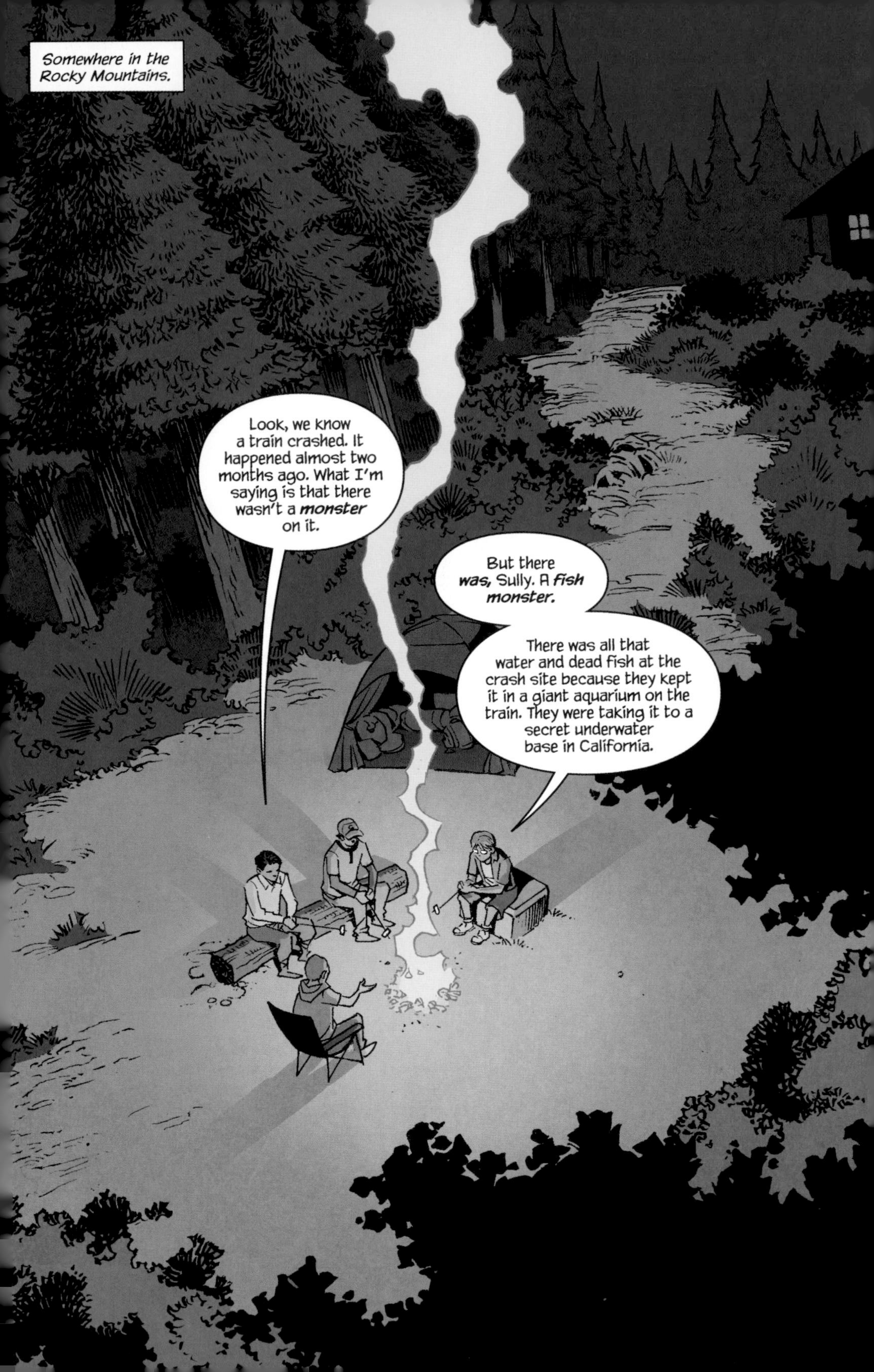
Somewhere in the Rocky Mountains.
Look, we know a train crashed. It happened almost two months ago. What I'm saying is that there wasn't a *monster* on it.
But there *was,* Sully. A *fish monster.*
There was all that water and dead fish at the crash site because they kept it in a giant aquarium on the train. They were taking it to a secret underwater base in California.

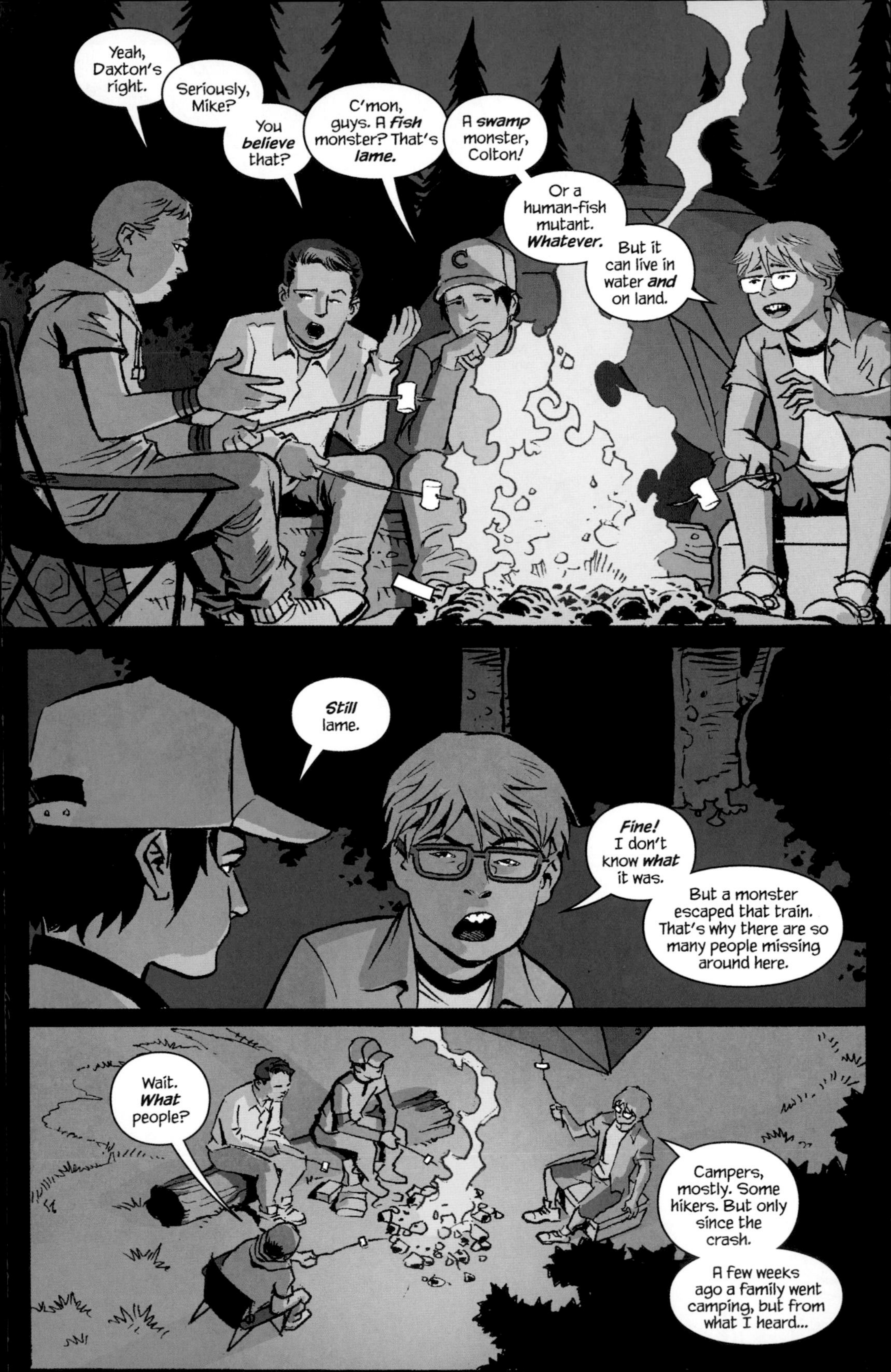
Yeah, Daxton's right.
Seriously, Mike?
You *believe* that?
C'mon, guys. A *fish* monster? That's *lame.*
A *swamp* monster, Colton!
Or a human-fish mutant. *Whatever.*
But it can live in water *and* on land.
Still lame.
Fine! I don't know *what* it was.
But a monster escaped that train. That's why there are so many people missing around here.
Wait. *What* people?
Campers, mostly. Some hikers. But only since the crash.
A few weeks ago a family went camping, but from what I heard...

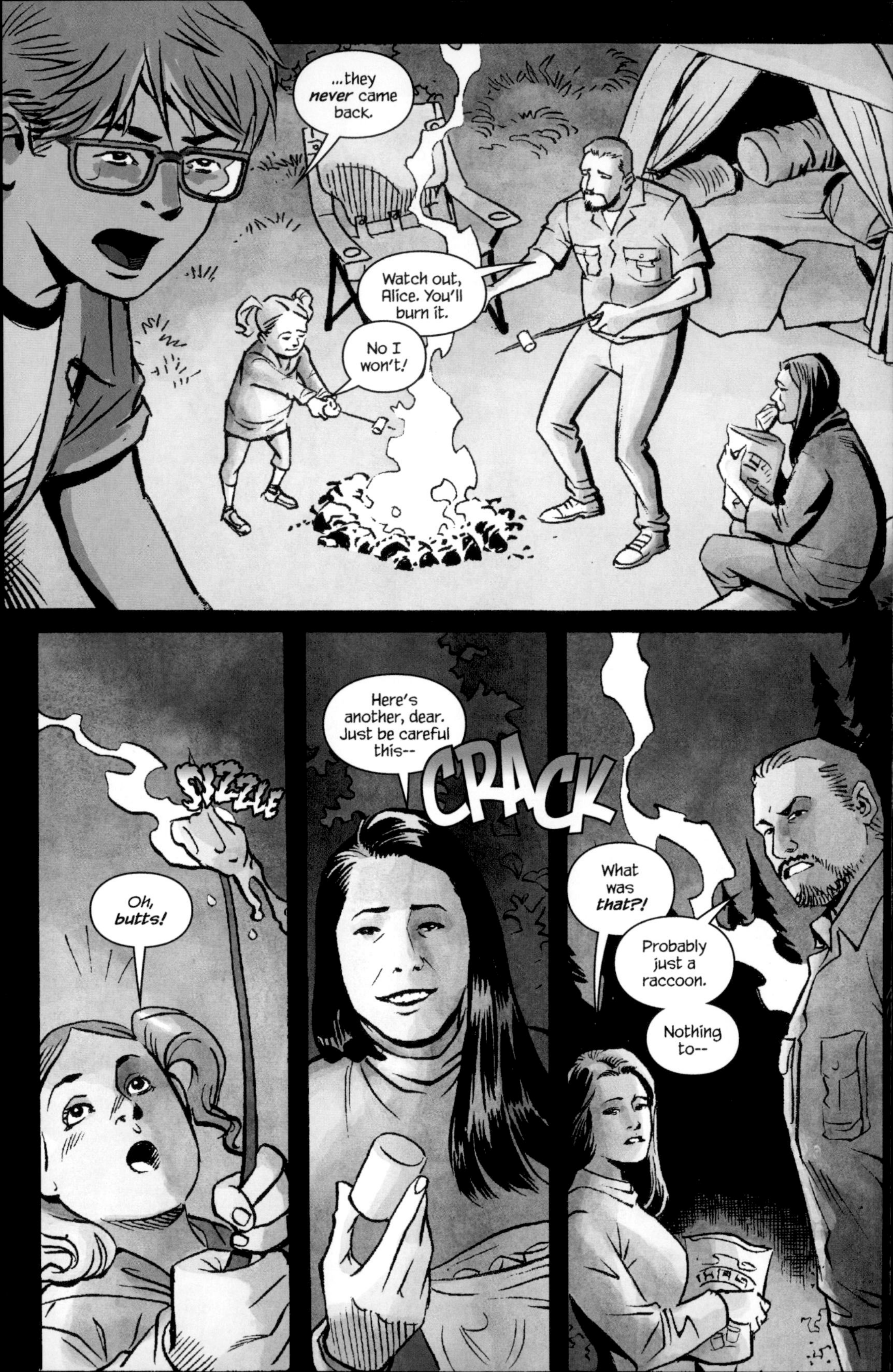
...they *never* came back.
Watch out, Alice. You'll burn it.
No I won't!
SIZZLE
Oh, *butts!*
Here's another, dear. Just be careful this--
CRACK
What was *that?!*
Probably just a raccoon.
Nothing to--

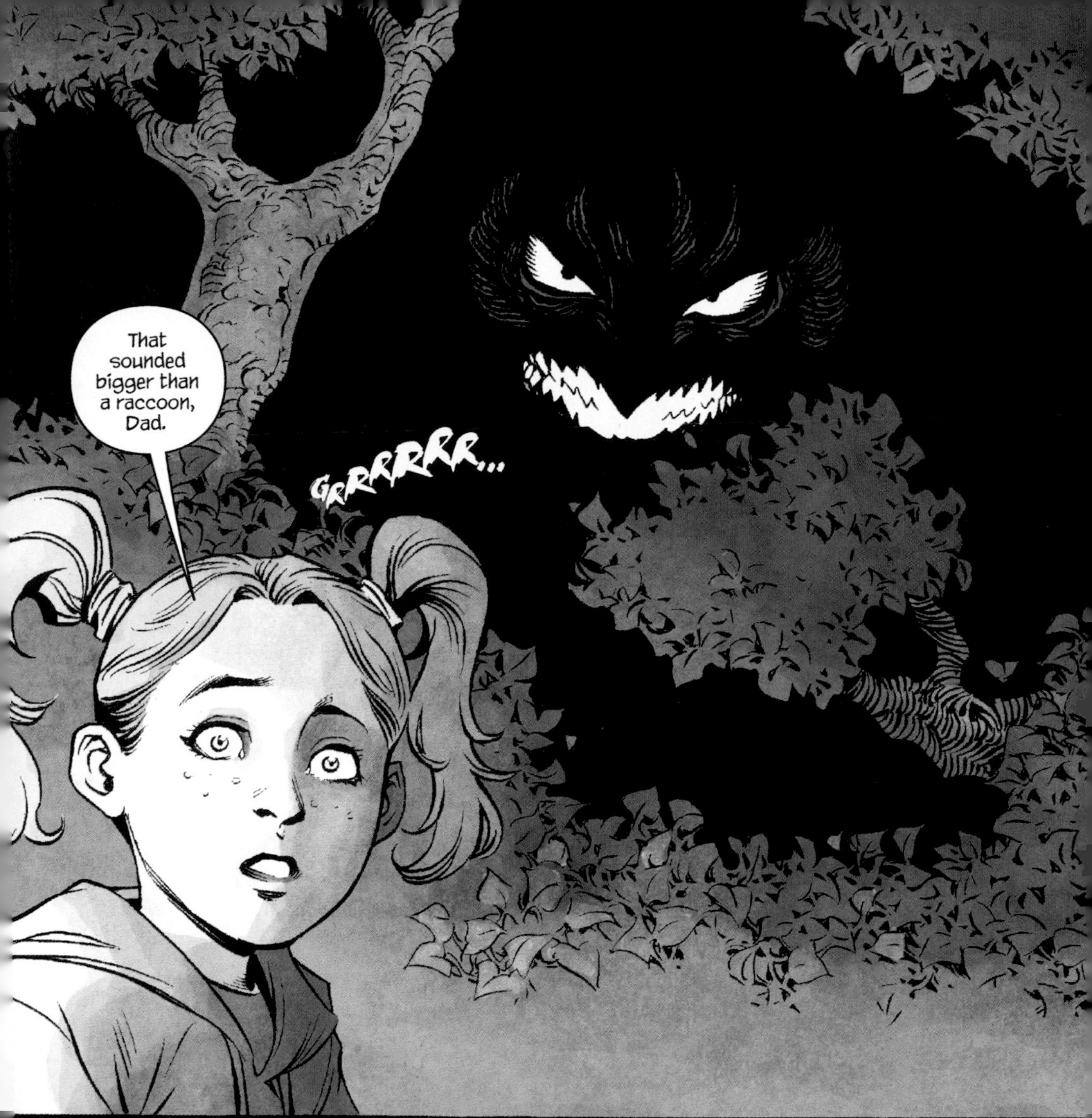
That sounded bigger than a raccoon, Dad.
GRRRRRR...

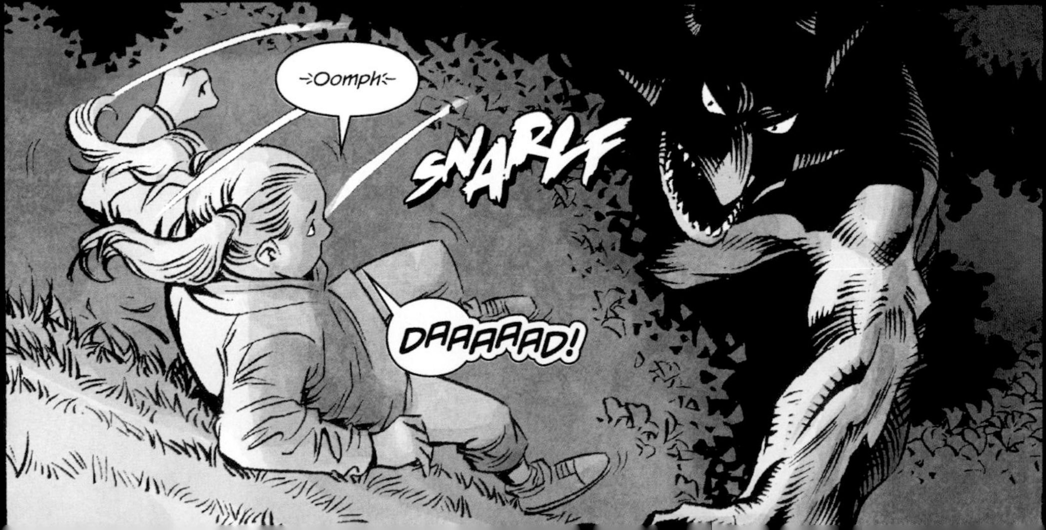
Oomph
SNARLF
DAAAAAD!

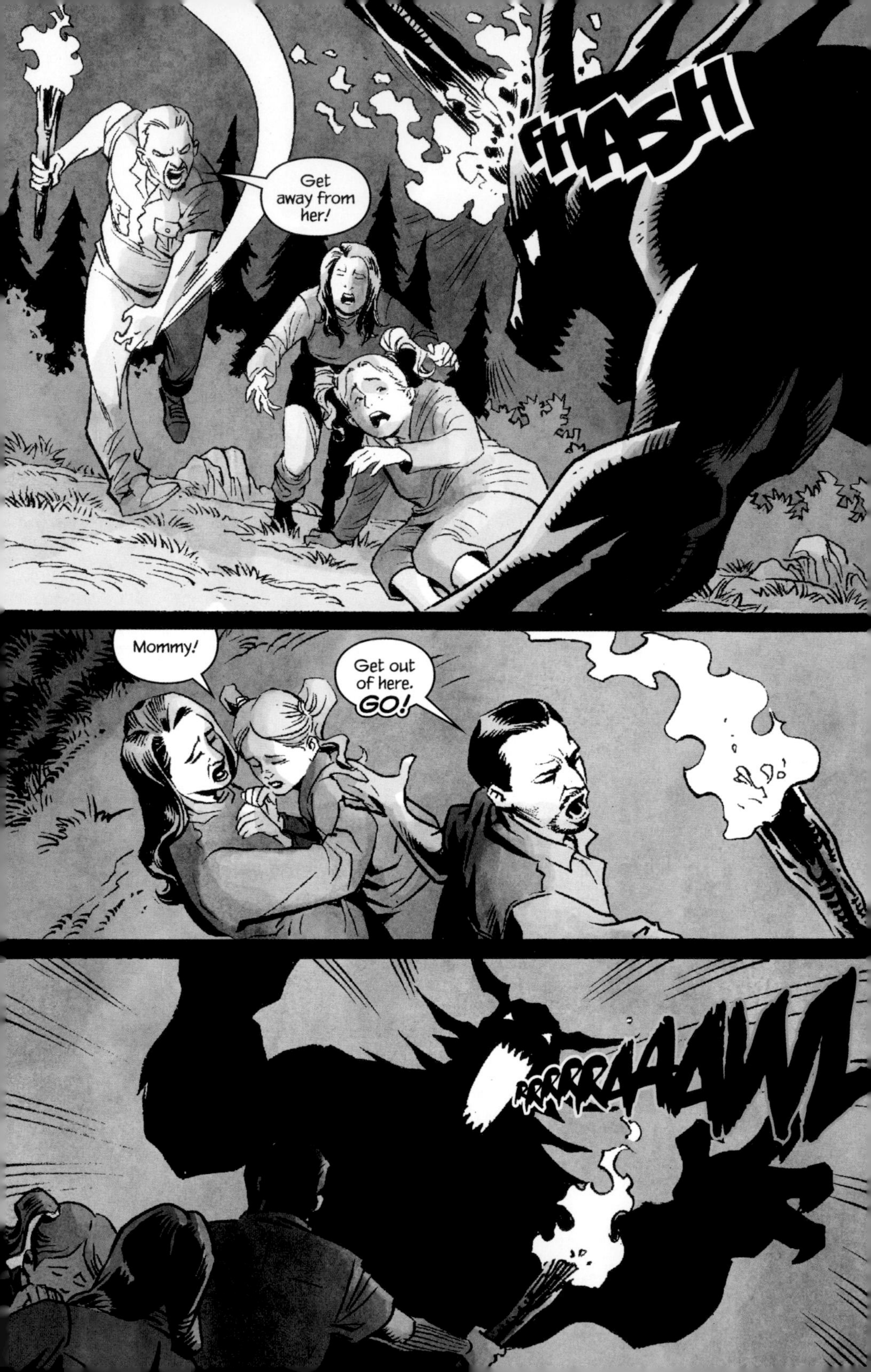
FHASH
Get away from her!
Mommy!
Get out of here. GO!
RRRRRAAAWL

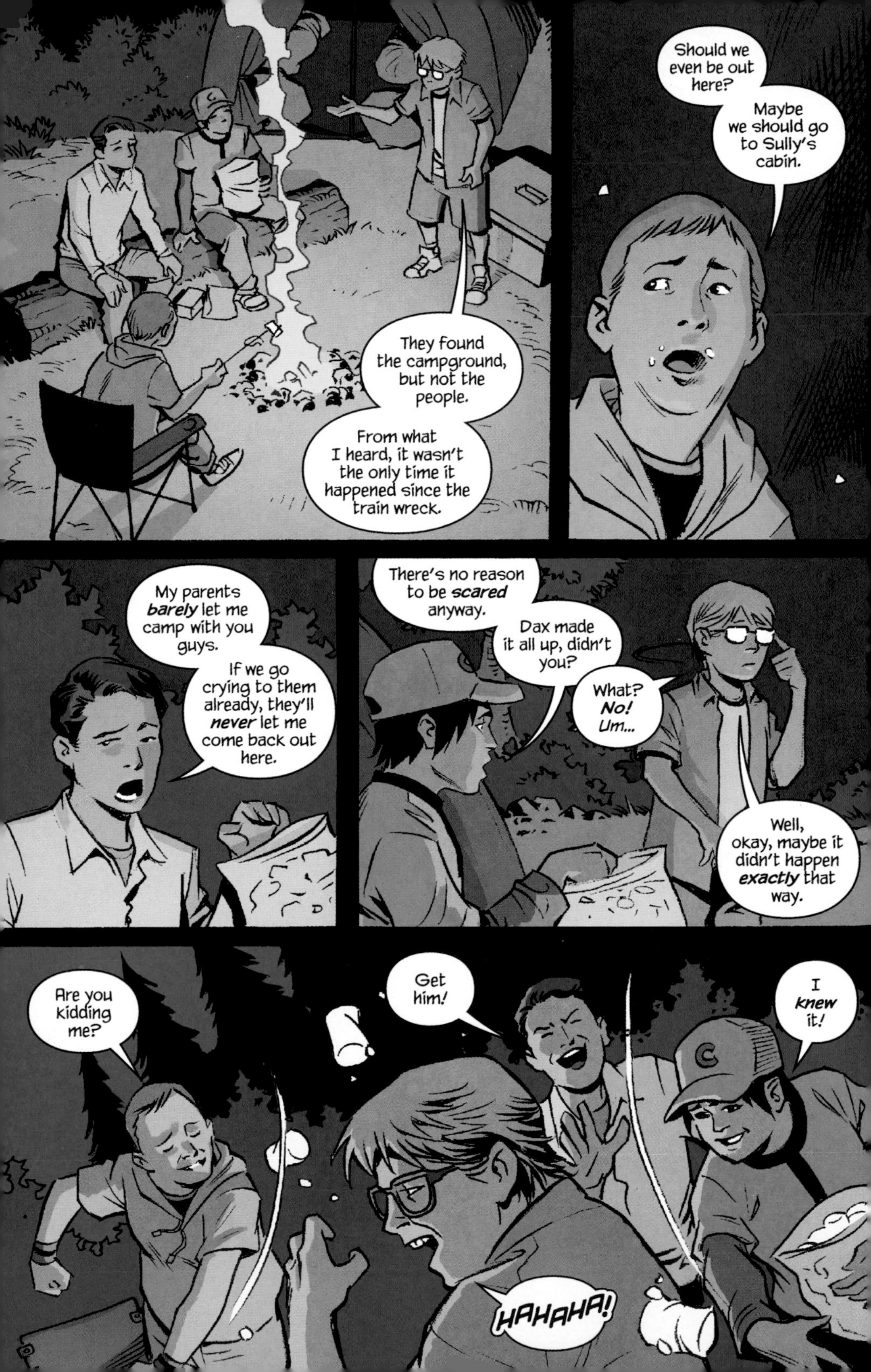
They found the campground, but not the people.
From what I heard, it wasn't the only time it happened since the train wreck.
Should we even be out here?
Maybe we should go to Sully's cabin.
My parents *barely* let me camp with you guys.
If we go crying to them already, they'll *never* let me come back out here.
There's no reason to be *scared* anyway.
Dax made it all up, didn't you?
What? *No!* Um...
Well, okay, maybe it didn't happen *exactly* that way.
Are you kidding me?
Get him!
I *knew* it!
HAHAHA!

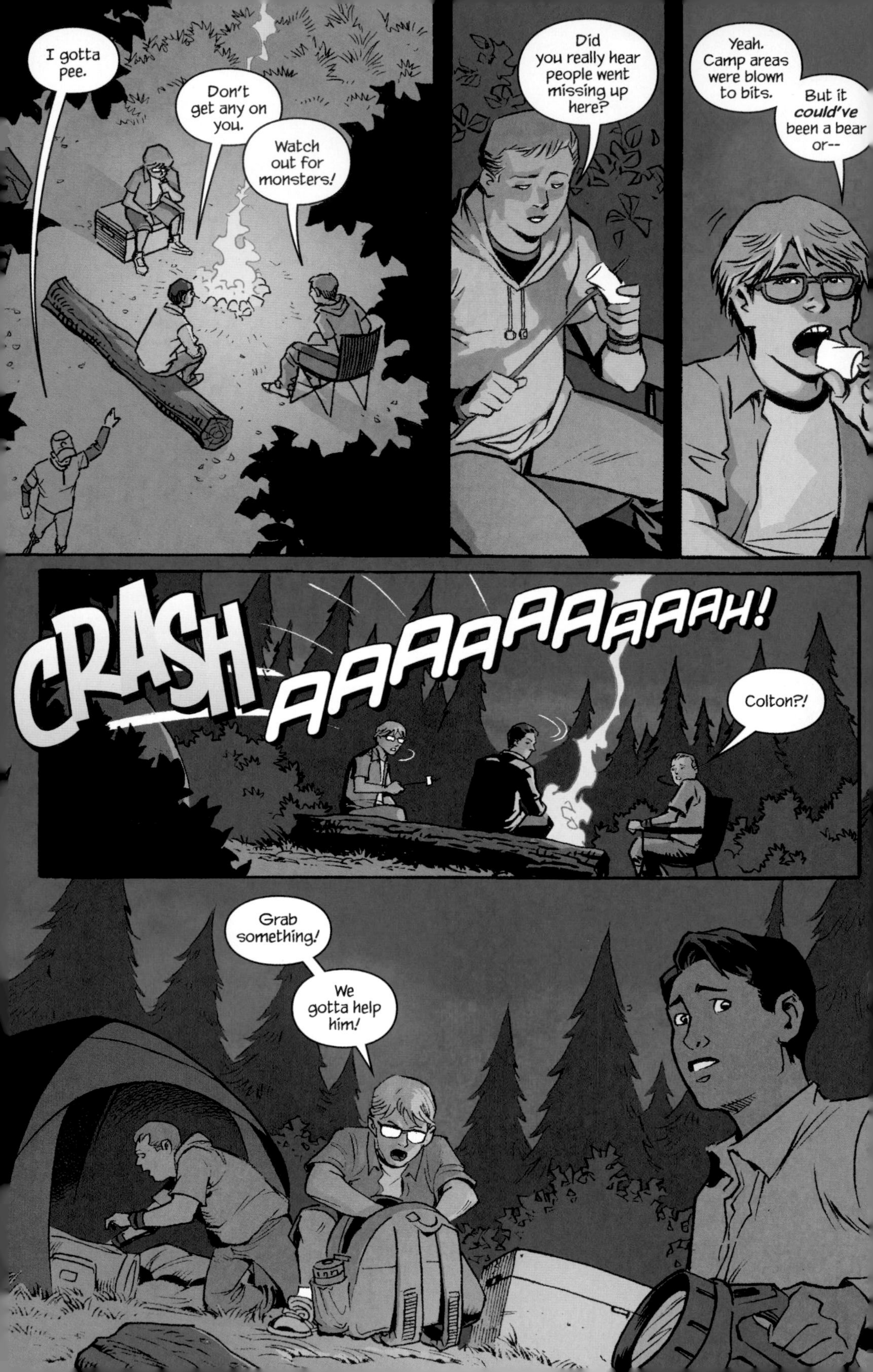
I gotta pee.
Don't get any on you.
Watch out for monsters!
Did you really hear people went missing up here?
Yeah. Camp areas were blown to bits.
But it *could've* been a bear or--
CRASH
AAAAAAAAAAAH!
Colton?!
Grab something!
We gotta help him!

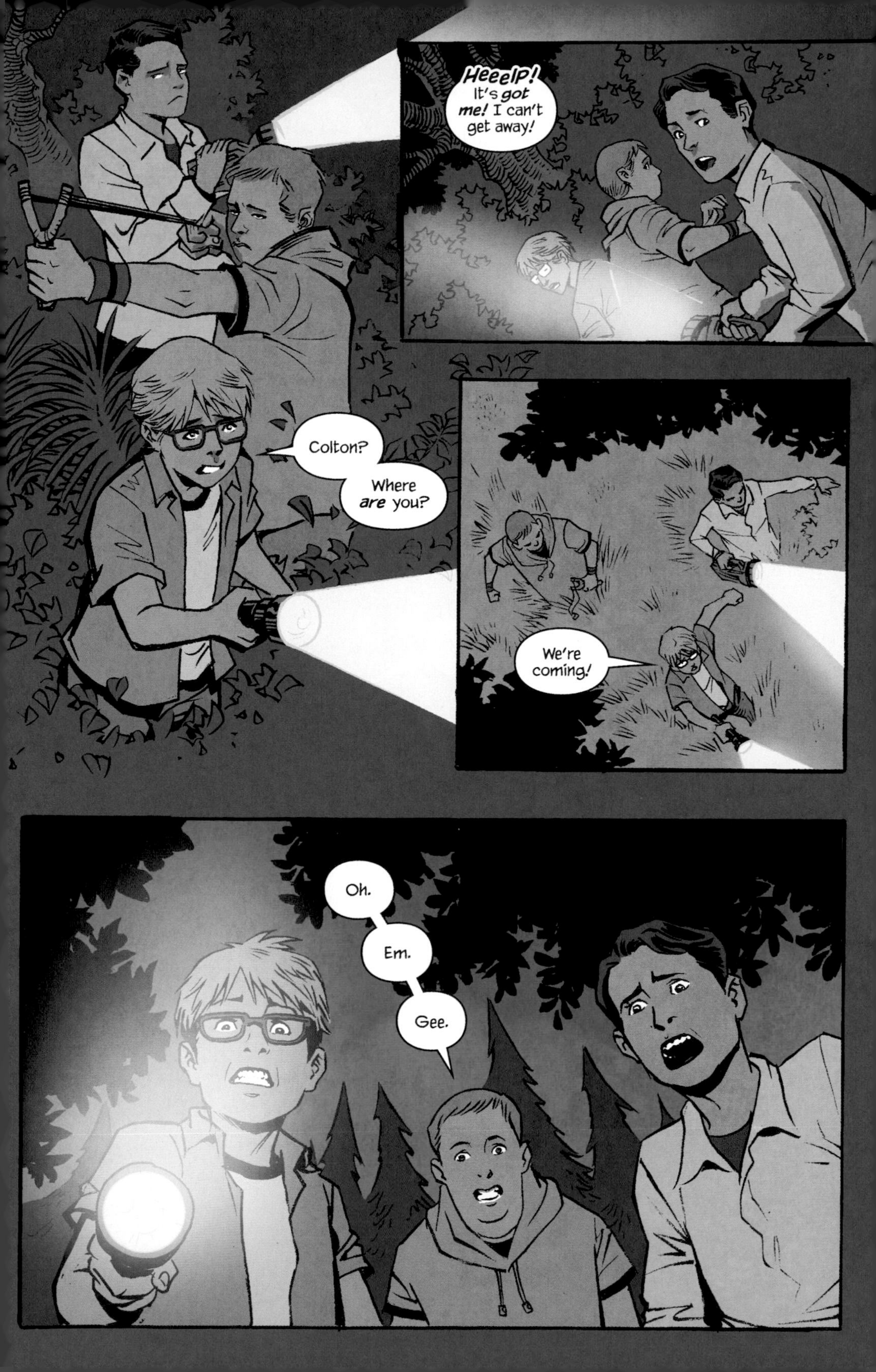
Heeelp! It's got me! I can't get away!
Colton?
Where are you?
We're coming!
Oh.
Em.
Gee.

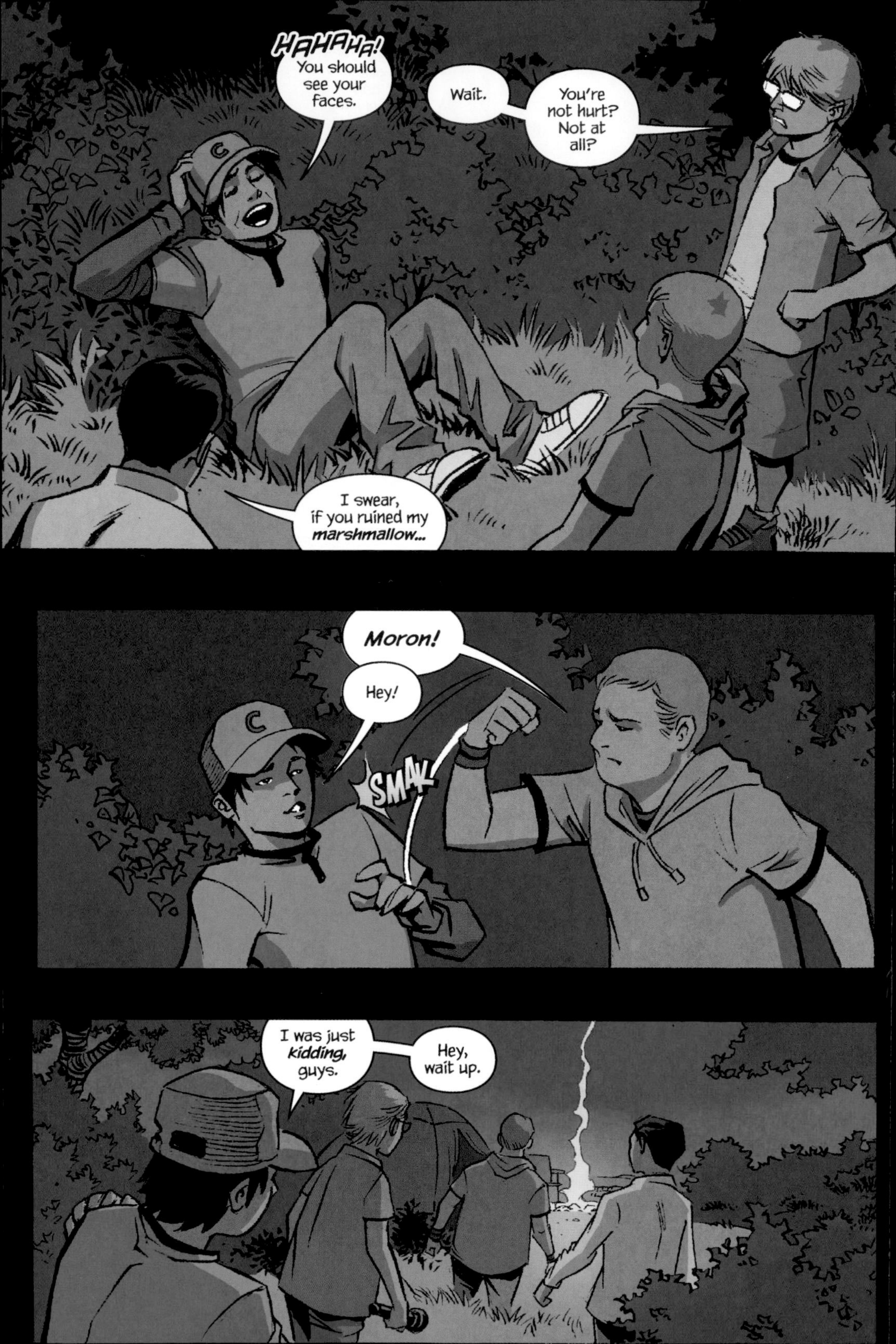
HAHAHA! You should see your faces.
Wait.
You're not hurt? Not at all?
I swear, if you ruined my *marshmallow...*
Moron!
Hey!
SMAK
I was just *kidding,* guys.
Hey, wait up.

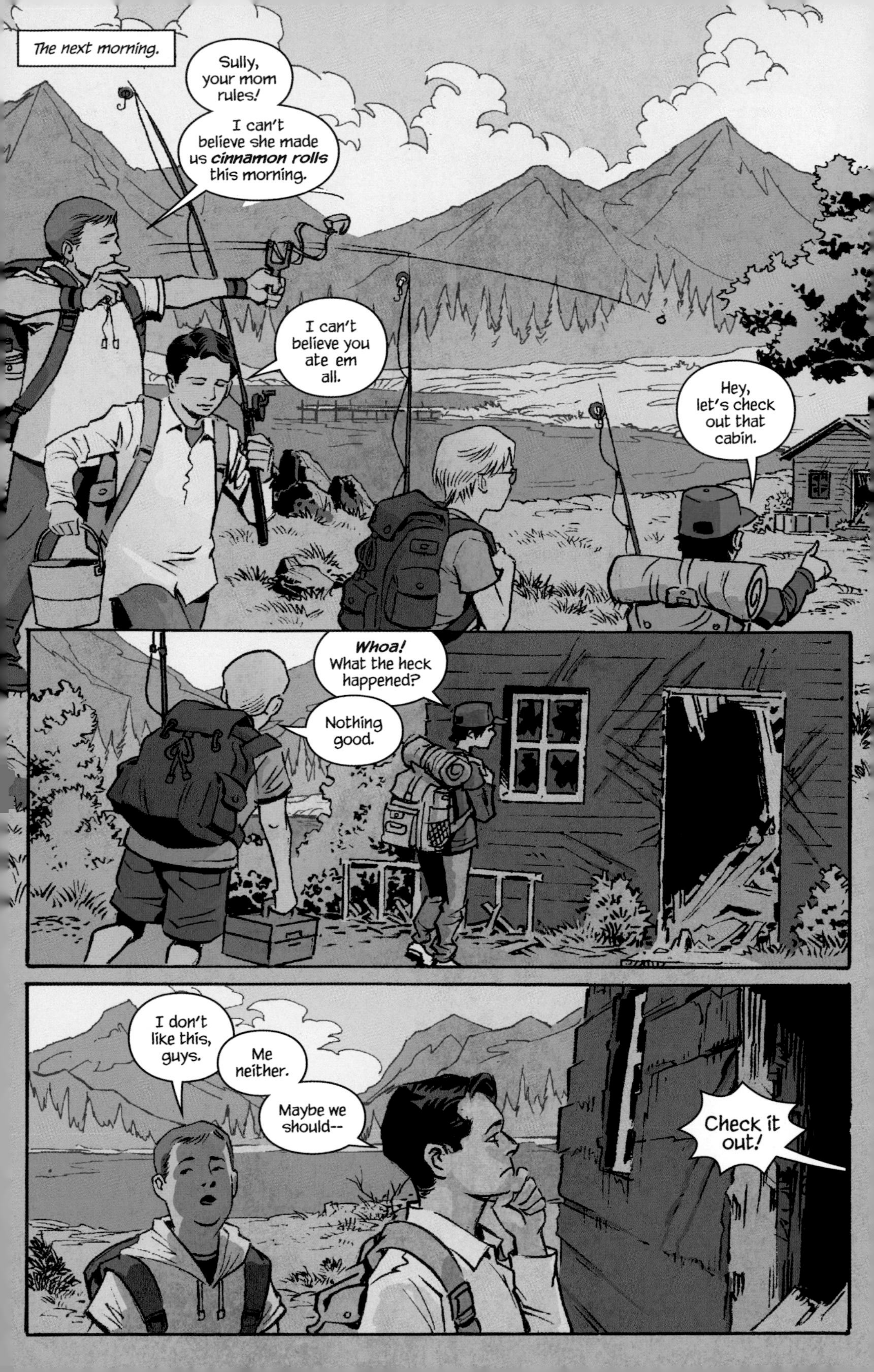
The next morning.
Sully, your mom rules!
I can't believe she made us *cinnamon rolls* this morning.
I can't believe you ate em all.
Hey, let's check out that cabin.
Whoa! What the heck happened?
Nothing good.
I don't like this, guys.
Me neither.
Maybe we should--
Check it out!

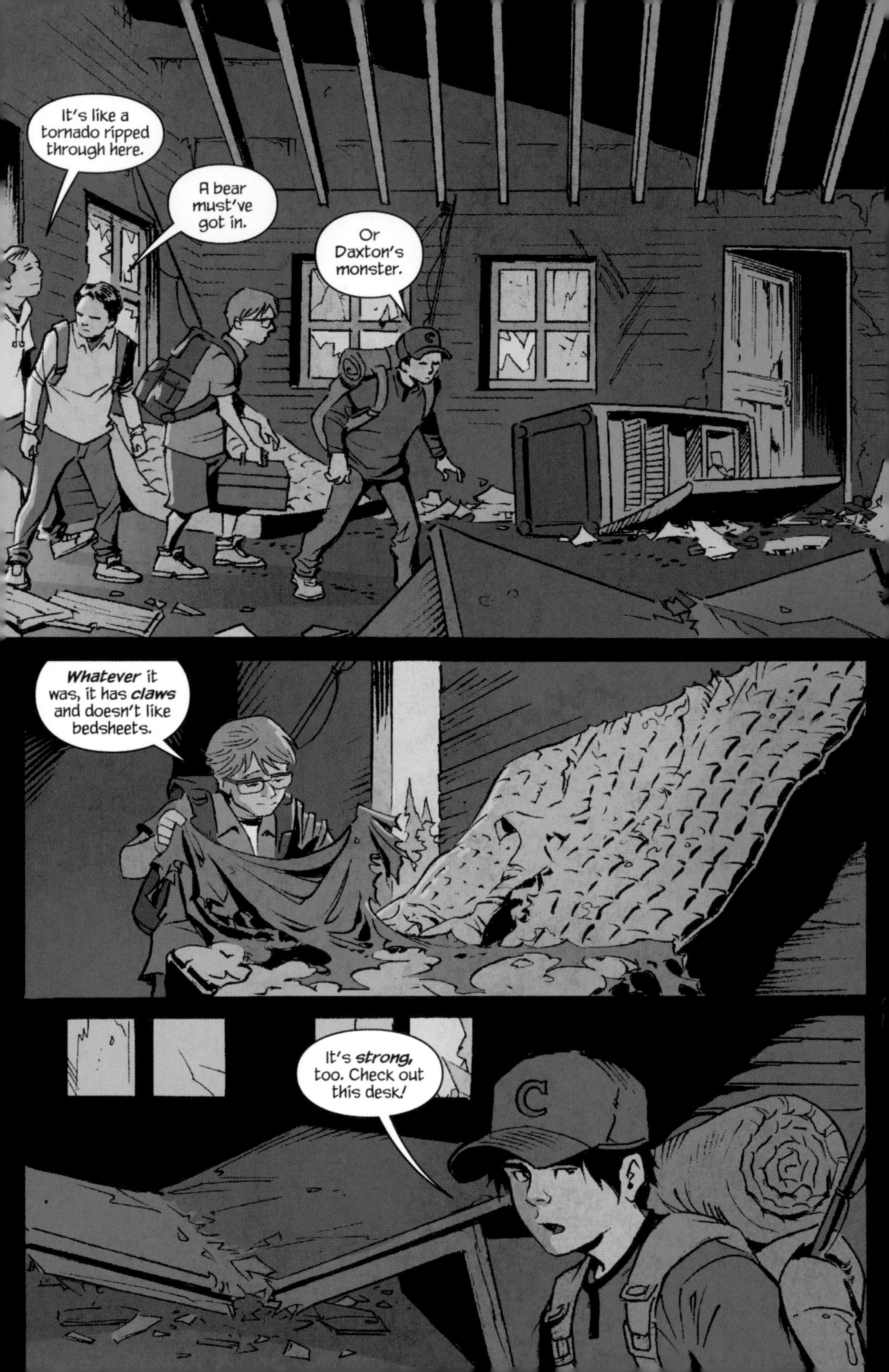
It's like a tornado ripped through here.
A bear must've got in.
Or Daxton's monster.
Whatever it was, it has *claws* and doesn't like bedsheets.
It's *strong,* too. Check out this desk!

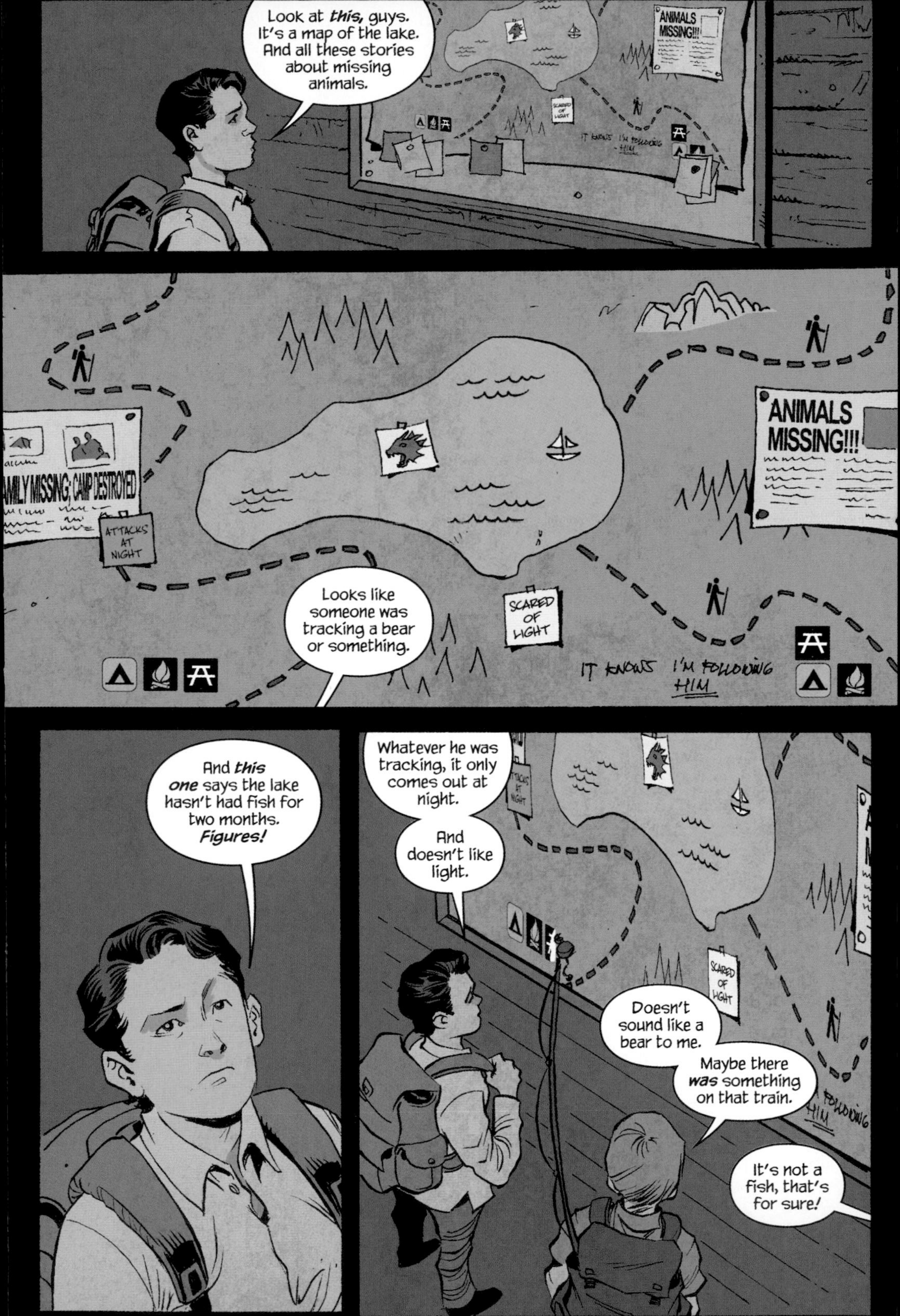

Look at *this,* guys. It's a map of the lake. And all these stories about missing animals.
ANIMALS MISSING!!!
SCARED OF LIGHT
IT KNOWS I'M FOLLOWING HIM
AMILY MISSING; CAMP DESTROYED
ATTACKS AT NIGHT
ANIMALS MISSING!!!
SCARED OF LIGHT
Looks like someone was tracking a bear or something.
IT KNOWS I'M FOLLOWING HIM
And *this one* says the lake hasn't had fish for two months. *Figures!*
Whatever he was tracking, it only comes out at night.
And doesn't like light.
SCARED OF LIGHT
Doesn't sound like a bear to me.
Maybe there *was* something on that train.
It's not a fish, that's for sure!

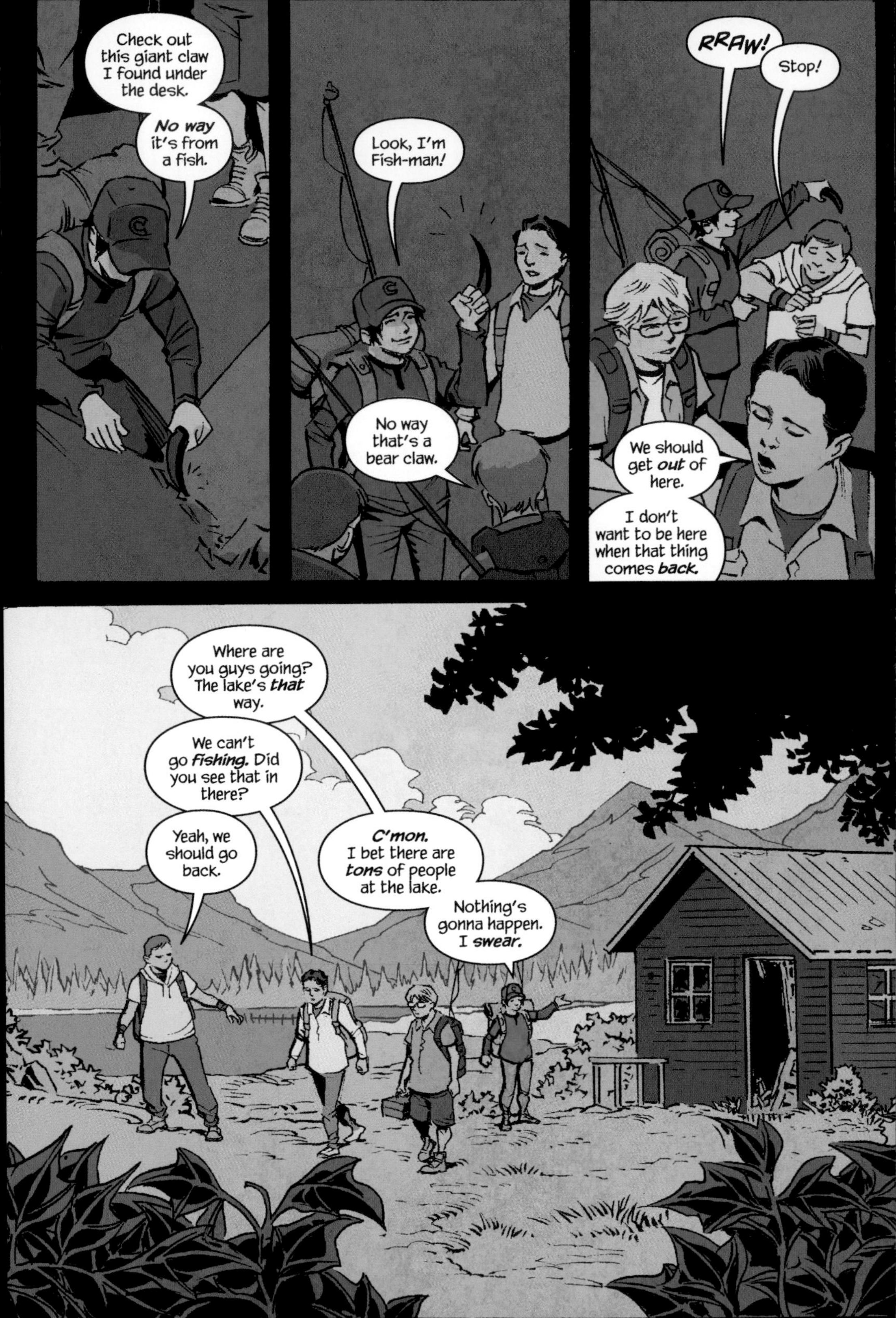

Check out this giant claw I found under the desk.
No way it's from a fish.
Look, I'm Fish-man!
No way that's a bear claw.
RRAW!
Stop!
We should get out of here.
I don't want to be here when that thing comes back.
Where are you guys going? The lake's that way.
We can't go fishing. Did you see that in there?
Yeah, we should go back.
C'mon. I bet there are tons of people at the lake.
Nothing's gonna happen. I swear.

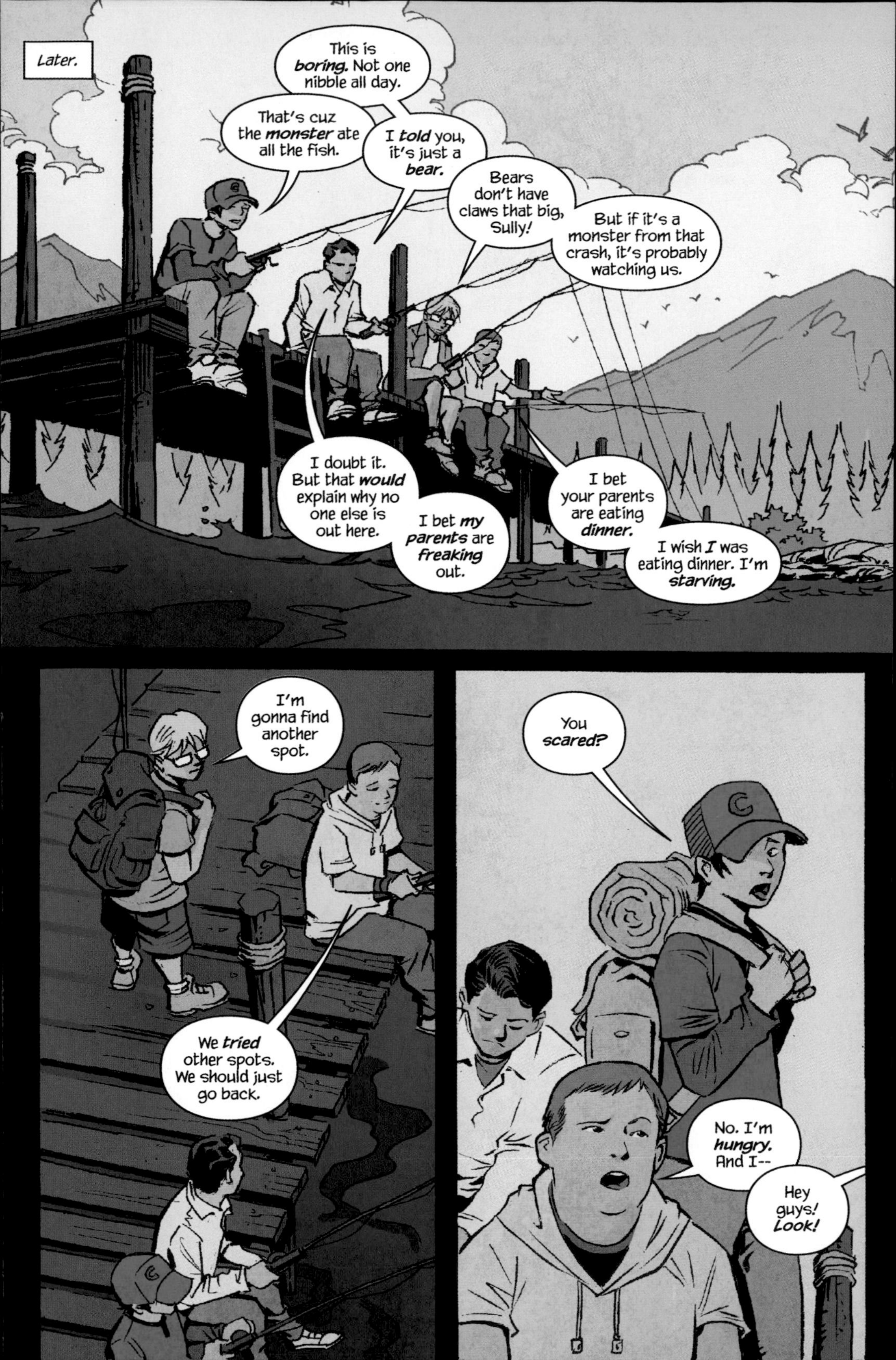
Later.
This is boring. Not one nibble all day.
That's cuz the monster ate all the fish.
I told you, it's just a bear.
Bears don't have claws that big, Sully!
But if it's a monster from that crash, it's probably watching us.
I doubt it. But that would explain why no one else is out here.
I bet my parents are freaking out.
I bet your parents are eating dinner.
I wish I was eating dinner. I'm starving.
I'm gonna find another spot.
We tried other spots. We should just go back.
You scared?
No. I'm hungry. And I--
Hey guys! Look!

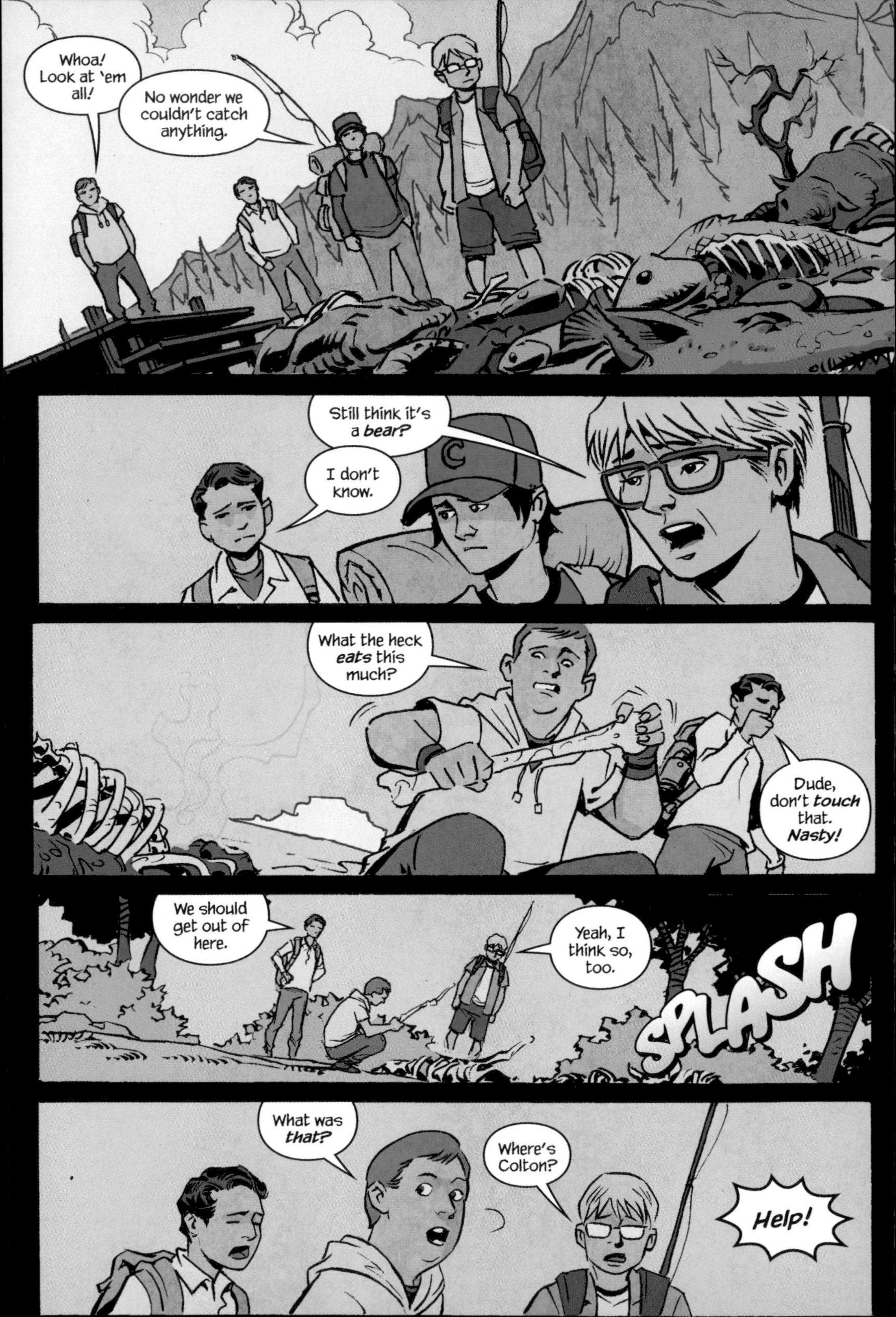
Whoa! Look at 'em all!
No wonder we couldn't catch anything.
Still think it's a *bear?*
I don't know.
What the heck *eats* this much?
Dude, don't *touch* that. *Nasty!*
We should get out of here.
Yeah, I think so, too.
SPLASH
What was *that?*
Where's Colton?
Help!

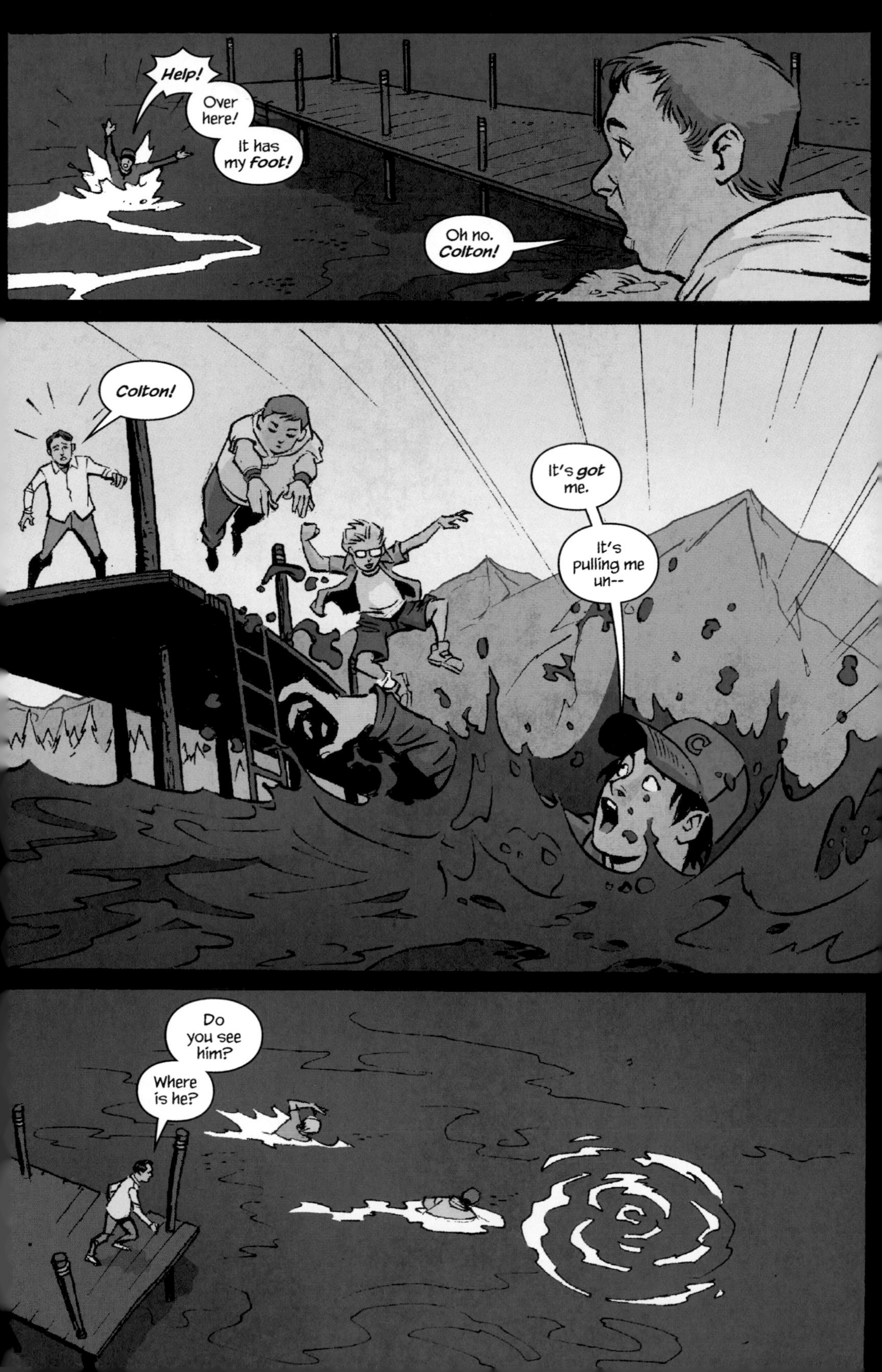
Help!
Over here!
It has my foot!
Oh no. Colton!
Colton!
It's got me.
It's pulling me un--
Do you see him?
Where is he?

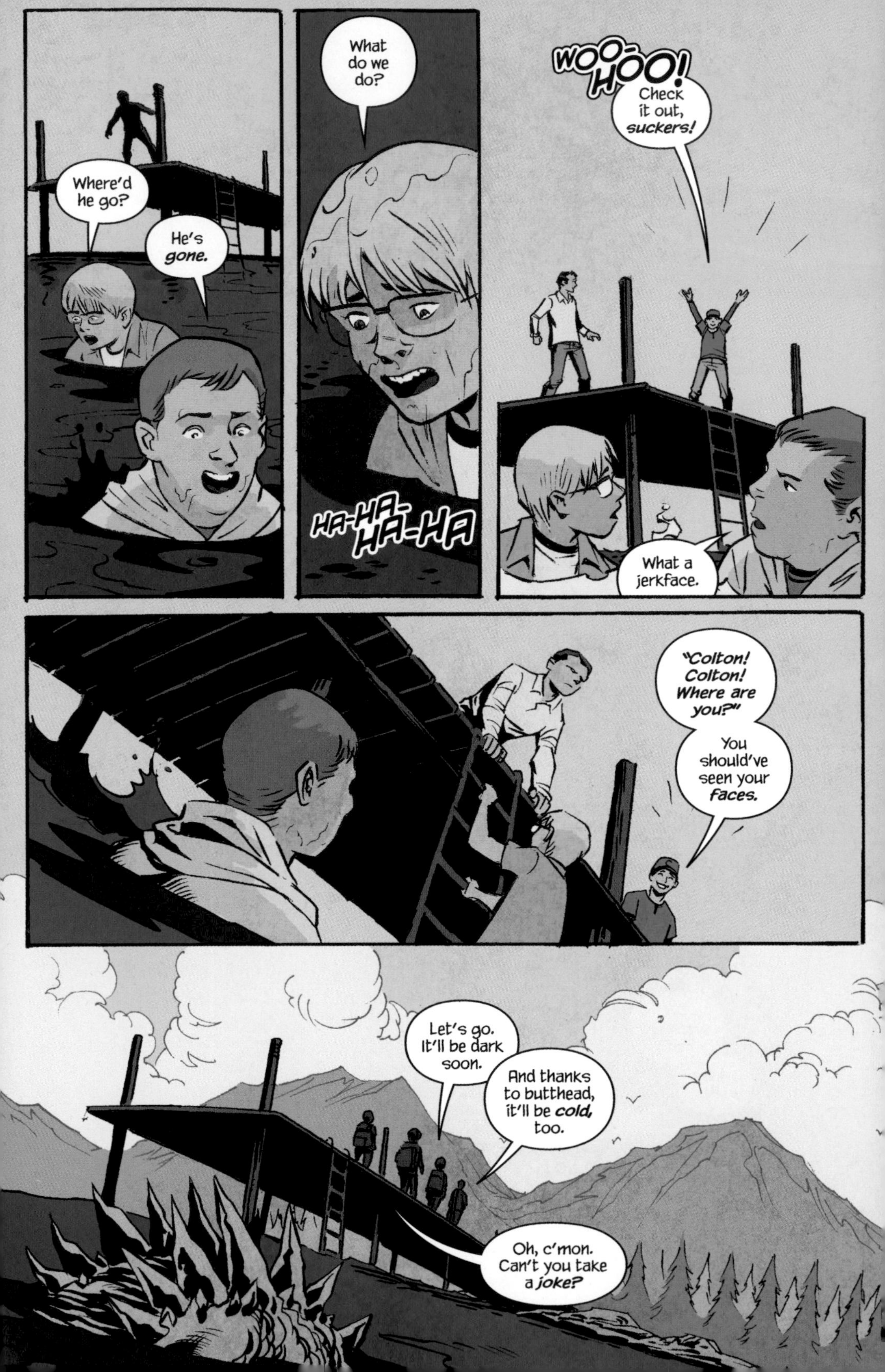
Where'd he go?
He's gone.
What do we do?
HA-HA-HA-HA
WOO-HOO!
Check it out, suckers!
What a jerkface.
"Colton! Colton! Where are you?"
You should've seen your faces.
Let's go. It'll be dark soon.
And thanks to butthead, it'll be cold, too.
Oh, c'mon. Can't you take a joke?

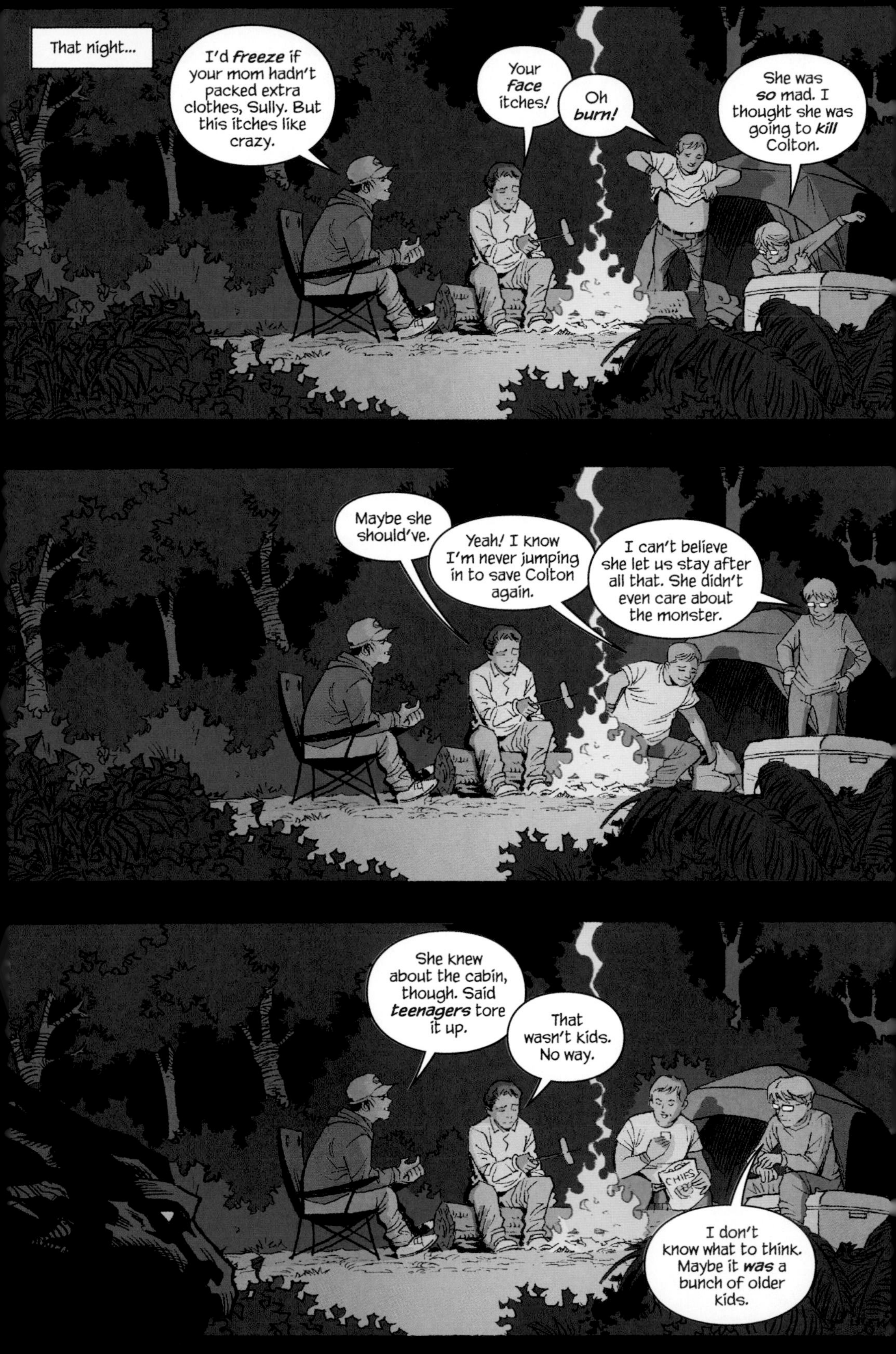
That night...
I'd *freeze* if your mom hadn't packed extra clothes, Sully. But this itches like crazy.
Your *face* itches!
Oh *burn!*
She was *so* mad. I thought she was going to *kill* Colton.
Maybe she should've.
Yeah! I know I'm never jumping in to save Colton again.
I can't believe she let us stay after all that. She didn't even care about the monster.
She knew about the cabin, though. Said *teenagers* tore it up.
That wasn't kids. No way.
CHIPS
I don't know what to think. Maybe it *was* a bunch of older kids.

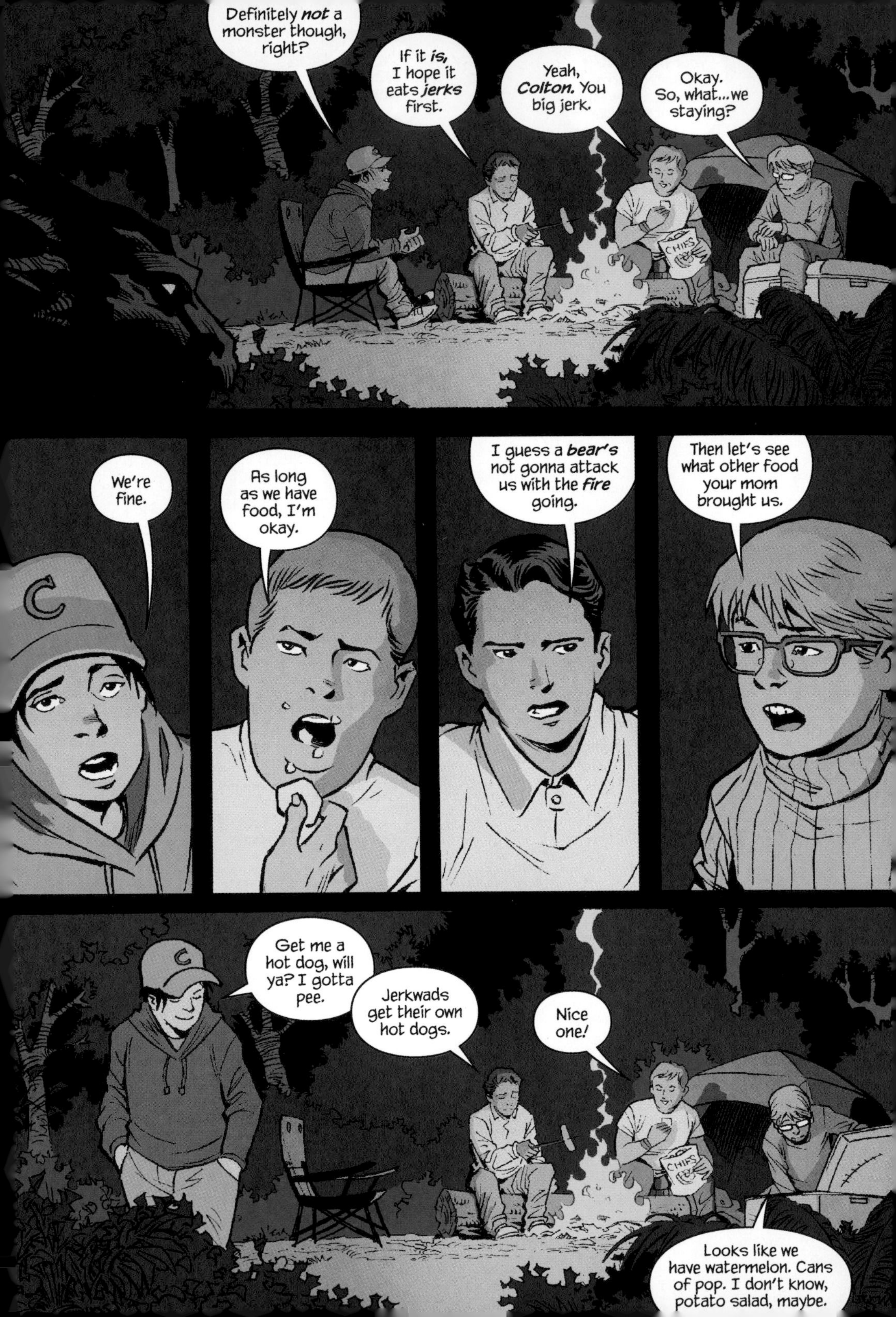

Definitely *not* a monster though, right?
If it *is,* I hope it eats *jerks* first.
Yeah, *Colton.* You big jerk.
Okay. So, what...we staying?
We're fine.
As long as we have food, I'm okay.
I guess a *bear's* not gonna attack us with the *fire* going.
Then let's see what other food your mom brought us.
Get me a hot dog, will ya? I gotta pee.
Jerkwads get their own hot dogs.
Nice one!
Looks like we have watermelon. Cans of pop. I don't know, potato salad, maybe.
CHIPS
CHIPS

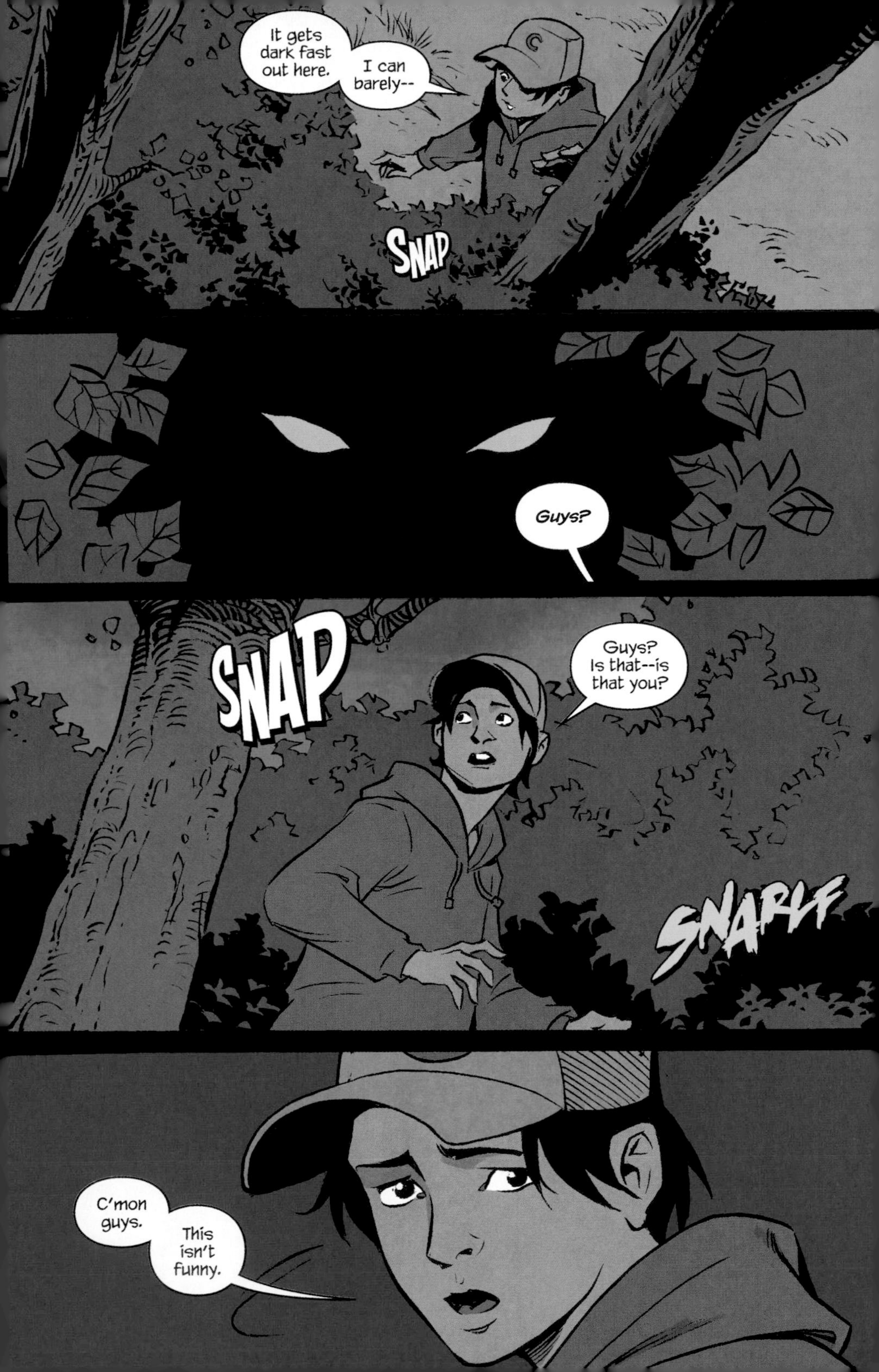
It gets dark fast out here.
I can barely--
SNAP
Guys?
SNAP
Guys? Is that--is that you?
SNARL
C'mon guys.
This isn't funny.

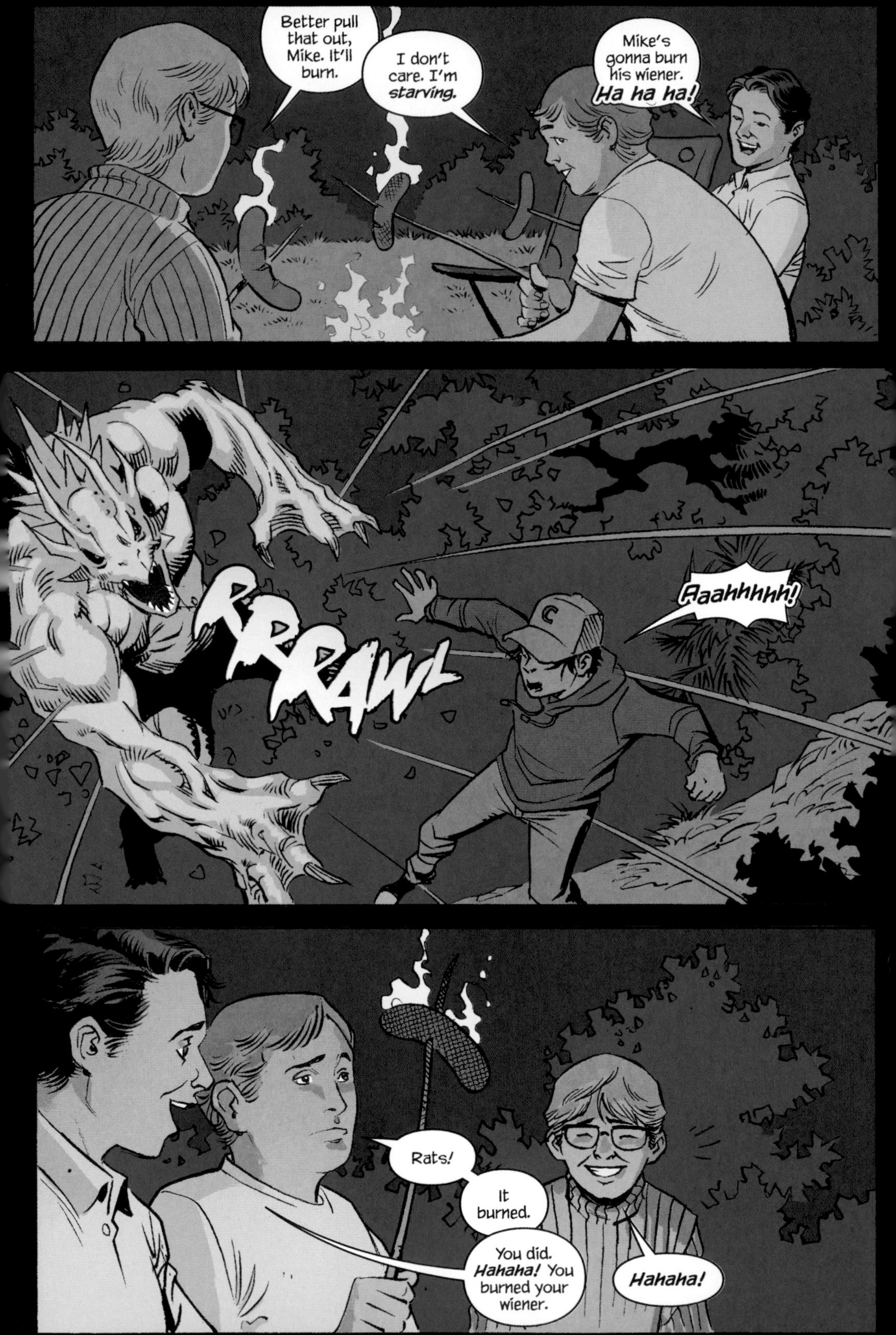

Better pull that out, Mike. It'll burn.
I don't care. I'm *starving.*
Mike's gonna burn his wiener. ***Ha ha ha!***
Aaahhhhh!
Rats!
It burned.
You did. ***Hahaha!*** You burned your wiener.
Hahaha!

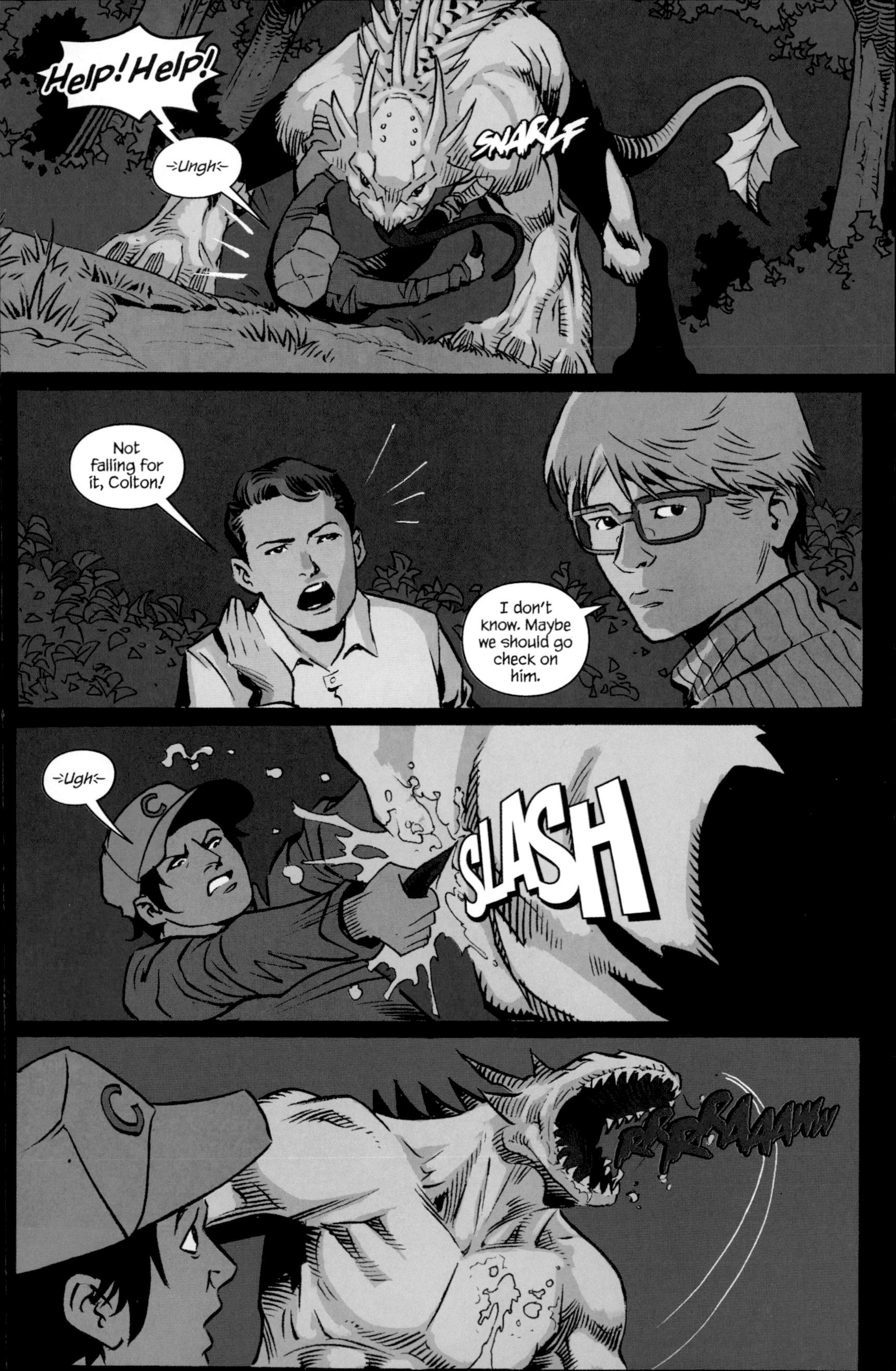

Help! Help!
Ungh
SNARLF
Not falling for it, Colton!
I don't know. Maybe we should go check on him.
Ungh
SLASH
RRRRAAAWW

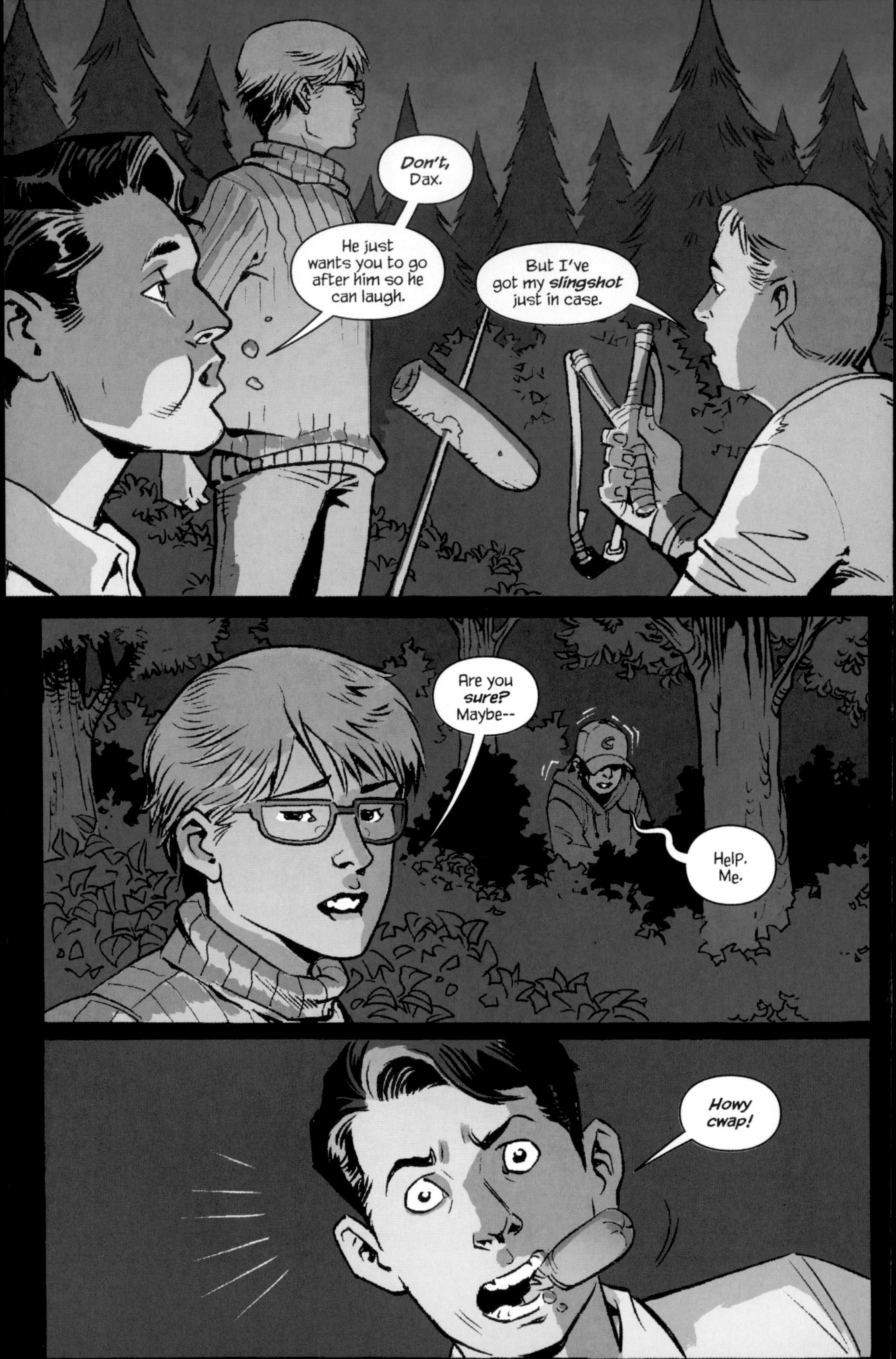
Don't, Dax.
He just wants you to go after him so he can laugh.
But I've got my slingshot just in case.
Are you sure? Maybe--
Help. Me.
Howy cwap!

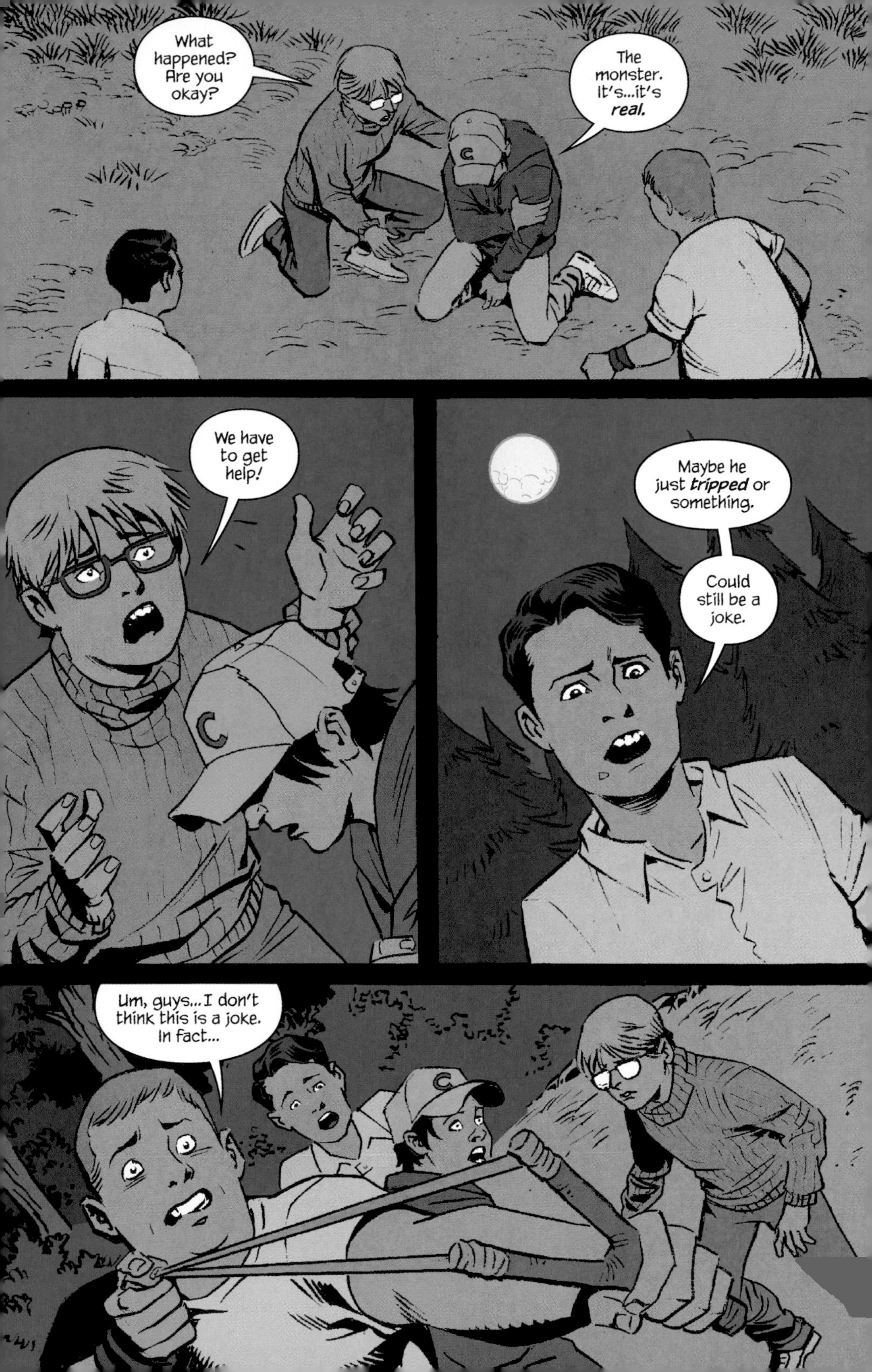
What happened? Are you okay?
The monster. It's...it's *real.*
We have to get help!
Maybe he just *tripped* or something.
Could still be a joke.
Um, guys...I don't think this is a joke. In fact...

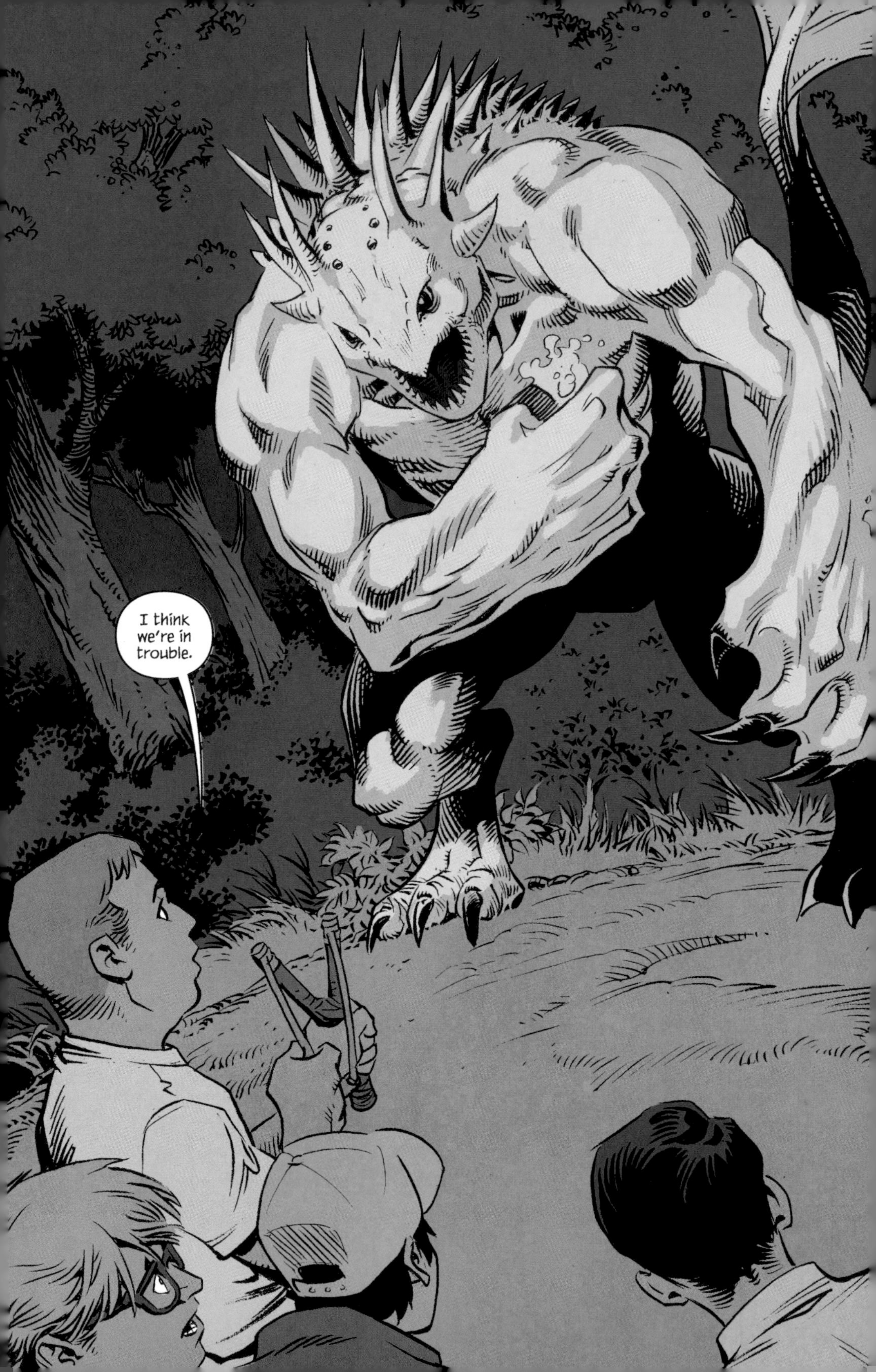
I think we're in trouble.

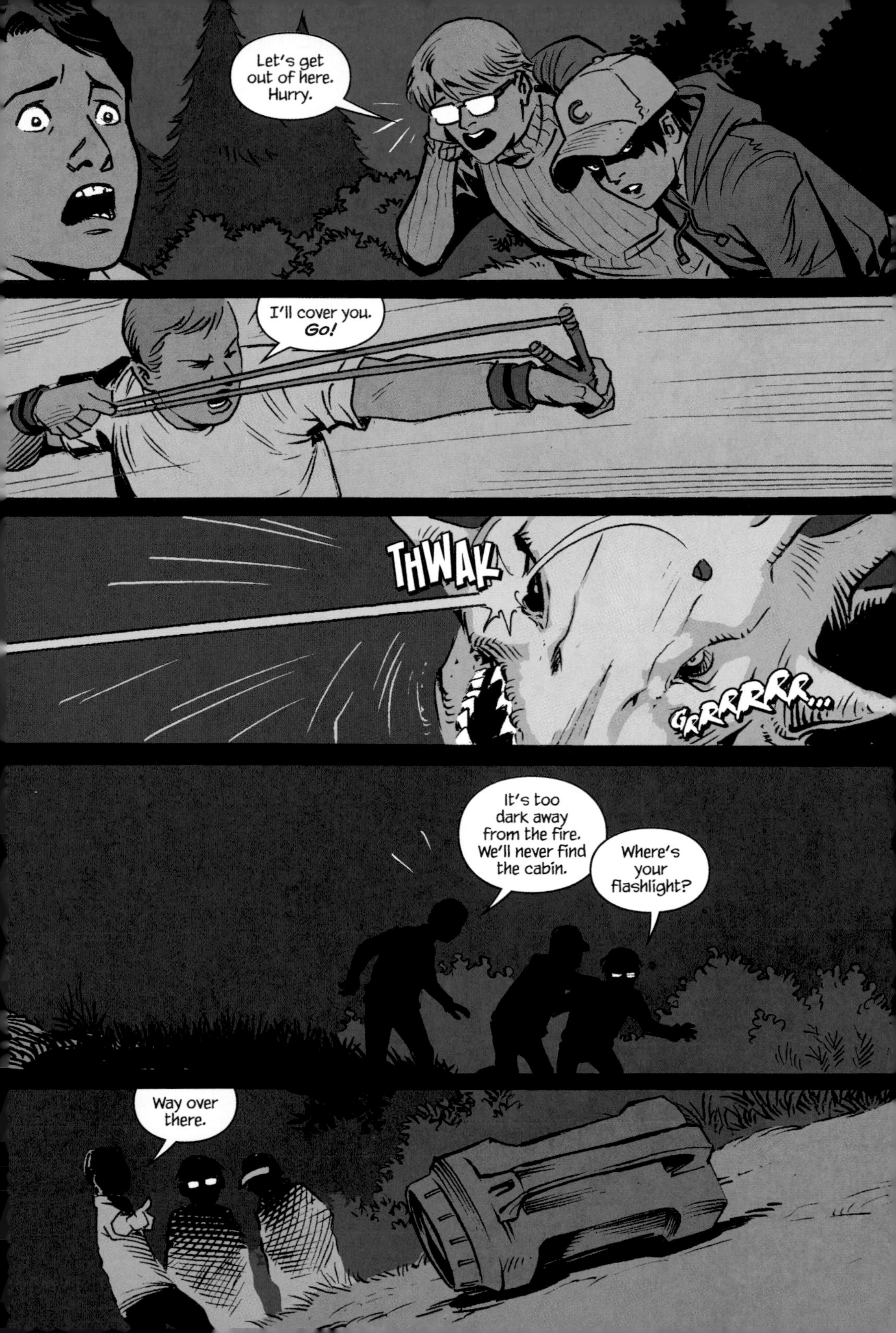
Let's get out of here. Hurry.
I'll cover you. *Go!*
THWAK
GRRRRRR...
It's too dark away from the fire. We'll never find the cabin.
Where's your flashlight?
Way over there.

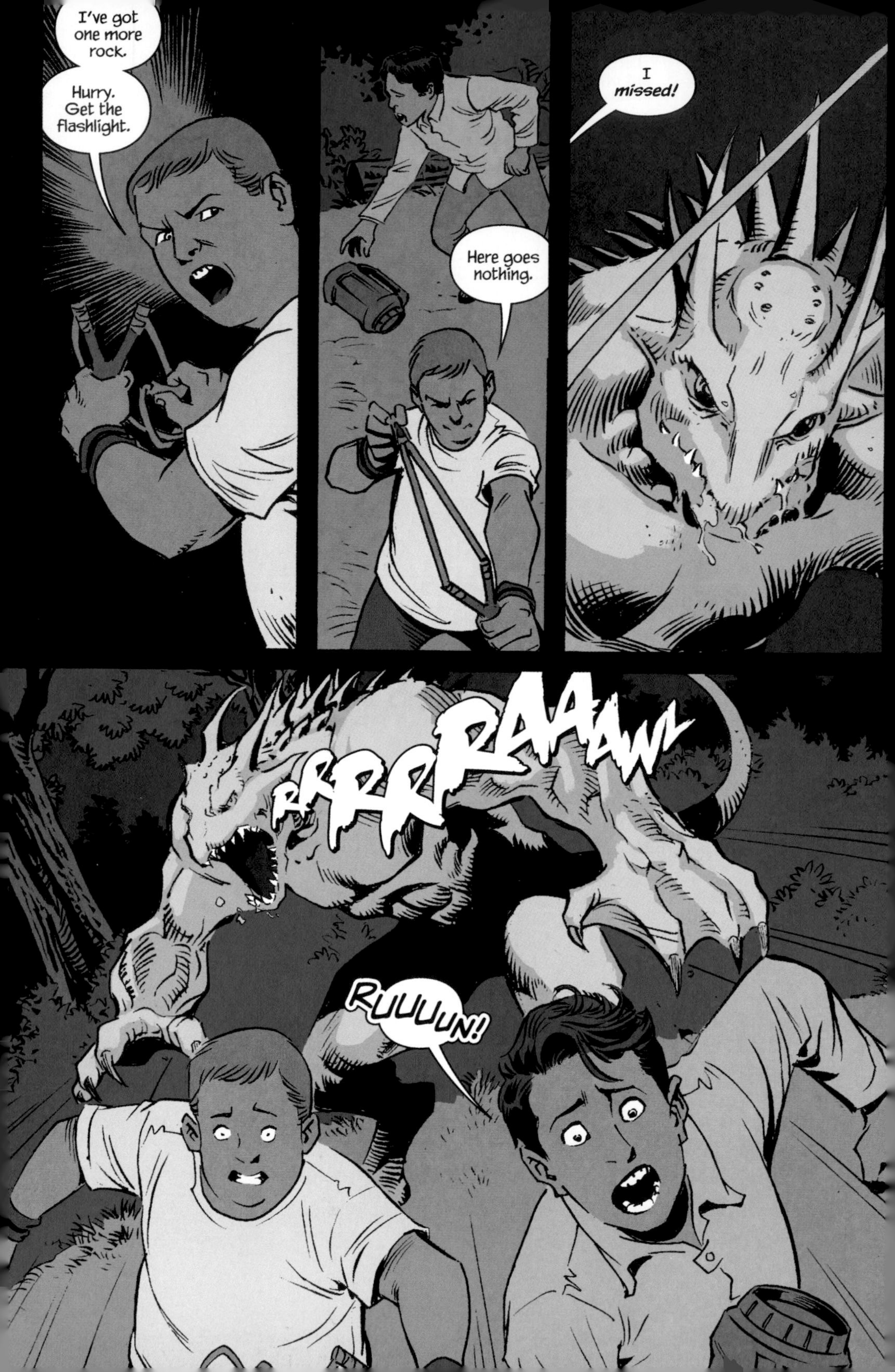

I've got one more rock.
Hurry. Get the flashlight.
Here goes nothing.
I missed!
RRRRRAAAAW!
RUUUUN!

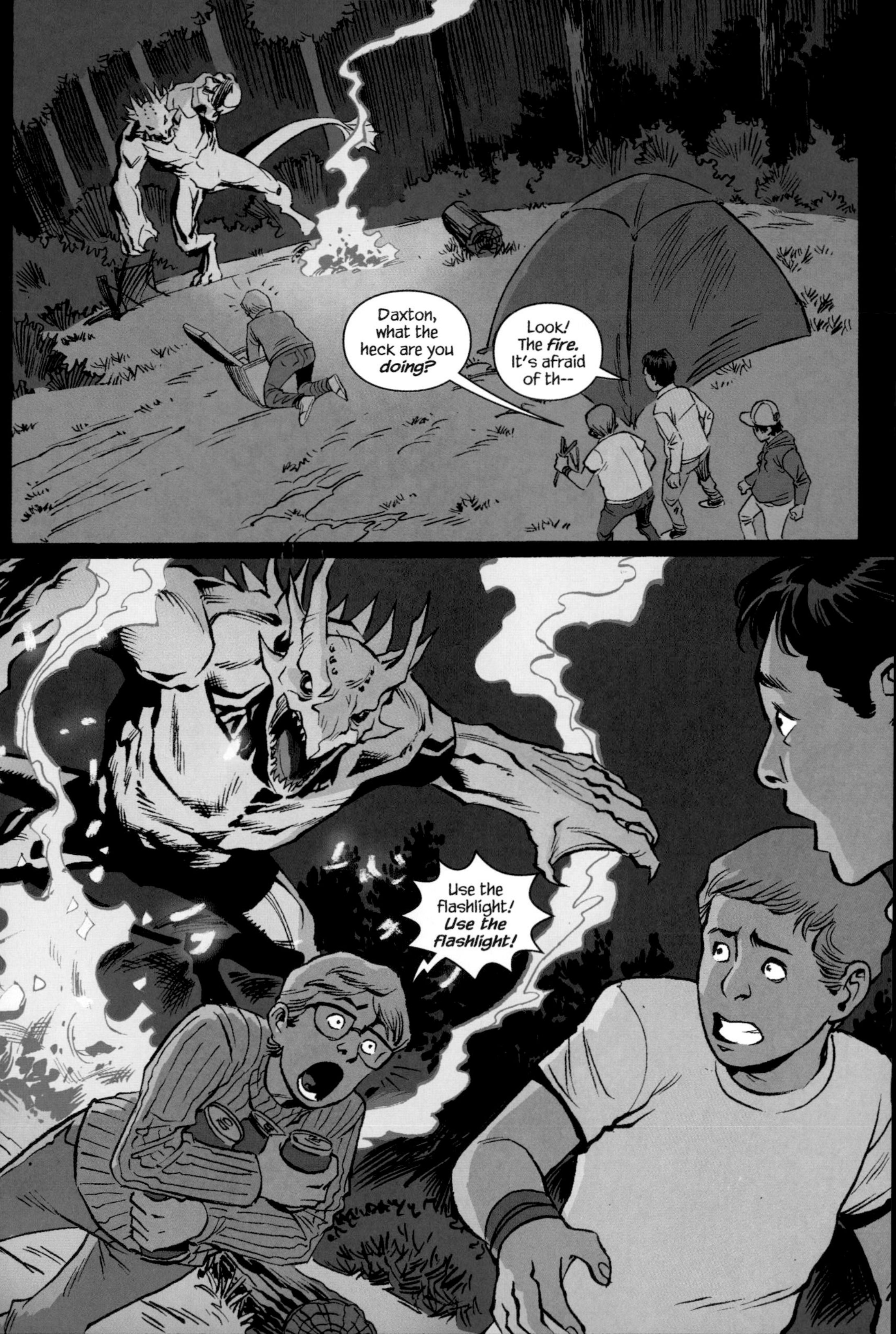
Daxton, what the heck are you *doing?*
Look! The *fire.* It's afraid of th--
Use the flashlight! *Use the flashlight!*

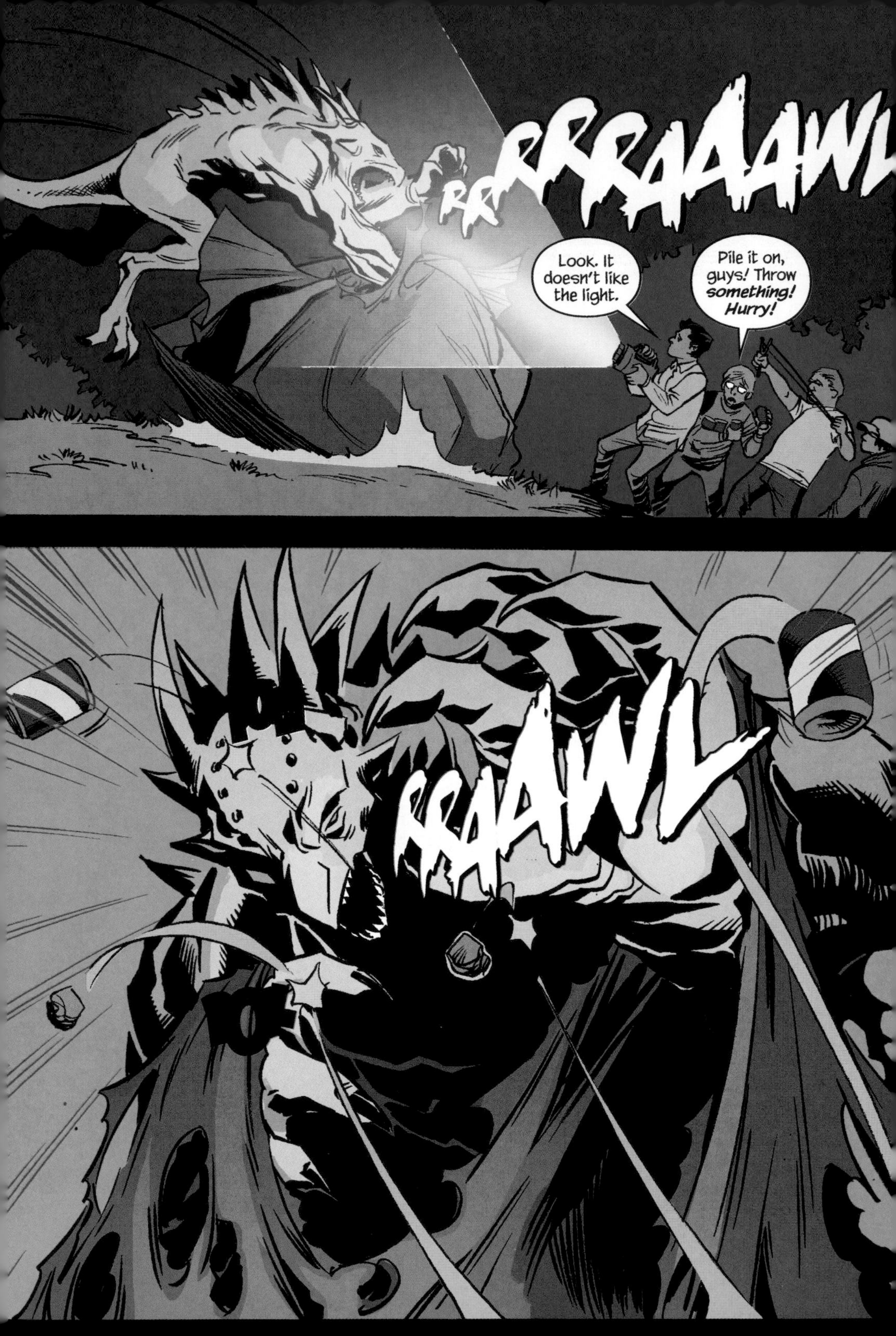
RRRRRAAAAWL
Look. It doesn't like the light.
Pile it on, guys! Throw *something! Hurry!*
RRAAWL

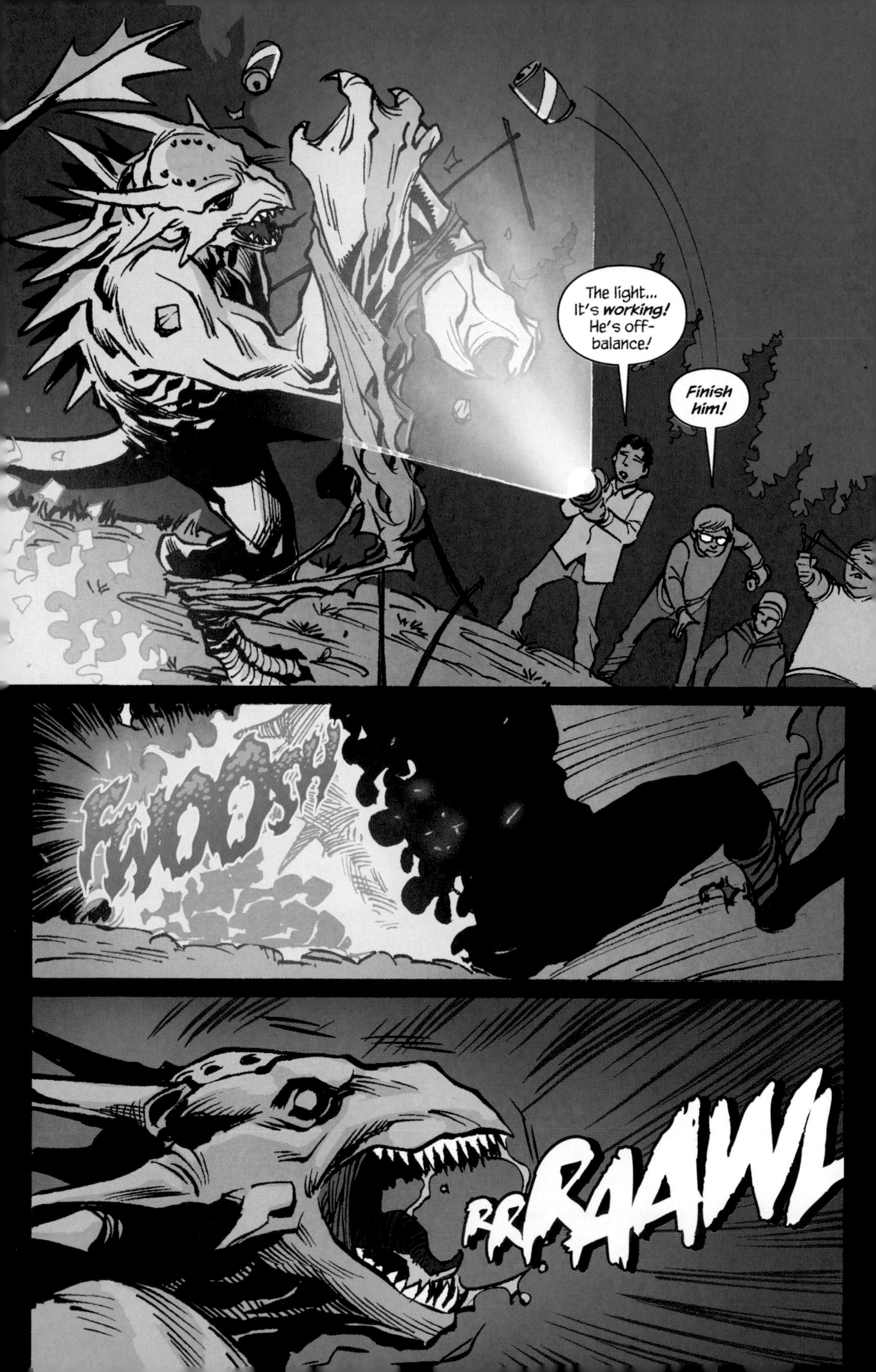
The light... It's *working!* He's off-balance!
Finish him!
RRRAAWL

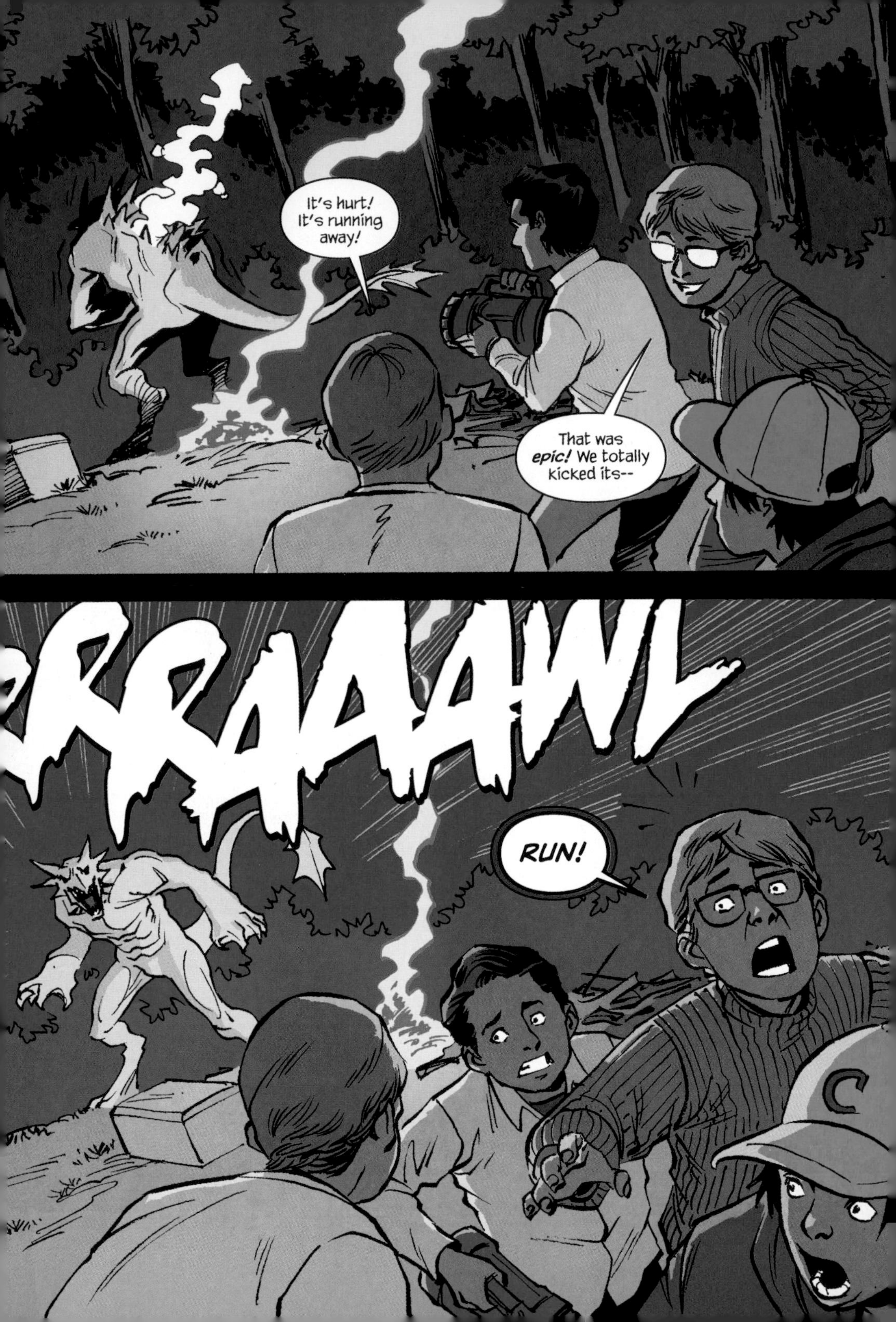
It's hurt! It's running away!
That was *epic!* We totally kicked its--
RRAAAWL
RUN!

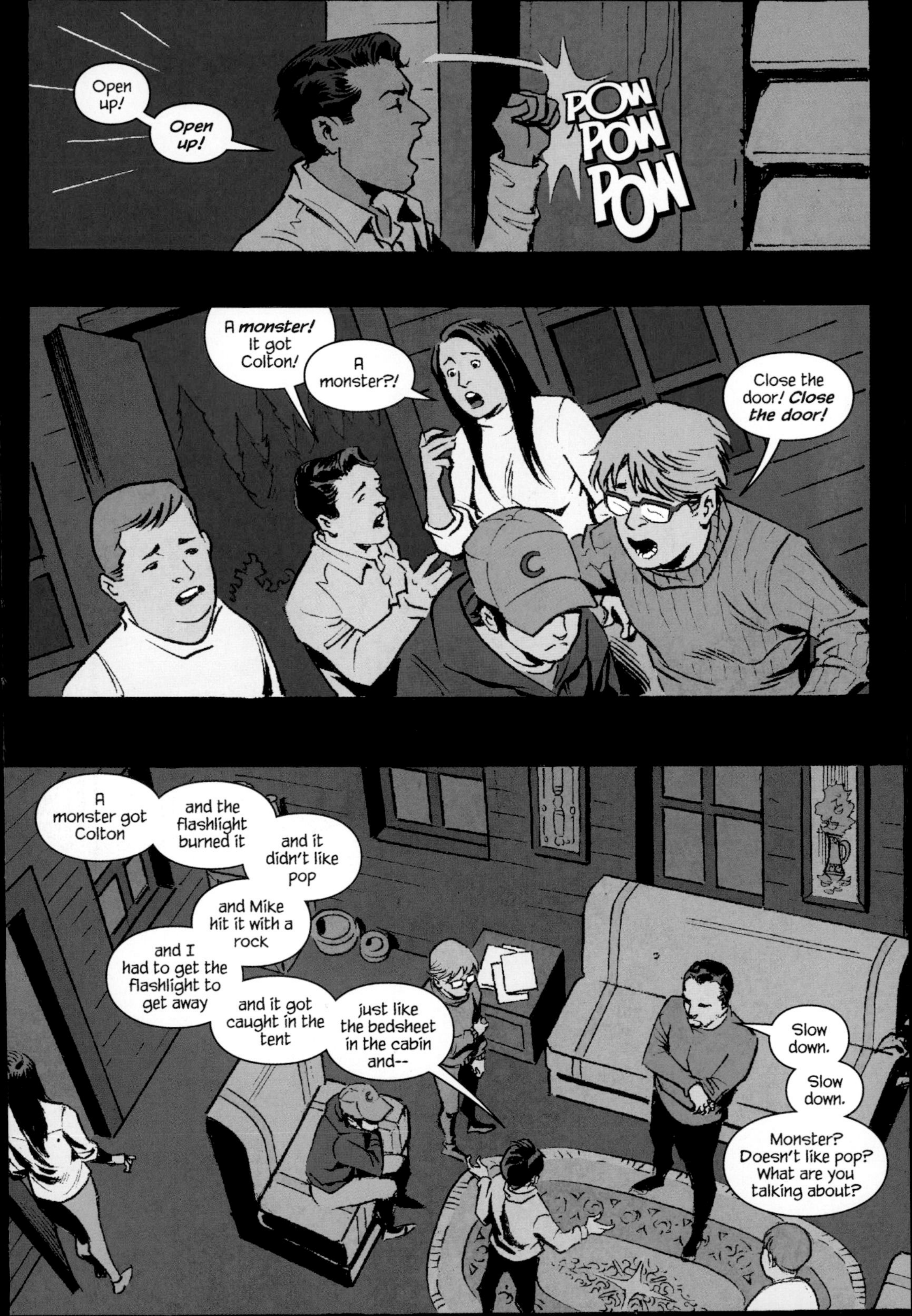
Open up!
Open up!
POW POW POW
A monster! It got Colton!
A monster?!
Close the door! Close the door!
A monster got Colton
and the flashlight burned it
and it didn't like pop
and Mike hit it with a rock
and I had to get the flashlight to get away
and it got caught in the tent
just like the bedsheet in the cabin and--
Slow down.
Slow down.
Monster? Doesn't like pop? What are you talking about?

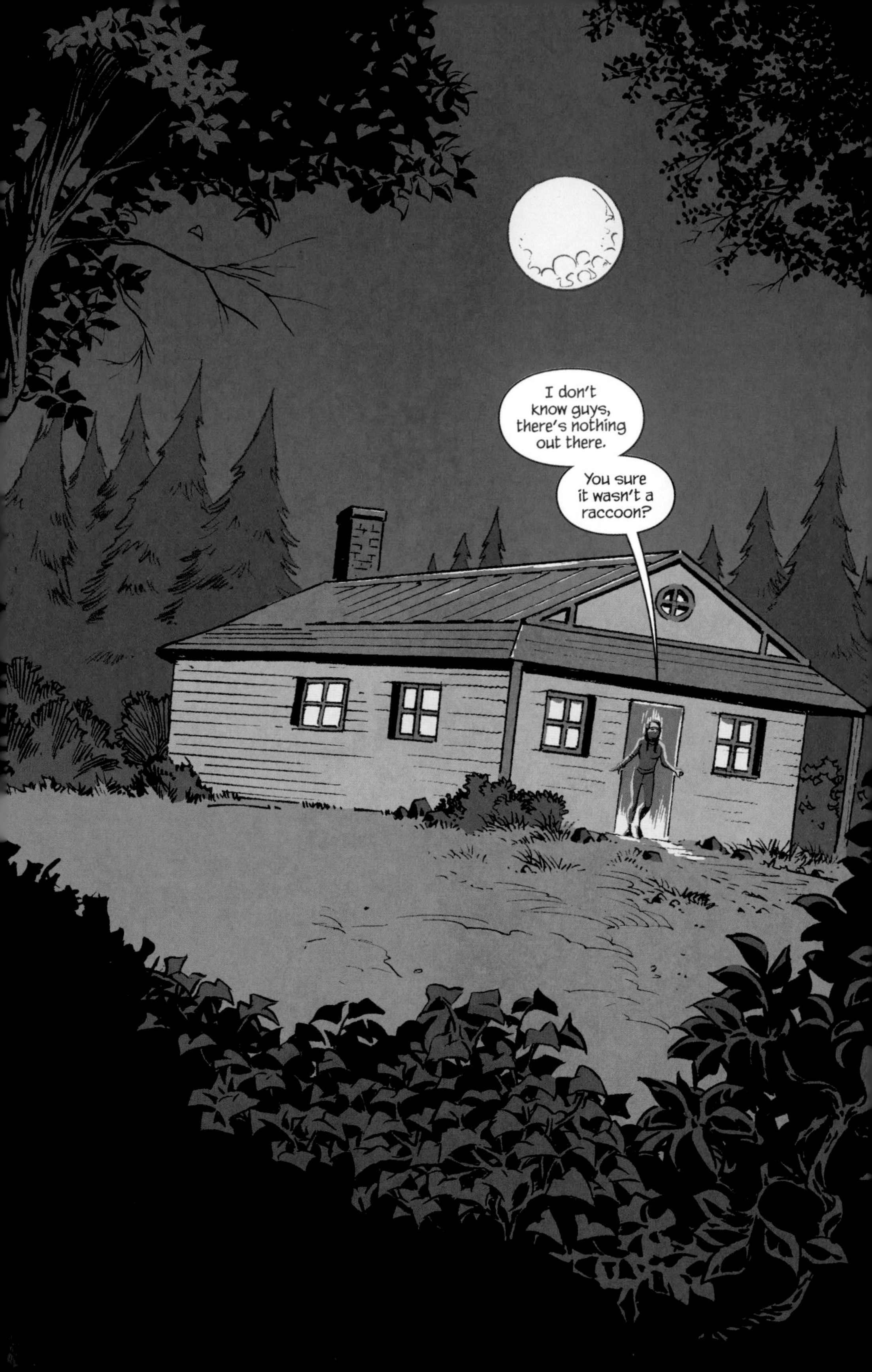
I don't know guys, there's nothing out there.
You sure it wasn't a raccoon?

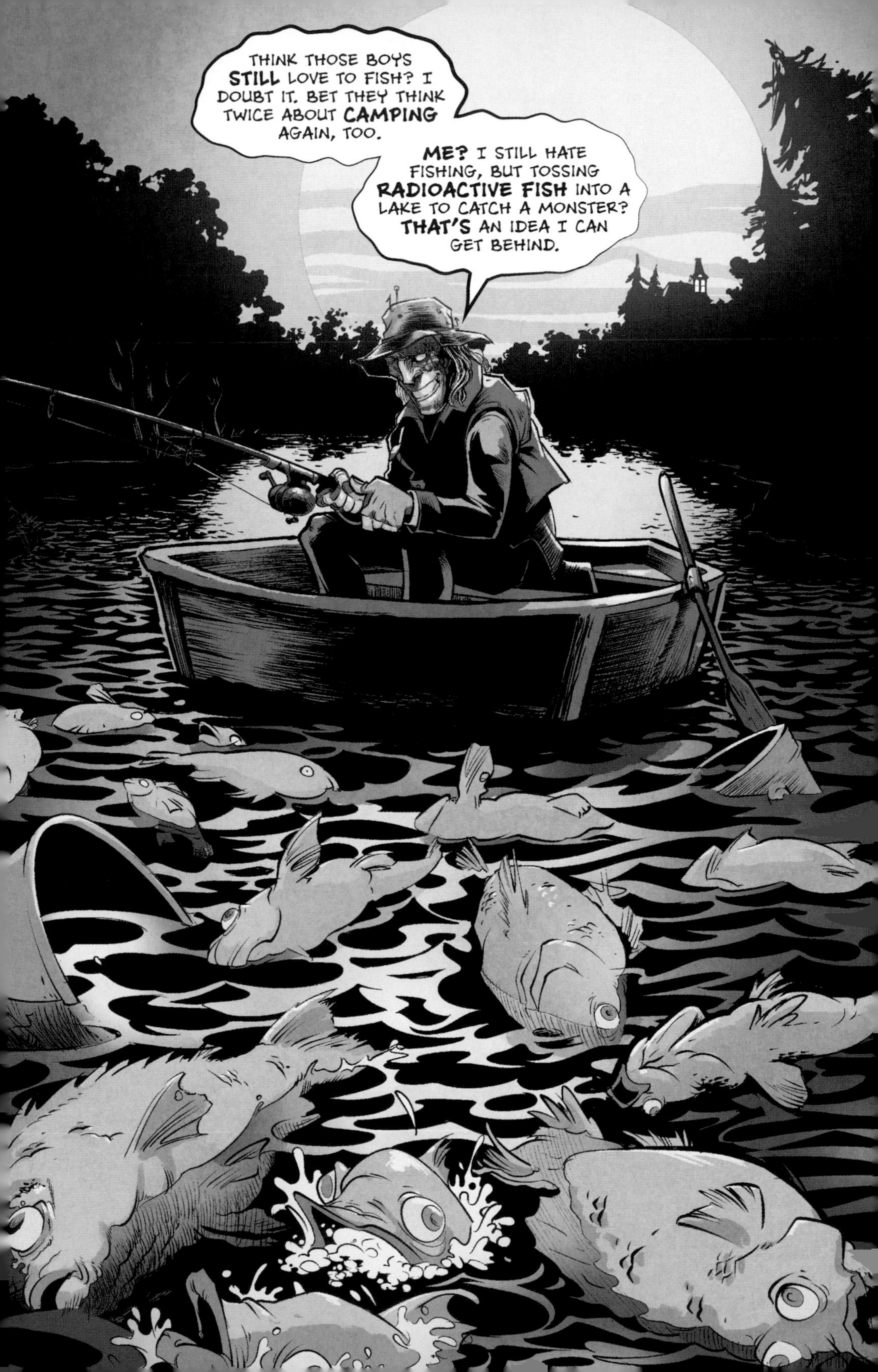
THINK THOSE BOYS STILL LOVE TO FISH? I DOUBT IT. BET THEY THINK TWICE ABOUT CAMPING AGAIN, TOO.
ME? I STILL HATE FISHING, BUT TOSSING RADIOACTIVE FISH INTO A LAKE TO CATCH A MONSTER? THAT'S AN IDEA I CAN GET BEHIND.

The LEAVING

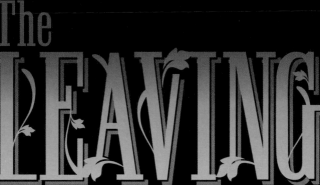

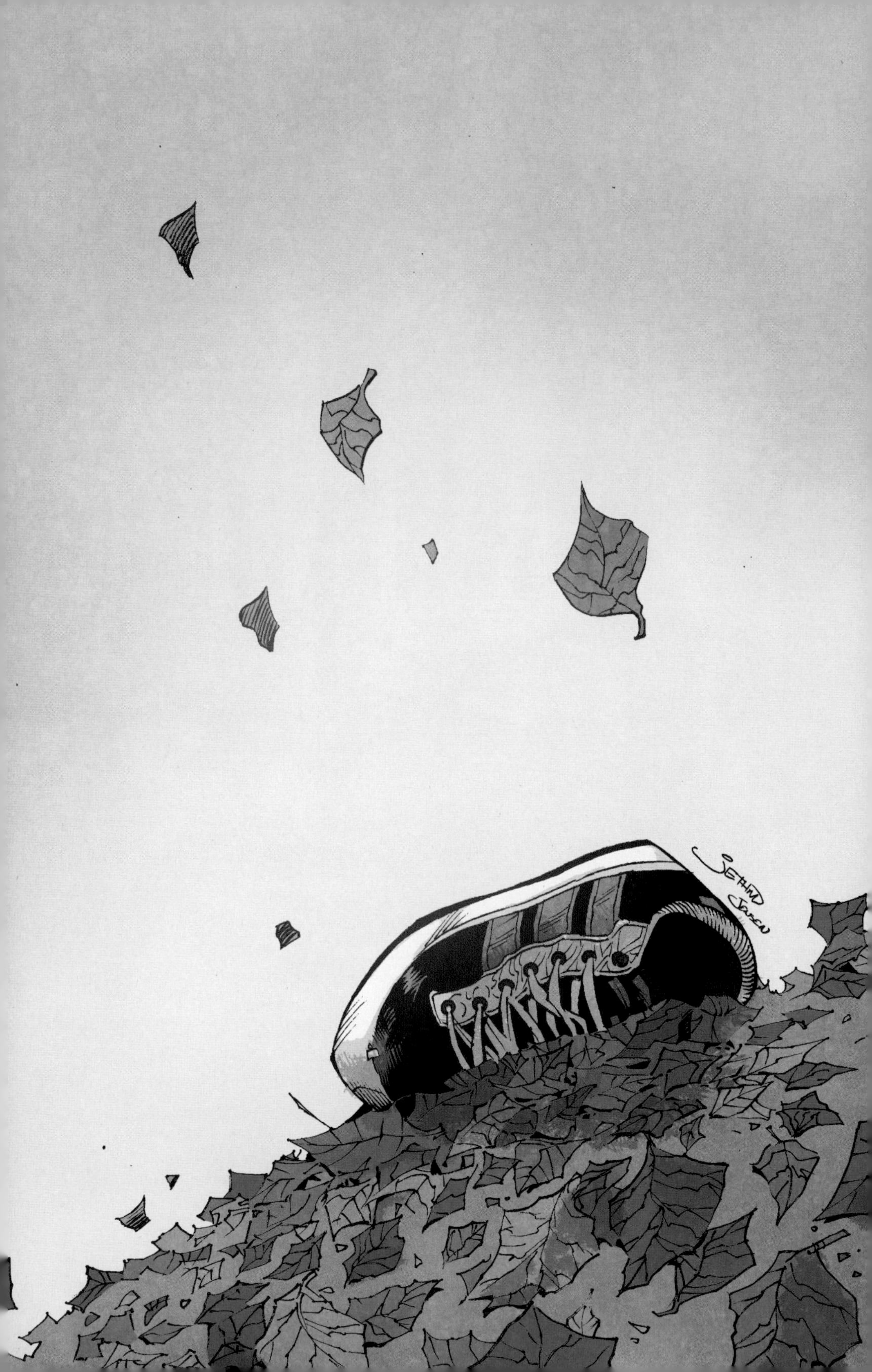

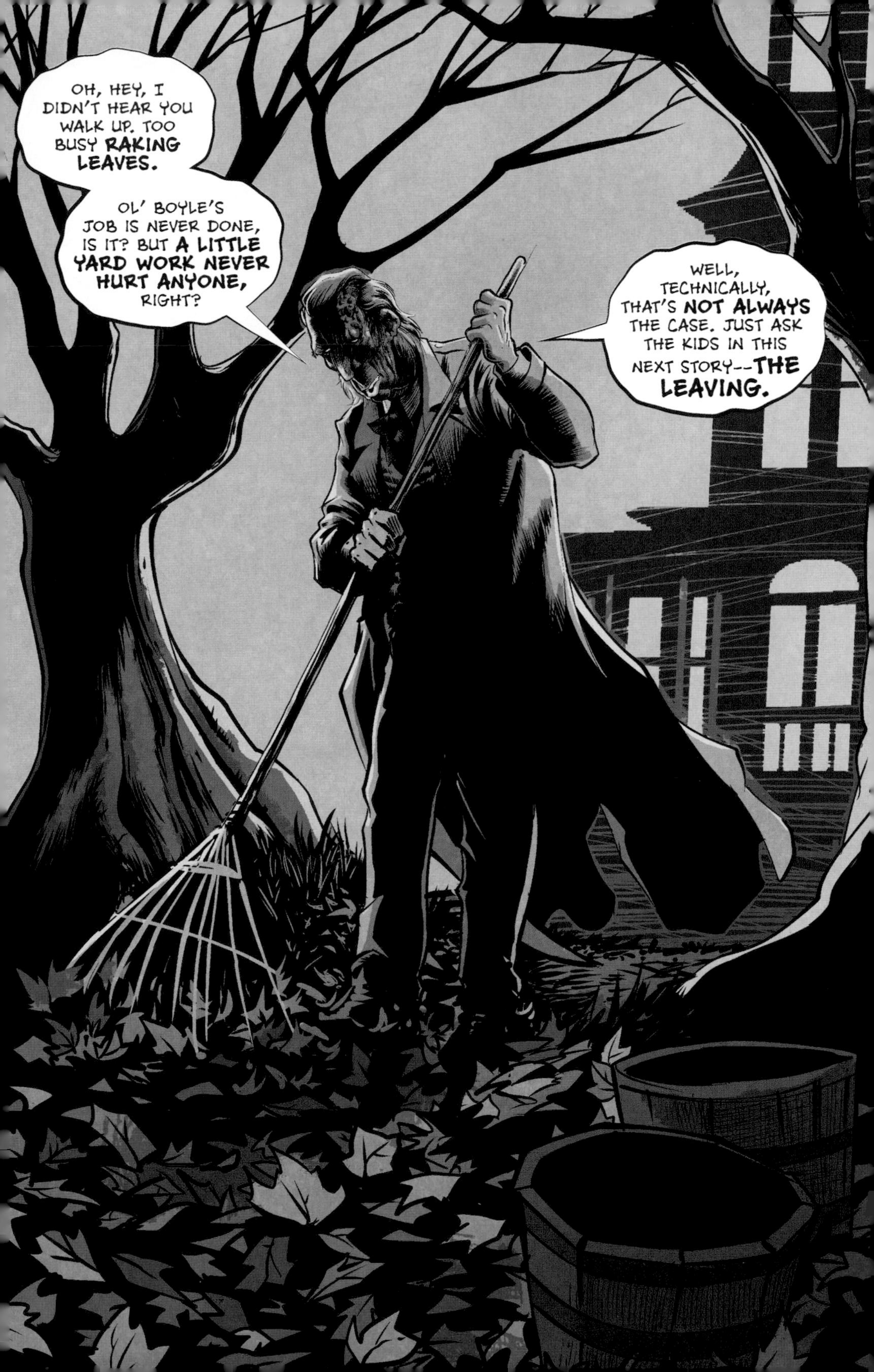
OH, HEY, I DIDN'T HEAR YOU WALK UP. TOO BUSY **RAKING LEAVES.**
OL' BOYLE'S JOB IS NEVER DONE, IS IT? BUT **A LITTLE YARD WORK NEVER HURT ANYONE,** RIGHT?
WELL, TECHNICALLY, THAT'S **NOT ALWAYS** THE CASE. JUST ASK THE KIDS IN THIS NEXT STORY--**THE LEAVING.**

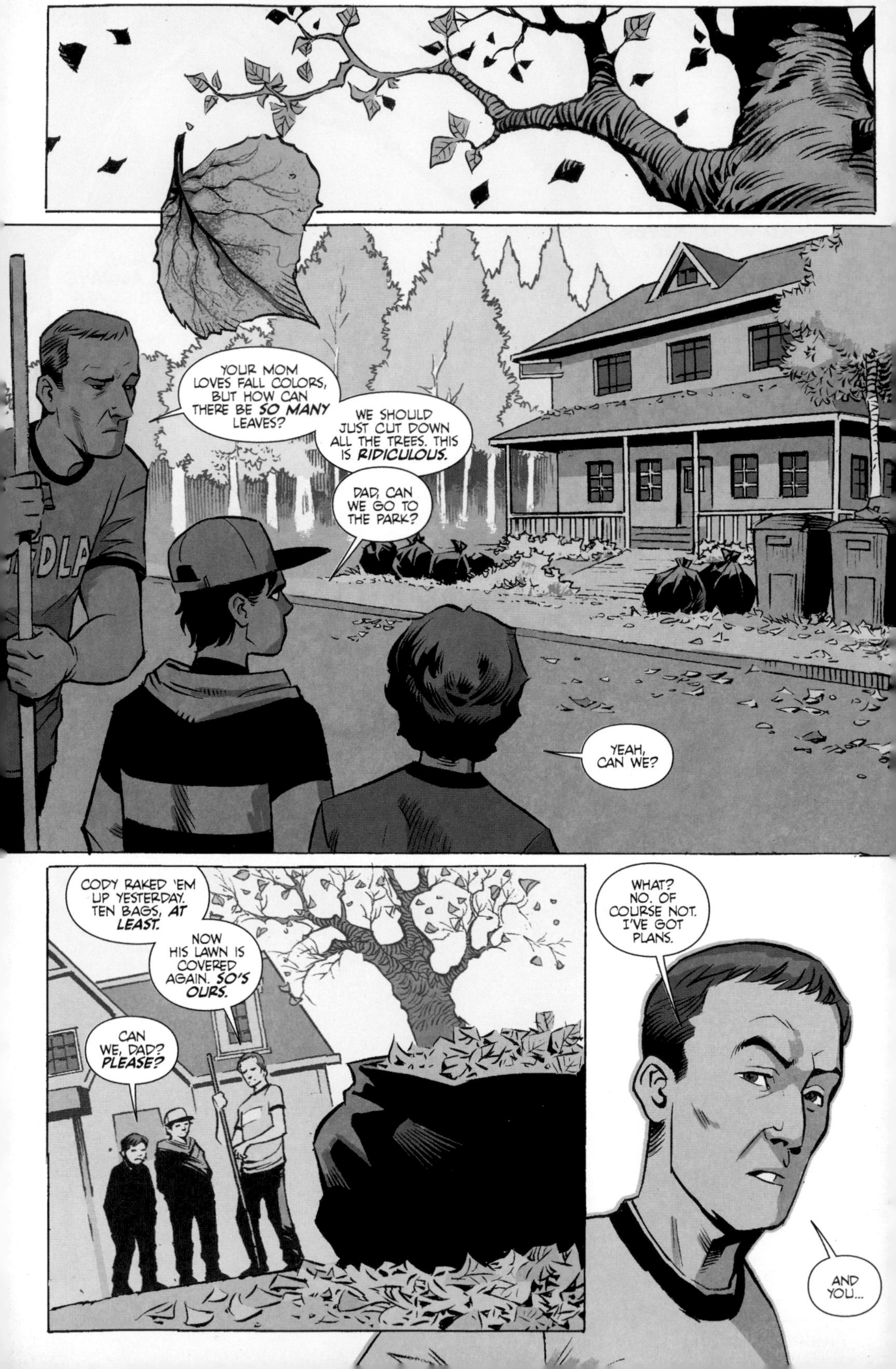
YOUR MOM LOVES FALL COLORS, BUT HOW CAN THERE BE SO MANY LEAVES?
WE SHOULD JUST CUT DOWN ALL THE TREES. THIS IS RIDICULOUS.
DAD, CAN WE GO TO THE PARK?
YEAH, CAN WE?
CODY RAKED 'EM UP YESTERDAY. TEN BAGS, AT LEAST.
NOW HIS LAWN IS COVERED AGAIN. SO'S OURS.
CAN WE, DAD? PLEASE?
WHAT? NO. OF COURSE NOT. I'VE GOT PLANS.
AND YOU...

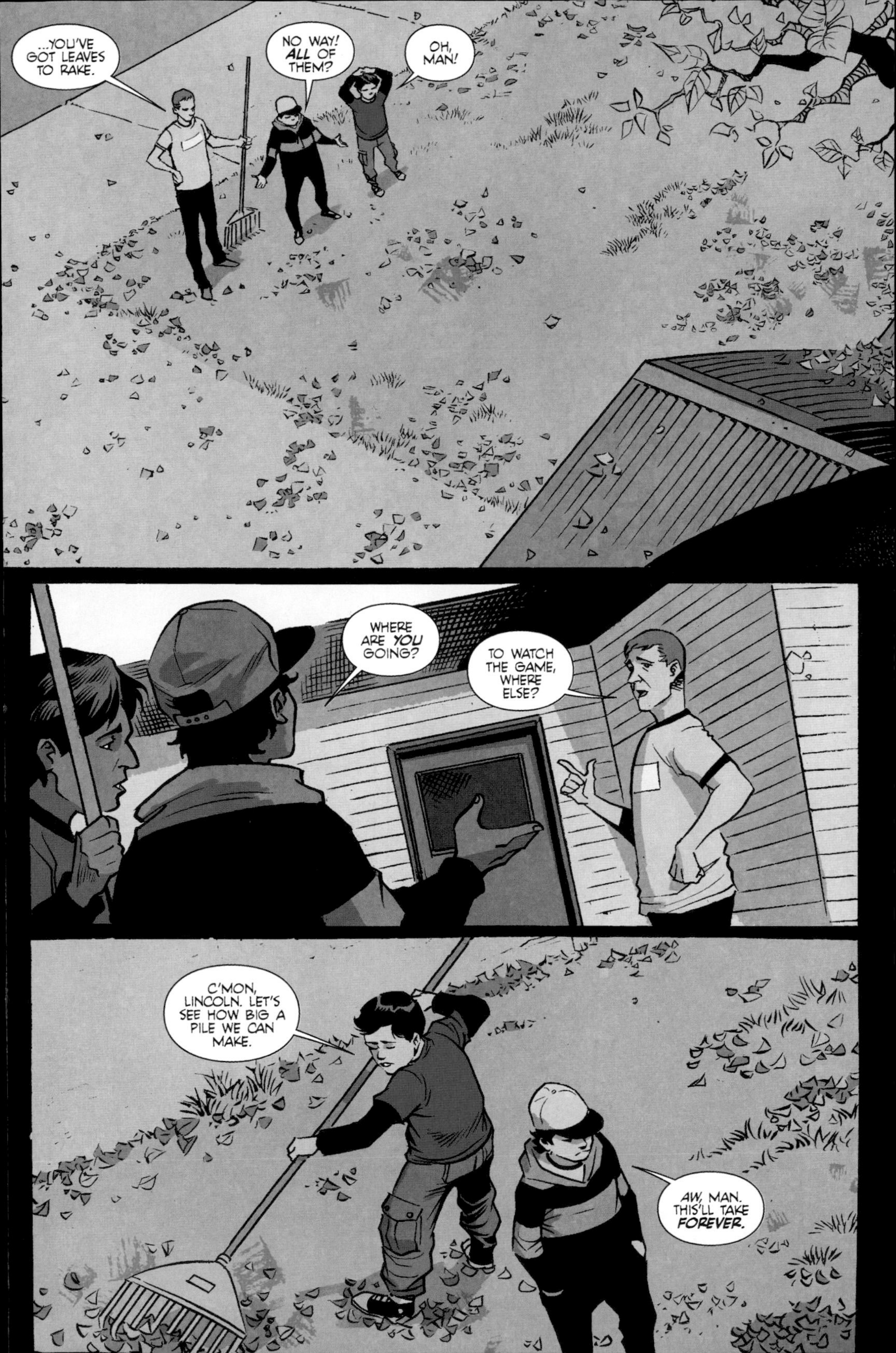
...YOU'VE GOT LEAVES TO RAKE.
NO WAY! **ALL** OF THEM?
OH, MAN!
WHERE ARE **YOU** GOING?
TO WATCH THE GAME, WHERE ELSE?
C'MON, LINCOLN. LET'S SEE HOW BIG A PILE WE CAN MAKE.
AW, MAN. THIS'LL TAKE ***FOREVER.***

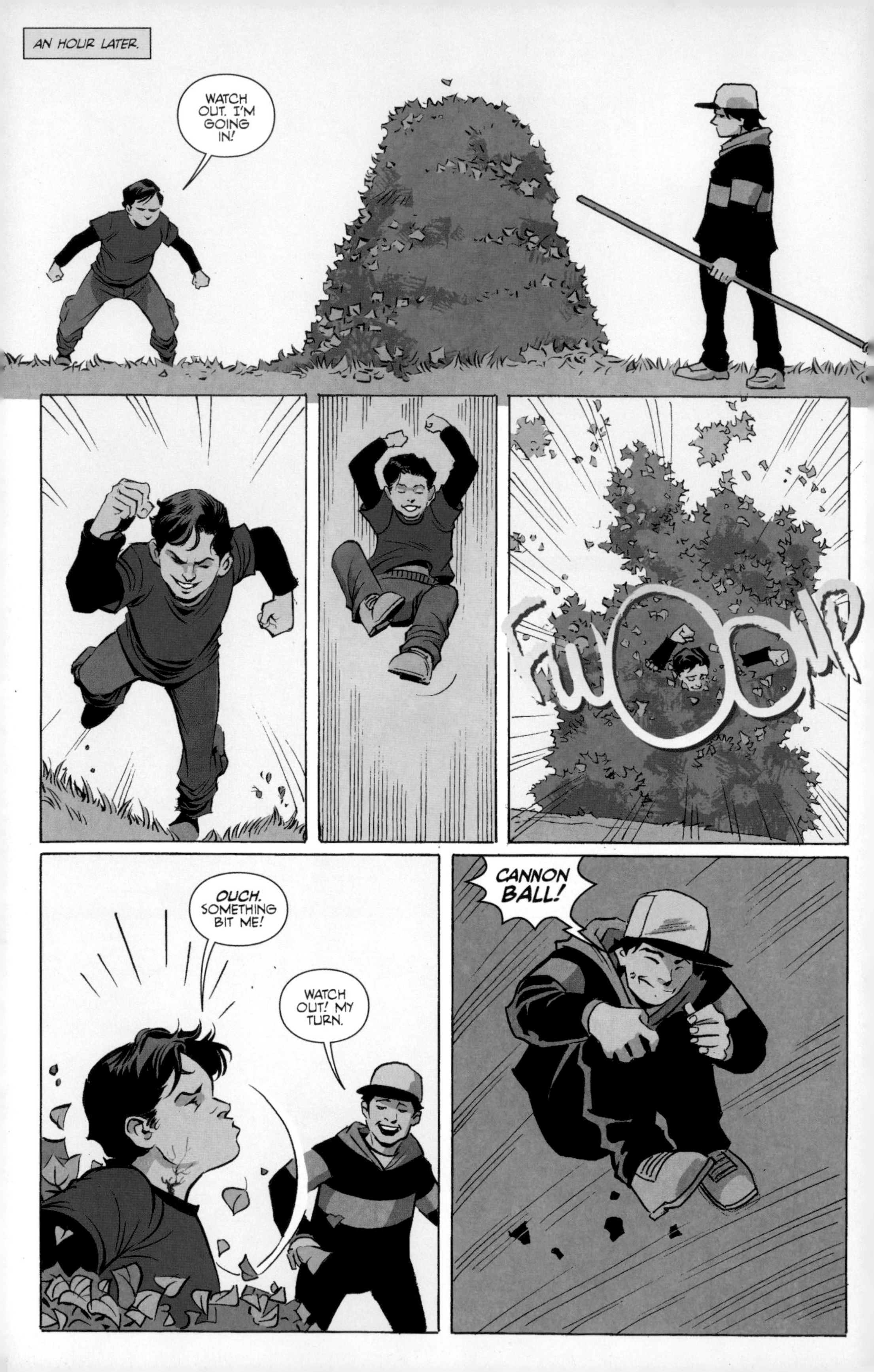
AN HOUR LATER.
WATCH OUT. I'M GOING IN!
FWOOMP
OUCH. SOMETHING BIT ME!
WATCH OUT! MY TURN.
CANNON BALL!

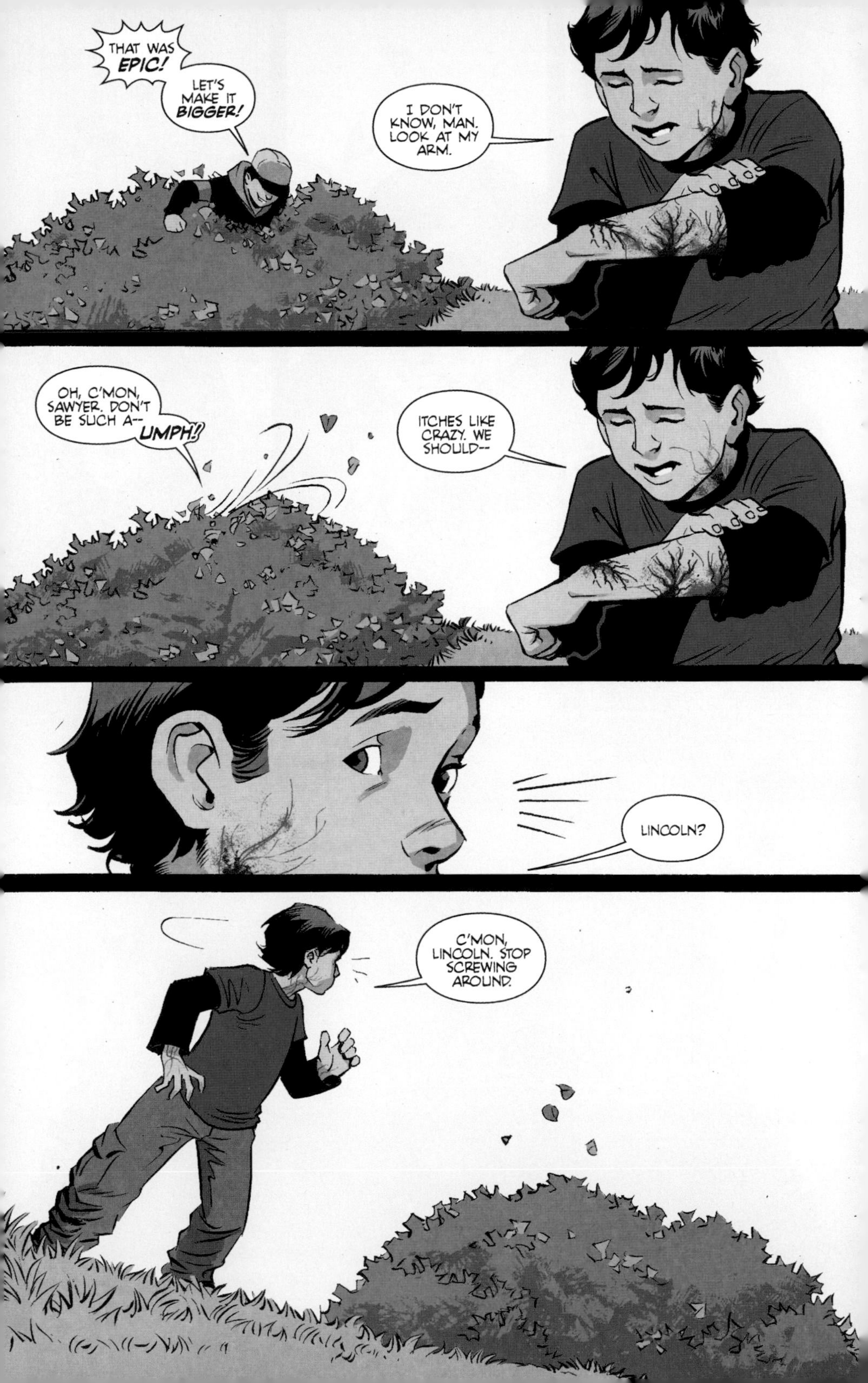
THAT WAS EPIC!
LET'S MAKE IT BIGGER!
I DON'T KNOW, MAN. LOOK AT MY ARM.
OH, C'MON, SAWYER. DON'T BE SUCH A--UMPH!
ITCHES LIKE CRAZY. WE SHOULD--
LINCOLN?
C'MON, LINCOLN. STOP SCREWING AROUND.

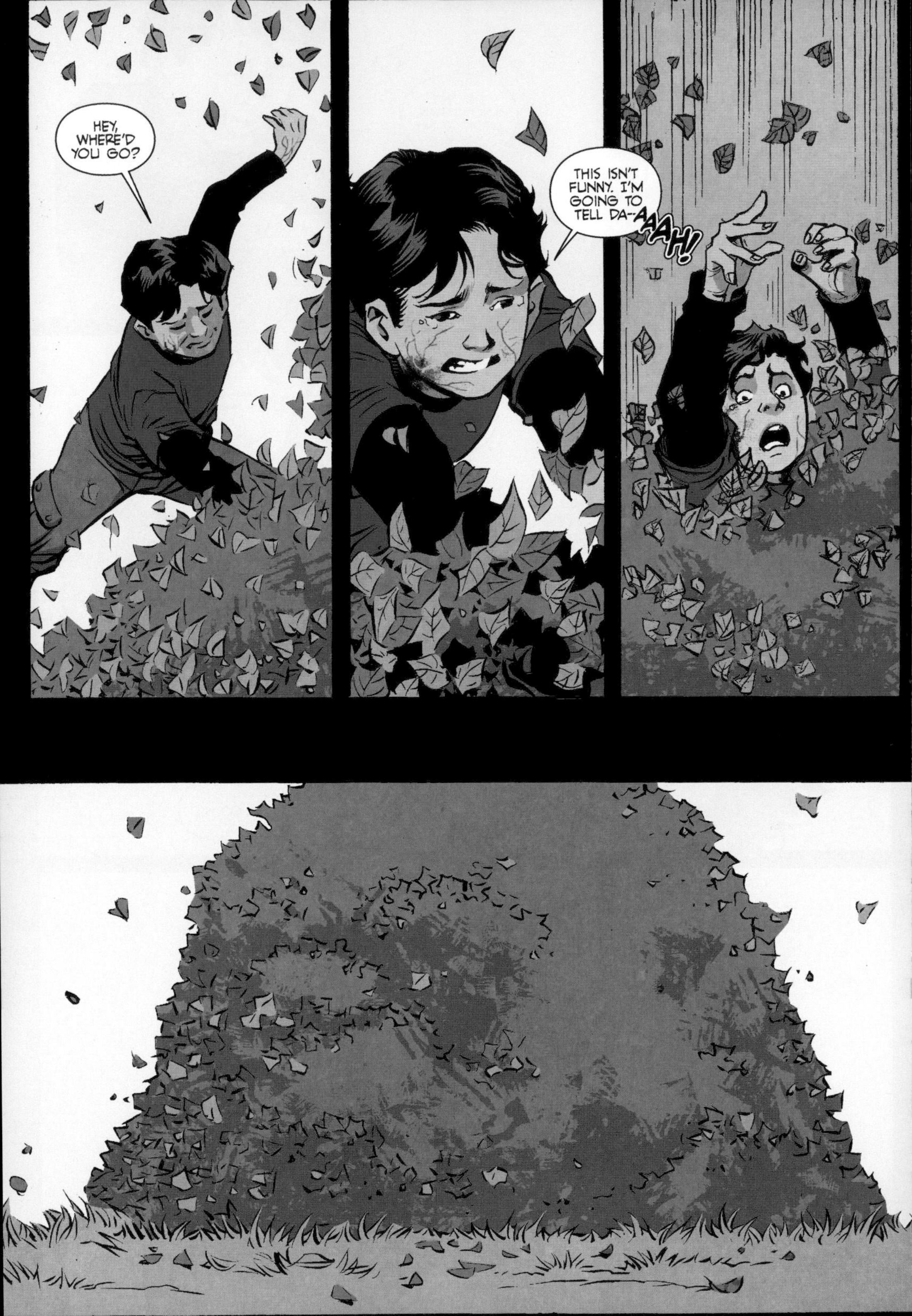
HEY, WHERE'D YOU GO?
THIS ISN'T FUNNY. I'M GOING TO TELL DA--
AAAH!

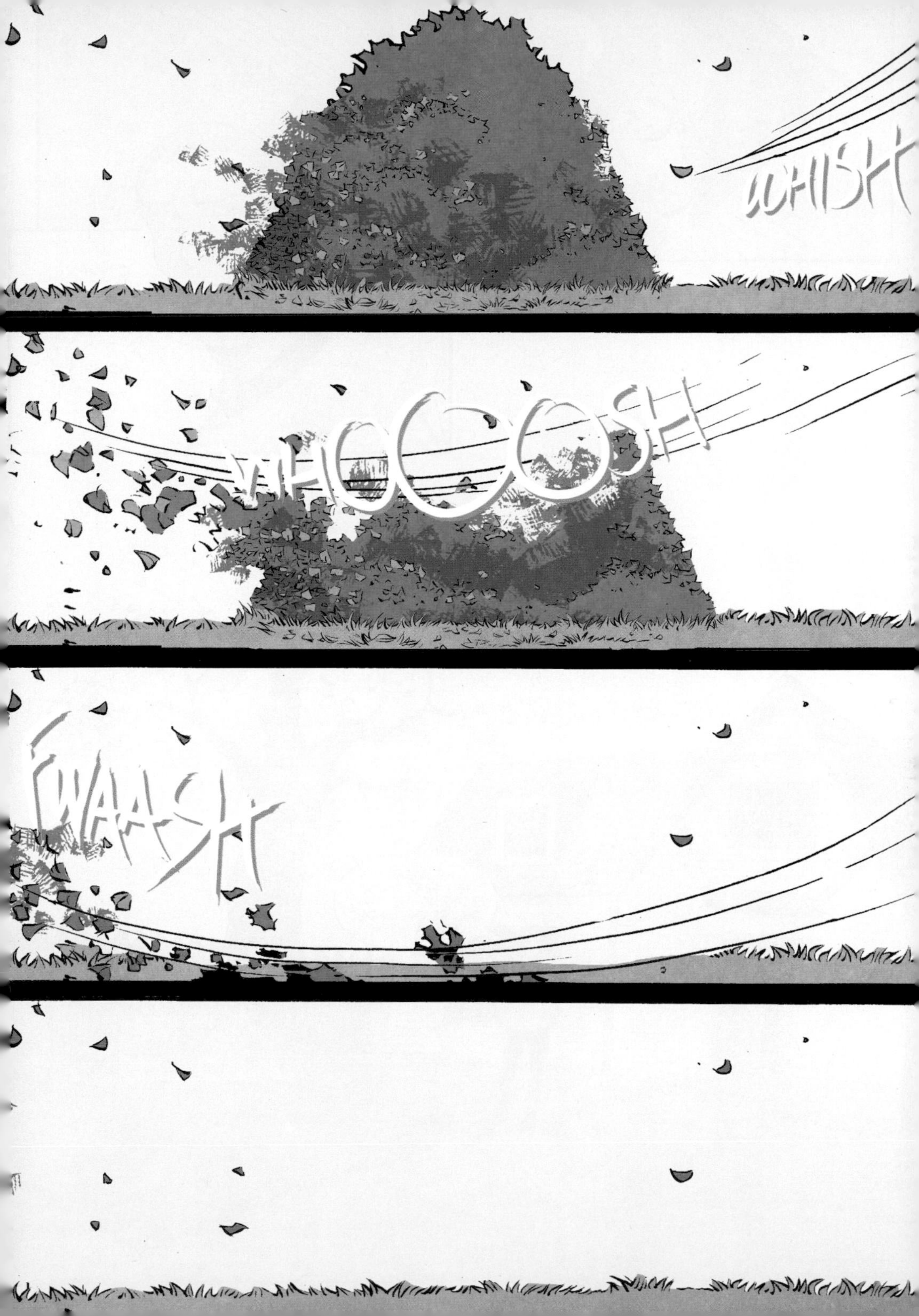
WHISH
WHOOOSH
FWAASH

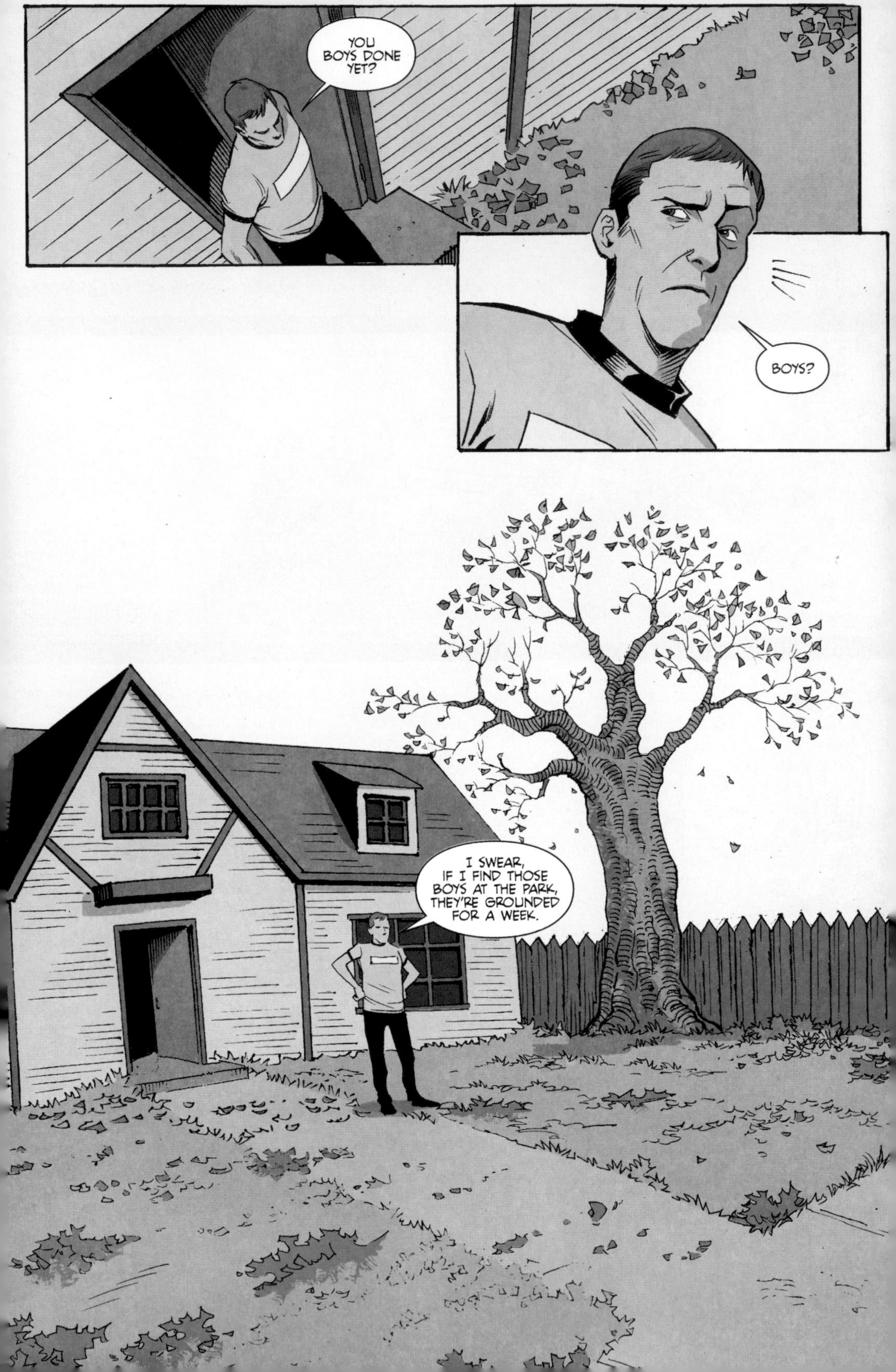
YOU BOYS DONE YET?
BOYS?
I SWEAR, IF I FIND THOSE BOYS AT THE PARK, THEY'RE GROUNDED FOR A WEEK.

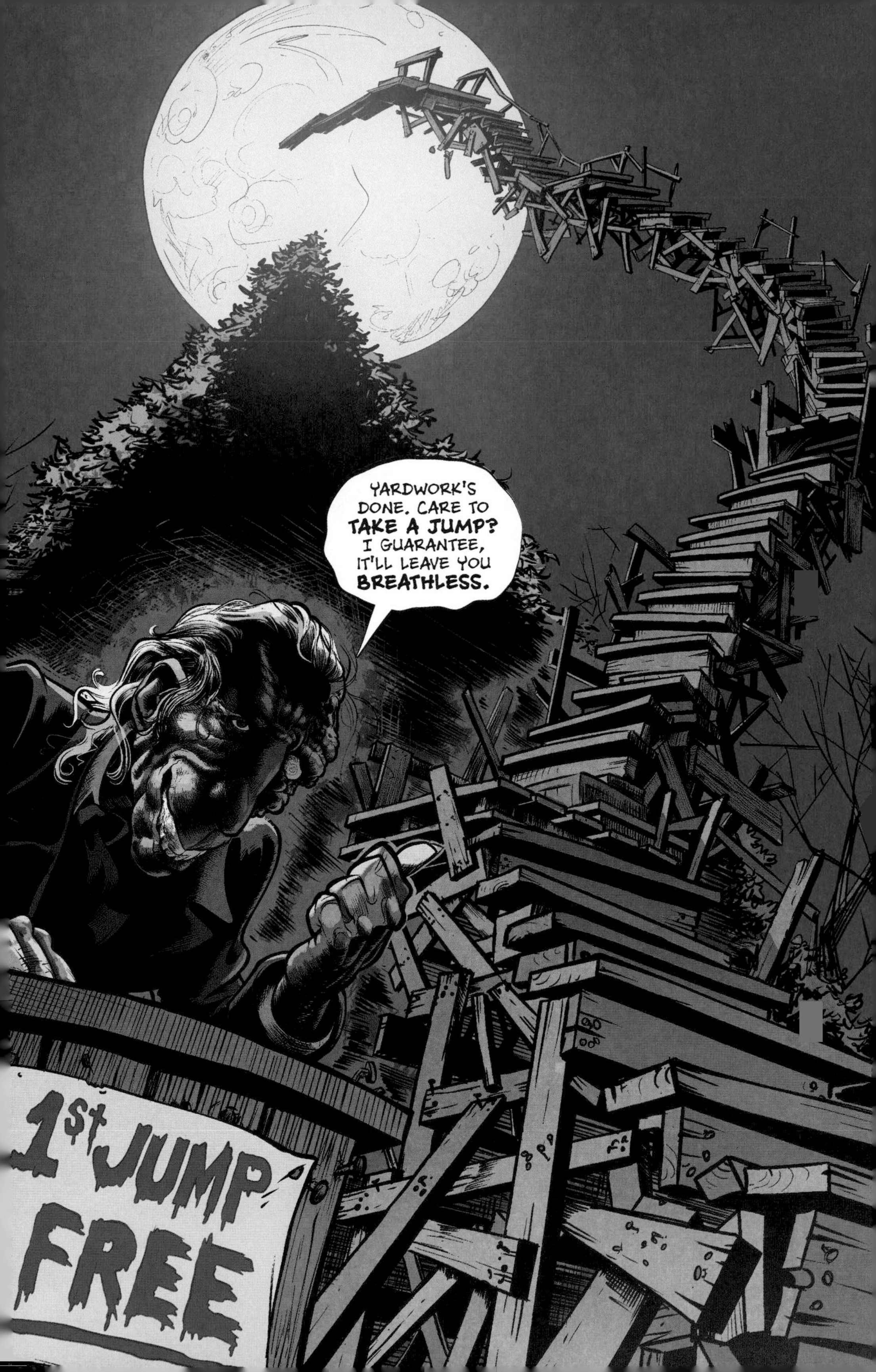
YARDWORK'S DONE. CARE TO TAKE A JUMP? I GUARANTEE, IT'LL LEAVE YOU BREATHLESS.
1st JUMP FREE

TEETH

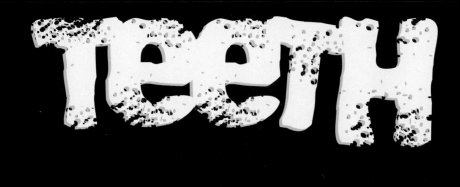

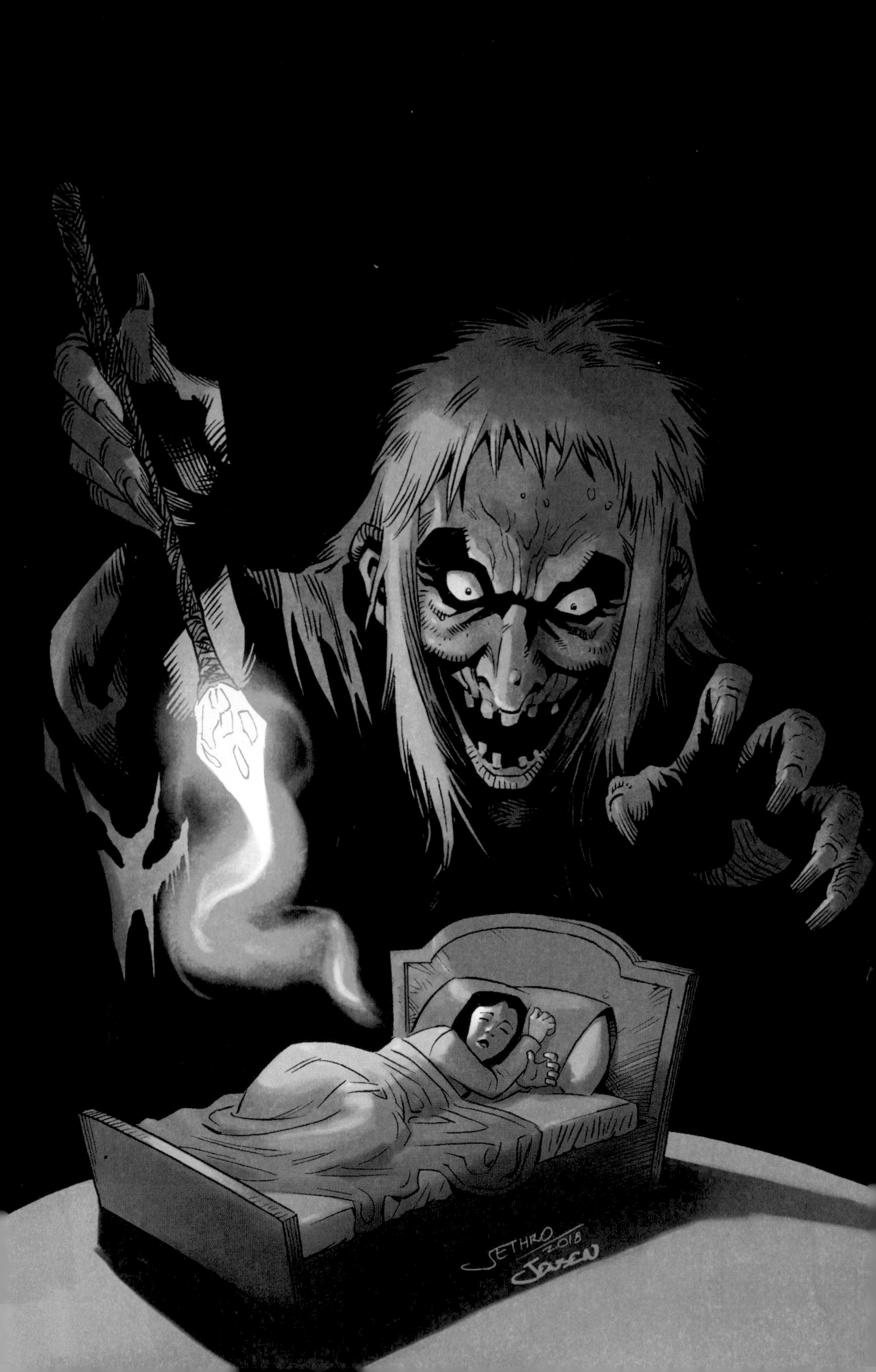
SETHRO 2018

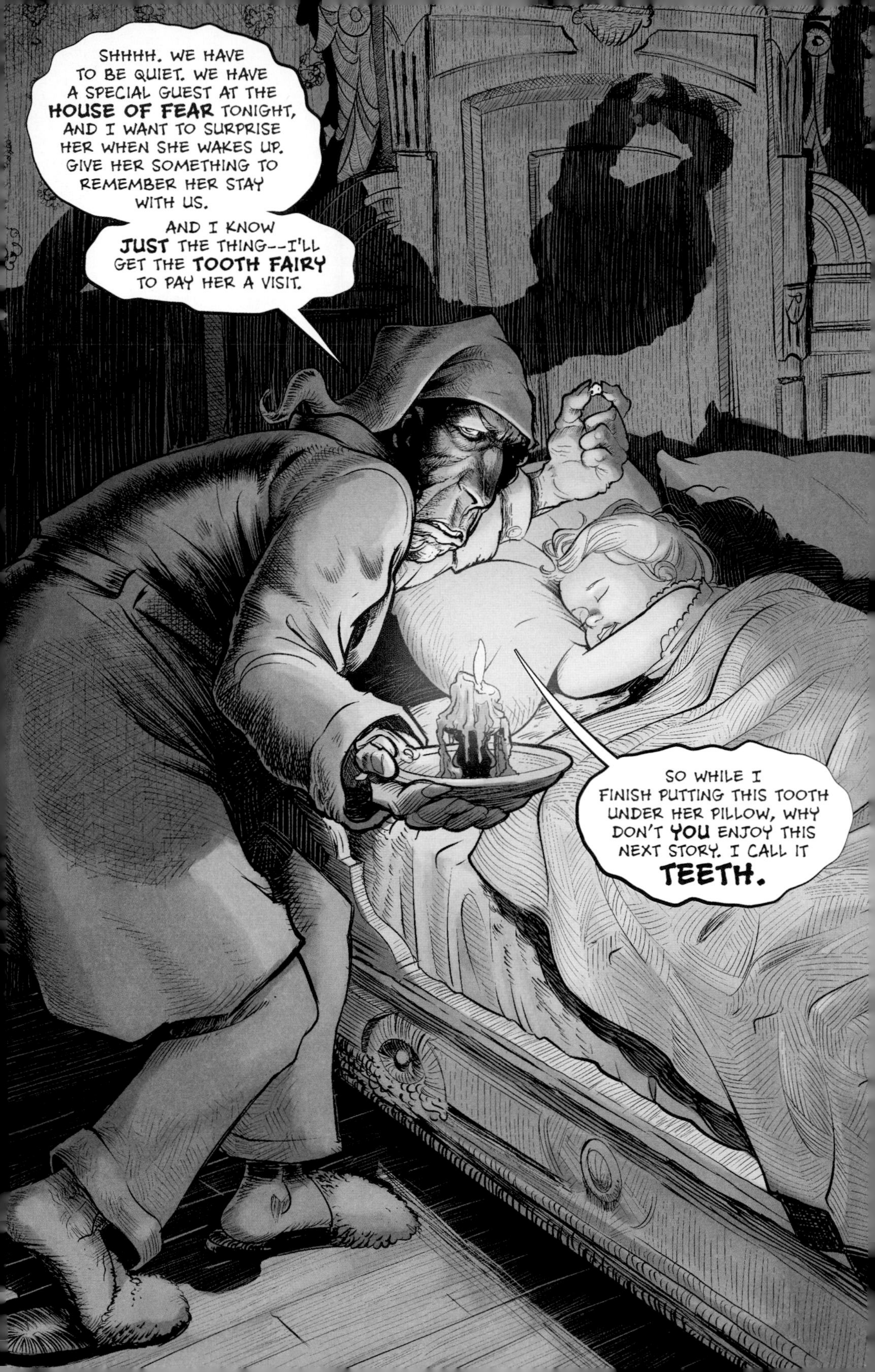
SHHHH. WE HAVE TO BE QUIET. WE HAVE A SPECIAL GUEST AT THE **HOUSE OF FEAR** TONIGHT, AND I WANT TO SURPRISE HER WHEN SHE WAKES UP. GIVE HER SOMETHING TO REMEMBER HER STAY WITH US.
AND I KNOW **JUST** THE THING--I'LL GET THE **TOOTH FAIRY** TO PAY HER A VISIT.
SO WHILE I FINISH PUTTING THIS TOOTH UNDER HER PILLOW, WHY DON'T **YOU** ENJOY THIS NEXT STORY. I CALL IT **TEETH.**

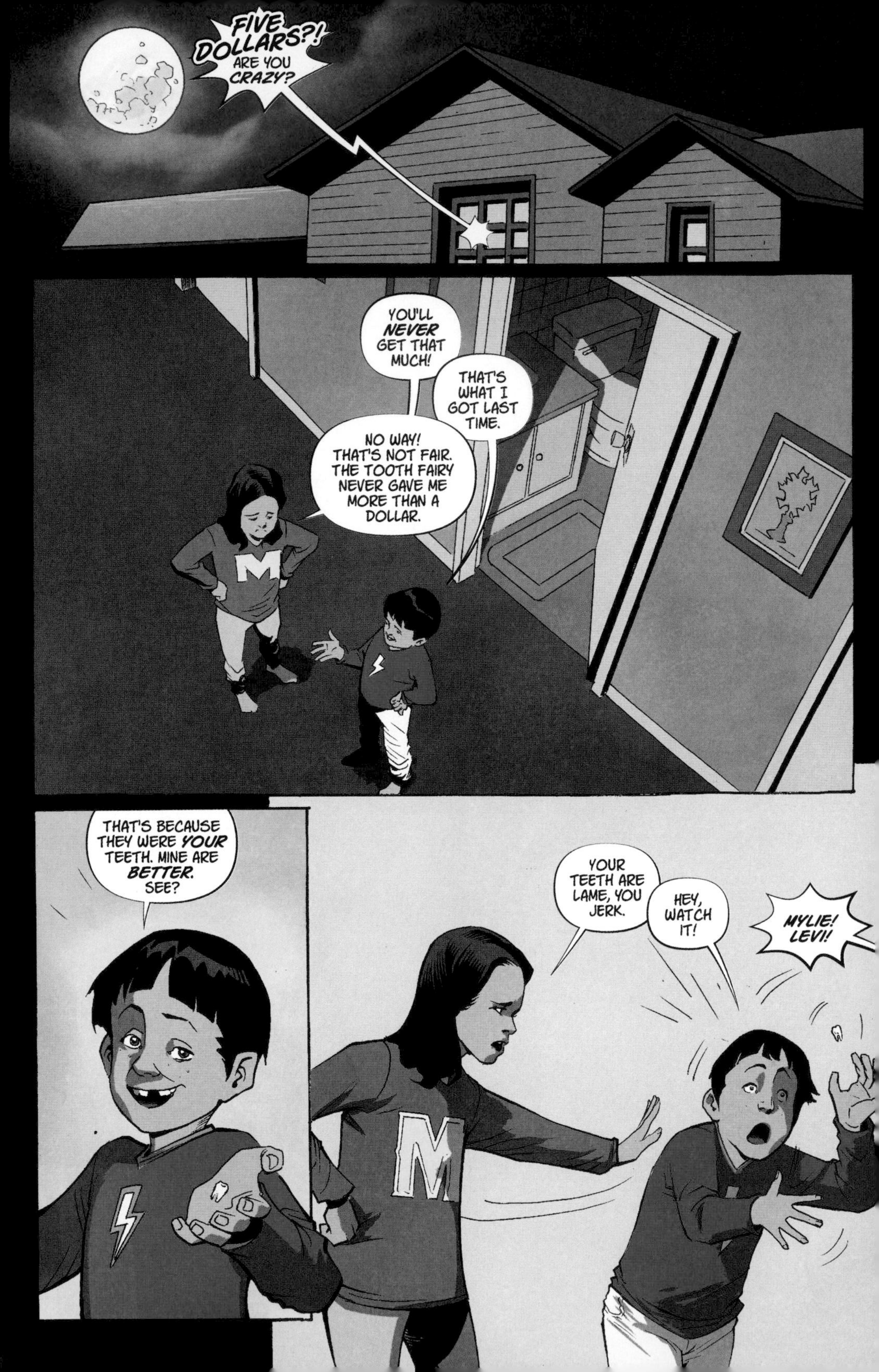
FIVE DOLLARS?! ARE YOU CRAZY?
YOU'LL NEVER GET THAT MUCH!
THAT'S WHAT I GOT LAST TIME.
NO WAY! THAT'S NOT FAIR. THE TOOTH FAIRY NEVER GAVE ME MORE THAN A DOLLAR.
THAT'S BECAUSE THEY WERE YOUR TEETH. MINE ARE BETTER. SEE?
YOUR TEETH ARE LAME, YOU JERK.
HEY, WATCH IT!
MYLIE! LEVI!

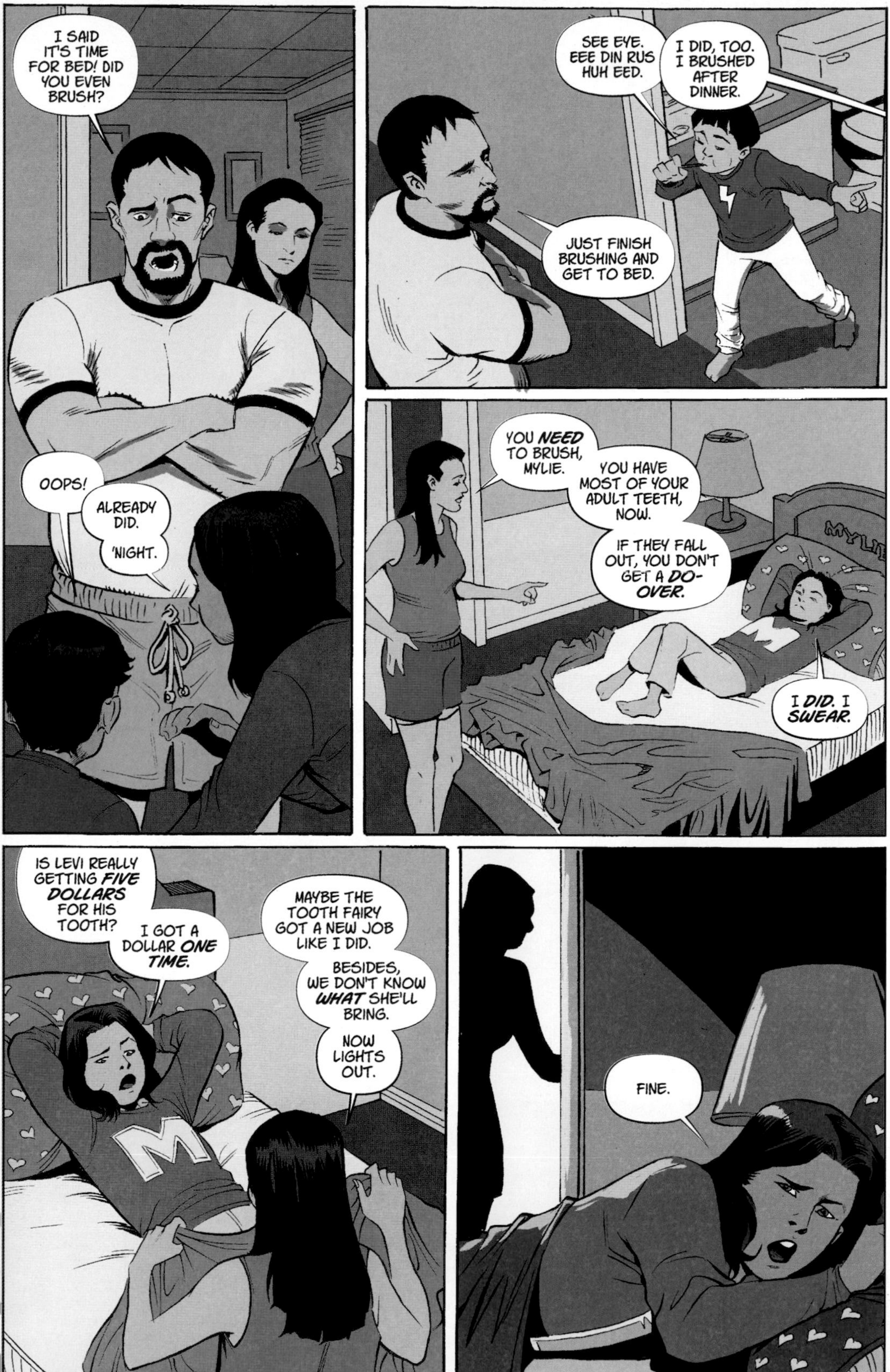
I SAID IT'S TIME FOR BED! DID YOU EVEN BRUSH?
OOPS!
ALREADY DID.
'NIGHT.
SEE EYE. EEE DIN RUS HUH EED.
I DID, TOO. I BRUSHED AFTER DINNER.
JUST FINISH BRUSHING AND GET TO BED.
YOU ***NEED*** TO BRUSH, MYLIE.
YOU HAVE MOST OF YOUR ADULT TEETH, NOW.
IF THEY FALL OUT, YOU DON'T GET A ***DO-OVER***.
I ***DID***. I ***SWEAR***.
IS LEVI REALLY GETTING ***FIVE DOLLARS*** FOR HIS TOOTH?
I GOT A DOLLAR ***ONE TIME***.
MAYBE THE TOOTH FAIRY GOT A NEW JOB LIKE I DID.
BESIDES, WE DON'T KNOW ***WHAT*** SHE'LL BRING.
NOW LIGHTS OUT.
FINE.

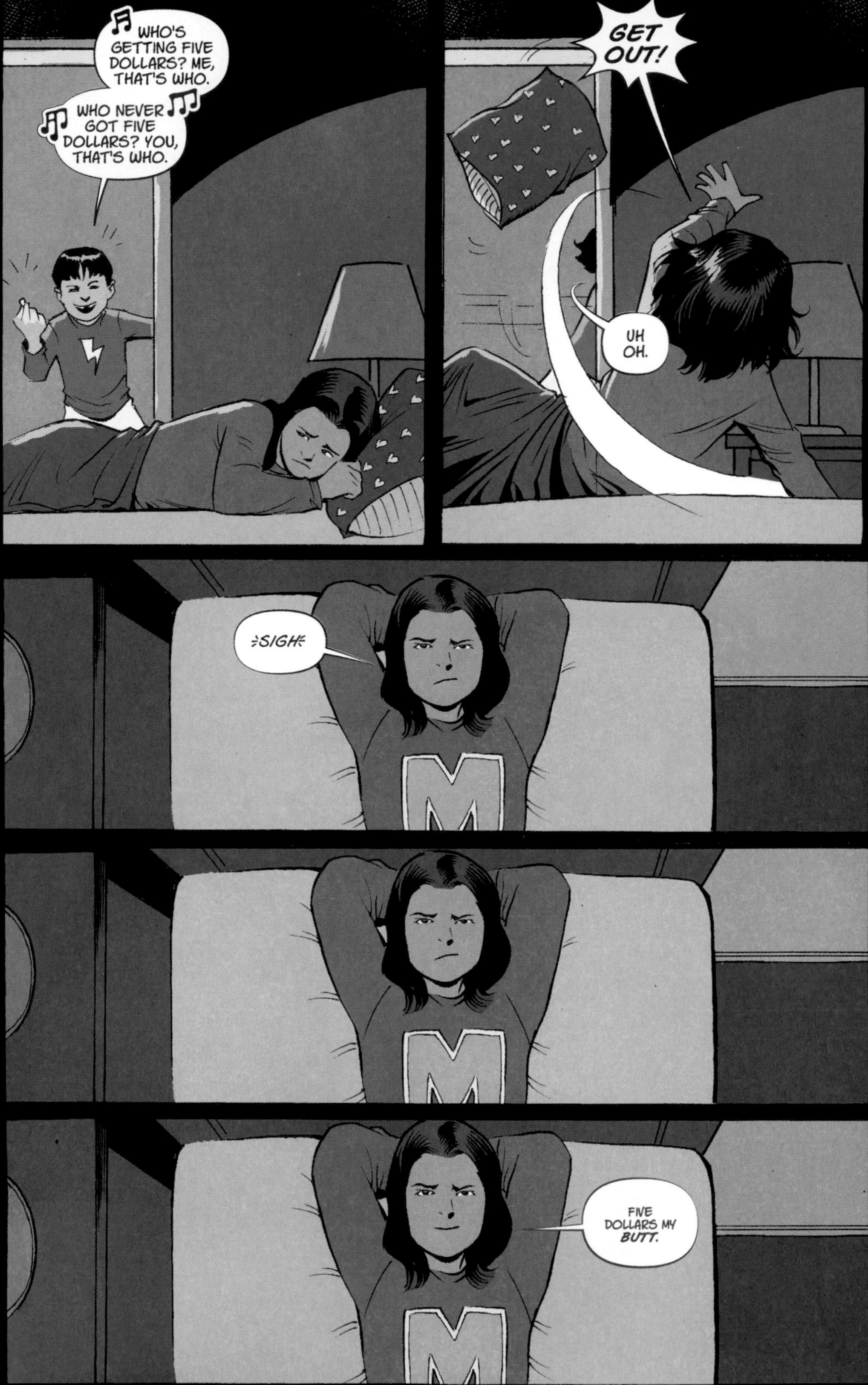

WHO'S GETTING FIVE DOLLARS? ME, THAT'S WHO.
WHO NEVER GOT FIVE DOLLARS? YOU, THAT'S WHO.
GET OUT!
UH OH.
SIGH
FIVE DOLLARS MY BUTT.

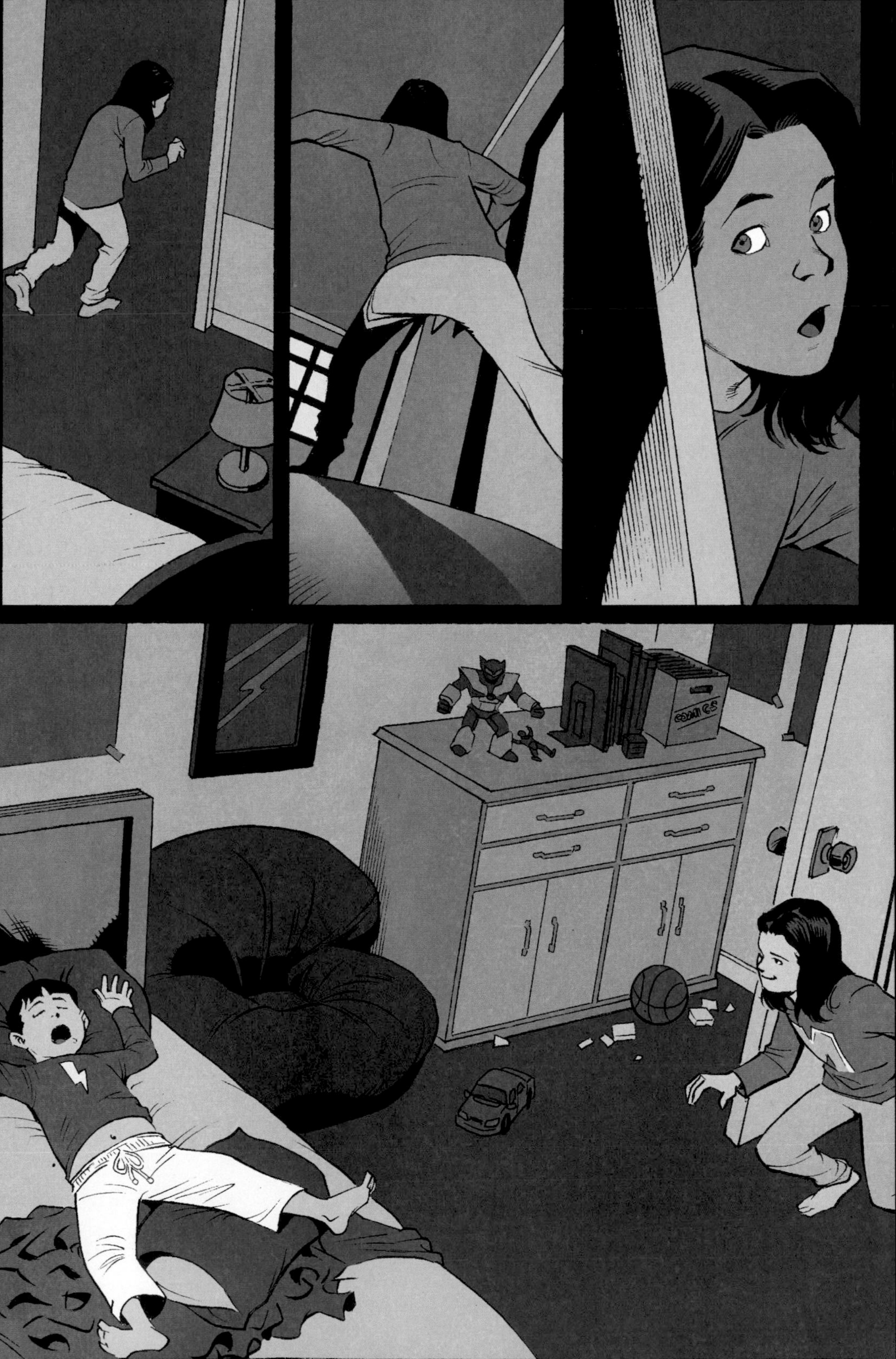
COMICS

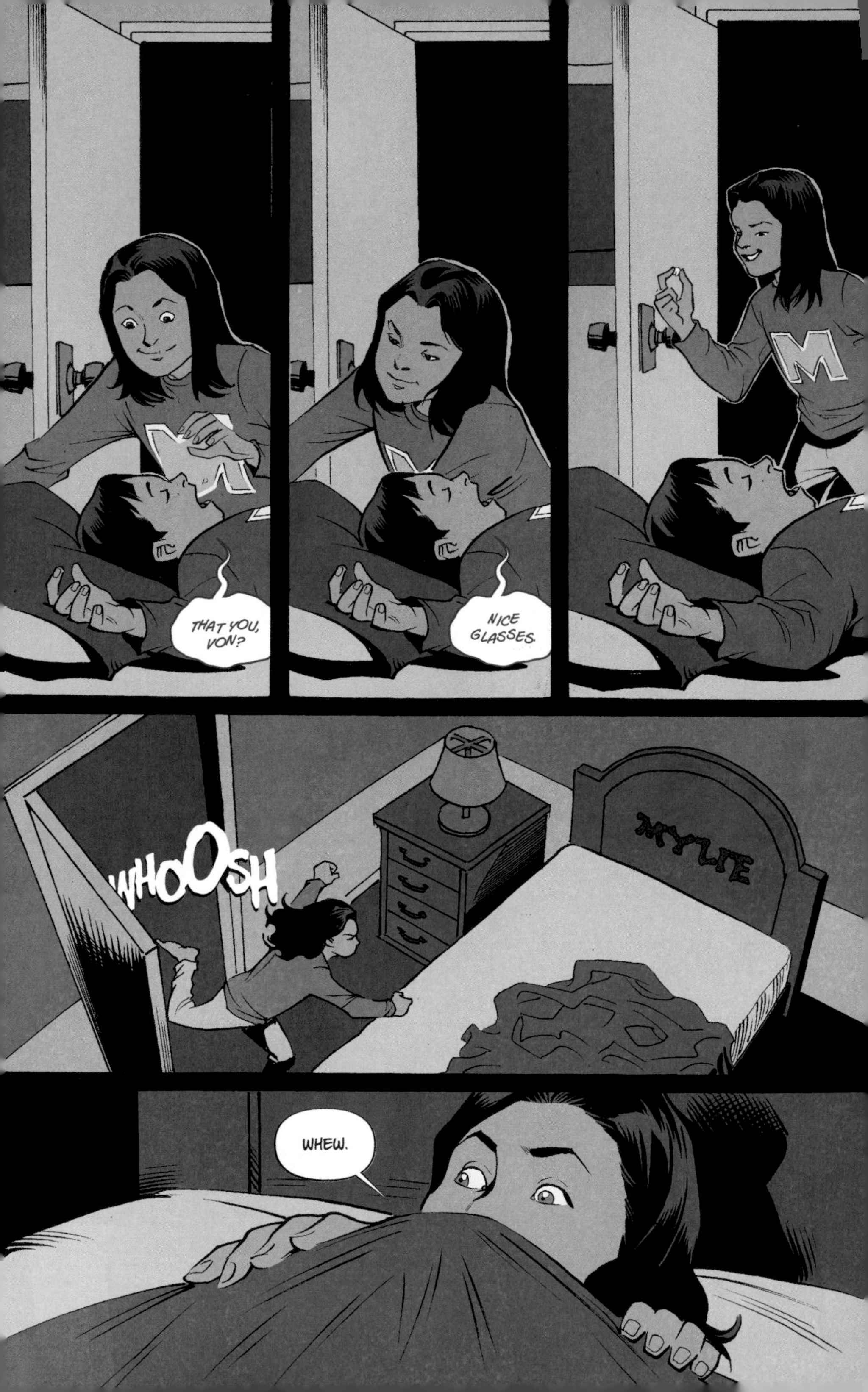
THAT YOU, VON?
NICE GLASSES.
WHOOOSH
MYLIFE
WHEW.

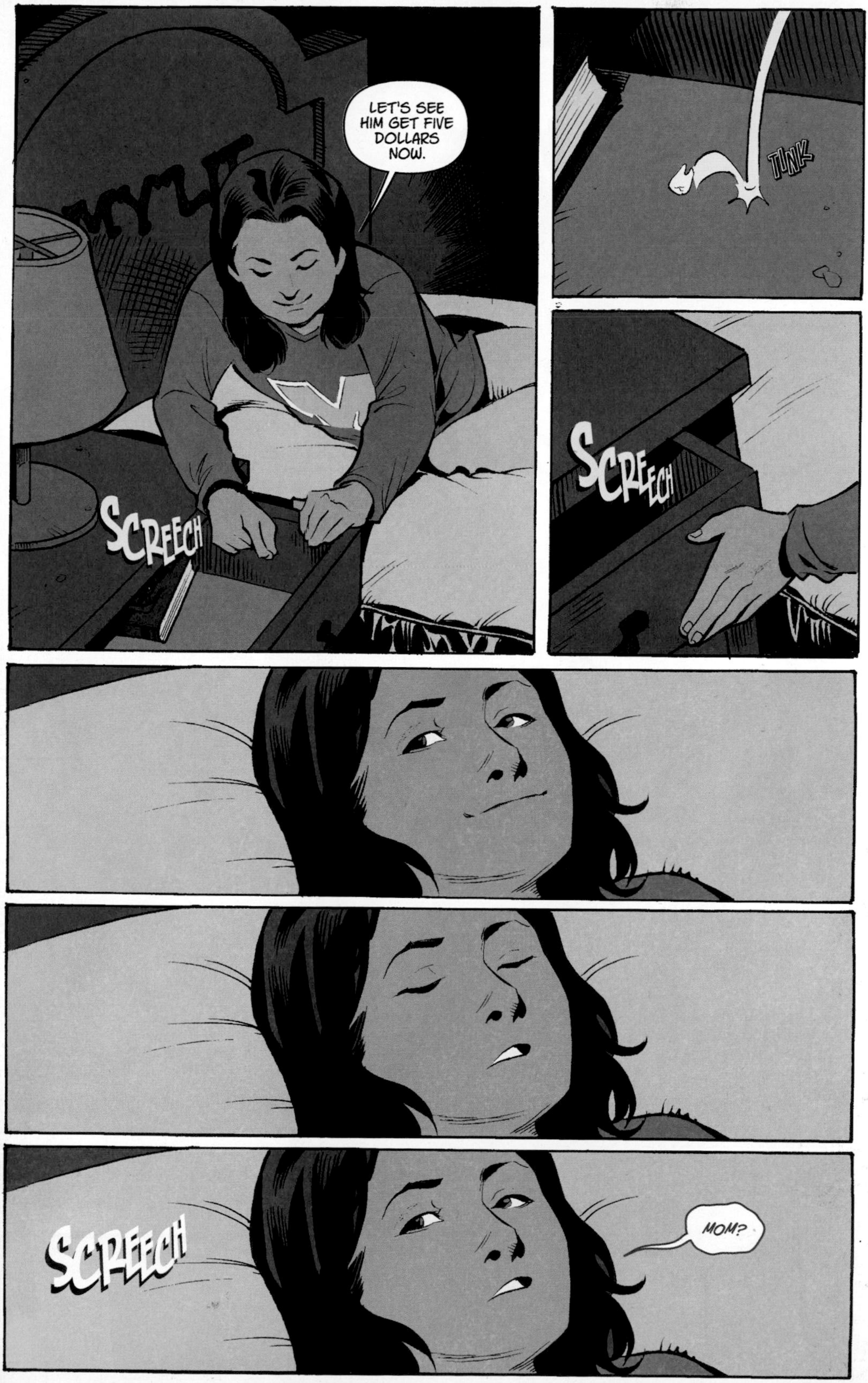
LET'S SEE HIM GET FIVE DOLLARS NOW.
SCREECH
TINK
SCREECH
SCREECH
MOM?

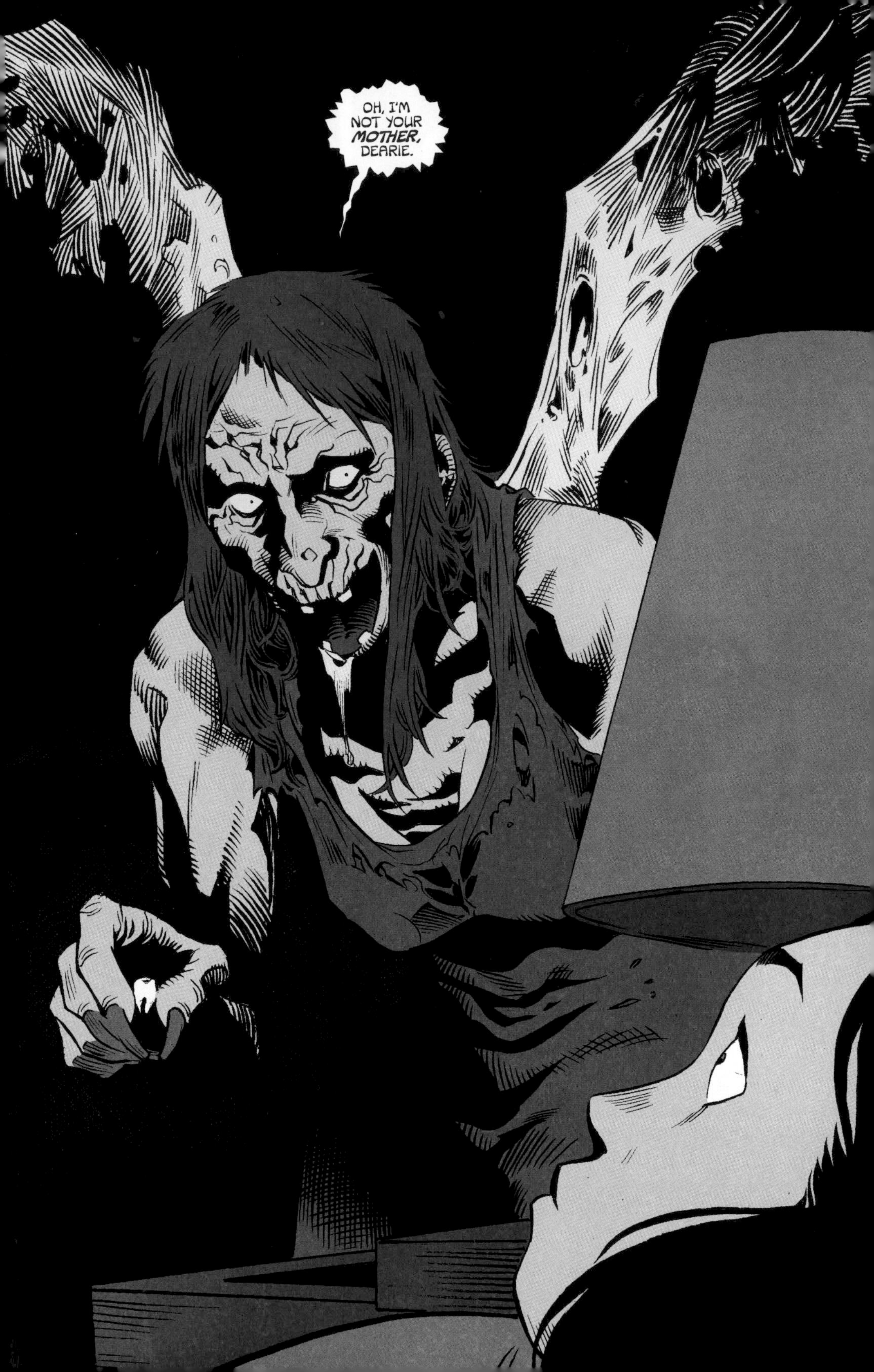
OH, I'M NOT YOUR *MOTHER,* DEARIE.

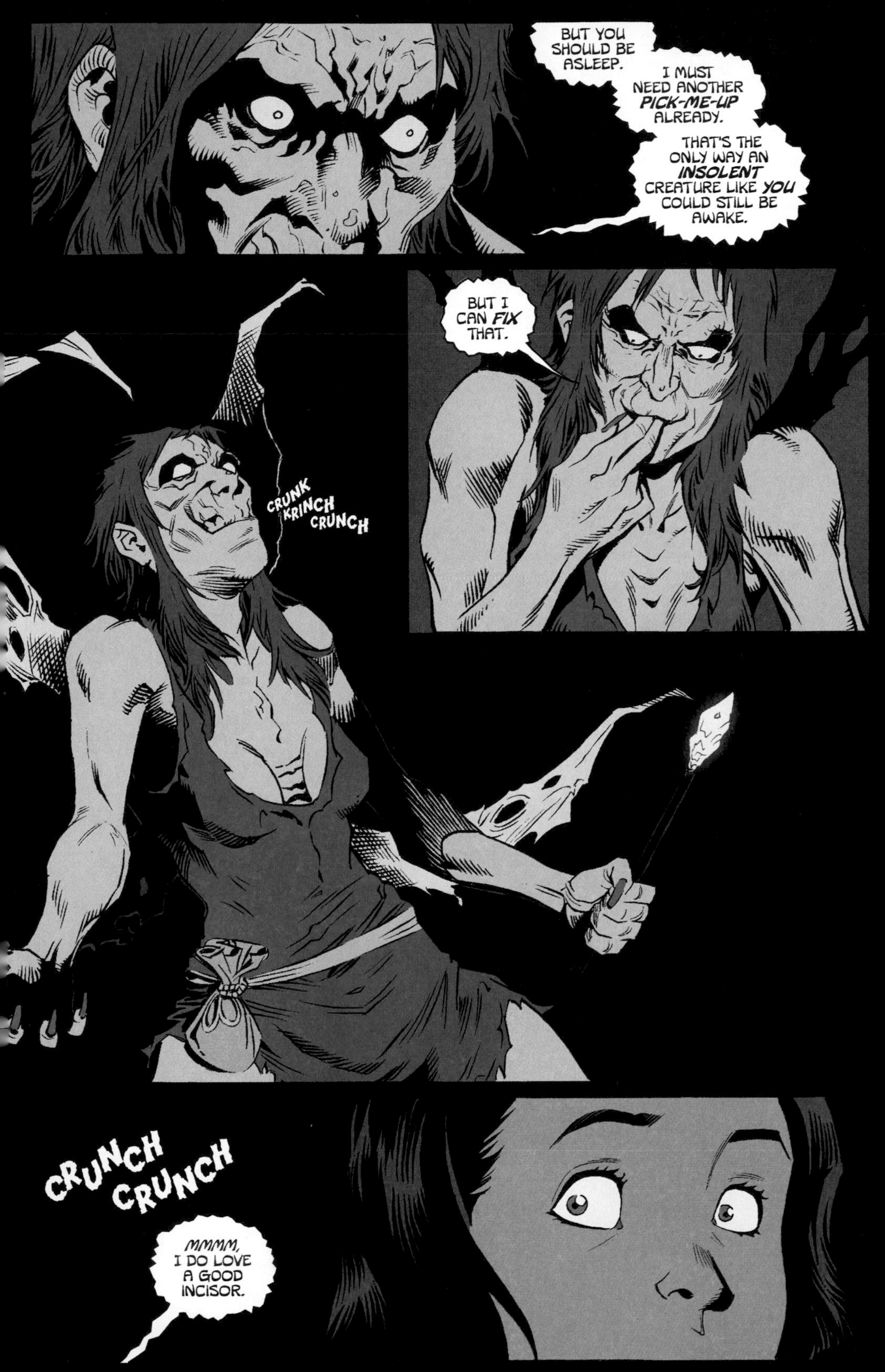
BUT YOU SHOULD BE ASLEEP.
I MUST NEED ANOTHER PICK-ME-UP ALREADY.
THAT'S THE ONLY WAY AN INSOLENT CREATURE LIKE YOU COULD STILL BE AWAKE.
BUT I CAN FIX THAT.
CRUNK KRINCH CRUNCH
CRUNCH CRUNCH
MMMM, I DO LOVE A GOOD INCISOR.

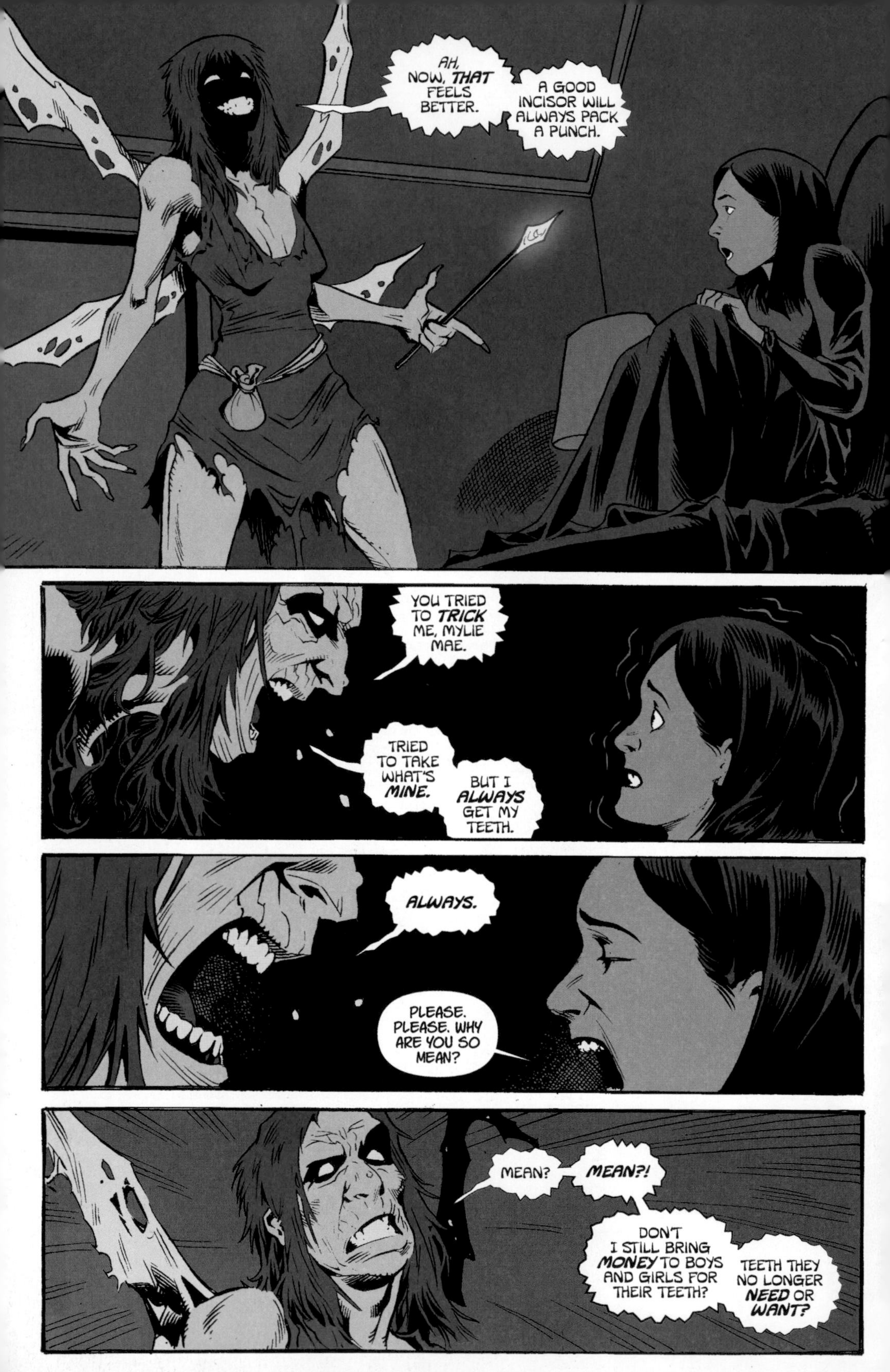
AH, NOW, THAT FEELS BETTER.
A GOOD INCISOR WILL ALWAYS PACK A PUNCH.
YOU TRIED TO TRICK ME, MYLIE MAE.
TRIED TO TAKE WHAT'S MINE.
BUT I ALWAYS GET MY TEETH.
ALWAYS.
PLEASE. PLEASE. WHY ARE YOU SO MEAN?
MEAN?
MEAN?!
DON'T I STILL BRING MONEY TO BOYS AND GIRLS FOR THEIR TEETH?
TEETH THEY NO LONGER NEED OR WANT?

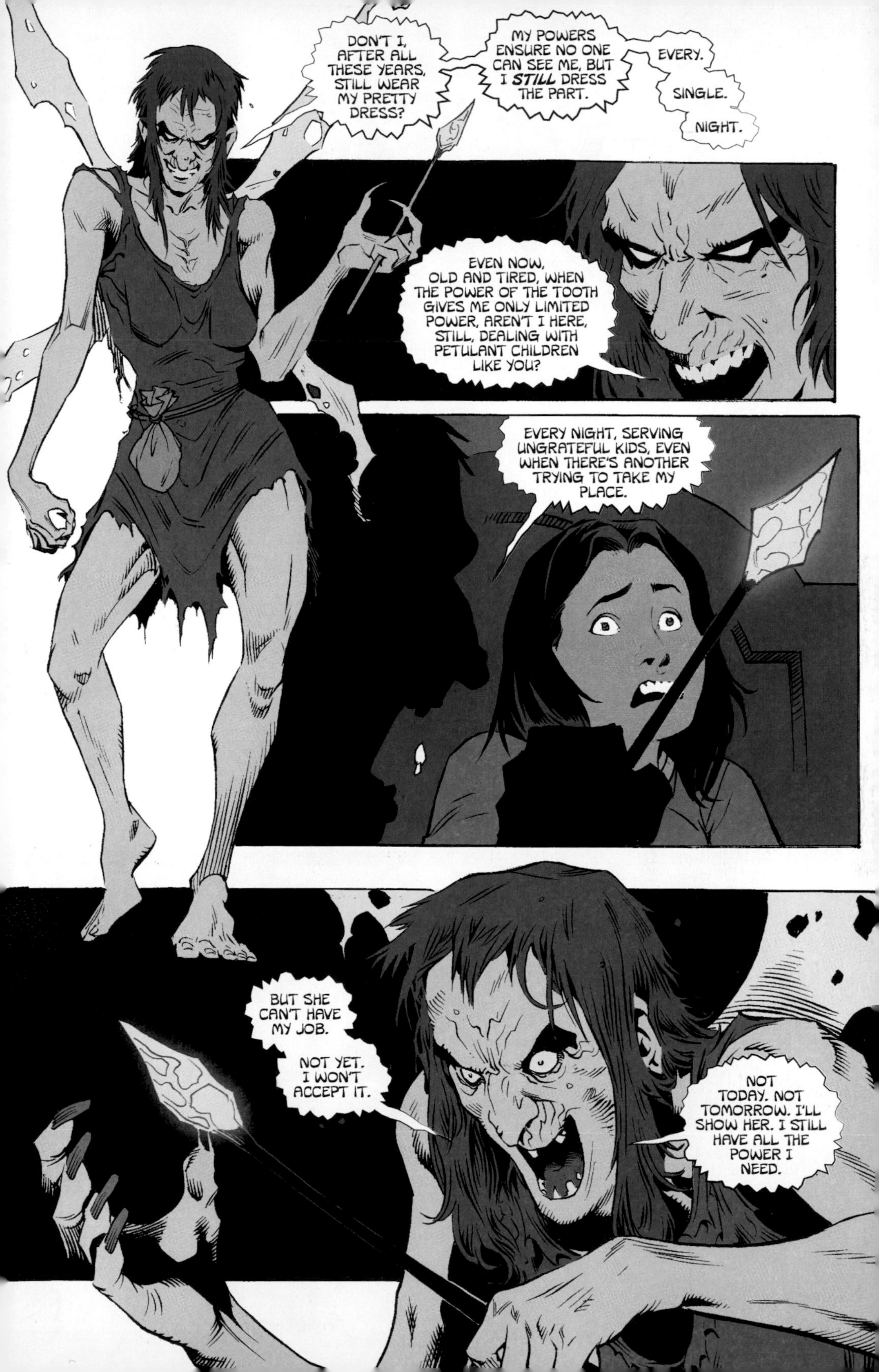
DON'T I, AFTER ALL THESE YEARS, STILL WEAR MY PRETTY DRESS?
MY POWERS ENSURE NO ONE CAN SEE ME, BUT I *STILL* DRESS THE PART.
EVERY.
SINGLE.
NIGHT.
EVEN NOW, OLD AND TIRED, WHEN THE POWER OF THE TOOTH GIVES ME ONLY LIMITED POWER, AREN'T I HERE, STILL, DEALING WITH PETULANT CHILDREN LIKE YOU?
EVERY NIGHT, SERVING UNGRATEFUL KIDS, EVEN WHEN THERE'S ANOTHER TRYING TO TAKE MY PLACE.
BUT SHE CAN'T HAVE MY JOB.
NOT YET. I WON'T ACCEPT IT.
NOT TODAY. NOT TOMORROW. I'LL SHOW HER. I STILL HAVE ALL THE POWER I NEED.

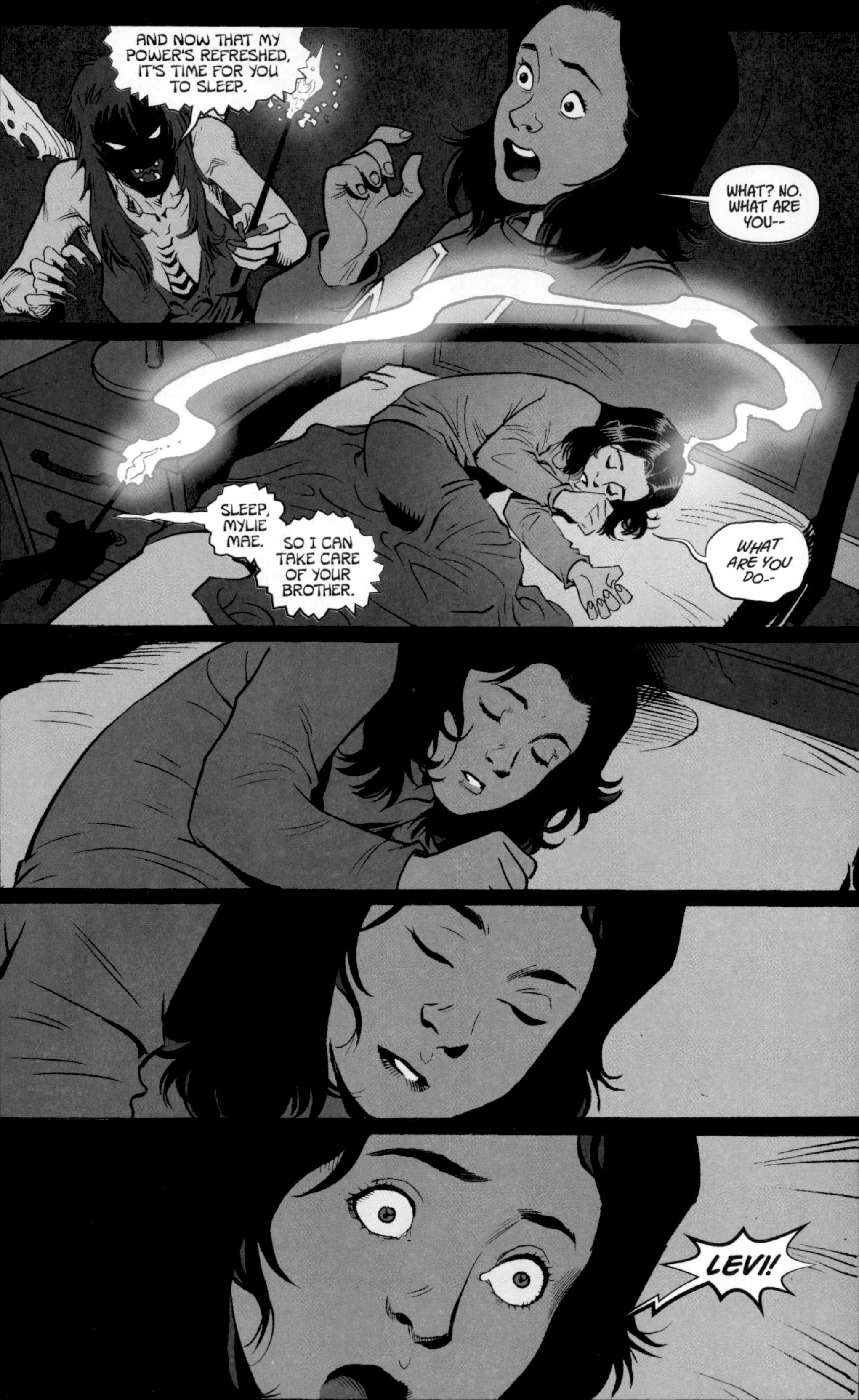
AND NOW THAT MY POWER'S REFRESHED, IT'S TIME FOR YOU TO SLEEP.
WHAT? NO. WHAT ARE YOU--
SLEEP, MYLIE MAE.
SO I CAN TAKE CARE OF YOUR BROTHER.
WHAT ARE YOU DO-
LEVI!

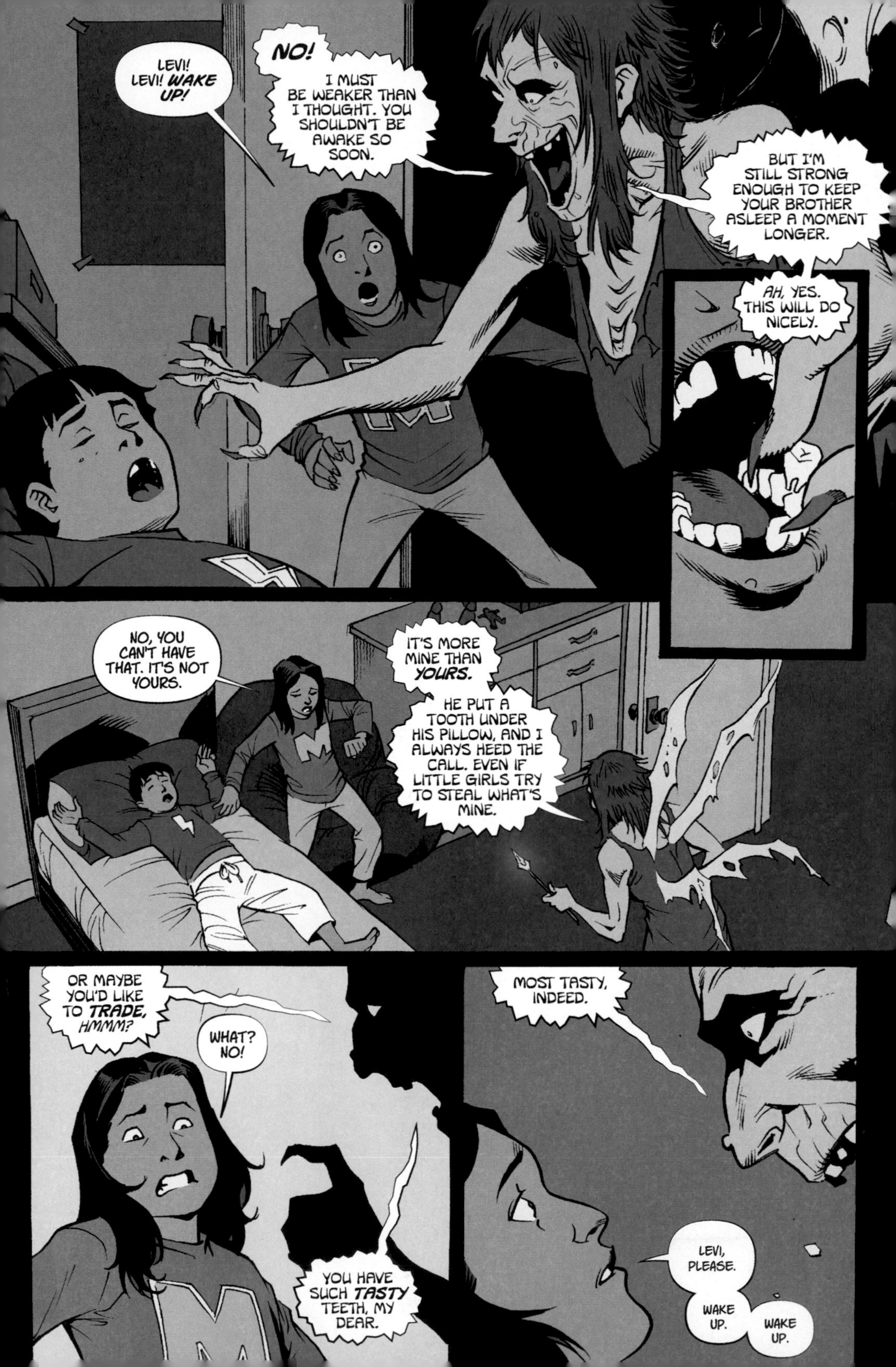
LEVI! LEVI! WAKE UP!
NO!
I MUST BE WEAKER THAN I THOUGHT. YOU SHOULDN'T BE AWAKE SO SOON.
BUT I'M STILL STRONG ENOUGH TO KEEP YOUR BROTHER ASLEEP A MOMENT LONGER.
AH, YES. THIS WILL DO NICELY.
NO, YOU CAN'T HAVE THAT. IT'S NOT YOURS.
IT'S MORE MINE THAN YOURS.
HE PUT A TOOTH UNDER HIS PILLOW, AND I ALWAYS HEED THE CALL. EVEN IF LITTLE GIRLS TRY TO STEAL WHAT'S MINE.
OR MAYBE YOU'D LIKE TO TRADE, HMMM?
WHAT? NO!
YOU HAVE SUCH TASTY TEETH, MY DEAR.
MOST TASTY, INDEED.
LEVI, PLEASE.
WAKE UP.
WAKE UP.

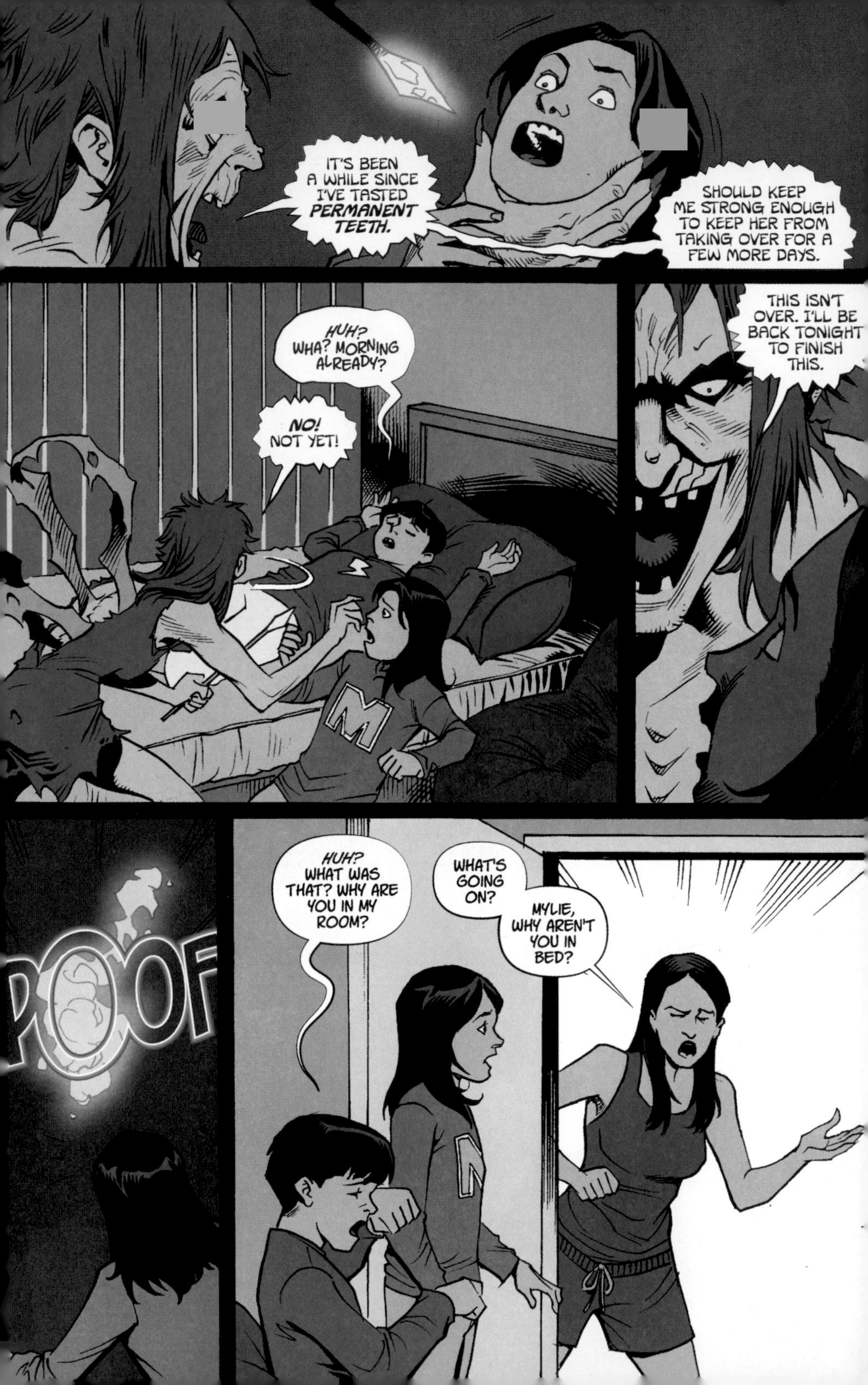
IT'S BEEN A WHILE SINCE I'VE TASTED *PERMANENT TEETH.*
SHOULD KEEP ME STRONG ENOUGH TO KEEP HER FROM TAKING OVER FOR A FEW MORE DAYS.
HUH? WHA? MORNING ALREADY?
NO! NOT YET!
THIS ISN'T OVER. I'LL BE BACK TONIGHT TO FINISH THIS.
POOF
HUH? WHAT WAS THAT? WHY ARE YOU IN MY ROOM?
WHAT'S GOING ON?
MYLIE, WHY AREN'T YOU IN BED?

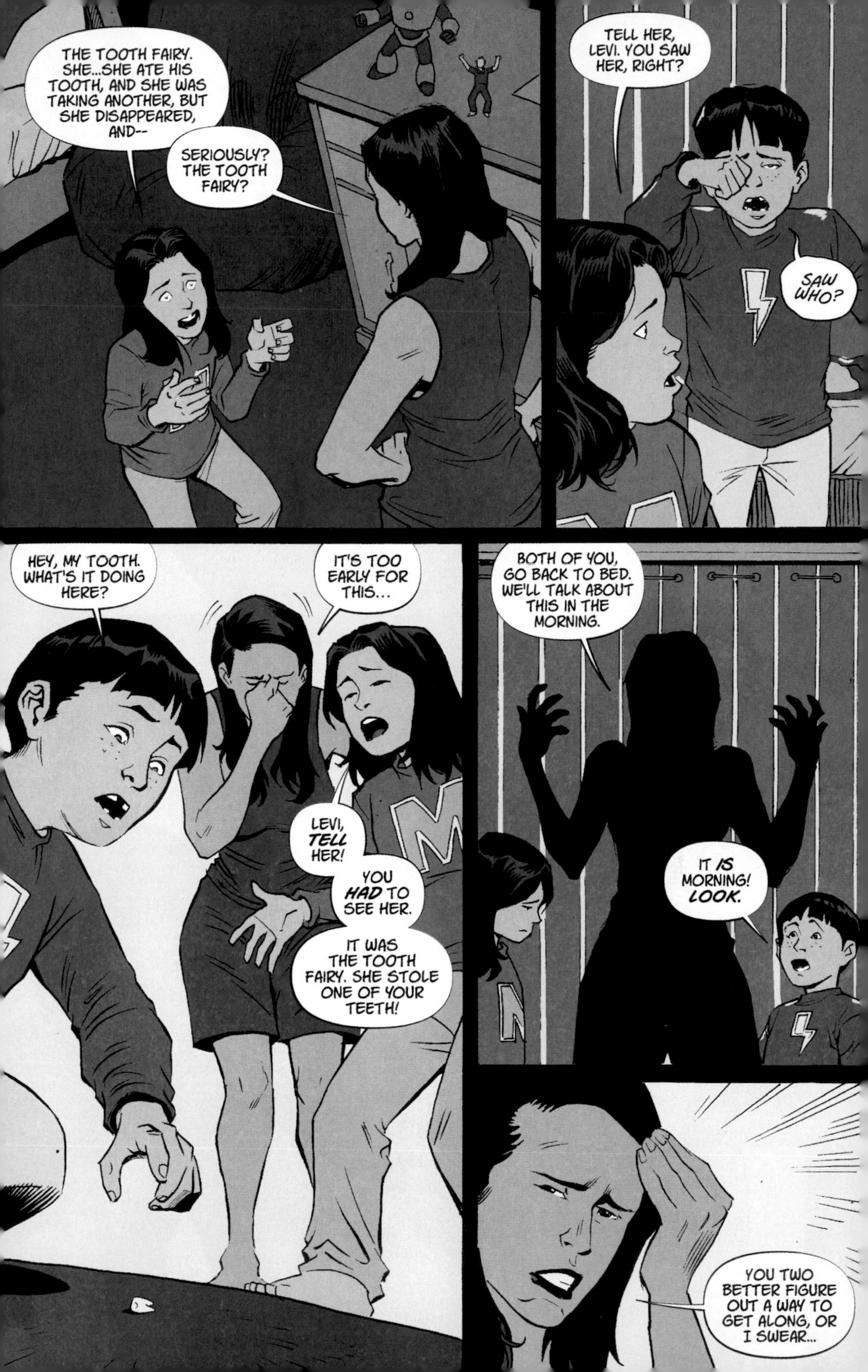
THE TOOTH FAIRY. SHE...SHE ATE HIS TOOTH, AND SHE WAS TAKING ANOTHER, BUT SHE DISAPPEARED, AND--
SERIOUSLY? THE TOOTH FAIRY?
TELL HER, LEVI. YOU SAW HER, RIGHT?
SAW WHO?
HEY, MY TOOTH. WHAT'S IT DOING HERE?
IT'S TOO EARLY FOR THIS...
LEVI, *TELL* HER!
YOU *HAD* TO SEE HER.
IT WAS THE TOOTH FAIRY. SHE STOLE ONE OF YOUR TEETH!
BOTH OF YOU, GO BACK TO BED. WE'LL TALK ABOUT THIS IN THE MORNING.
IT *IS* MORNING! *LOOK.*
YOU TWO BETTER FIGURE OUT A WAY TO GET ALONG, OR I SWEAR...

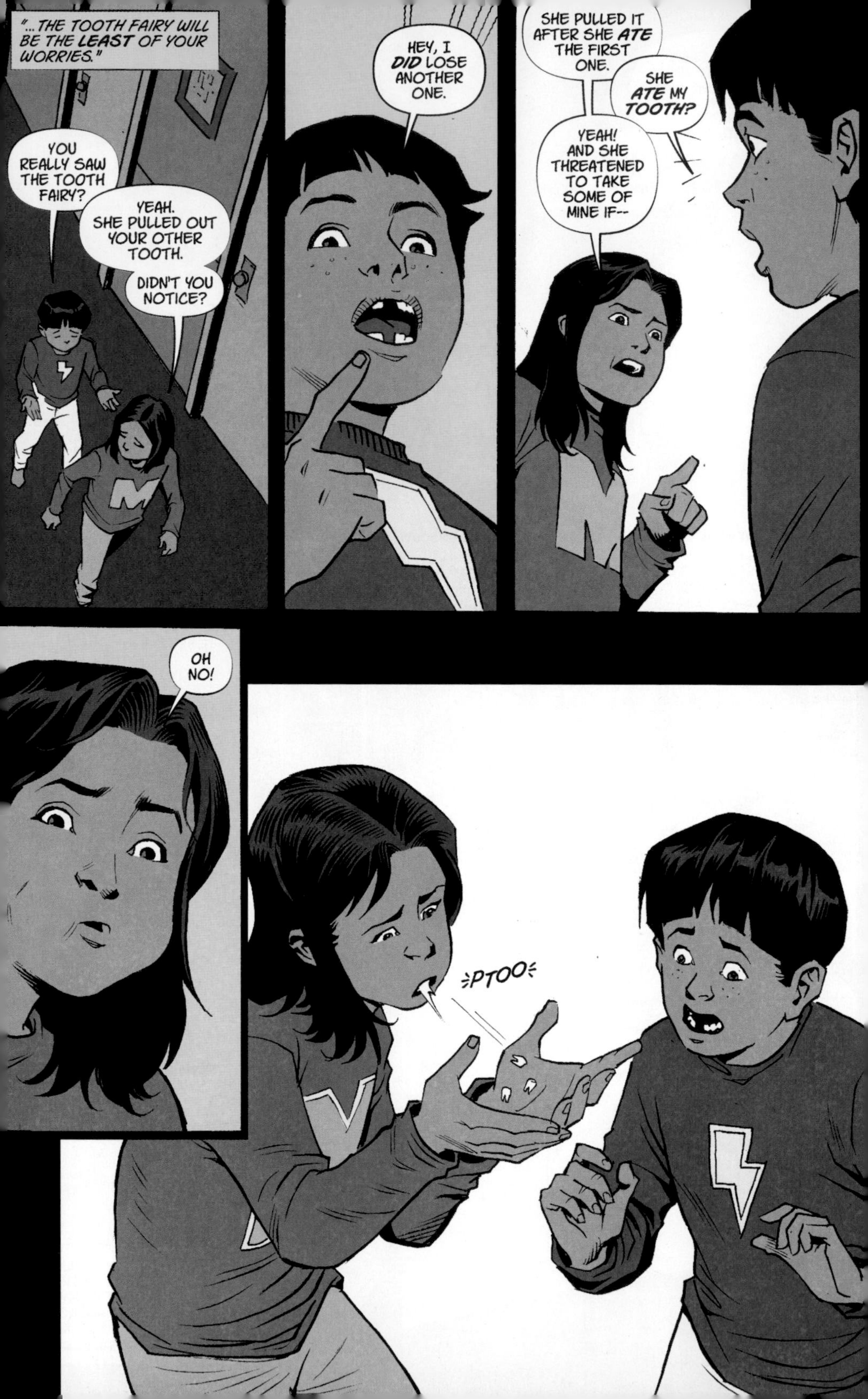
"...THE TOOTH FAIRY WILL BE THE LEAST OF YOUR WORRIES."
YOU REALLY SAW THE TOOTH FAIRY?
YEAH. SHE PULLED OUT YOUR OTHER TOOTH.
DIDN'T YOU NOTICE?
HEY, I DID LOSE ANOTHER ONE.
SHE PULLED IT AFTER SHE ATE THE FIRST ONE.
SHE ATE MY TOOTH?
YEAH! AND SHE THREATENED TO TAKE SOME OF MINE IF--
OH NO!
PTOO

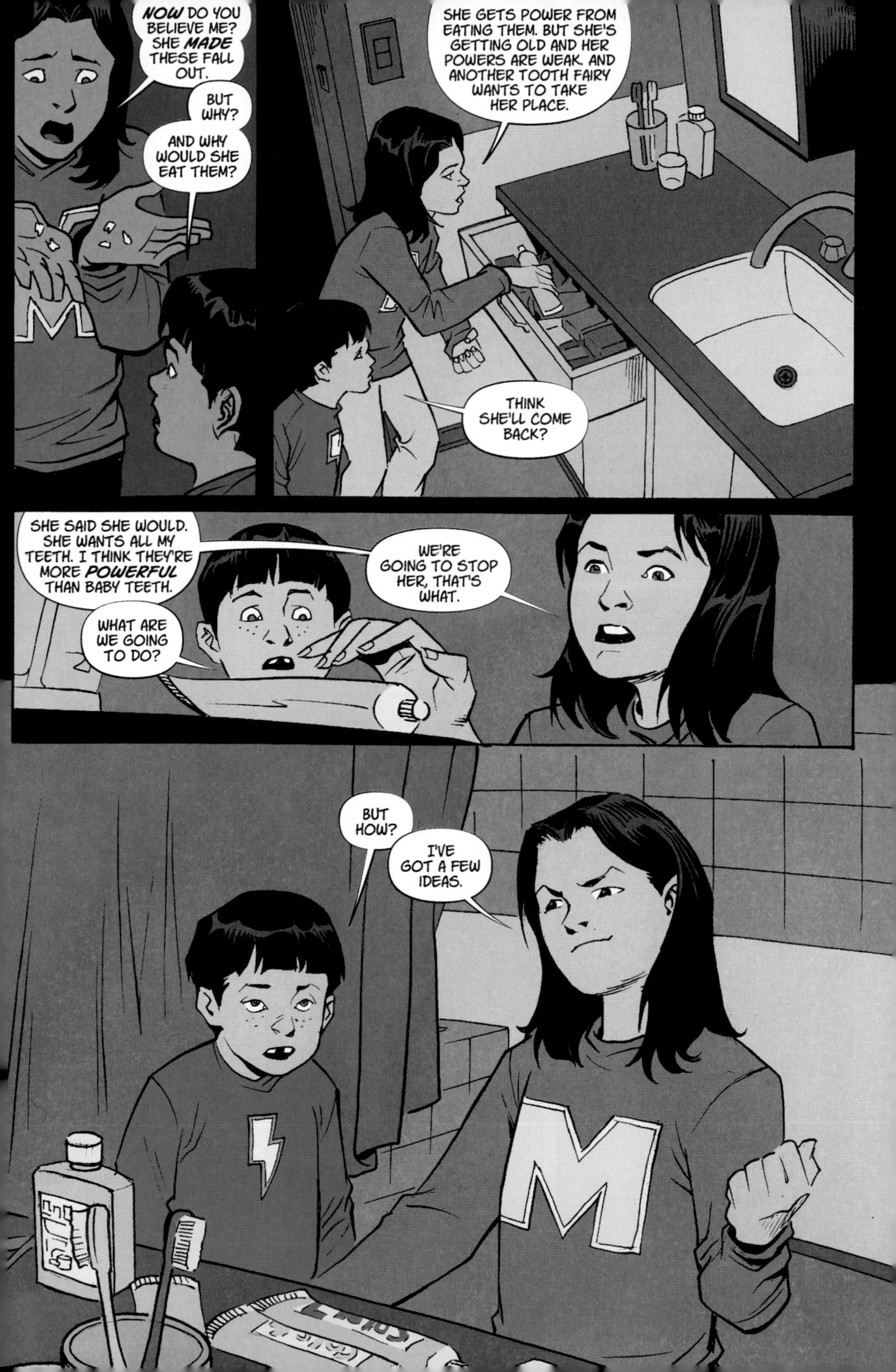
NOW DO YOU BELIEVE ME? SHE MADE THESE FALL OUT.
BUT WHY?
AND WHY WOULD SHE EAT THEM?
SHE GETS POWER FROM EATING THEM. BUT SHE'S GETTING OLD AND HER POWERS ARE WEAK. AND ANOTHER TOOTH FAIRY WANTS TO TAKE HER PLACE.
THINK SHE'LL COME BACK?
SHE SAID SHE WOULD. SHE WANTS ALL MY TEETH. I THINK THEY'RE MORE POWERFUL THAN BABY TEETH.
WHAT ARE WE GOING TO DO?
WE'RE GOING TO STOP HER, THAT'S WHAT.
BUT HOW?
I'VE GOT A FEW IDEAS.

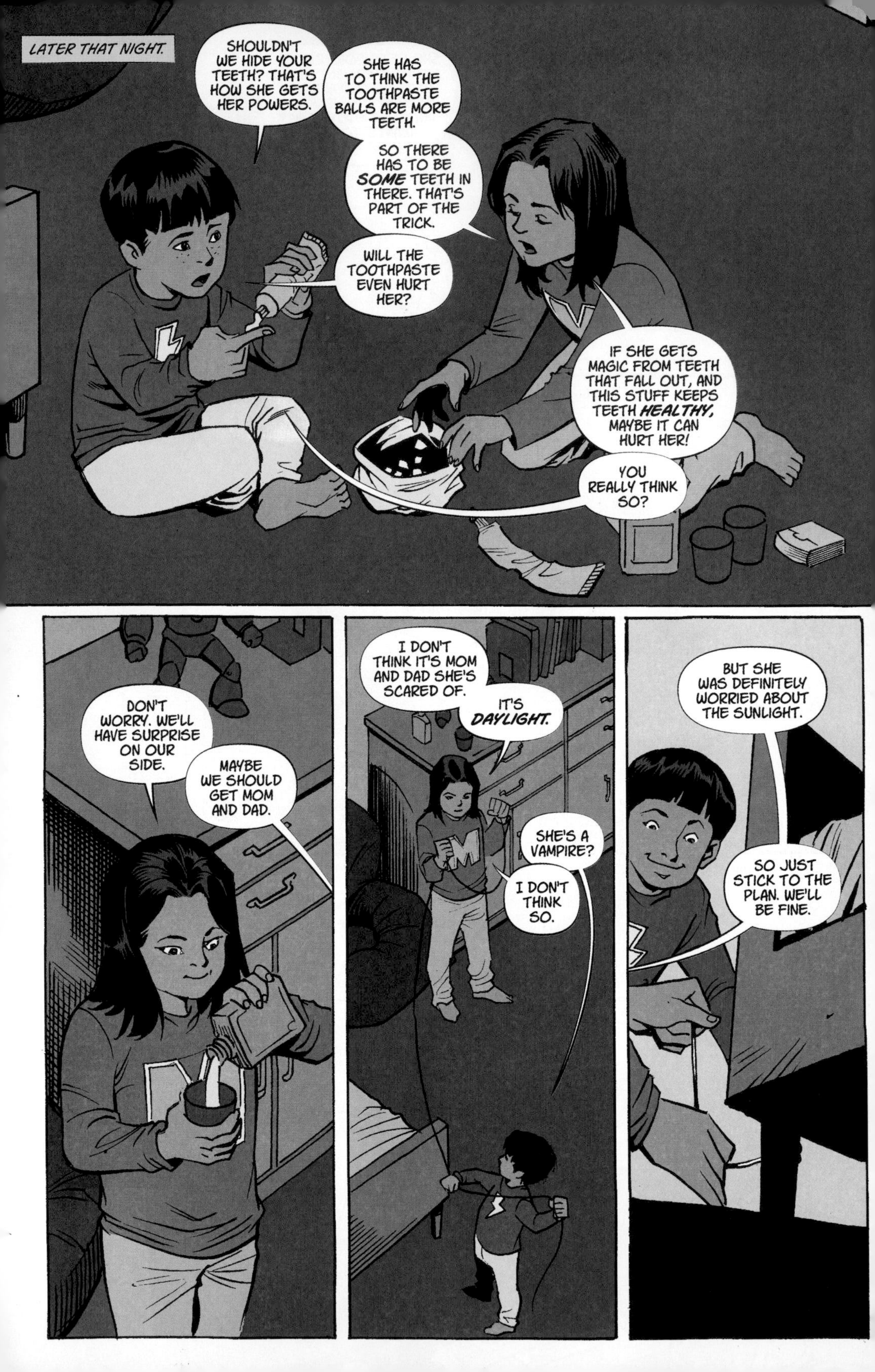
LATER THAT NIGHT.
SHOULDN'T WE HIDE YOUR TEETH? THAT'S HOW SHE GETS HER POWERS.
SHE HAS TO THINK THE TOOTHPASTE BALLS ARE MORE TEETH.
SO THERE HAS TO BE SOME TEETH IN THERE. THAT'S PART OF THE TRICK.
WILL THE TOOTHPASTE EVEN HURT HER?
IF SHE GETS MAGIC FROM TEETH THAT FALL OUT, AND THIS STUFF KEEPS TEETH HEALTHY, MAYBE IT CAN HURT HER!
YOU REALLY THINK SO?
DON'T WORRY. WE'LL HAVE SURPRISE ON OUR SIDE.
MAYBE WE SHOULD GET MOM AND DAD.
I DON'T THINK IT'S MOM AND DAD SHE'S SCARED OF.
IT'S DAYLIGHT.
SHE'S A VAMPIRE?
I DON'T THINK SO.
BUT SHE WAS DEFINITELY WORRIED ABOUT THE SUNLIGHT.
SO JUST STICK TO THE PLAN. WE'LL BE FINE.

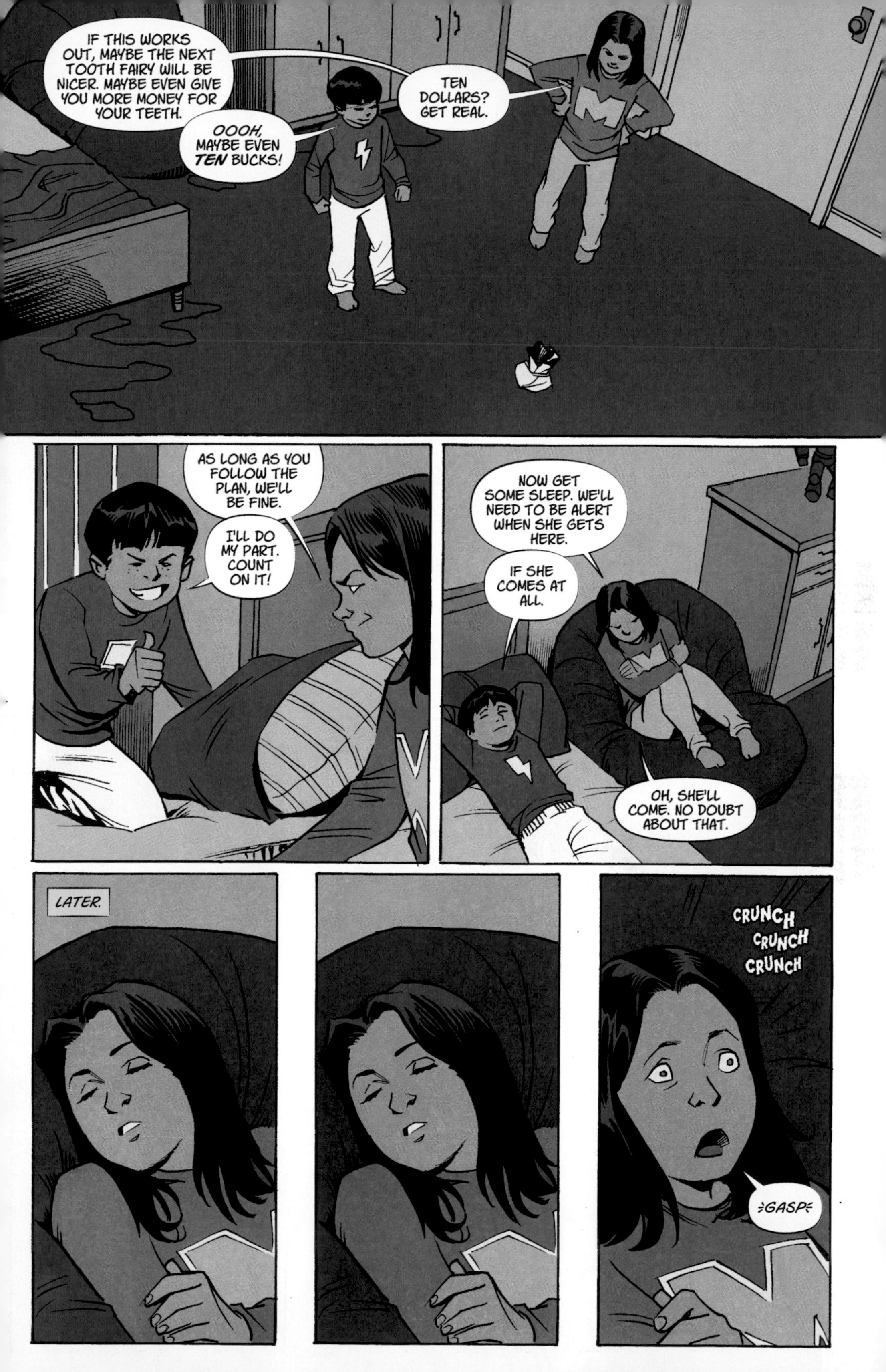

IF THIS WORKS OUT, MAYBE THE NEXT TOOTH FAIRY WILL BE NICER. MAYBE EVEN GIVE YOU MORE MONEY FOR YOUR TEETH.
OOOH, MAYBE EVEN TEN BUCKS!
TEN DOLLARS? GET REAL.
AS LONG AS YOU FOLLOW THE PLAN, WE'LL BE FINE.
I'LL DO MY PART. COUNT ON IT!
NOW GET SOME SLEEP. WE'LL NEED TO BE ALERT WHEN SHE GETS HERE.
IF SHE COMES AT ALL.
OH, SHE'LL COME. NO DOUBT ABOUT THAT.
LATER.
CRUNCH
CRUNCH
CRUNCH
GASP

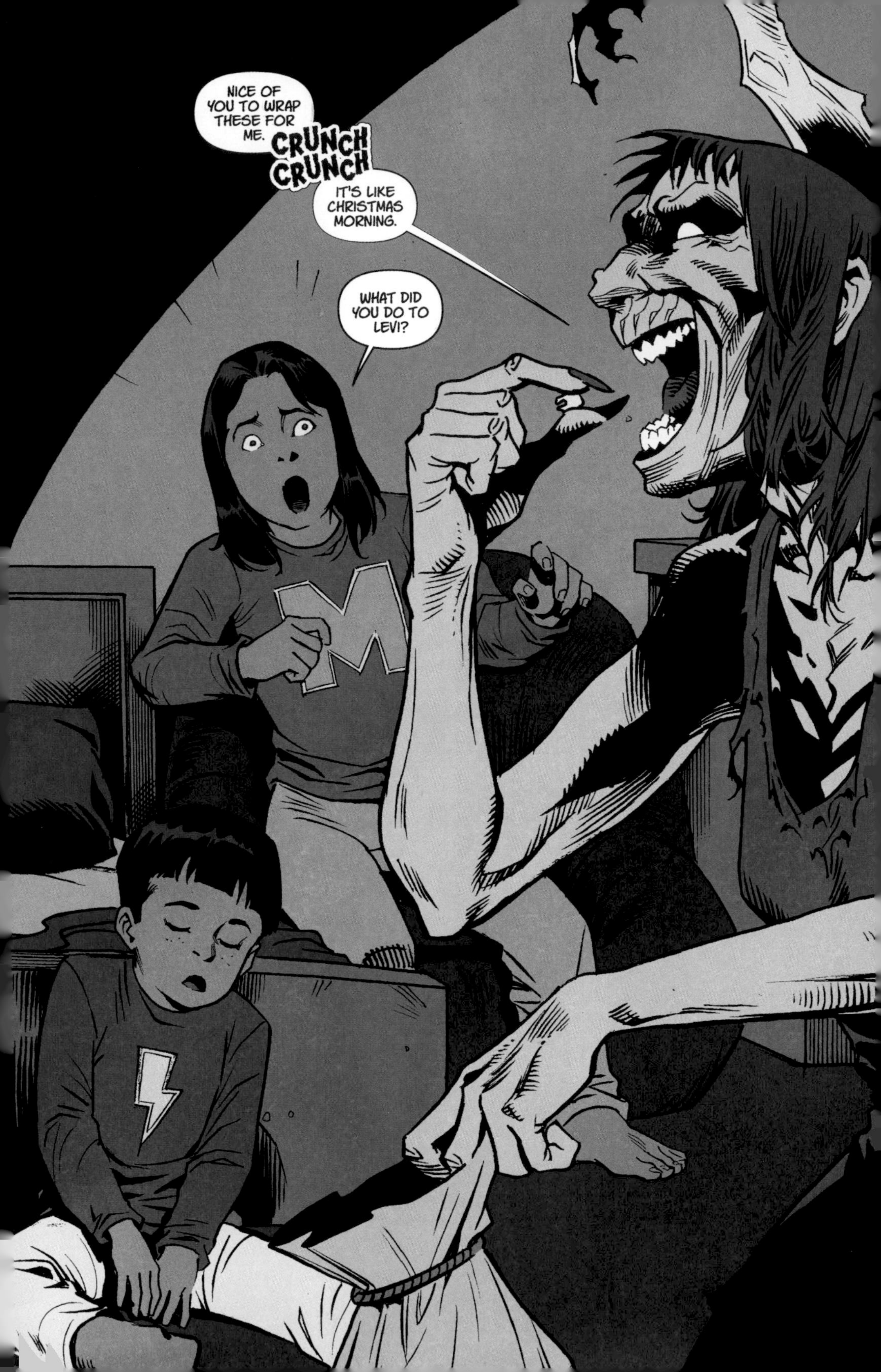
NICE OF YOU TO WRAP THESE FOR ME.
CRUNCH CRUNCH
IT'S LIKE CHRISTMAS MORNING.
WHAT DID YOU DO TO LEVI?

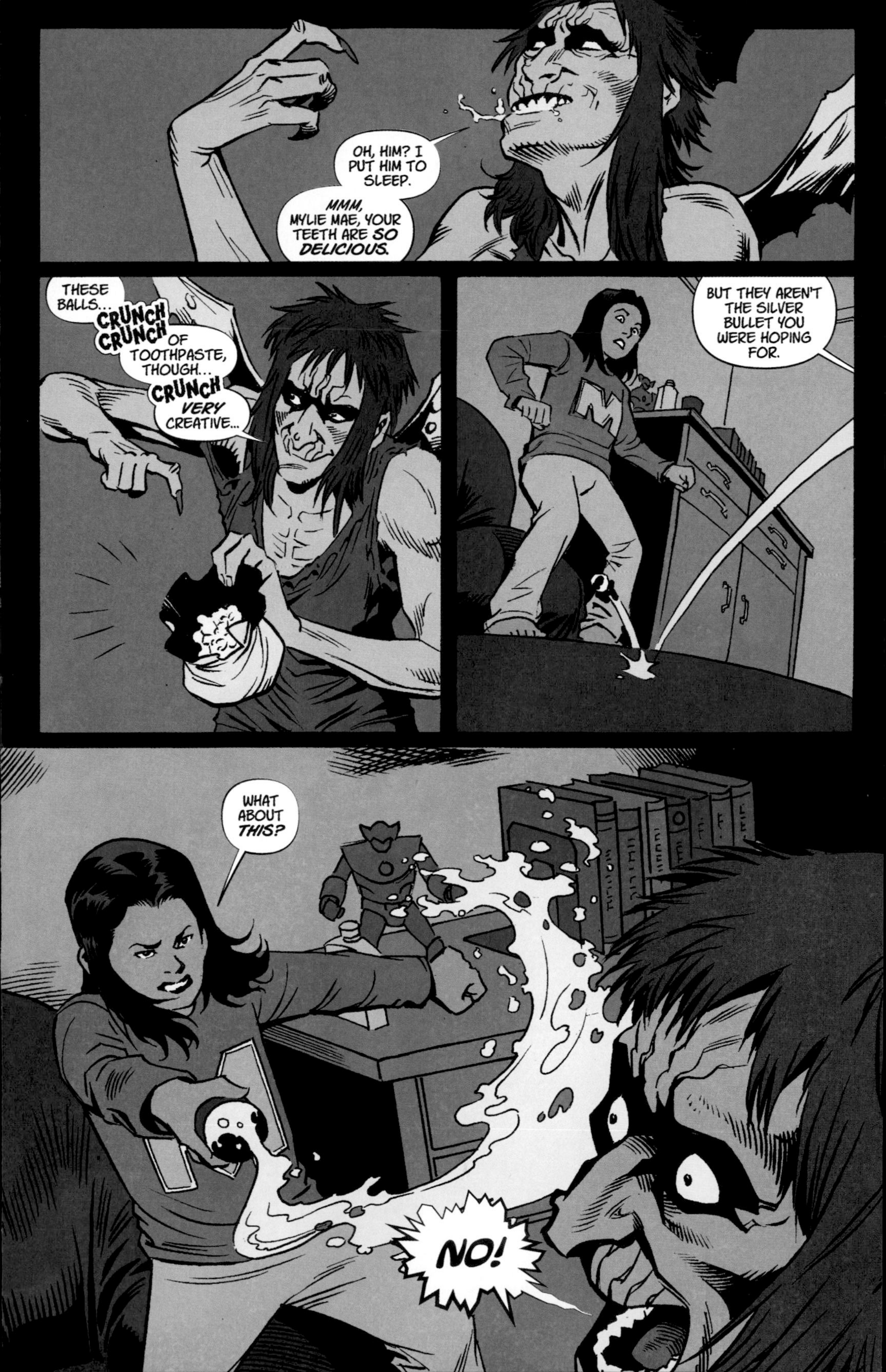
OH, HIM? I PUT HIM TO SLEEP.
MMM, MYLIE MAE, YOUR TEETH ARE SO DELICIOUS.
THESE BALLS...
CRUNCH CRUNCH
OF TOOTHPASTE, THOUGH...
CRUNCH
VERY CREATIVE...
BUT THEY AREN'T THE SILVER BULLET YOU WERE HOPING FOR.
WHAT ABOUT THIS?
NO!

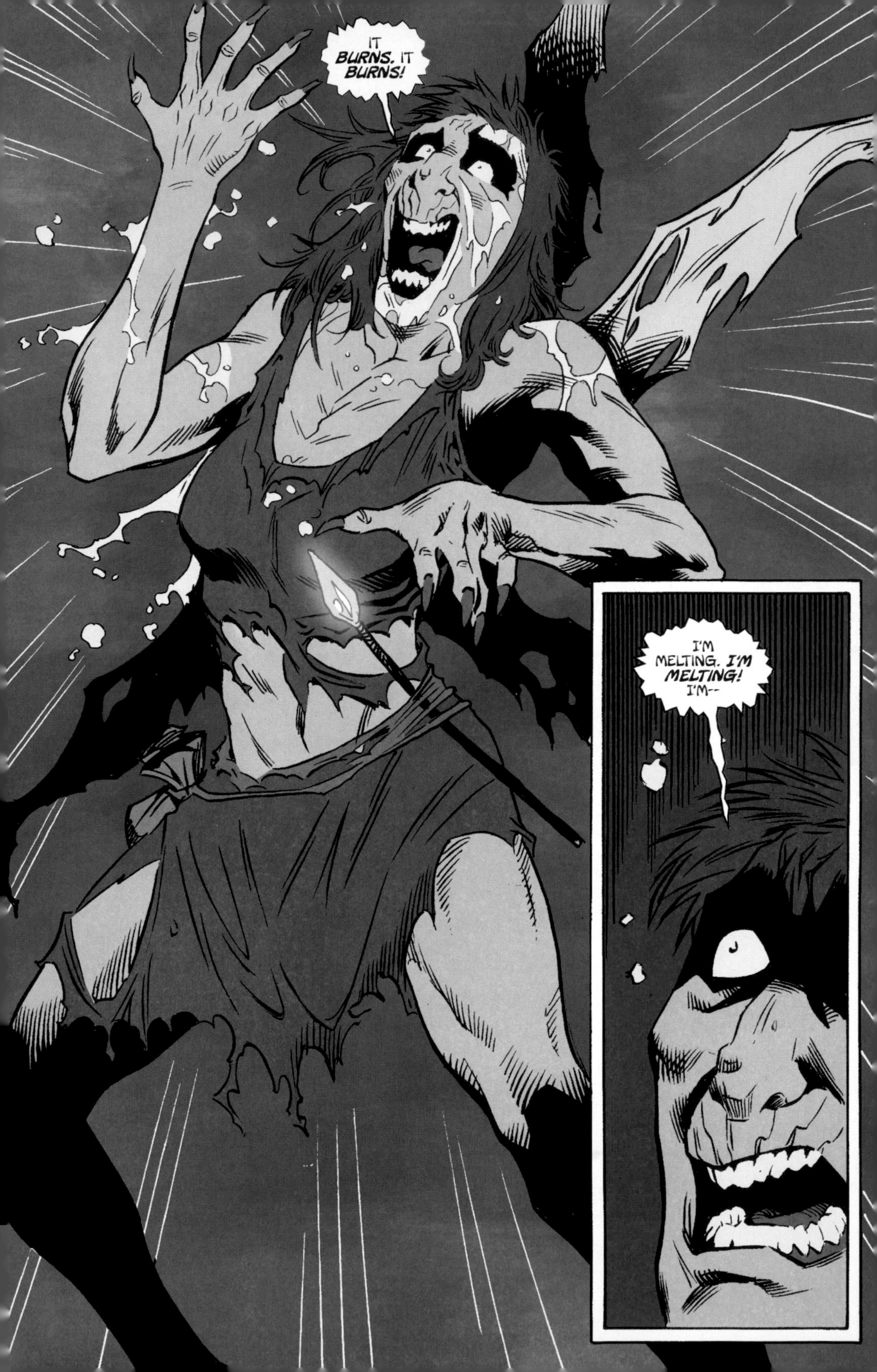
IT BURNS. IT BURNS!
I'M MELTING. I'M MELTING! I'M--

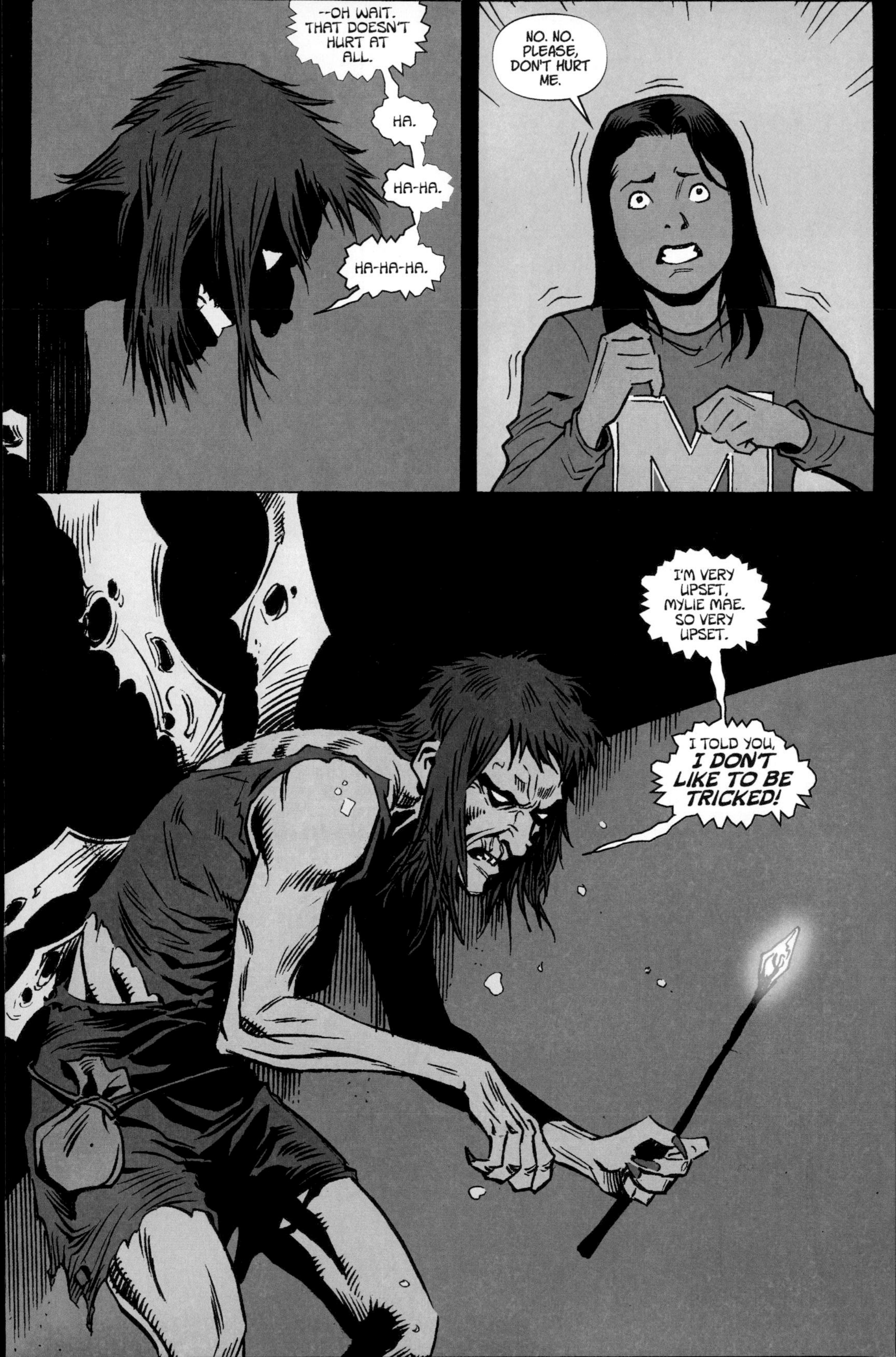
--OH WAIT. THAT DOESN'T HURT AT ALL.
HA.
HA-HA.
HA-HA-HA.
NO. NO. PLEASE, DON'T HURT ME.
I'M VERY UPSET, MYLIE MAE. SO VERY UPSET.
I TOLD YOU, ***I DON'T LIKE TO BE TRICKED!***

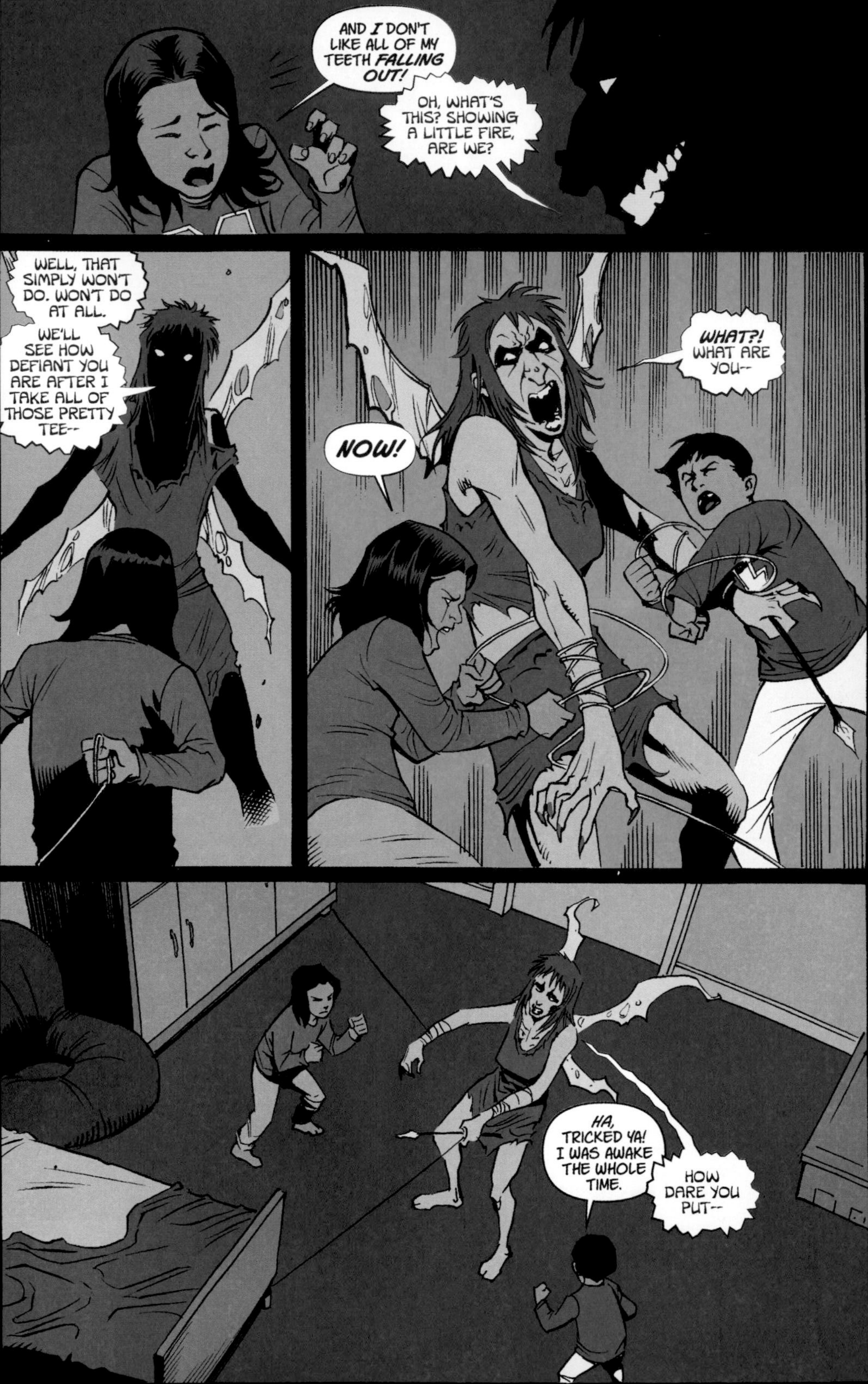
AND *I* DON'T LIKE ALL OF MY TEETH *FALLING OUT!*
OH, WHAT'S THIS? SHOWING A LITTLE FIRE, ARE WE?
WELL, THAT SIMPLY WON'T DO. WON'T DO AT ALL.
WE'LL SEE HOW DEFIANT YOU ARE AFTER I TAKE ALL OF THOSE PRETTY TEE--
WHAT?! WHAT ARE YOU--
NOW!
HA, TRICKED YA! I WAS AWAKE THE WHOLE TIME.
HOW DARE YOU PUT--

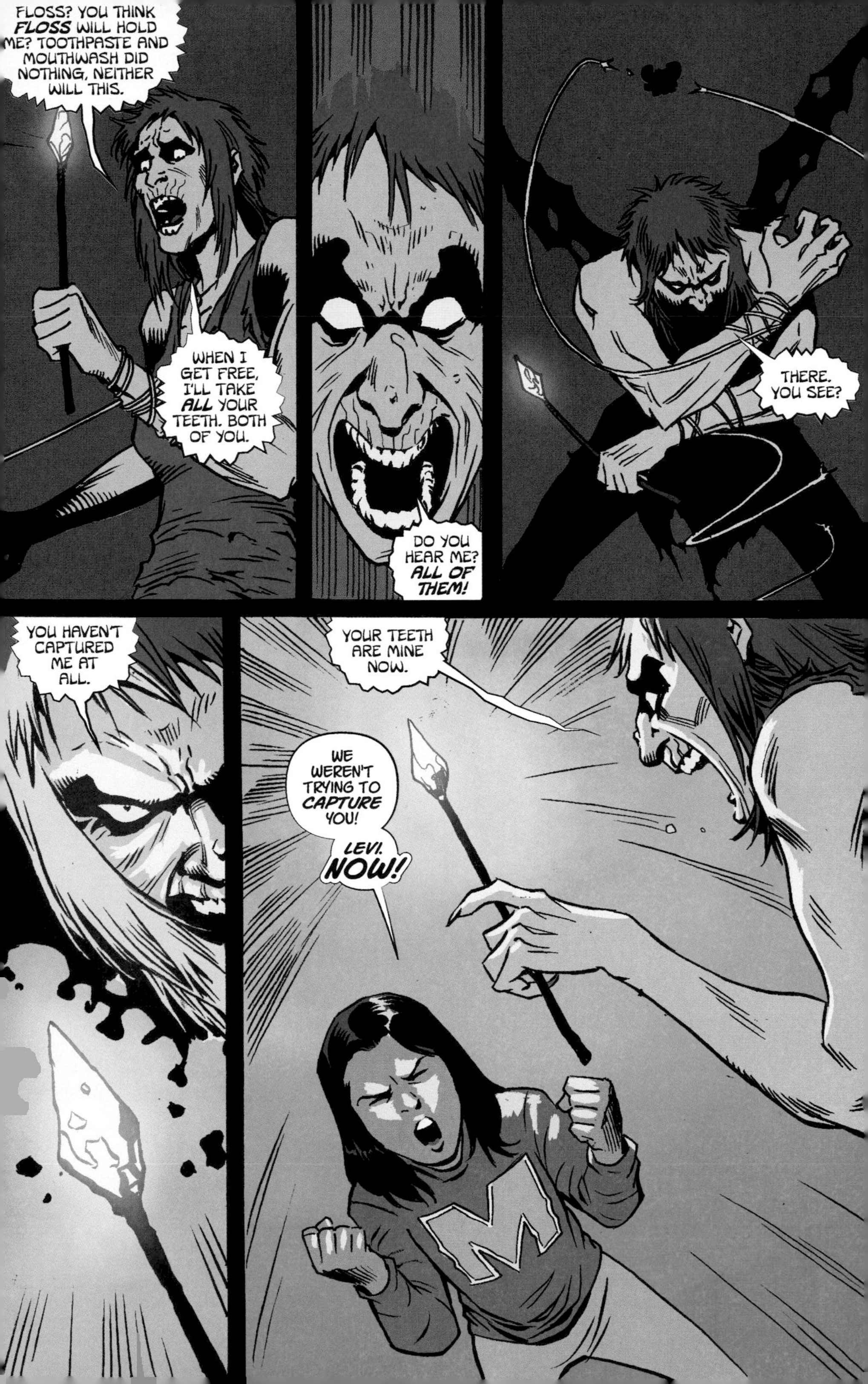
FLOSS? YOU THINK FLOSS WILL HOLD ME? TOOTHPASTE AND MOUTHWASH DID NOTHING, NEITHER WILL THIS.
WHEN I GET FREE, I'LL TAKE ALL YOUR TEETH. BOTH OF YOU.
DO YOU HEAR ME? ALL OF THEM!
THERE. YOU SEE?
YOU HAVEN'T CAPTURED ME AT ALL.
YOUR TEETH ARE MINE NOW.
WE WEREN'T TRYING TO CAPTURE YOU!
LEVI. NOW!

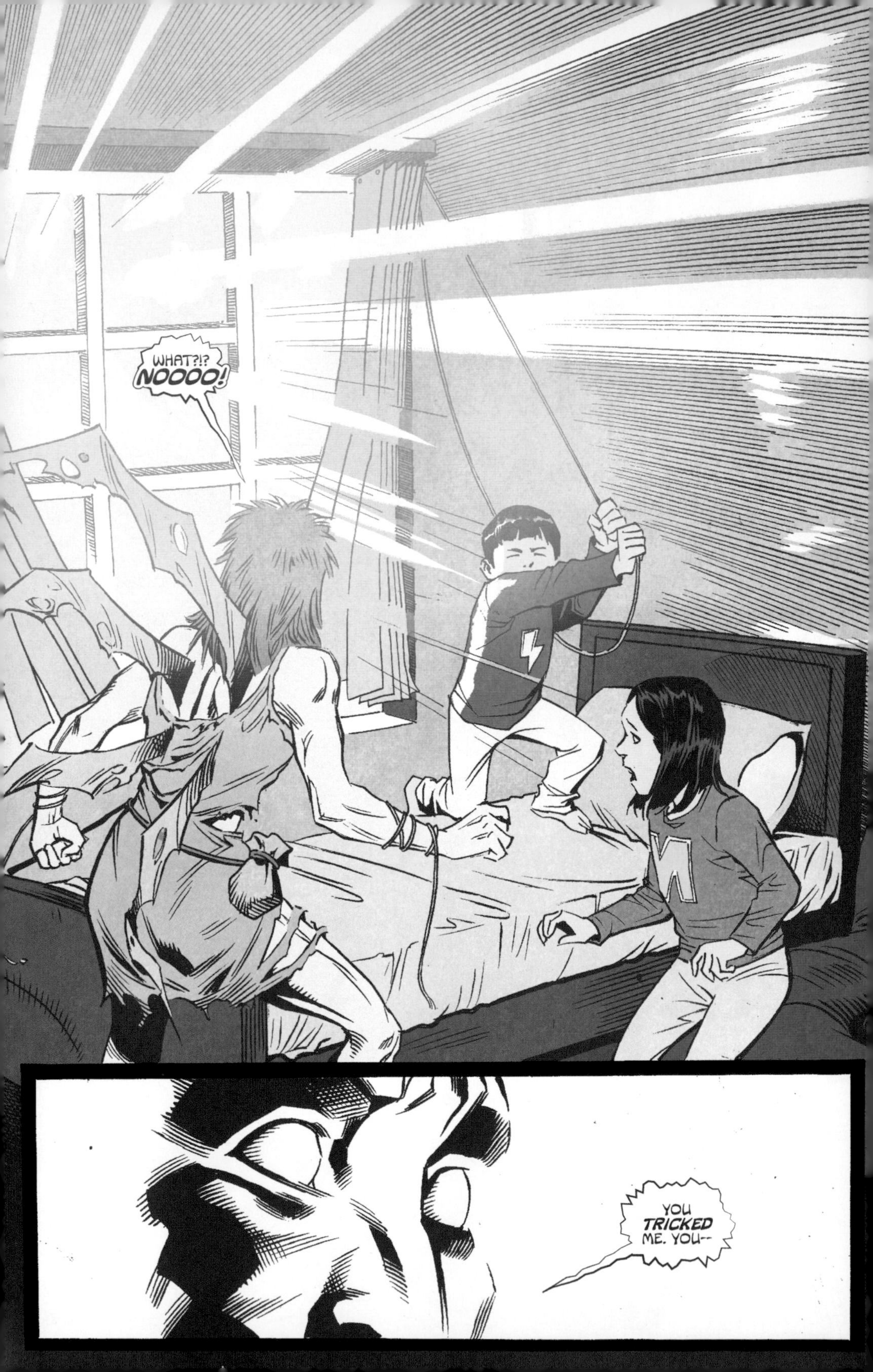
WHAT?!? NOOOO!
YOU TRICKED ME. YOU--

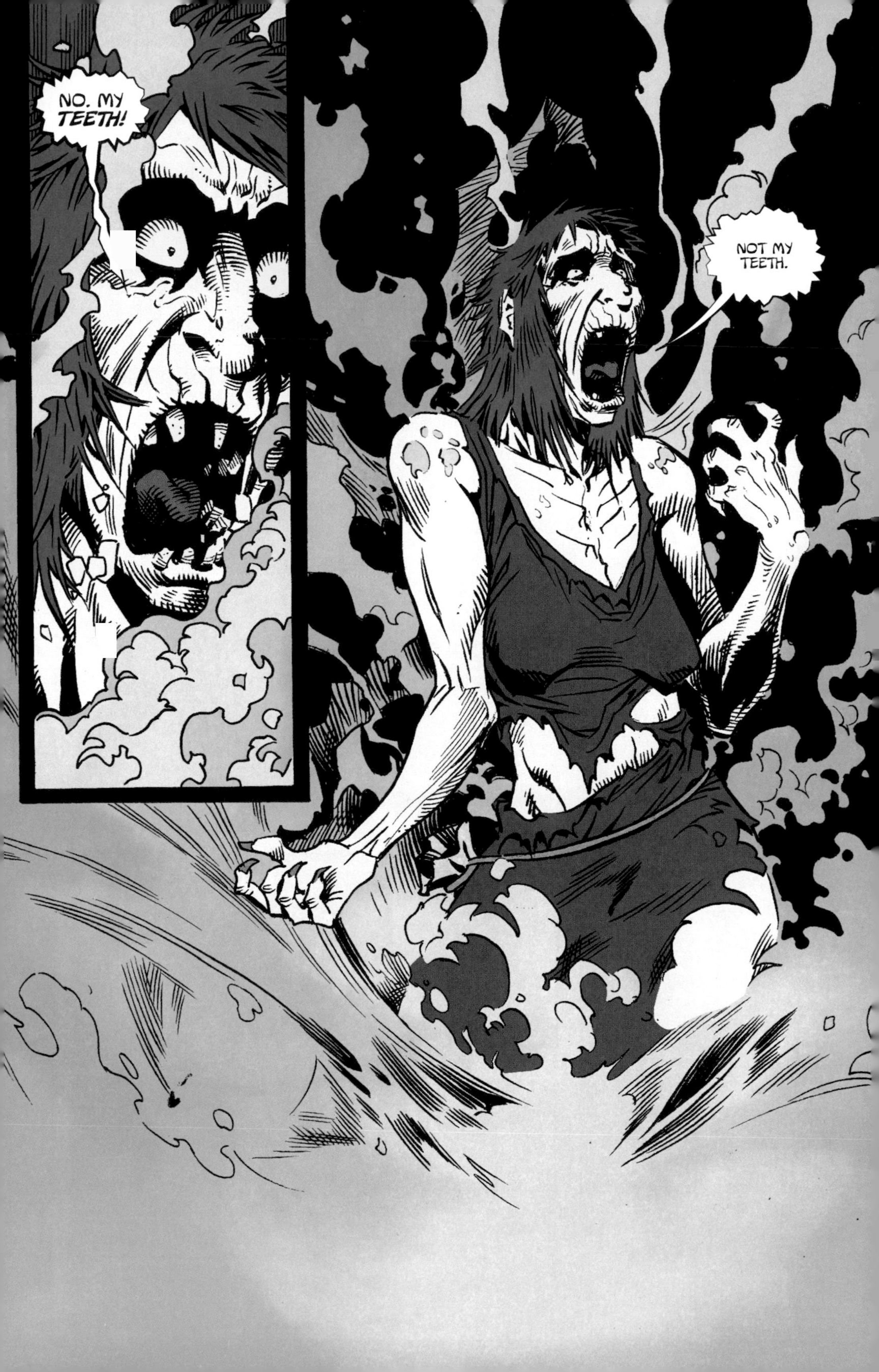
NO. MY TEETH!
NOT MY TEETH.

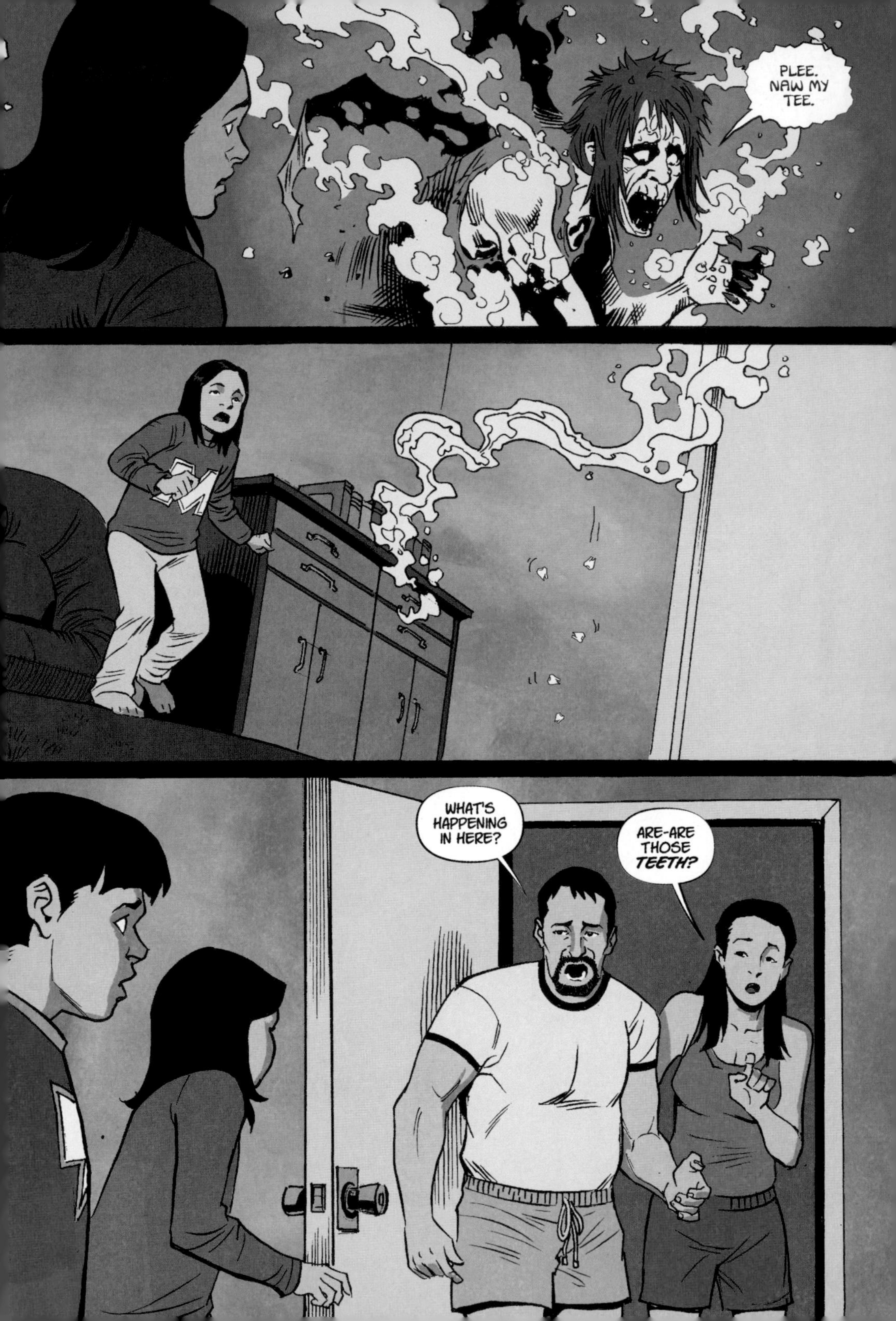
PLEE. NAW MY TEE.
WHAT'S HAPPENING IN HERE?
ARE-ARE THOSE *TEETH?*

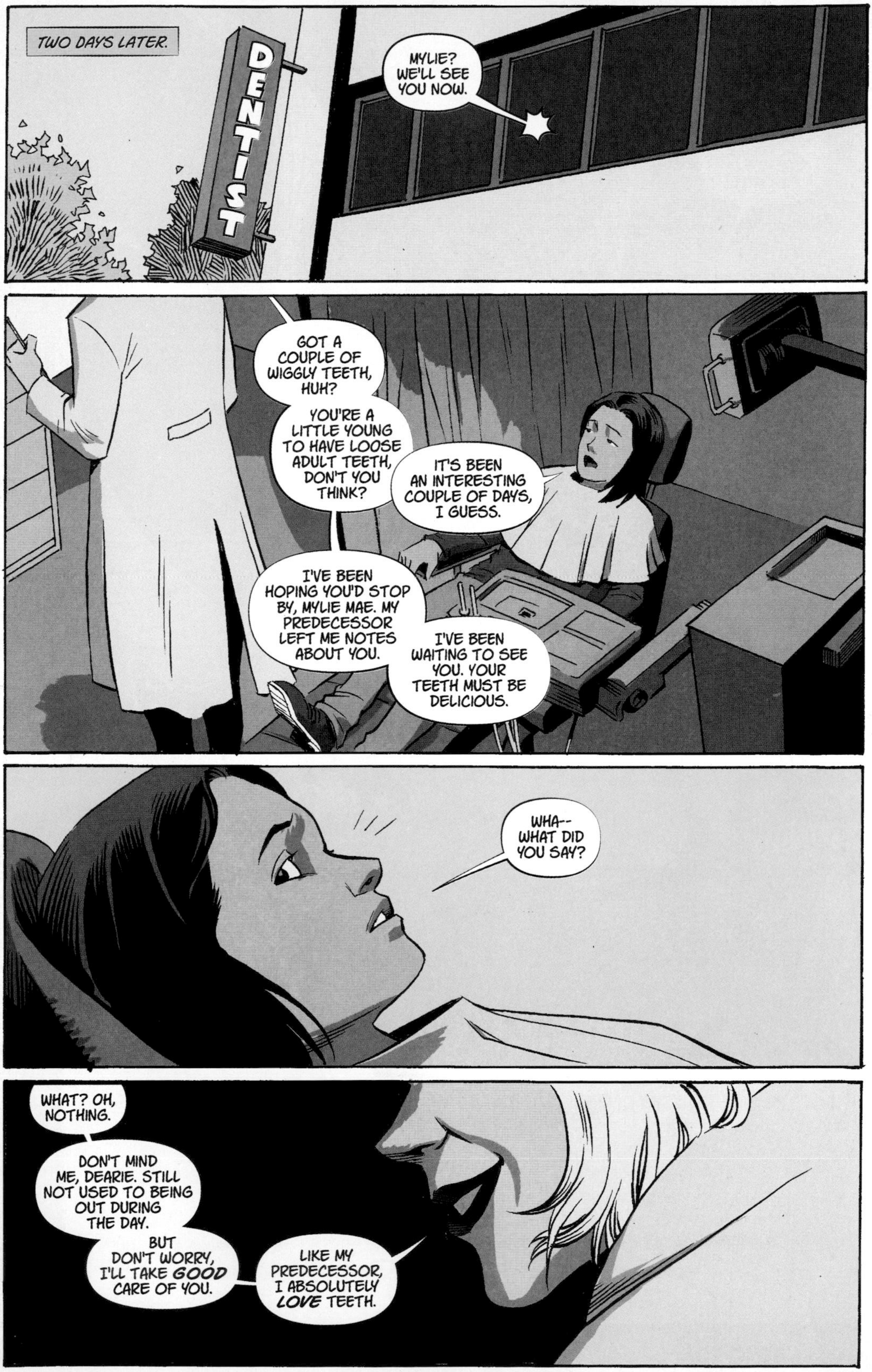
TWO DAYS LATER.
DENTIST
MYLIE? WE'LL SEE YOU NOW.
GOT A COUPLE OF WIGGLY TEETH, HUH?
YOU'RE A LITTLE YOUNG TO HAVE LOOSE ADULT TEETH, DON'T YOU THINK?
IT'S BEEN AN INTERESTING COUPLE OF DAYS, I GUESS.
I'VE BEEN HOPING YOU'D STOP BY, MYLIE MAE. MY PREDECESSOR LEFT ME NOTES ABOUT YOU.
I'VE BEEN WAITING TO SEE YOU. YOUR TEETH MUST BE DELICIOUS.
WHA-- WHAT DID YOU SAY?
WHAT? OH, NOTHING.
DON'T MIND ME, DEARIE. STILL NOT USED TO BEING OUT DURING THE DAY.
BUT DON'T WORRY, I'LL TAKE GOOD CARE OF YOU.
LIKE MY PREDECESSOR, I ABSOLUTELY LOVE TEETH.

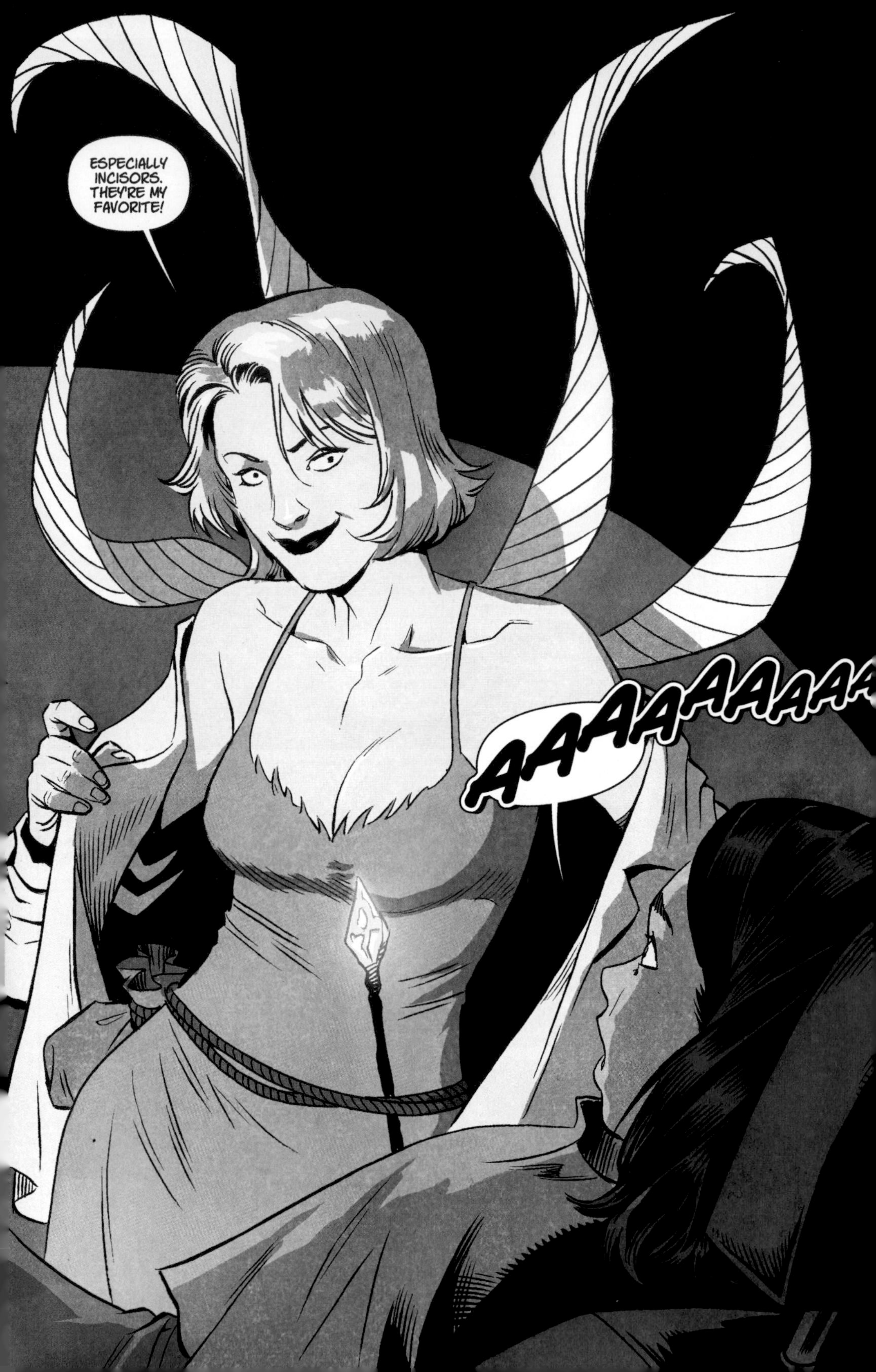
ESPECIALLY INCISORS. THEY'RE MY FAVORITE!
AAAAAAAAAA

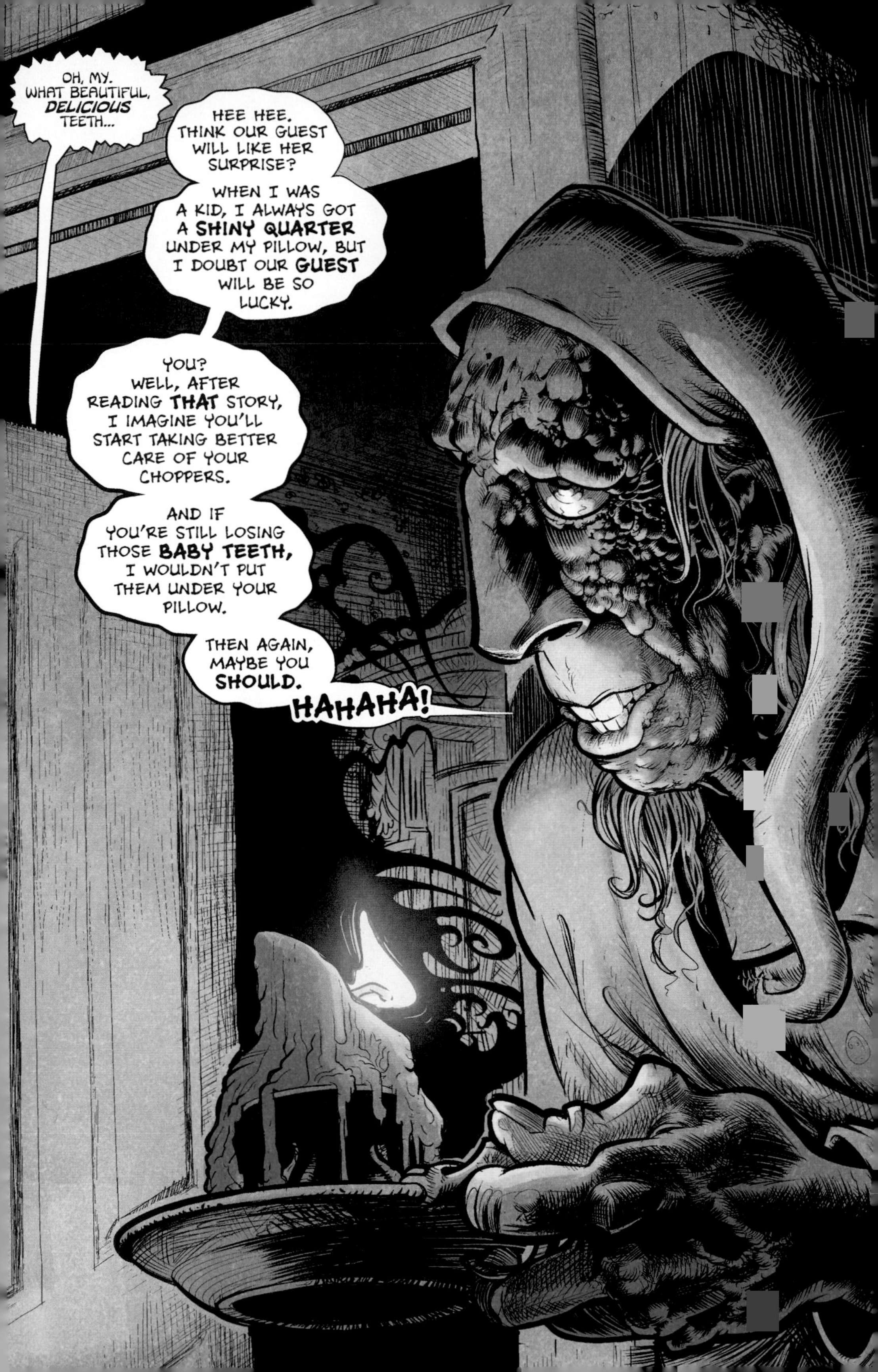
OH, MY. WHAT BEAUTIFUL, DELICIOUS TEETH...
HEE HEE. THINK OUR GUEST WILL LIKE HER SURPRISE?
WHEN I WAS A KID, I ALWAYS GOT A SHINY QUARTER UNDER MY PILLOW, BUT I DOUBT OUR GUEST WILL BE SO LUCKY.
YOU? WELL, AFTER READING THAT STORY, I IMAGINE YOU'LL START TAKING BETTER CARE OF YOUR CHOPPERS.
AND IF YOU'RE STILL LOSING THOSE BABY TEETH, I WOULDN'T PUT THEM UNDER YOUR PILLOW.
THEN AGAIN, MAYBE YOU SHOULD.
HAHAHA!

THE CURSE OF COTTONWOOD COURT!

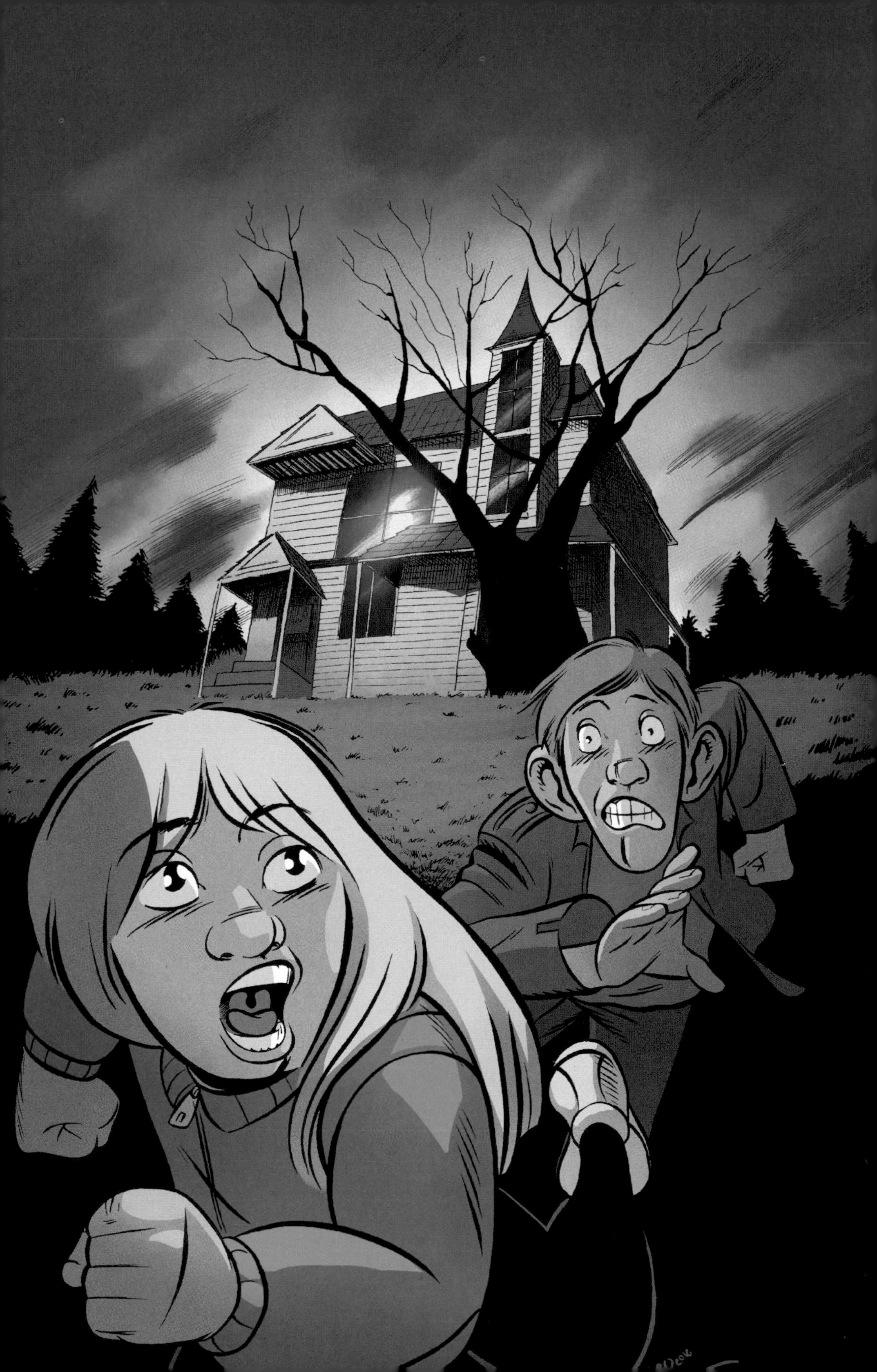

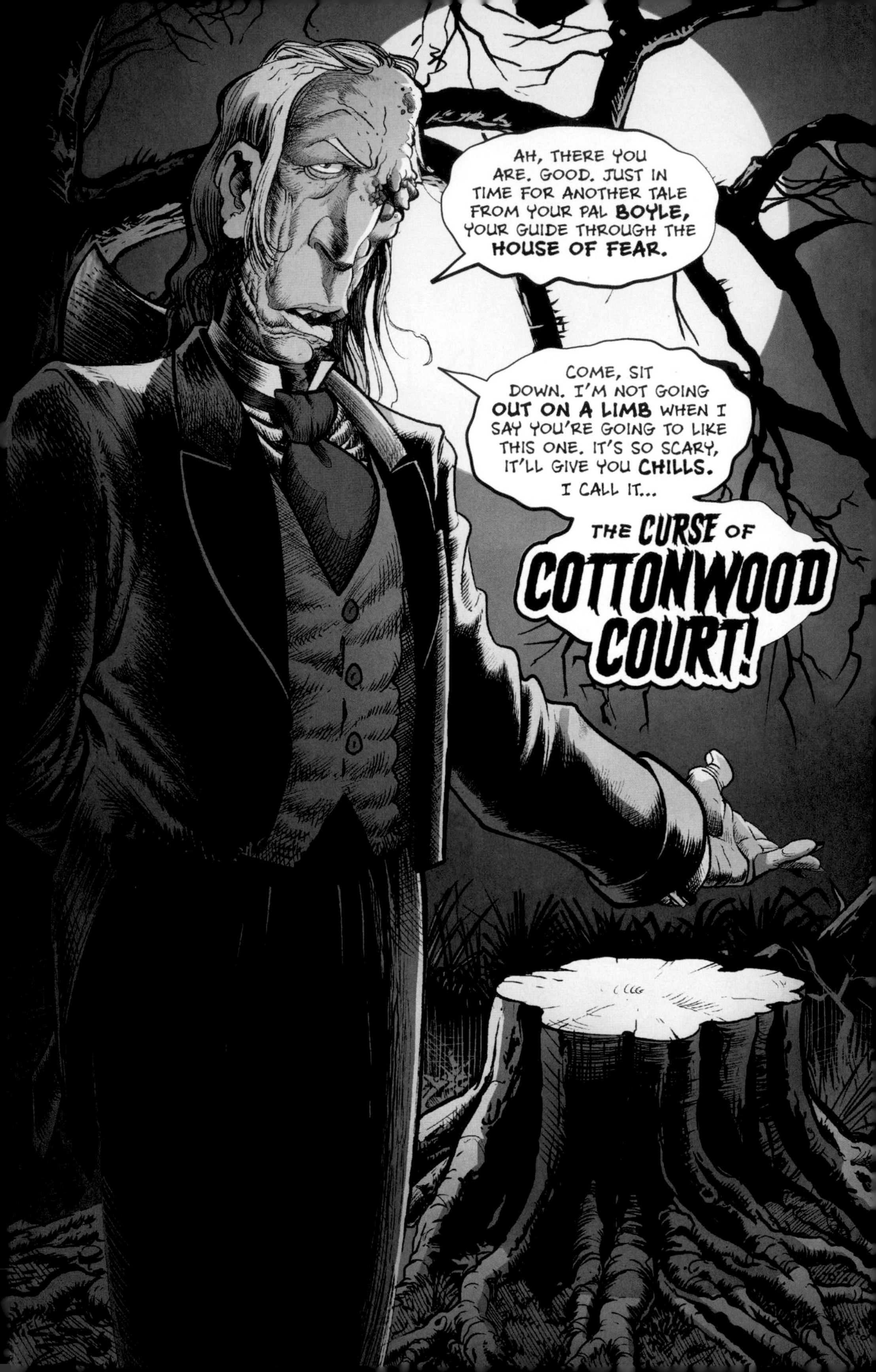
AH, THERE YOU ARE. GOOD. JUST IN TIME FOR ANOTHER TALE FROM YOUR PAL BOYLE, YOUR GUIDE THROUGH THE HOUSE OF FEAR.
COME, SIT DOWN. I'M NOT GOING OUT ON A LIMB WHEN I SAY YOU'RE GOING TO LIKE THIS ONE. IT'S SO SCARY, IT'LL GIVE YOU CHILLS.
I CALL IT...
THE CURSE OF COTTONWOOD COURT!

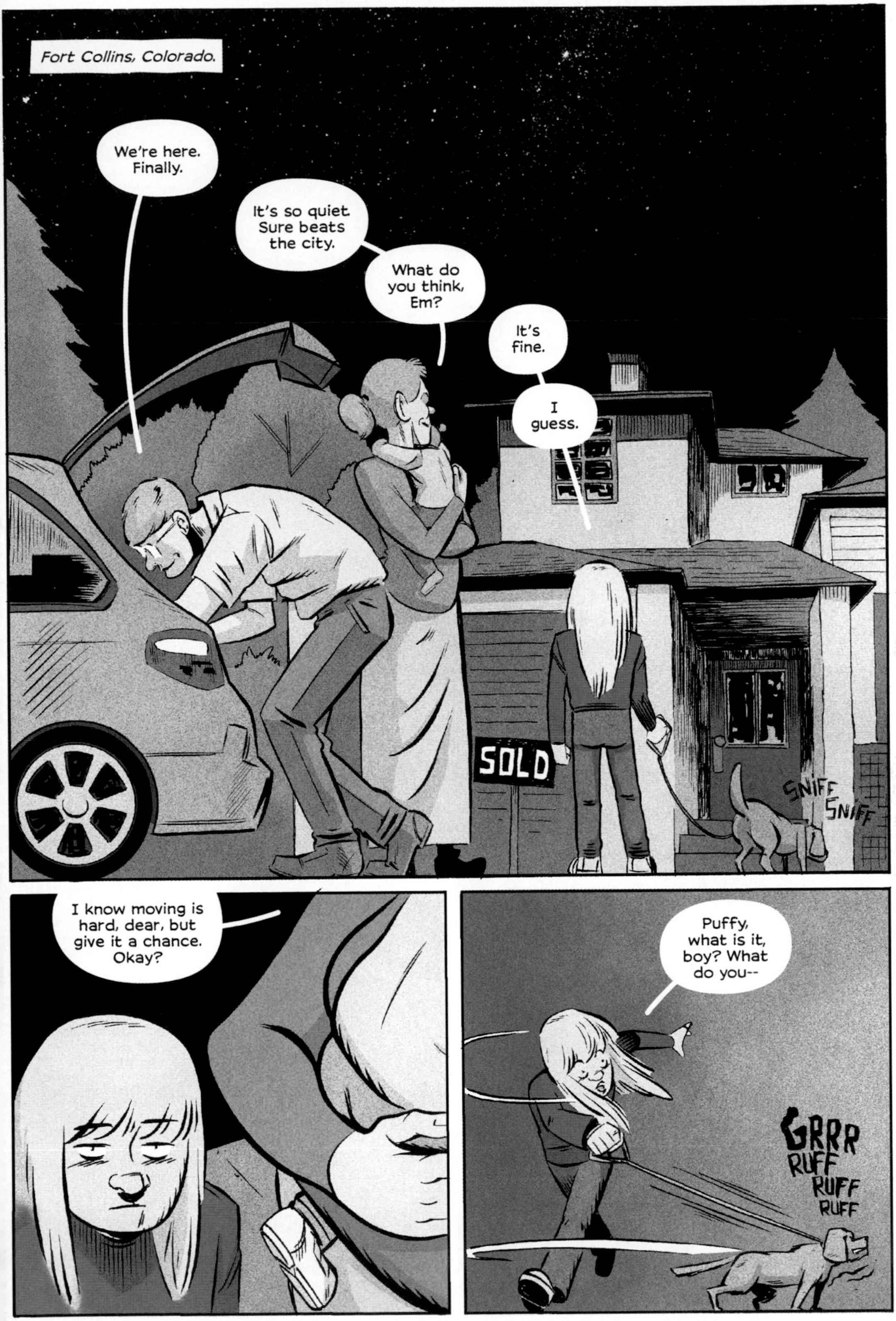
Fort Collins, Colorado.
We're here. Finally.
It's so quiet Sure beats the city.
What do you think, Em?
It's fine.
I guess.
SOLD
SNIFF SNIFF
I know moving is hard, dear, but give it a chance. Okay?
Puffy, what is it, boy? What do you--
GRRR RUFF RUFF RUFF

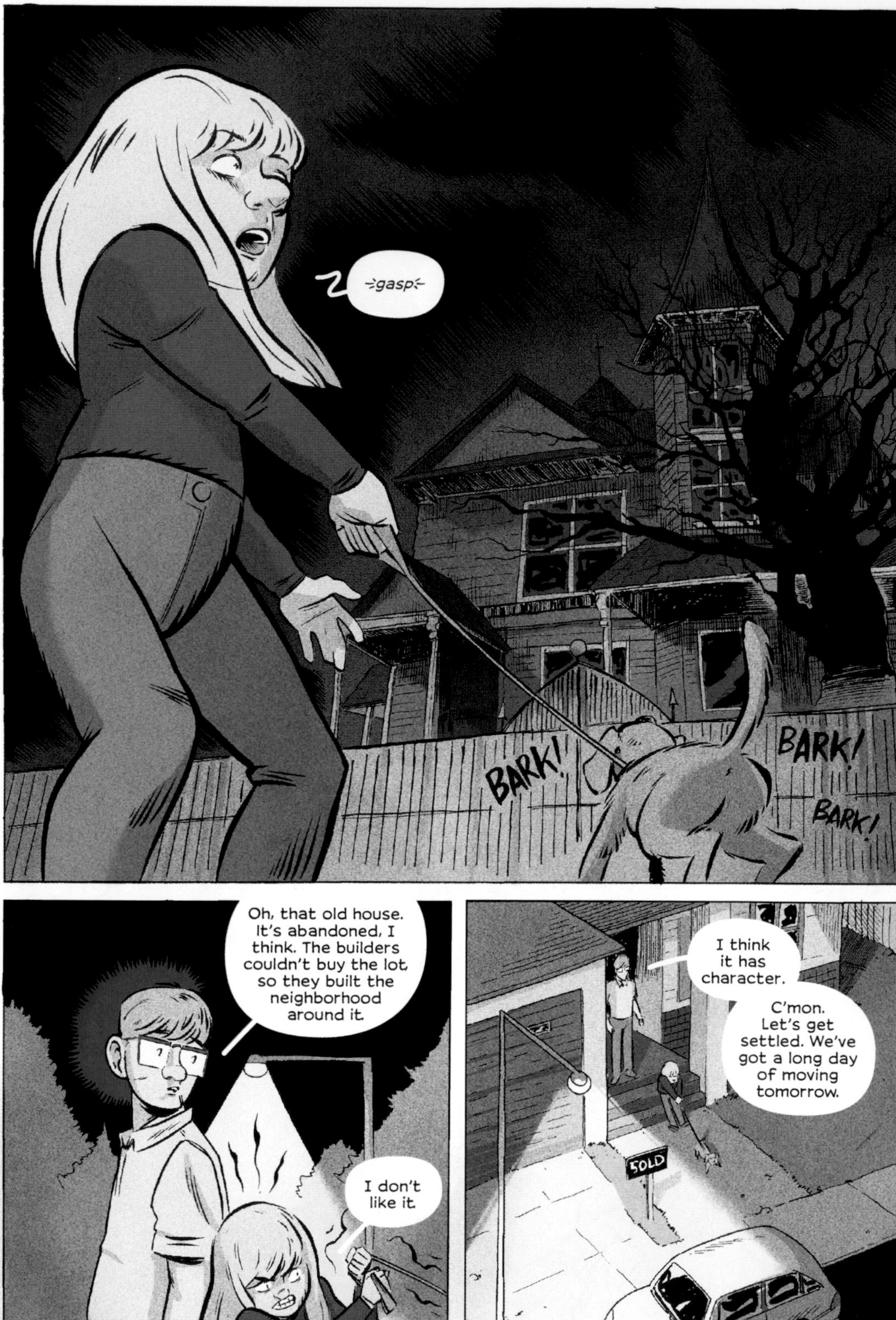
gasp
BARK!
BARK!
BARK!
Oh, that old house. It's abandoned, I think. The builders couldn't buy the lot so they built the neighborhood around it.
I don't like it.
I think it has character.
C'mon. Let's get settled. We've got a long day of moving tomorrow.
SOLD

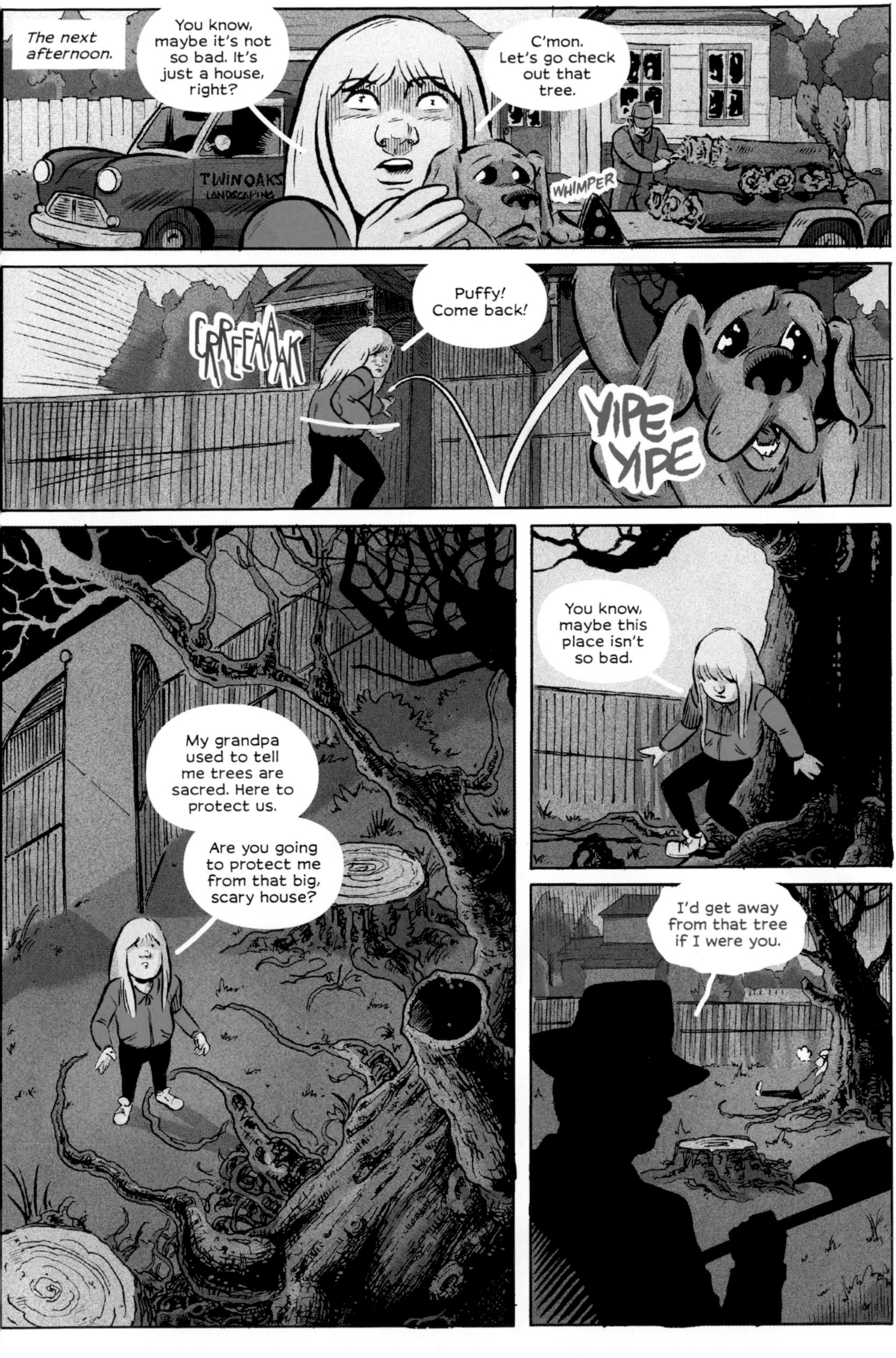
The next afternoon.
You know, maybe it's not so bad. It's just a house, right?
C'mon. Let's go check out that tree.
TWIN OAKS LANDSCAPING
WHIMPER
CRREEAAAK
Puffy! Come back!
YIPE YIPE
My grandpa used to tell me trees are sacred. Here to protect us.
Are you going to protect me from that big, scary house?
You know, maybe this place isn't so bad.
I'd get away from that tree if I were you.

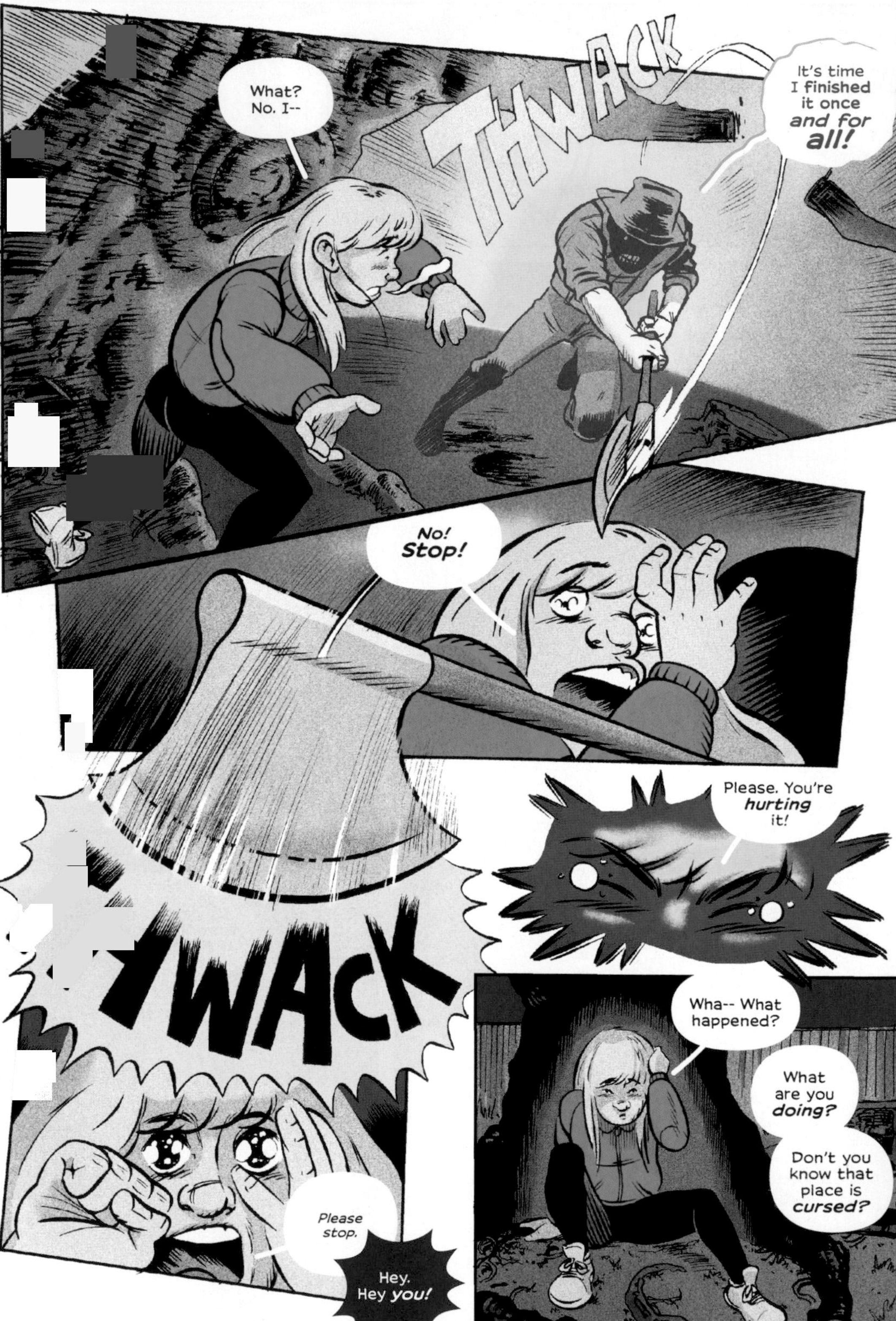
What? No. I--
THWACK
It's time I finished it once *and for* ***all!***
No! Stop!
THWACK
Please. You're *hurting* it!
Please stop.
Hey. Hey *you!*
Wha-- What happened?
What are you *doing?*
Don't you know that place is *cursed?*

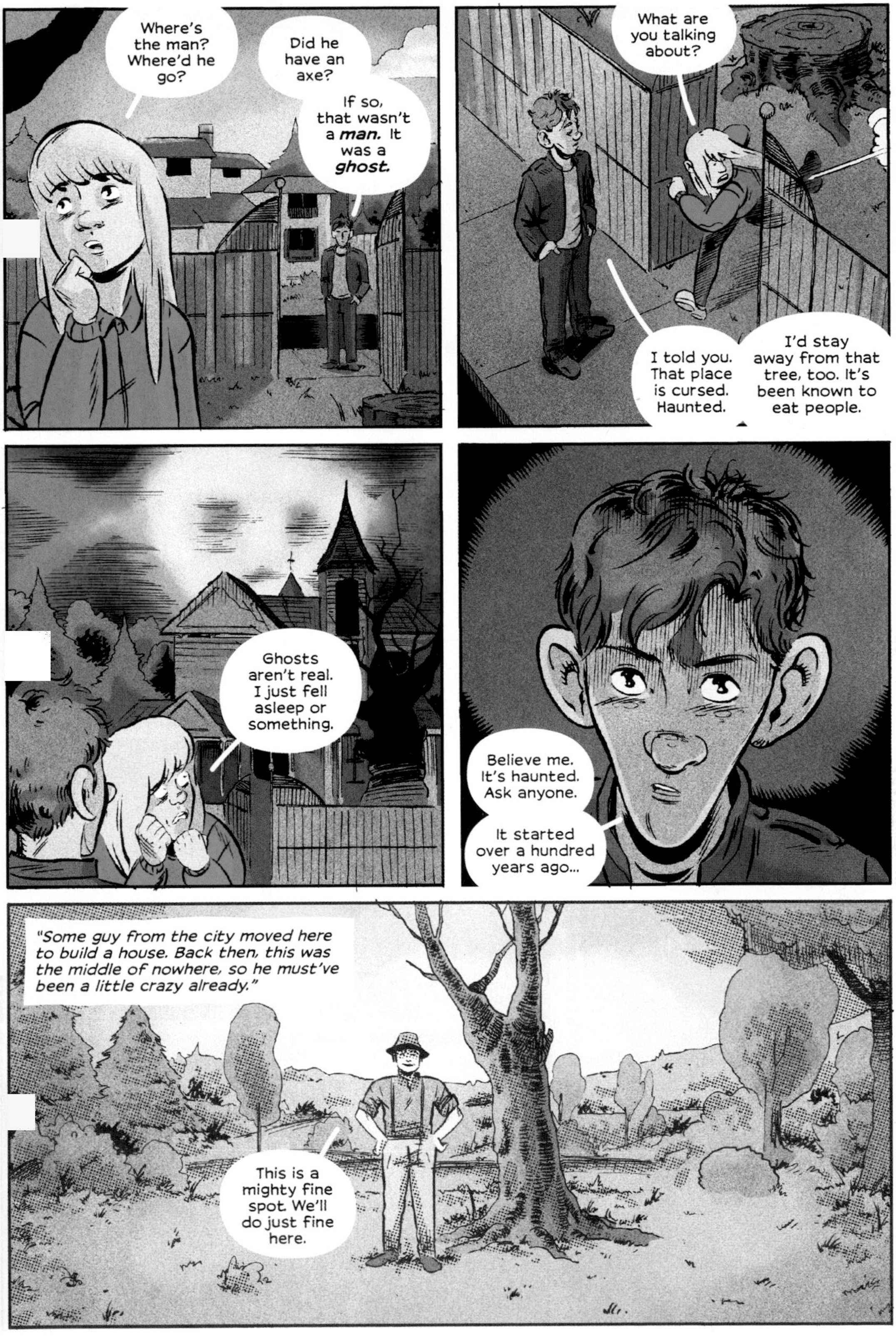
Where's the man? Where'd he go?
Did he have an axe?
If so, that wasn't a *man.* It was a ***ghost.***
What are you talking about?
I told you. That place is cursed. Haunted.
I'd stay away from that tree, too. It's been known to eat people.
Ghosts aren't real. I just fell asleep or something.
Believe me. It's haunted. Ask anyone.
It started over a hundred years ago...
"Some guy from the city moved here to build a house. Back then, this was the middle of nowhere, so he must've been a little crazy already."
This is a mighty fine spot. We'll do just fine here.

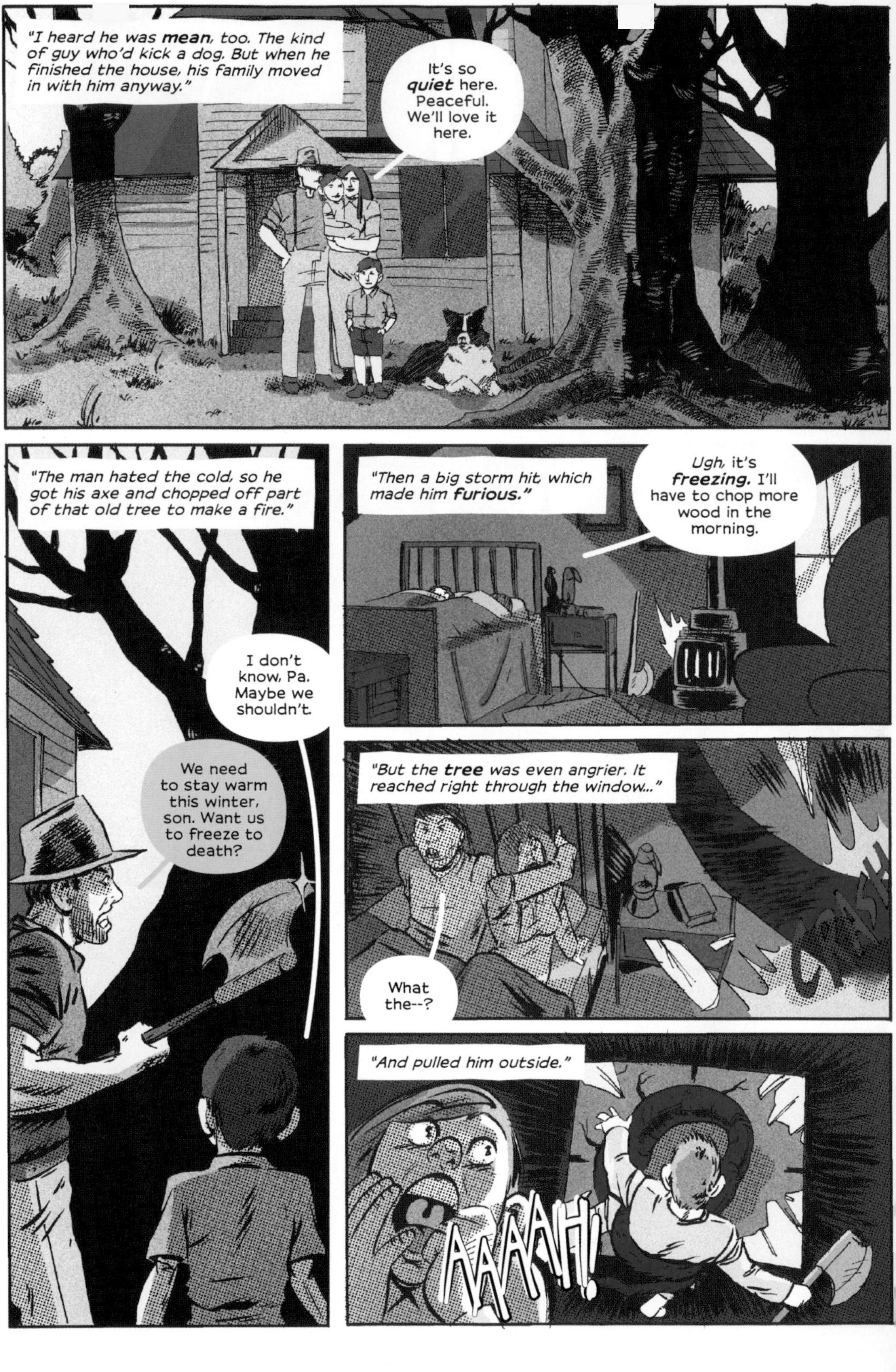
"I heard he was **mean**, too. The kind of guy who'd kick a dog. But when he finished the house, his family moved in with him anyway."
It's so ***quiet*** here. Peaceful. We'll love it here.
"The man hated the cold, so he got his axe and chopped off part of that old tree to make a fire."
I don't know, Pa. Maybe we shouldn't.
We need to stay warm this winter, son. Want us to freeze to death?
"Then a big storm hit which made him ***furious.***"
Ugh, it's ***freezing.*** I'll have to chop more wood in the morning.
"But the **tree** was even angrier. It reached right through the window..."
CRASH
What the--?
"And pulled him outside."
AAAAH!

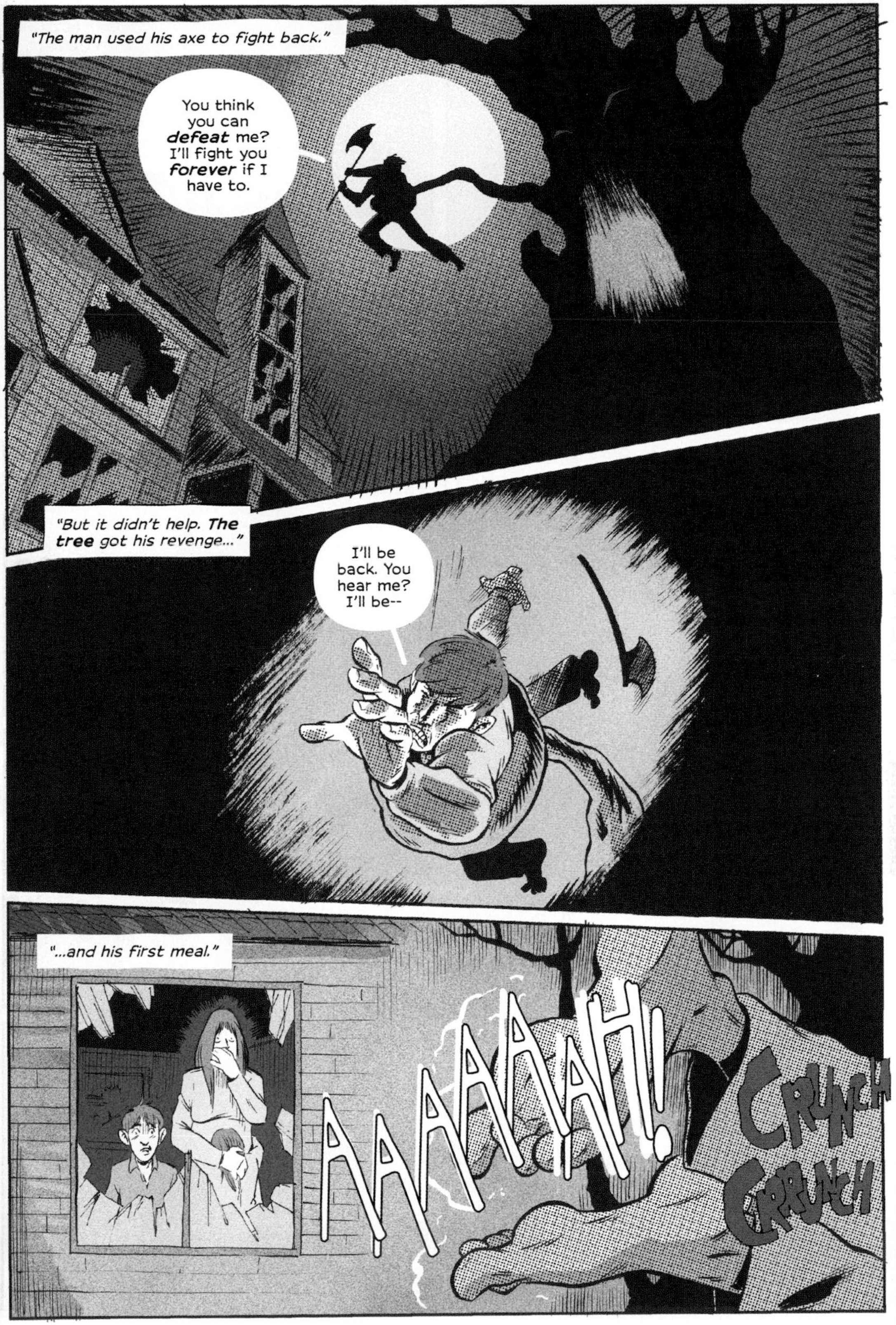
"The man used his axe to fight back."
You think you can **defeat** me? I'll fight you **forever** if I have to.
"But it didn't help. **The tree** got his revenge..."
I'll be back. You hear me? I'll be--
"...and his first meal."
AAAAAAAH!
CRUNCH
CRRUNCH

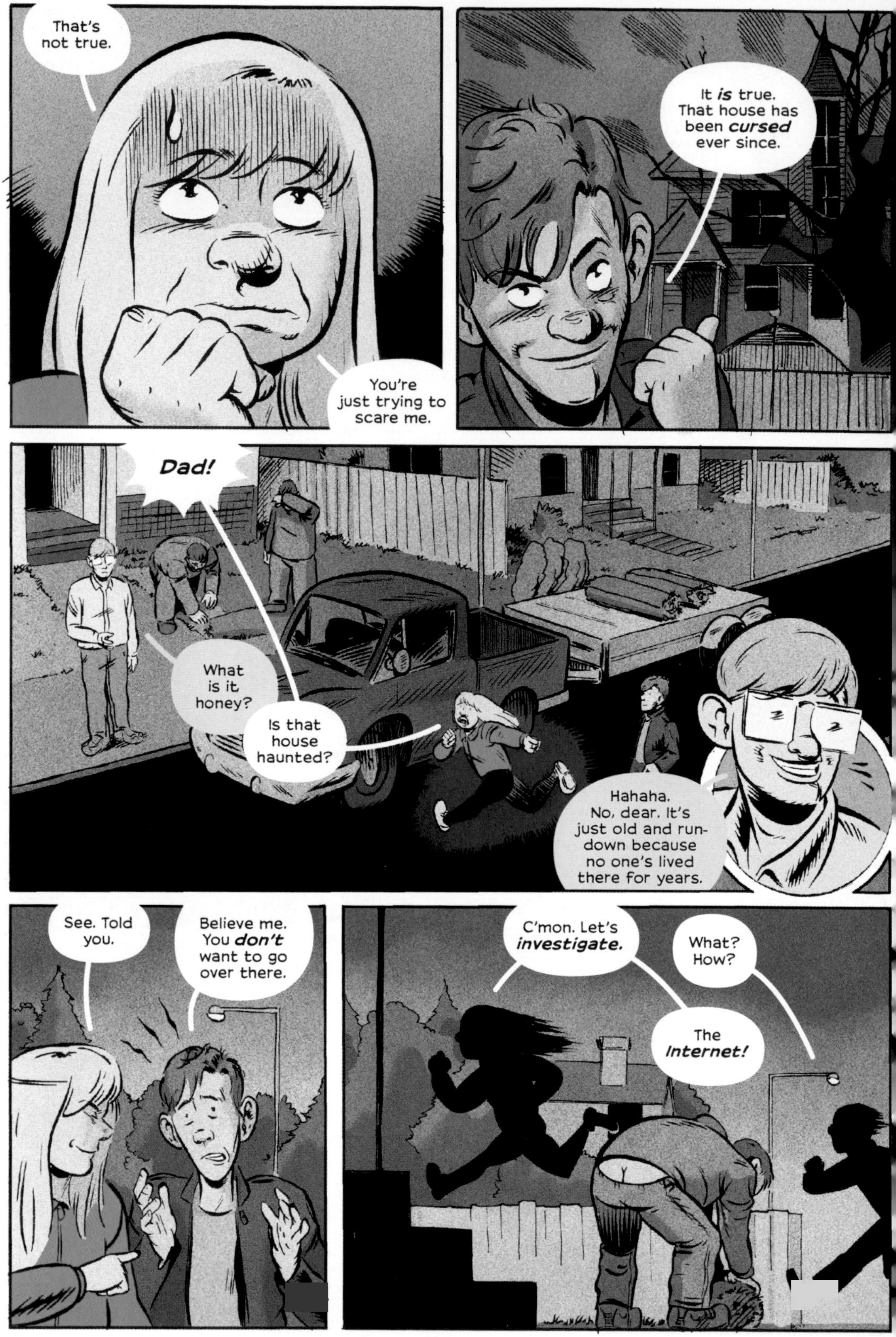
That's not true.
You're just trying to scare me.
It *is* true. That house has been *cursed* ever since.
Dad!
What is it honey?
Is that house haunted?
Hahaha. No, dear. It's just old and run-down because no one's lived there for years.
See. Told you.
Believe me. You *don't* want to go over there.
C'mon. Let's *investigate.*
What? How?
The *Internet!*

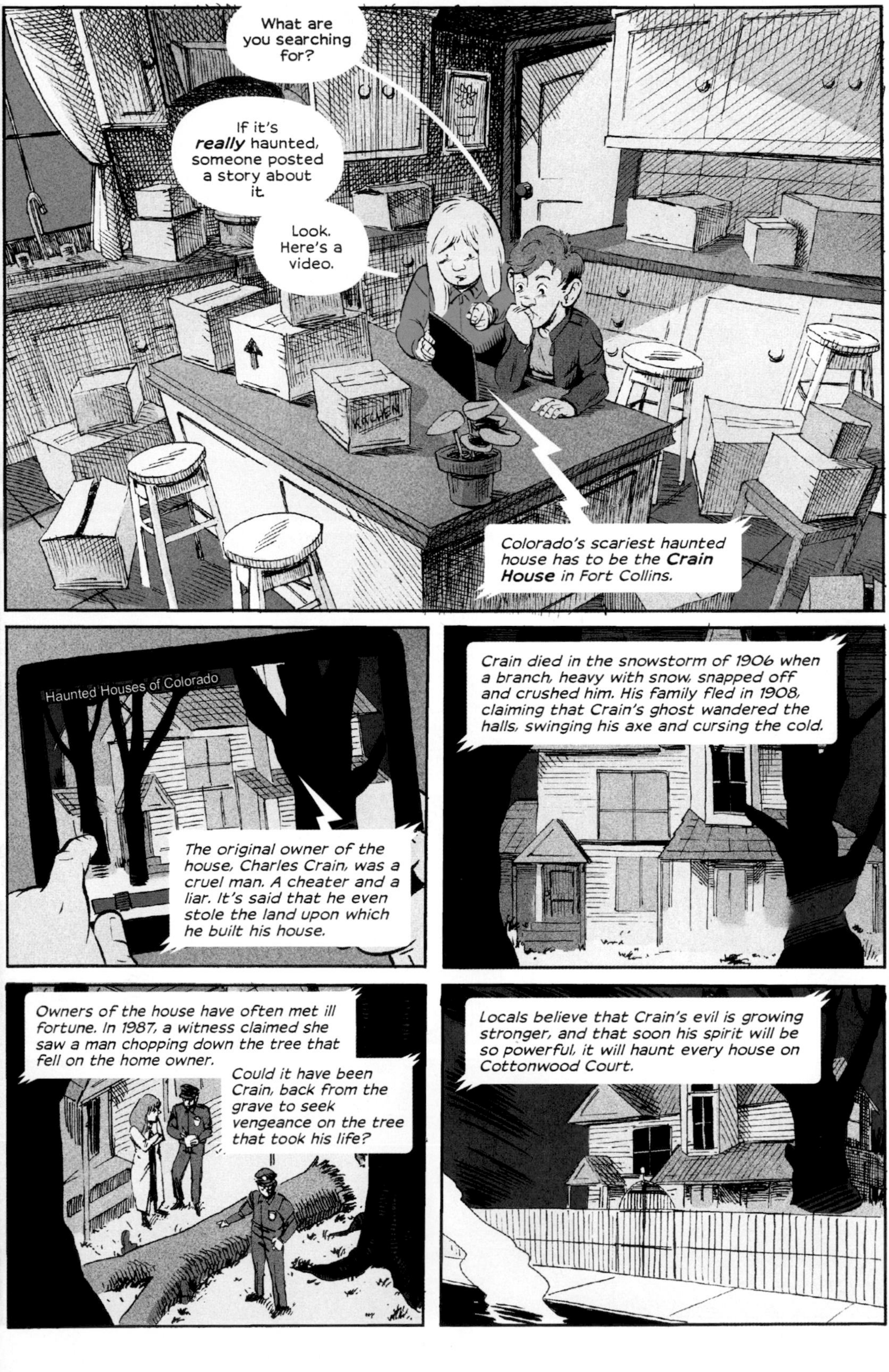
What are you searching for?
If it's ***really*** haunted, someone posted a story about it.
Look. Here's a video.
KITCHEN
Colorado's scariest haunted house has to be the ***Crain House*** *in Fort Collins.*
Haunted Houses of Colorado
The original owner of the house, Charles Crain, was a cruel man. A cheater and a liar. It's said that he even stole the land upon which he built his house.
Crain died in the snowstorm of 1906 when a branch, heavy with snow, snapped off and crushed him. His family fled in 1908, claiming that Crain's ghost wandered the halls, swinging his axe and cursing the cold.
Owners of the house have often met ill fortune. In 1987, a witness claimed she saw a man chopping down the tree that fell on the home owner.
Could it have been Crain, back from the grave to seek vengeance on the tree that took his life?
Locals believe that Crain's evil is growing stronger, and that soon his spirit will be so powerful, it will haunt every house on Cottonwood Court.

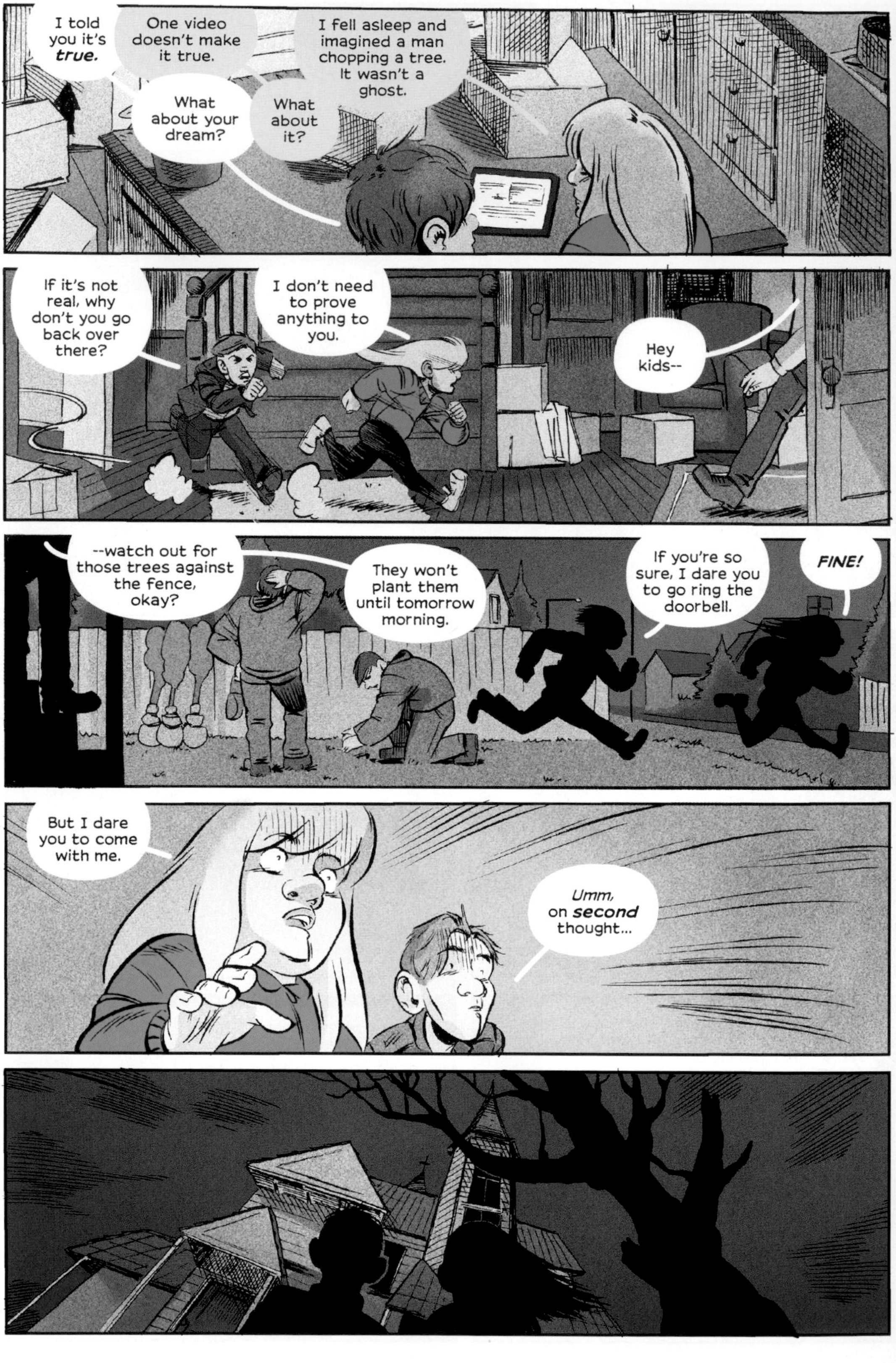
I told you it's *true.*
One video doesn't make it true.
I fell asleep and imagined a man chopping a tree. It wasn't a ghost.
What about your dream?
What about it?
If it's not real, why don't you go back over there?
I don't need to prove anything to you.
Hey kids--
--watch out for those trees against the fence, okay?
They won't plant them until tomorrow morning.
If you're so sure, I dare you to go ring the doorbell.
FINE!
But I dare you to come with me.
Umm, on ***second*** thought...

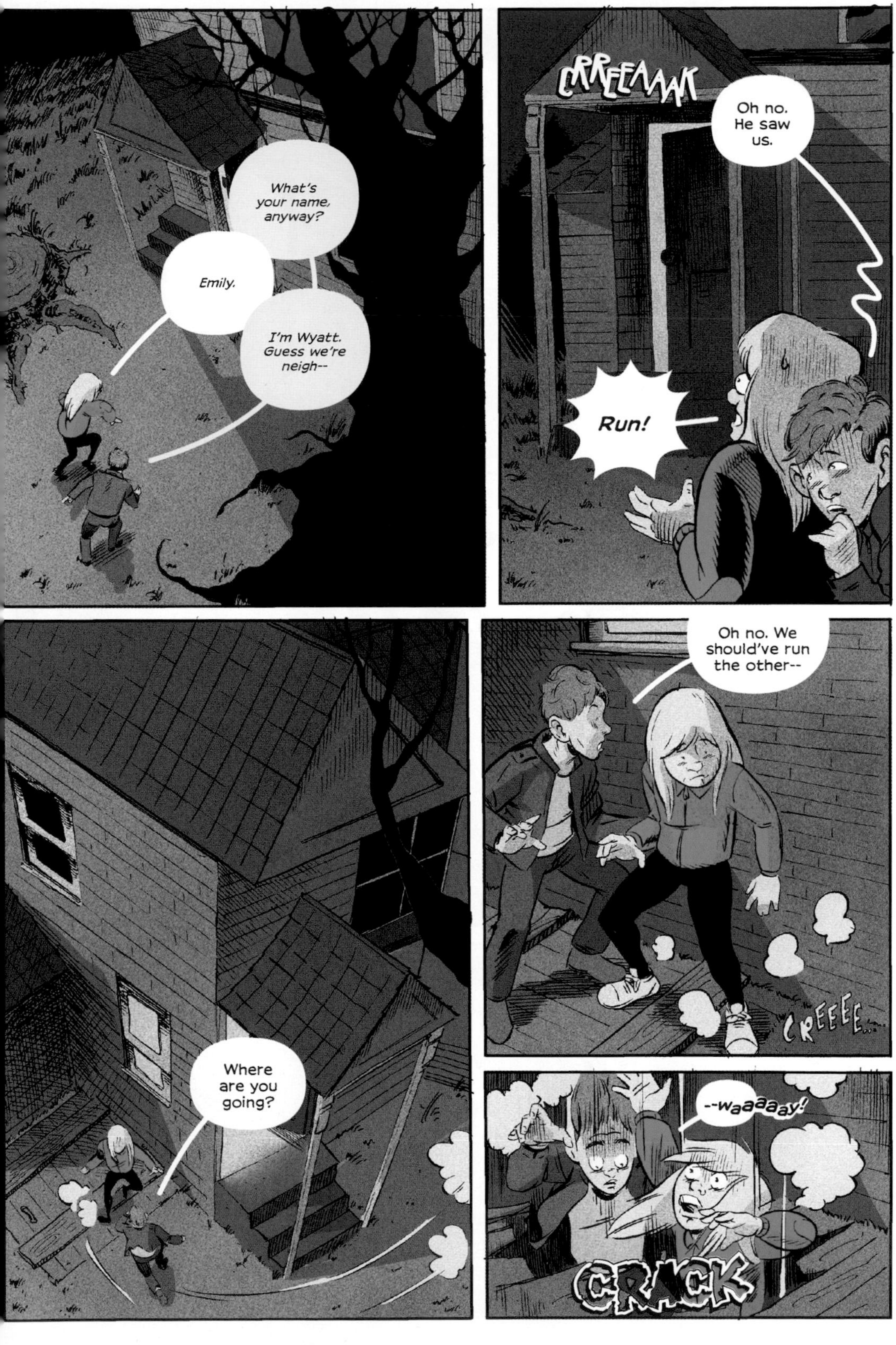
What's your name, anyway?
Emily.
I'm Wyatt. Guess we're neigh--
CRREEAAAK
Oh no. He saw us.
Run!
Where are you going?
Oh no. We should've run the other--
CREEEE...
--waaaaay!
CRACK

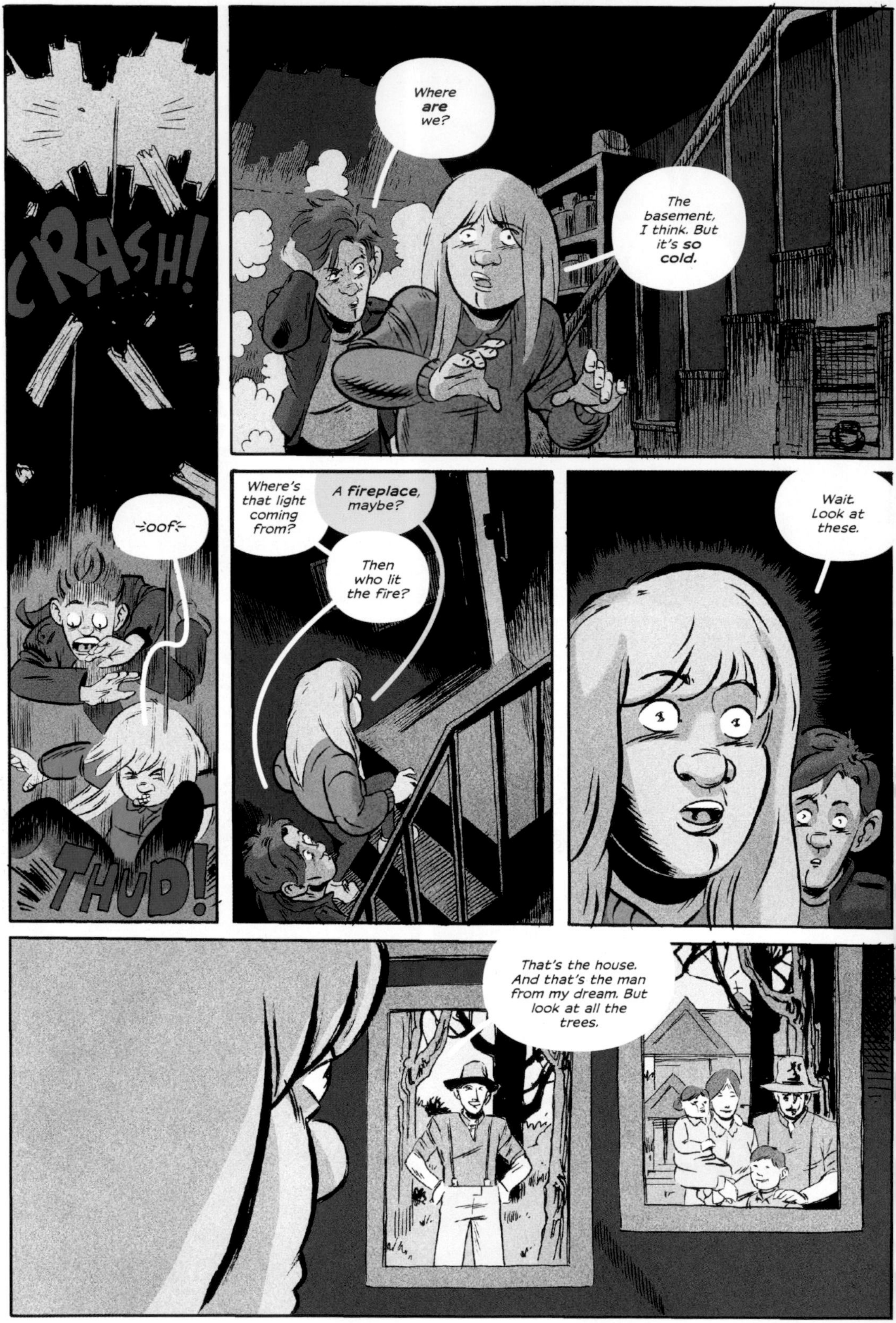
CRASH!
-oof-
THUD!
Where are we?
The basement, I think. But it's so cold.
Where's that light coming from?
A fireplace, maybe?
Then who lit the fire?
Wait Look at these.
That's the house. And that's the man from my dream. But look at all the trees.

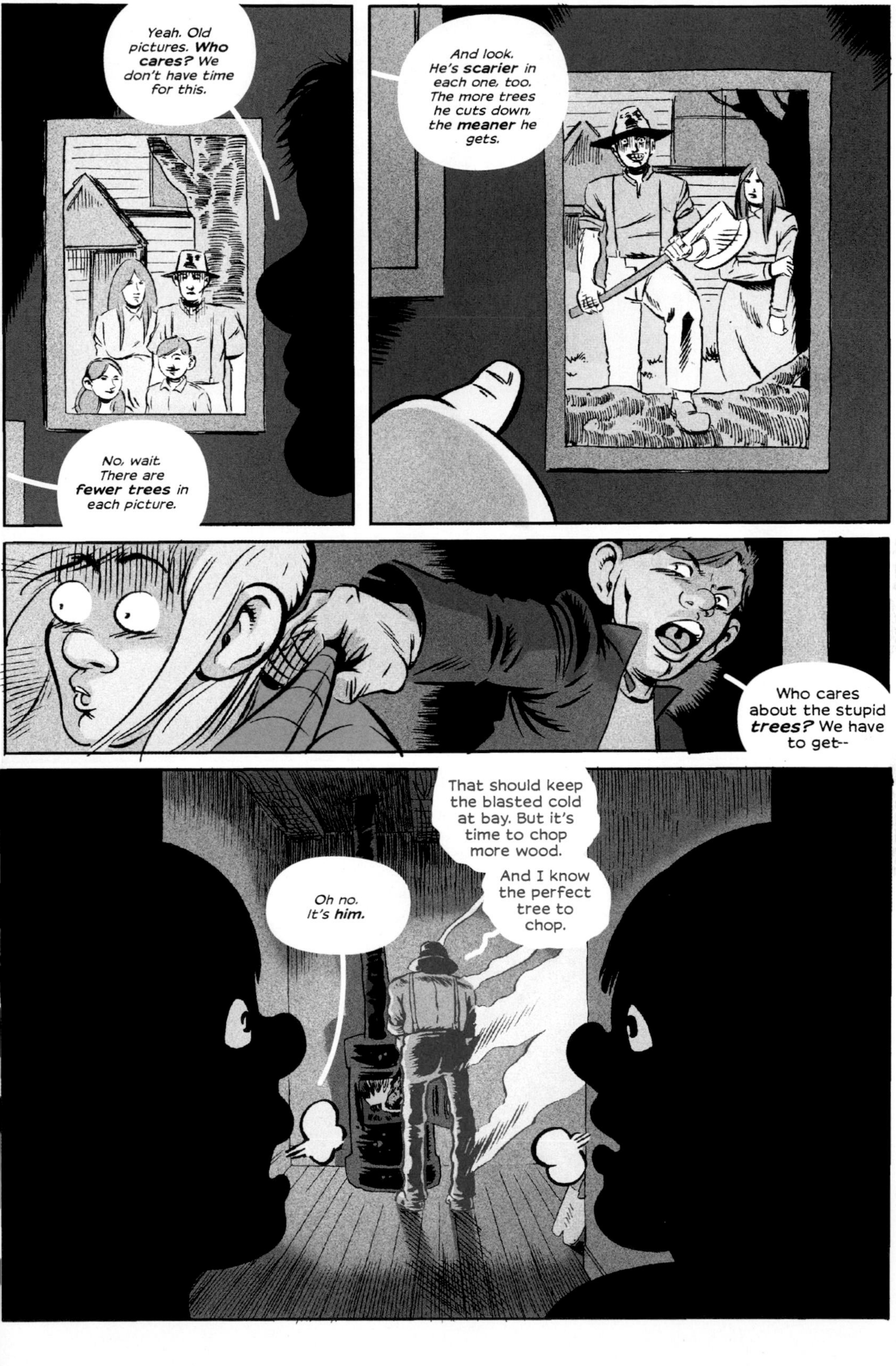
Yeah. Old pictures. **Who cares?** We don't have time for this.
No, wait. There are **fewer trees** in each picture.
And look. He's **scarier** in each one, too. The more trees he cuts down, the **meaner** he gets.
Who cares about the stupid ***trees?*** We have to get--
That should keep the blasted cold at bay. But it's time to chop more wood.
And I know the perfect tree to chop.
Oh no. It's **him.**

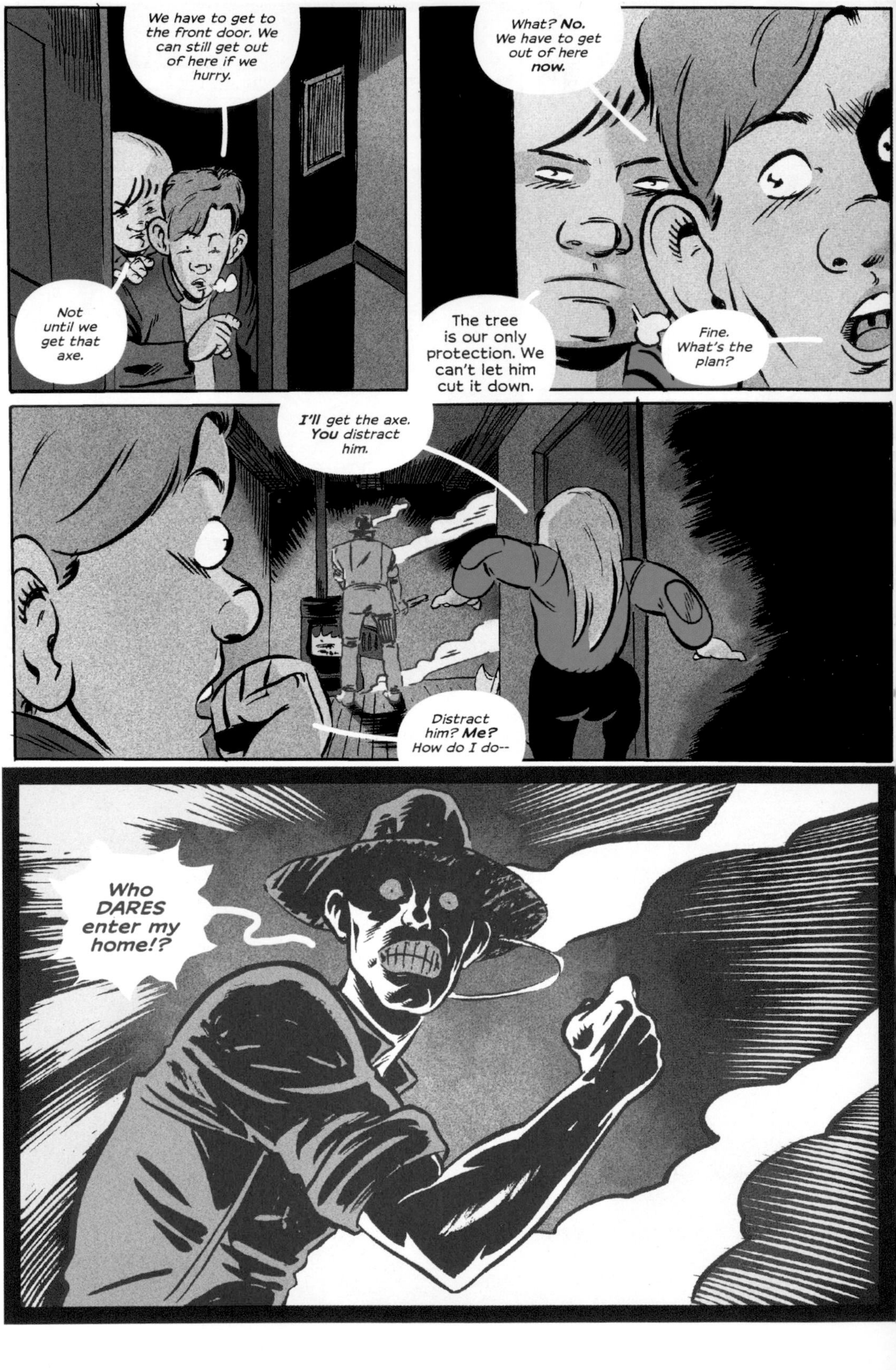

We have to get to the front door. We can still get out of here if we hurry.
Not until we get that axe.
What? **No.** We have to get out of here **now.**
The tree is our only protection. We can't let him cut it down.
Fine. What's the plan?
I'll get the axe. ***You*** distract him.
Distract him? ***Me?*** How do I do--
Who DARES enter my home!?

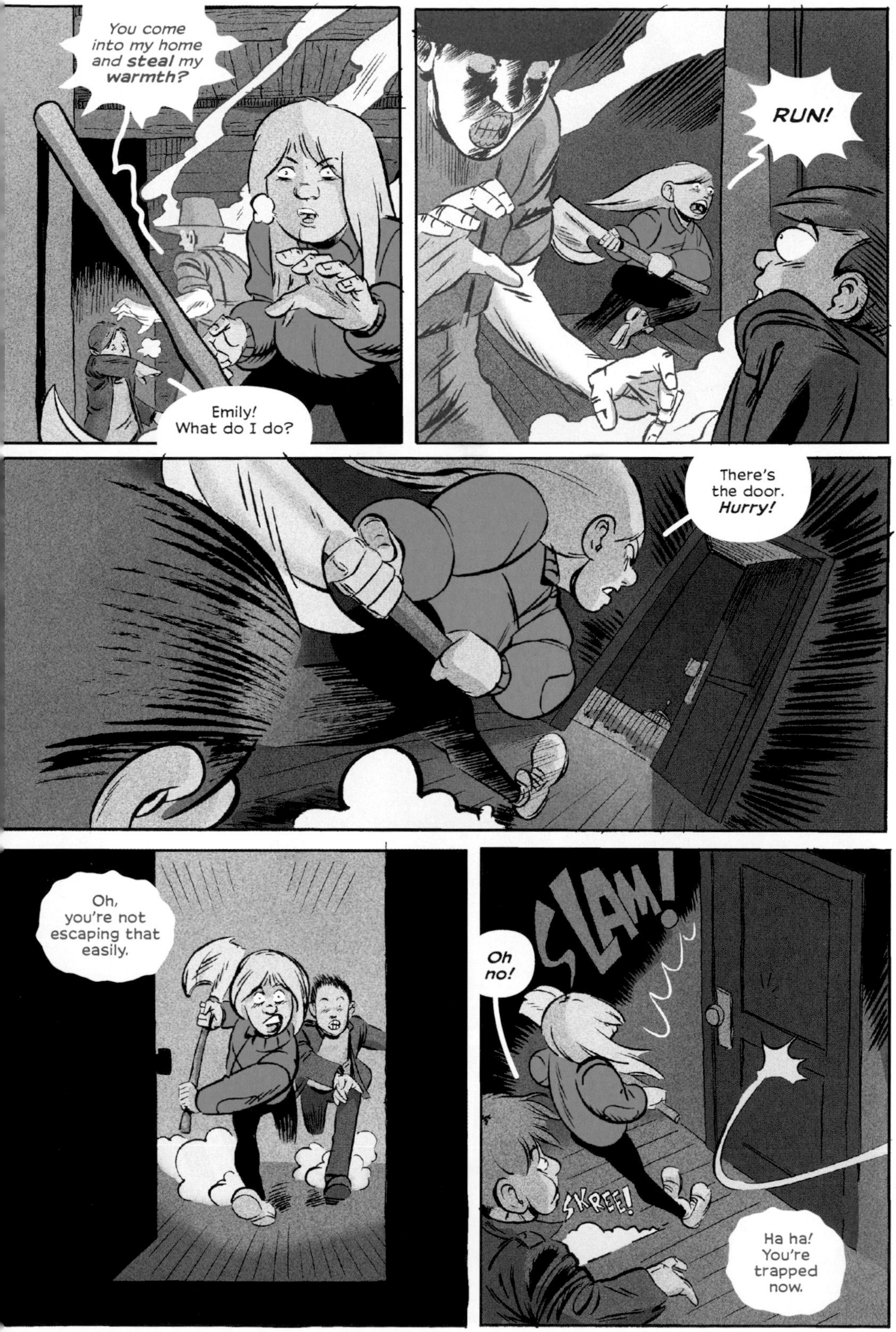
You come into my home and steal my warmth?
Emily! What do I do?
RUN!
There's the door. Hurry!
Oh, you're not escaping that easily.
SLAM!
Oh no!
SKREE!
Ha ha! You're trapped now.

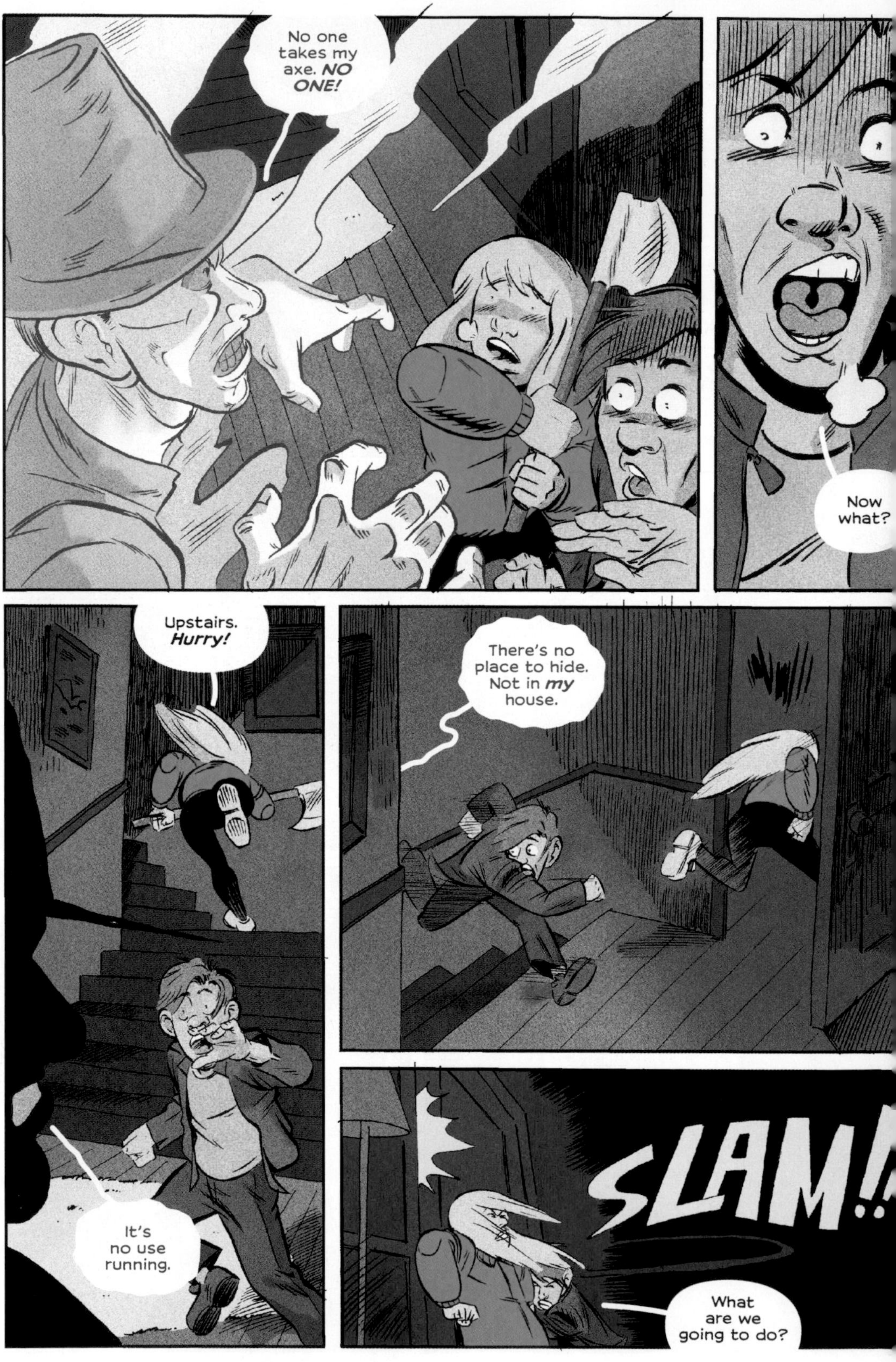
No one takes my axe. NO ONE!
Now what?
Upstairs. Hurry!
It's no use running.
There's no place to hide. Not in my house.
SLAM!!
What are we going to do?

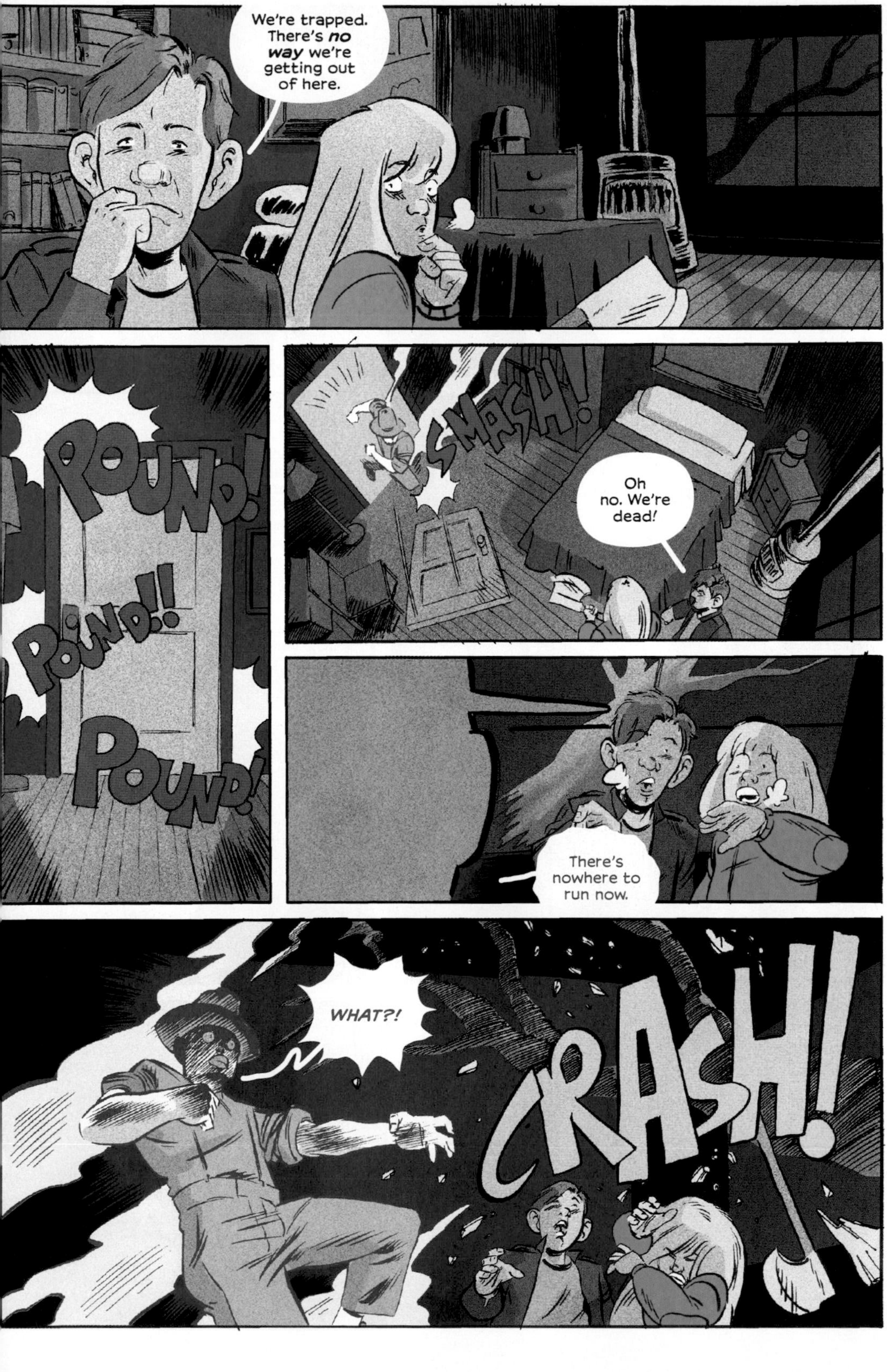
We're trapped. There's *no way* we're getting out of here.
POUND!
POUND!!
POUND!
SMASH!
Oh no. We're dead!
There's nowhere to run now.
WHAT?!
CRASH!

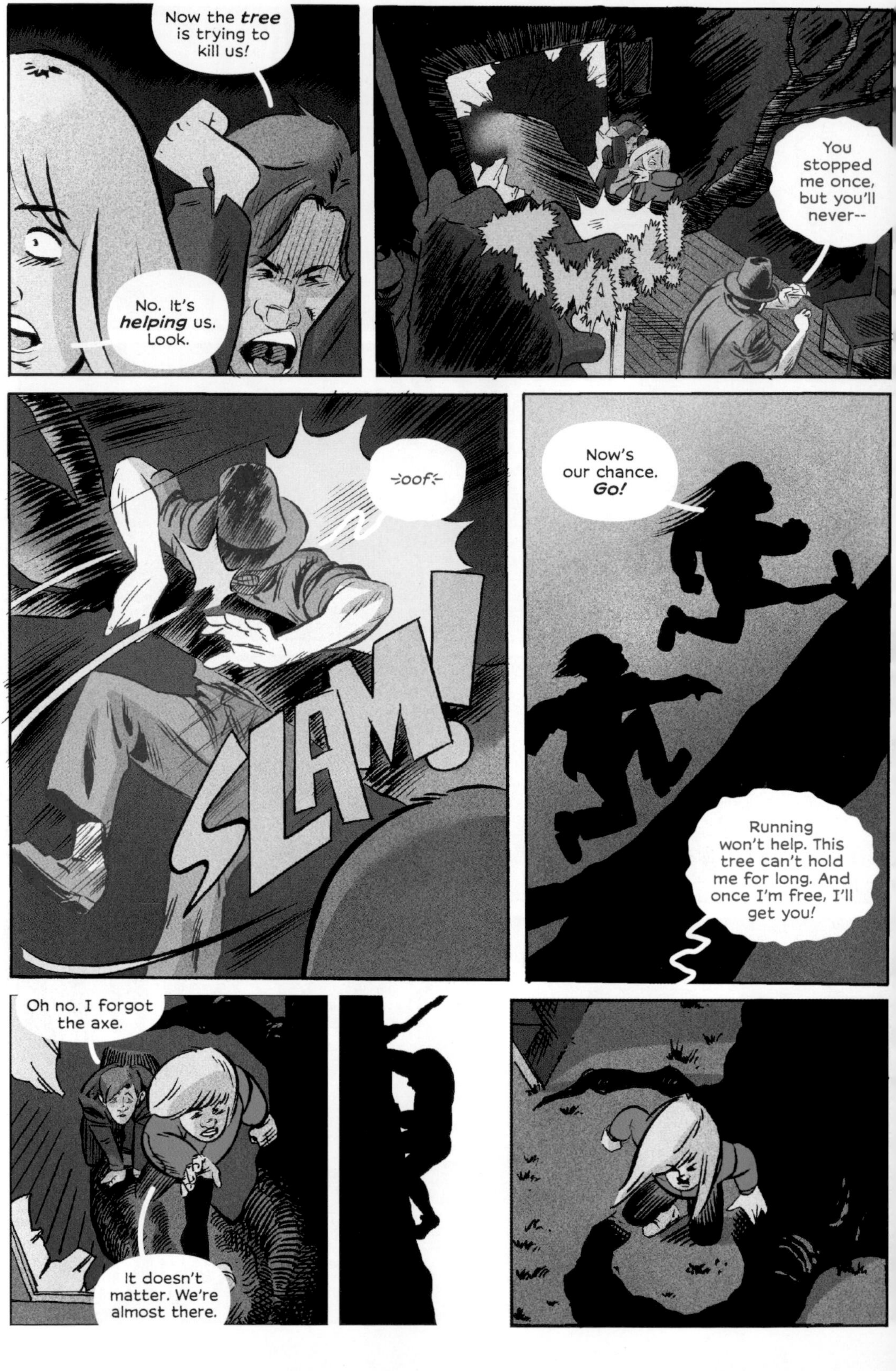
Now the *tree* is trying to kill us!
No. It's ***helping*** us. Look.
THACK!
You stopped me once, but you'll never--
oof
SLAM!
Now's our chance. ***Go!***
Running won't help. This tree can't hold me for long. And once I'm free, I'll get you!
Oh no. I forgot the axe.
It doesn't matter. We're almost there.

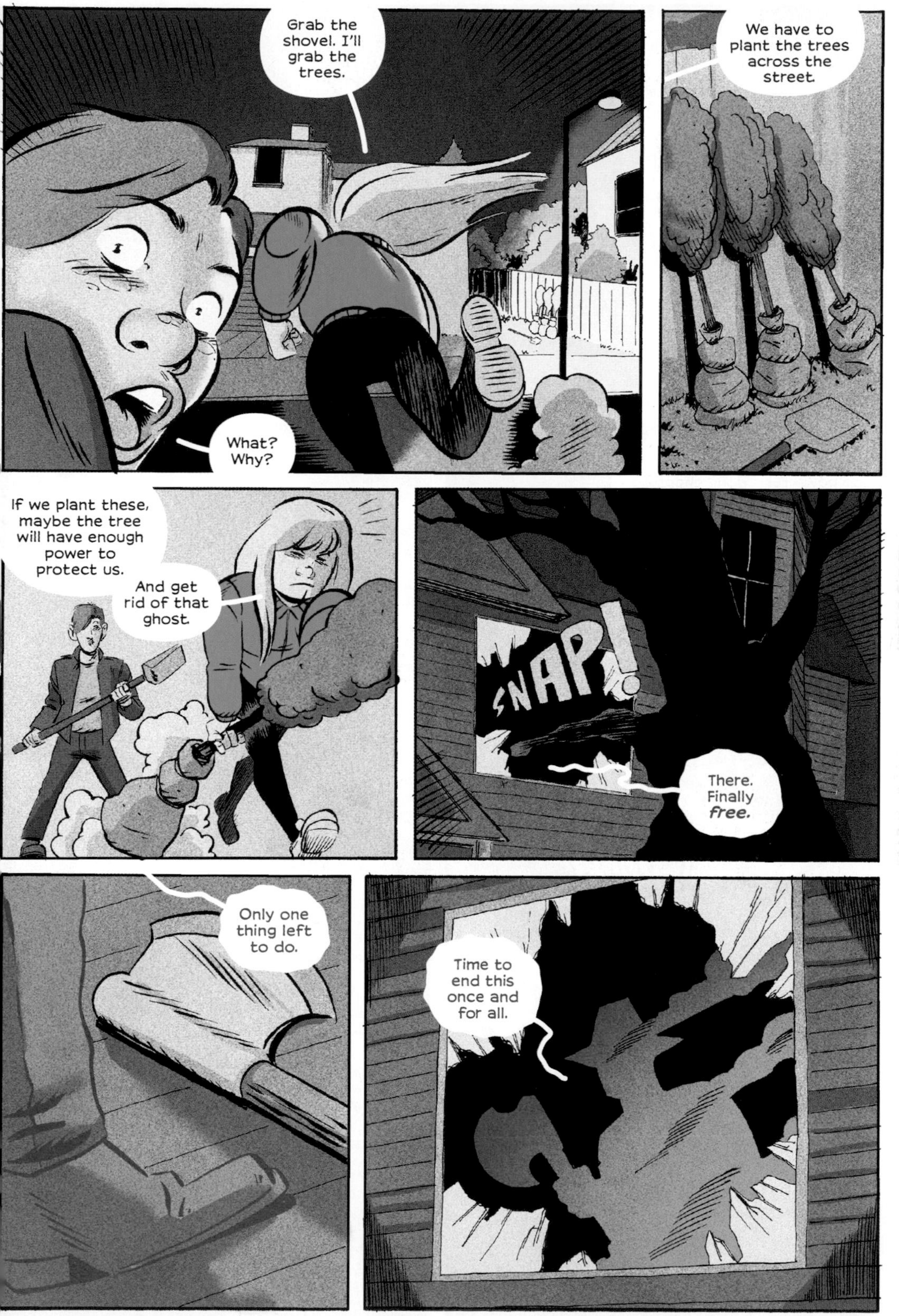
Grab the shovel. I'll grab the trees.
What? Why?
We have to plant the trees across the street.
If we plant these, maybe the tree will have enough power to protect us.
And get rid of that ghost.
SNAP!
There. Finally *free.*
Only one thing left to do.
Time to end this once and for all.

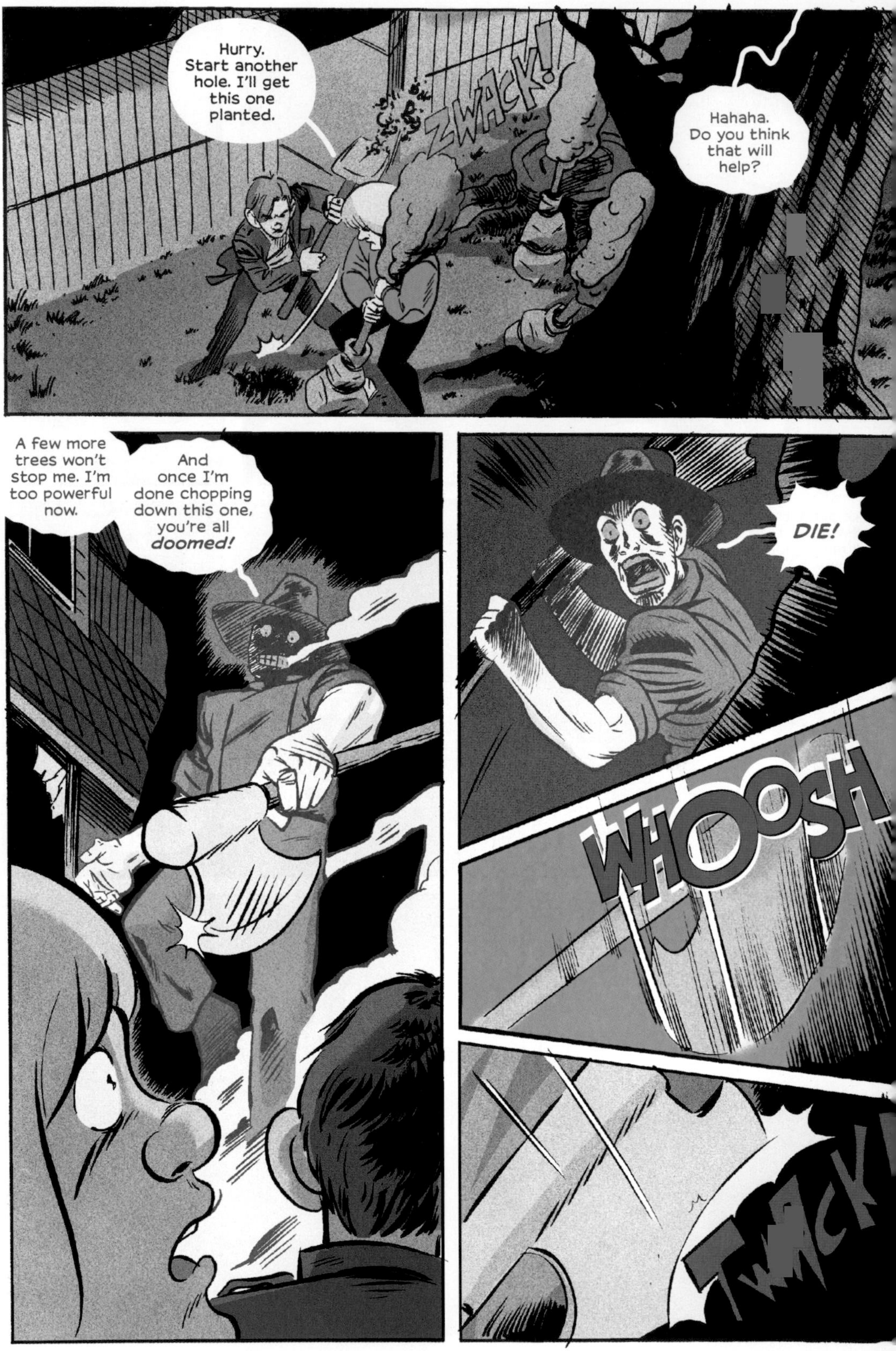
Hurry. Start another hole. I'll get this one planted.
ZWACK!
Hahaha. Do you think that will help?
A few more trees won't stop me. I'm too powerful now.
And once I'm done chopping down this one, you're all *doomed!*
DIE!
WHOOSH

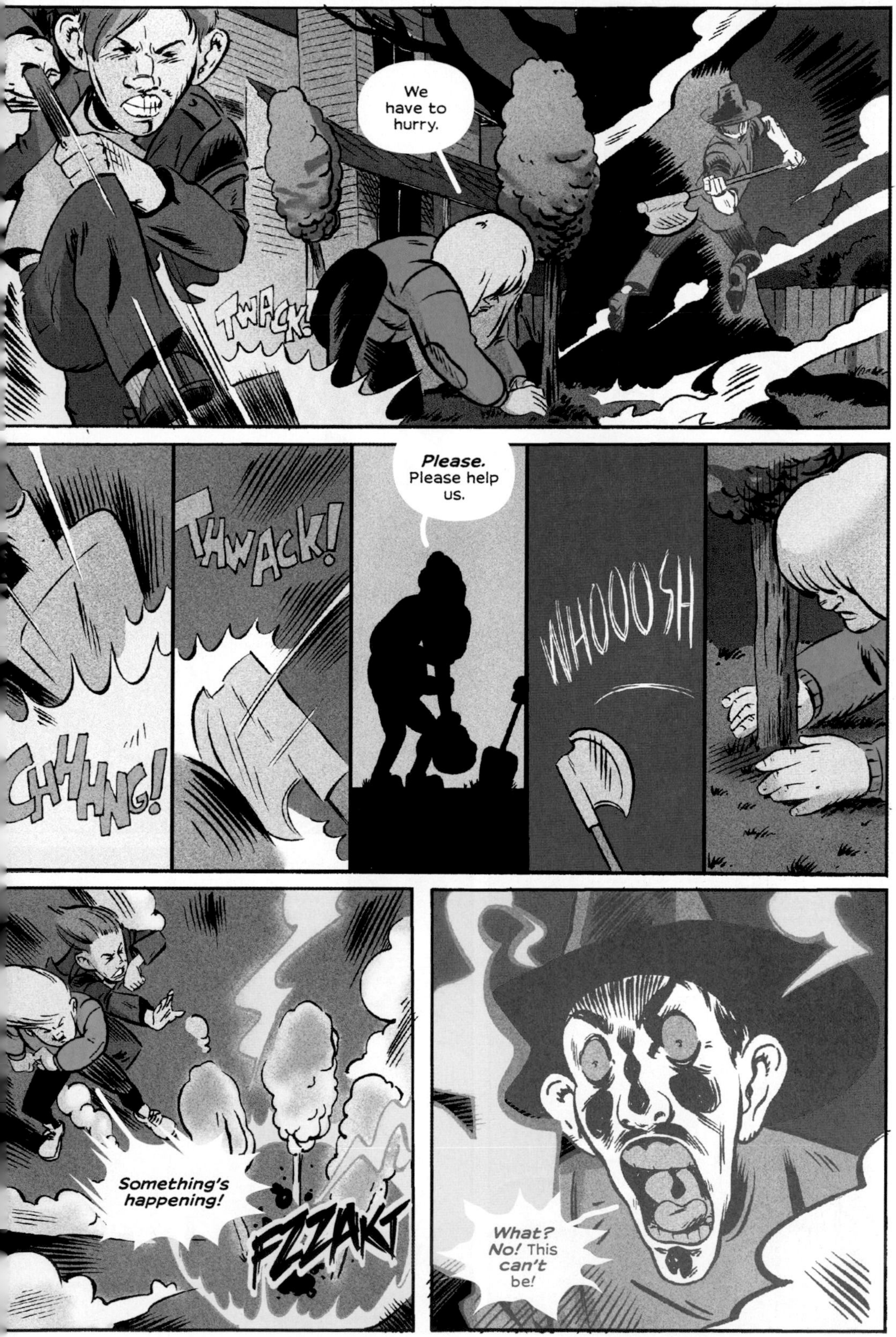

We have to hurry.
TWACK!
CHHHNG!
THWACK!
Please. Please help us.
WHOOOSH
Something's happening!
FZZAKT
What? No! This *can't* be!

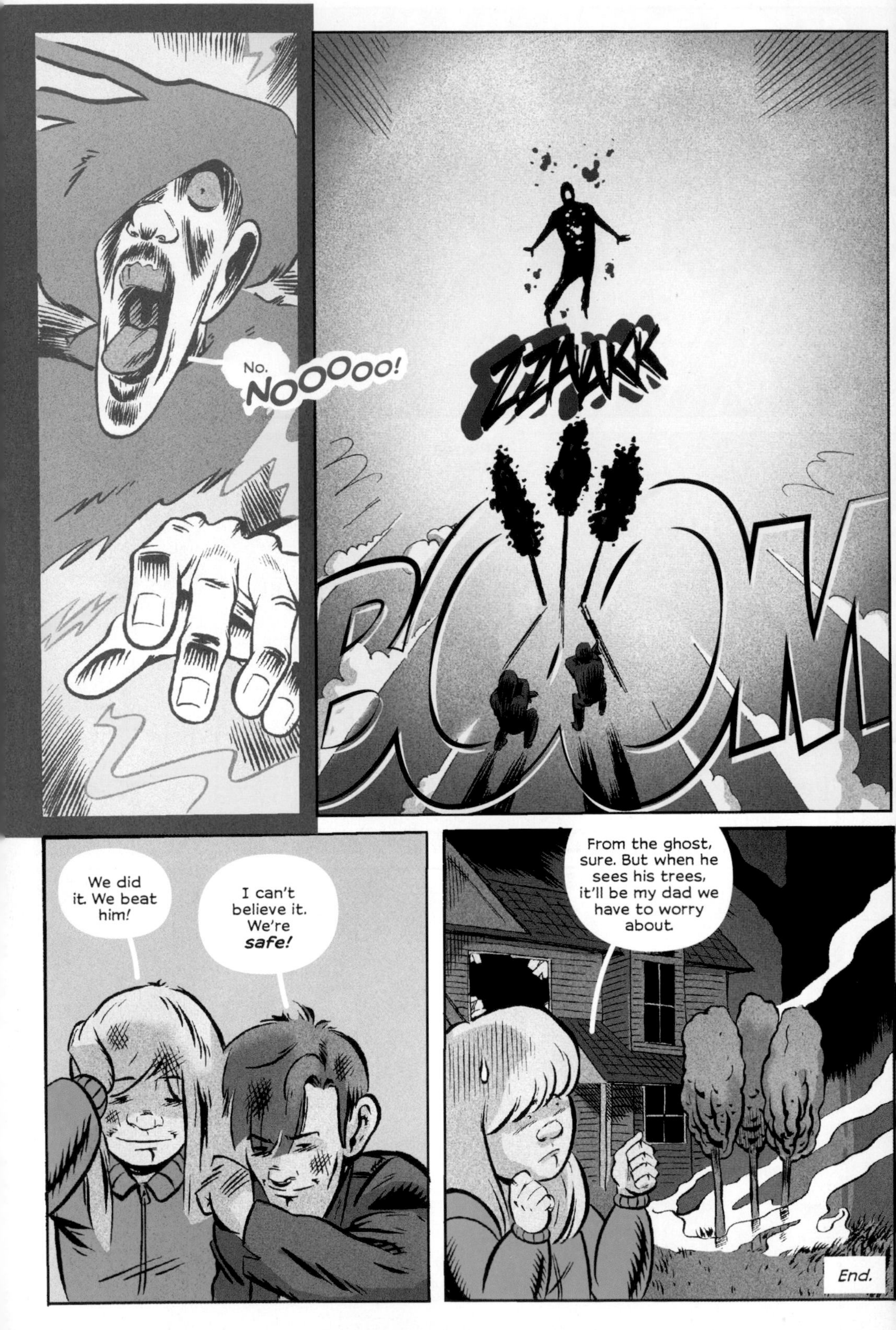
No.
NOOOOO!
ZZAAKK
BOOM
We did it. We beat him!
I can't believe it. We're *safe!*
From the ghost, sure. But when he sees his trees, it'll be my dad we have to worry about.
End.

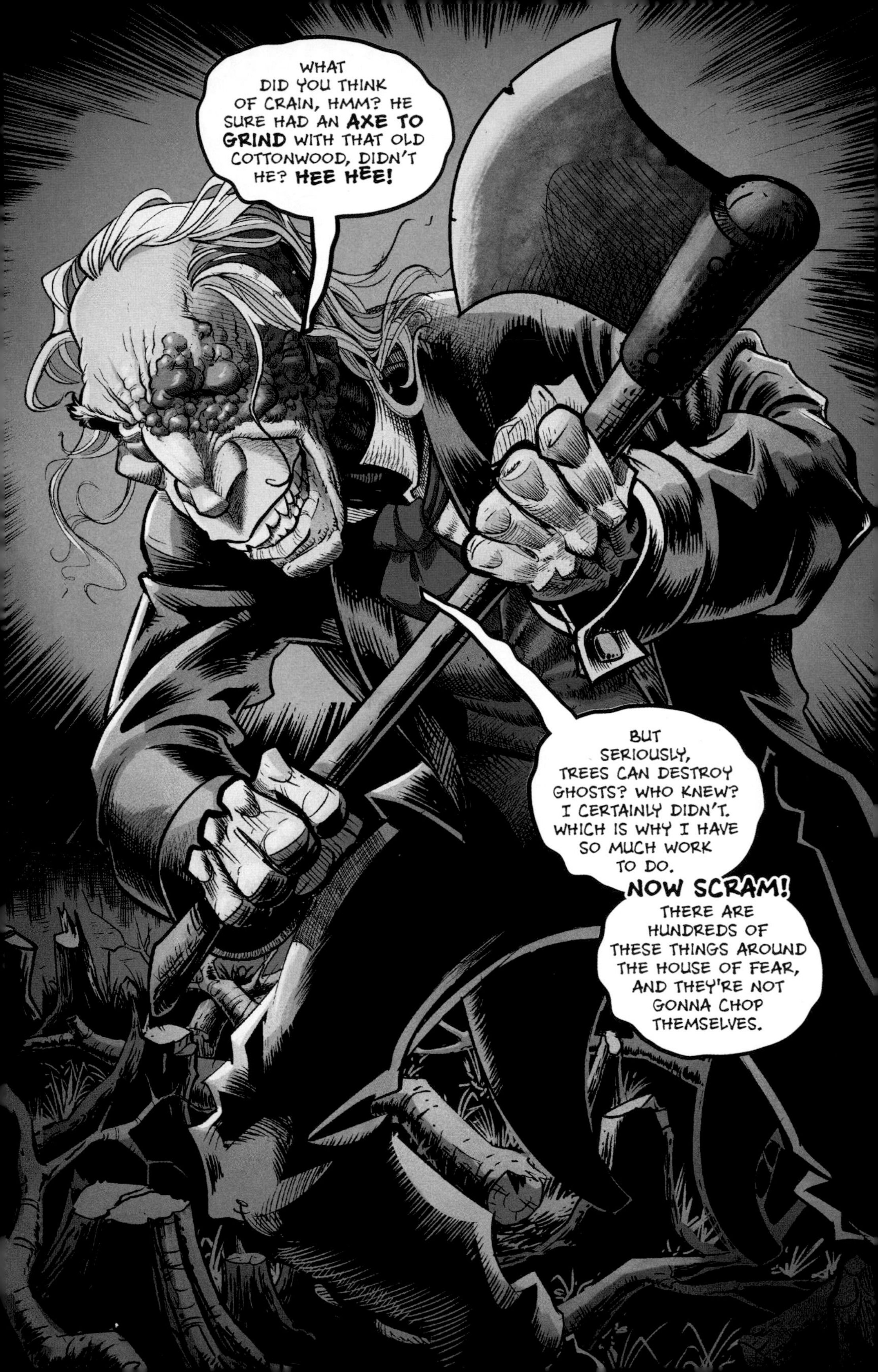
WHAT DID YOU THINK OF CRAIN, HMM? HE SURE HAD AN **AXE TO GRIND** WITH THAT OLD COTTONWOOD, DIDN'T HE? **HEE HEE!**
BUT SERIOUSLY, TREES CAN DESTROY GHOSTS? WHO KNEW? I CERTAINLY DIDN'T. WHICH IS WHY I HAVE SO MUCH WORK TO DO.
NOW SCRAM!
THERE ARE HUNDREDS OF THESE THINGS AROUND THE HOUSE OF FEAR, AND THEY'RE NOT GONNA CHOP THEMSELVES.

LEARN HOW TO MAKE COMICS!

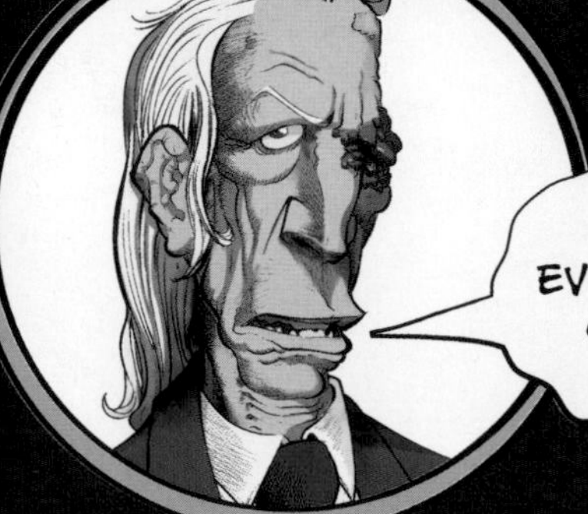
HEY KIDS, EVER MAKE YOUR OWN **COMIC** BOOK?
IT'S **SIMPLE.** ALL IT TAKES IS **CREATIVITY** AND A FEW PIECES OF **PAPER.**

STEP ONE: WRITE!

First you need to write the story. In comics, the story is called the **SCRIPT.**

Writing it out helps you decide what to draw on each page. Be sure to write the dialog for each scene.

DIALOG is what your characters say to each other.

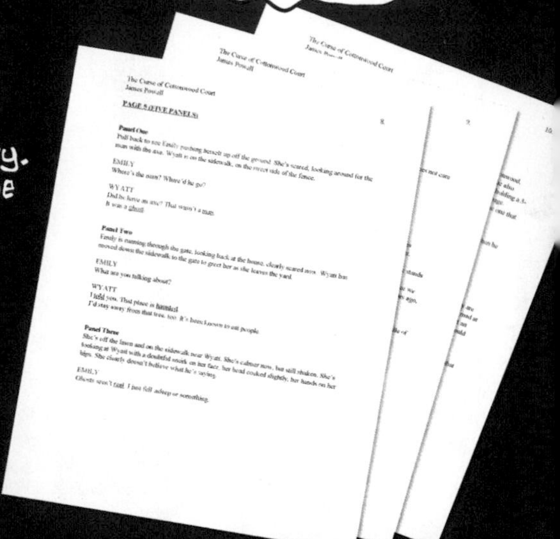
The Curse of Cottonwood Court
James Powell

PAGE 8 (FIVE PANELS)

8

Panel One
Pull back to see Emily pushing herself up off the ground. She's scared, looking around for the man with the axe. Wyatt is on the sidewalk, on the street side of the fence.

EMILY
Where's the man? Where'd he go?

WYATT
Did he have an axe? That wasn't a man.
It was a ghost.

Panel Two
Emily is running through the gate, looking back at the house, clearly scared now. Wyatt has moved down the sidewalk to the gate to greet her as she leaves the yard.

EMILY
What are you talking about?

WYATT
I told you. That place is haunted.
I'd stay away from that tree, too. It's been known to eat people.

Panel Three
She's off the lawn and on the sidewalk near Wyatt. She's calmer now, but still shaken. She's looking at Wyatt with a doubtful smirk on her face, her head cocked slightly, her hands on her hips. She clearly doesn't believe what he's saying.

EMILY
Ghosts aren't real. I just fell asleep or something.

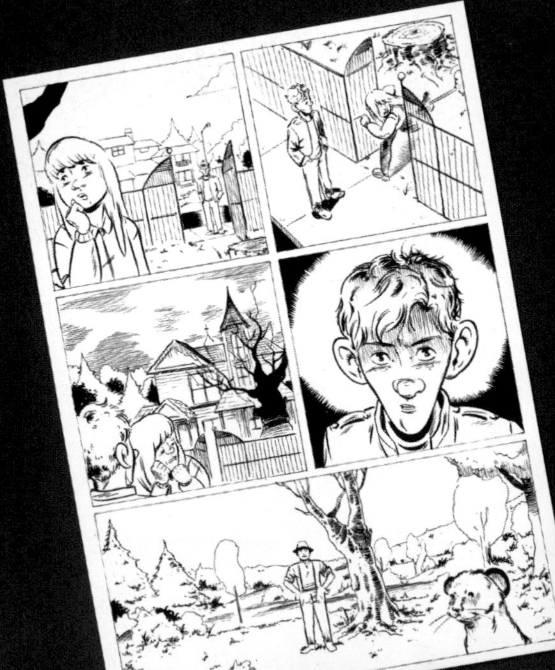

STEP TWO: DRAW!

Next, **DRAW** the comic based on what you wrote. In this step, sketch out each drawing in pencil.

When you like how it looks, trace the lines with **INK,** using a pen, marker, or brush.

STEP THREE: COLOR!

Now you need to **COLOR** your comic.

Many artists use the computer to color comics, but you can color right on top of your art, too.

Use whatever you have: crayons, colored pencils, pens, or paint.

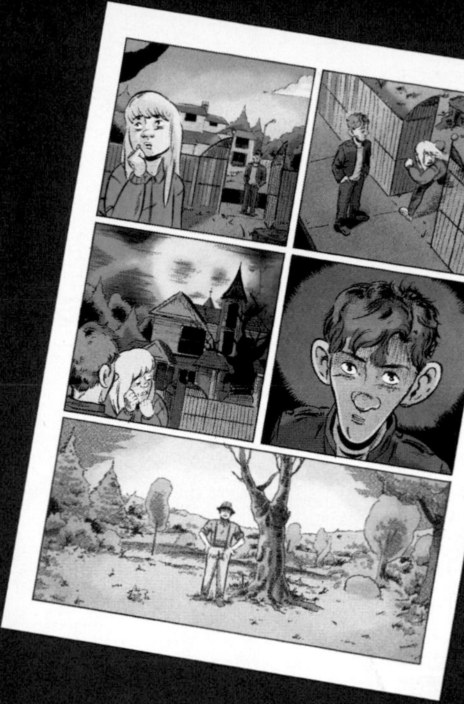

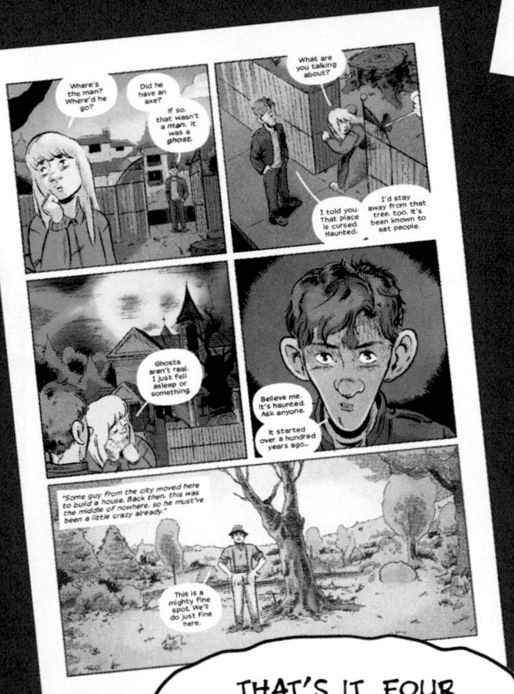
Where's the man? Where'd he go?
Did he have an axe?
If so, that wasn't a *man*. It was a *ghost*.
What are you talking about?
I told you. That place is cursed. Haunted.
I'd stay away from that tree, too. It's been known to eat people.
Ghosts aren't real. I just fell asleep or something.
Believe me. It's haunted. Ask anyone.
It started over a hundred years ago...
"Some guy from the city moved here to build a house. Back then, this was the middle of nowhere, so he must've been a little crazy already."
This is a mighty fine spot. We'll do just fine here.

STEP FOUR: LETTER!

The final step is to add the words. This is called **LETTERING.**

In this step, create word balloons for each character, and write the **dialog** in them.

Don't forget to add the **SOUND EFFECTS!**

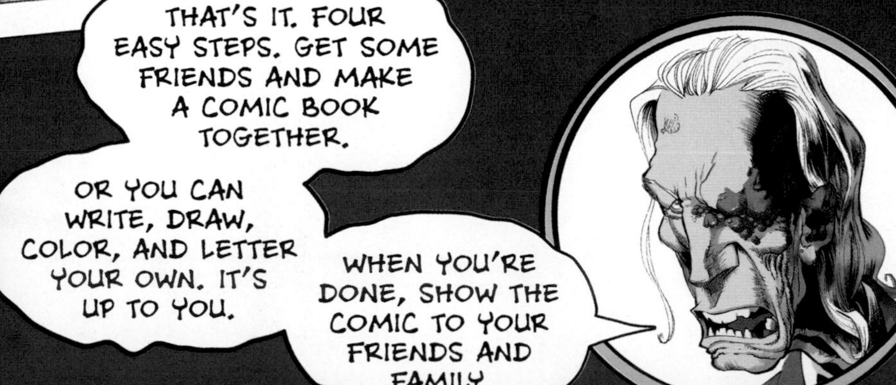
THAT'S IT. FOUR EASY STEPS. GET SOME FRIENDS AND MAKE A COMIC BOOK TOGETHER.
OR YOU CAN WRITE, DRAW, COLOR, AND LETTER YOUR OWN. IT'S UP TO YOU.
WHEN YOU'RE DONE, SHOW THE COMIC TO YOUR FRIENDS AND FAMILY.

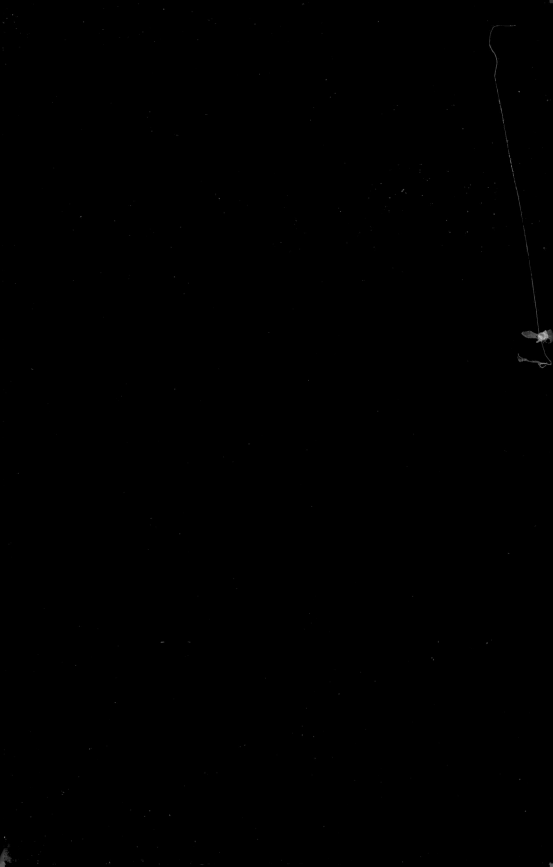